T0272682

Tidal
Creatures

ALSO BY SEANAN McGUIRE

SEANAN McGUIRE

Tidal Creatures

TOR PUBLISHING GROUP
NEW YORK

TIDAL CREATURES

Copyright © 2024 by Seanan McGuire

All rights reserved.

A Tordotcom Book
Published by Tom Doherty Associates / Tor Publishing Group
120 Broadway
New York, NY 10271

www.torpublishinggroup.com

Tor® is a registered trademark of Macmillan Publishing Group, LLC.

The Library of Congress Cataloging-in-Publication Data is available upon request.

ISBN 978-1-250-33355-1 (hardcover)
ISBN 978-1-250-33358-2 (ebook)

Our books may be purchased in bulk for promotional, educational, or business use. Please contact your local bookseller or the Macmillan Corporate and Premium Sales Department at 1-800-221-7945, extension 5442, or by email at MacmillanSpecialMarkets@macmillan.com.

First Edition: 2024

Printed in the United States of America

0 9 8 7 6 5 4 3 2 1

For Jess, who may or may not understand why.
And for Crystal, in the name of the moon.

We have left the territory of once upon a time at this point. Once upon a time is for the beginning of stories, and we are now well and truly mired in the sticky, unpredictable middle. There is a commonality to beginnings. We meet people; we learn their names and the sketches of their stories; we see the situation beginning to unfold in front of them; we either decide we're interested enough to follow them over the woodward wall or down the road of glistening nacre, like the trail of some fairy-kissed snail slithering through a world of impossible things, or we turn back and let them be. Not every story is for every person, you see, and if a tale baits its hook and dangles it in front of us and we feel no temptation to bite, there is no shame in walking away. There are many fish in the sea. There are many hooks as well.

If you are still here with me now, then when the scrimshaw hook etched with the names "Avery" and "Zib" was dangled in front of you, you were happy to slide it between your lips and into the space between your cheek and your teeth. You bit down, and have since been pulled out of the shallows and safe harbor of once upon a time, and now swim the choppy seas of the middle of the story with the rest of us. I am not sorry. I am glad, in fact, that you are here, for stories cannot be nothing but beginnings: they must have a vast and terrible middle to get them from hook to home. Thank you for allowing me to catch you. We have so far left to go.

But as the beginning is some distance behind us now, it seems proper for me to remind you, at least a little, of where we are going and how we have reached this point. I promise I will not take long, as the story itself is on the other side of this digression, and we would all prefer to get there quickly. . . .

—From *Into the Windwracked Wilds,* by A. Deborah Baker

BOOK I

New Moon

Do not swear by the moon, for she changes constantly.
Then your love would also change.

—William Shakespeare, *Romeo and Juliet*

Lady Moon, will you dance with me
Just once while I am mortal?
For there is no woman I would rather
Gather in my arms.

—Talis Kimberley, "Lady Moon"

Sinus Asperitatis

Always there was the moon.

Before humanity drew breath, the moon was there, shining in the sky, waxing and waning as it circled the world. It did not think. It did not dream. It was only the moon, endless and eternal.

With time, new creatures stirred and rose on the planet below. They saw the skies and were enchanted; they saw the seas and were afraid. Some saw the connections between the two, and they were lauded as wise ones and burned as witches, and still there was the moon. The moon, which watched but did not see, not yet, for no one had considered or suggested that it should.

Those new creatures saw the world so clearly and so strangely that it began to change itself to suit them. In tiny ways at first, but the world was very new; it had many tiny ways in which to change. Bit by bit they changed it through observance, until aspects of the universe itself began to take on the forms of these new beings, wearing their skins and seeing their reality through the eyes of the creatures, who called themselves "people."

Those people looked up, and they saw the moon. They wondered what might live there, what glories and wonders the moon might conceal, and as they wondered, the universe changed again. Gods were born, gods who had just now come into being but had suddenly been there from the very beginning of everything, as reality adjusted to accommodate the always-present nature of things that hadn't been only a moment before.

And for the first time, exactly as it had done every night since time began, the Moon rose.

There was little difference between the moon and the Moon, at least to the eye; they shone the same, hung in the sky the same, illuminated the night the same. They were one. But the Moon also walked the world; it lived the short, temporary lives of the people who had dreamt it into being, and while the moon was eternal, the Moon was temporary, waxing and waning from existence even as the moon waxed and waned from the sky.

Reality, self-organizing as ever, marched on, and the Moon split itself into innumerable pieces, each one with a body and mind of its own, and they continued, born and dying and mortal and eternal, all at the same time.

Always there is the Moon.

*   *   *

Aske is a goddess, and she walks down a tunnel filled with flashes of rainbow light against a background of dark so profound that it transcends darkness, becoming something else altogether. This is the everything, the glorious tunnel between worlds where she is called to do her duty as a divine reflection of the midnight sky.

Aske is also a nineteen-year-old girl from Minnesota, currently studying early childhood education in California. She had been considering colleges when the moon began speaking to her through her bedroom window, suggesting she consider Berkeley. *Great things in Berkeley,* the moon had said, before she had understood that she *was* the moon, the moon was *her,* and together, they were going to shine. *Great things for you to learn and know and understand. Go to Berkeley.*

Her grades had been good enough and her college fund had been healthy enough, and her desire to be away from her parents had been pronounced enough, and so off she'd gone, a suitcase in one hand and a transcript in the other, the moon whispering in the back of her thoughts like an imaginary friend. She'd worried at first about the growing clarity of that voice, wondering if she was losing her mind, and then one day the moon had become the Moon had become Aske, the goddess herself, sitting cross-legged on the edge of the dorm-room bed with her hands on her ankles, glowing with a faint silver-white light and smiling a hopeful, uneven smile.

"Your name is Eliza Benson, and my name is Aske, and you are nineteen years old, and I am without age, outside of time, and we are the same person, or we will be, if you allow us to be," she'd said, voice earnest and soft and layered with an accent Eliza hadn't known at the time. It's not an accent that still walks the world; it has worn away by centuries of conquest and social unrest and change. "I am the moon goddess of the Sámi people, and you are a daughter of those same people, and I am here because we are meant to be combined."

"Oh, no," said Eliza. "I'm the daughter of a dentist and a school secretary from Minnesota."

"Not in such immediate terms, silly," said Aske, and laughed, and her laughter was like moonlight on the snow, shimmering and perfect, utterly unblemished by the world around her. "They were your ancestors, long and long ago. Not all who carry me are descended from my kind, but I prefer it when you are. It makes it easier for us to understand each other, if I embody a Moon whose tides your blood remembers."

Eliza had stared at the girl for a while, then leaned over and poked her on the shoulder. Her skin had been cool and slightly yielding, like she was a well-built doll that just *looked* like a living woman. Aske had responded with a sigh and a sorrowful look, catching Eliza's hand in her own.

"Let me tell you a story," she'd said.

And Eliza, who was studying early childhood education for a reason, had settled on the bed, willing to listen to this impossible girl in this impossible situation as she said more impossible things. Somatic satiation of the soul is a thing, after all; once a concept has been repeated a sufficient number of times, it becomes easier to accept, to incorporate, to stop being seen as anything out of the ordinary. When Aske had first appeared on the bed, Eliza very nearly panicked. Now, after relatively little time, she was accepting the presence of a glowing girl who claimed to be the moon with surprising ease.

Even then, something about it had felt right. And the voice of the girl in front of her had been so similar to the voice that had been speaking inside her head that it seemed almost easier to just sit back and listen.

Aske had nodded as she watched her, and said, "A very, very, *very* long time ago, the world began. It was full of all manner of things, and it needed all manner of forces if it was going to operate properly and not collapse in on itself in a tangle of contradictions. Those forces worked very hard to do their jobs, but they didn't *know* they were doing jobs; they didn't *know* anything, because they weren't people. Nothing was people yet. It was only the world, and the unthinking advance of life and time and evolution.

"But then, bit by bit, some of the things that lived in the world got to be so good at living that they started to look at their environment and wonder things about it. They started to become people. Not just humans, although humans didn't have much going for them beyond being able to wonder things—elephants were people, too, and dolphins, and a bunch of other species. It was a race no one realized they were running, and everyone was racing for the first big prize that no one knew existed: they were running for the right to tell the universe what to be."

Eliza had blinked without interrupting, trying to understand the story unspooling in front of her, trying to recognize why it felt so *right*. It was like she was listening to a report on a topic she'd been studying extensively for her entire life, even though she'd never heard any of this before.

"Humans got there first. They started telling each other stories, fables where the moon was a maiden crossing the sky in a coracle boat, or the winter was a cruel king who killed the crops in the fields because he couldn't be with his one true love, the queen of the summer. They set the universe in terms they could understand, and the universe was listening, the whole time. The universe was learning what they wanted it to be.

"No one knows, not even the gods ourselves, which idea was the first one to find fertile soil. But one day, one of those forces the universe needed to contain if it wanted to keep working decided it was going to put on a fancy face and a pair of legs and go walking around the world. And it found it worked better that way. Oh, it was limited, because humans are always limited when you compare them to dispassionate cosmic forces, but it was limited in a way that helped it do its job. It understood itself, and in understanding itself, it could be *more* than itself. Do you understand?"

Eliza both did and didn't, and so she had shrugged, trying to express complexity in silence. Aske had only smiled in response, and then gone back to her story.

"Some of the forces were so big, so essential, that they appeared more than once. There's not just one Winter in the world, not just one Ocean. They began curating vessels they could inhabit, began watching the humans who spoke of them to see which ones might have the right seeds, the right sympathies, to carry them through their lives. And bit by bit, they built a system. Now sometimes, when it's time for a force to seek embodiment, they can go to those people and ask them whether they're willing to be something more than mortal."

And with that, Eliza had finally, truly begun to understand. She was a woman, and a student, and a vessel, and Aske was the thing she had been missing for her entire life. That was when she had held her hand out to Aske, and Aske had taken it, laughing again, and then Eliza had been alone but not alone, Aske still laughing in the back of her head, the air around her glittering silver-white with the divinity that poured off of her own skin, lighting up her suddenly shared room.

(The other gods—and there are *so many* other gods, moon gods from all over the world, and the number in Berkeley with her isn't even a fragment of the greater pantheon, oh, no. Even if it were, gods are like seasons: they manifest dozens of times at once, putting the weight of themselves into the world. Aske is a relatively minor goddess in the modern pantheon, and she exists dozens of times right now. Eliza is only the newest. Eliza hopes to meet those other Askes someday. She thinks they would be good friends. But. The other gods call the process of manifesting divinity into the real world "stepping up," meaning their godly sides step up while their human sides step back, allowing the divine to take the stage. When she lets Aske move to the front of their shared awareness, it's like she's watching everything from the other side of a wall, not quite in control of herself. She never really liked drinking in high school. Now she wishes she'd done it more, because it's the best comparison she has for the process of standing back and letting a god control her body.)

So Aske is a goddess and Aske is Eliza and Eliza is a goddess, and the both of them are also the one of them, and that one is traveling along the rainbow-streaked corridor that leads them through the everything, away from their own private window onto the Impossible City. The City is something out of a children's book, quite literally, but it's also real, it's *real,* it's the most real thing Eliza-who-is-Aske has ever seen, and the first time she looked at it, she started crying, because it was so beautiful that it made her understand that she'd never seen beauty before, not once in her whole entire life.

Chang'e, who isn't the senior or most powerful goddess in Berkeley—that honor goes to Diana, who's been doing this so long she's a *professor,* with *tenure,* teaching art classes; Eliza is planning to take a class with her next semester—but is the goddess who seems to handle most of the administrative side of things, says it's like that for everyone the first time they see the City. They're so stunned by the proof that humans really do shape the universe that it takes their breath away.

(Eliza was surprised, at first, to realize that gods had paperwork, had to keep records and set schedules and generally take all the magic out of divinity. Her surprise faded quickly when she remembered that Aske's initial explanation had included telling her how the universe sought out humanity as an organizational force; maybe there were pure gods somewhere in the actual heavens, divinities who didn't spend half their time as ordinary mortals, but if so, they were something she would never need to understand. The members of her pantheon are gods. They're also people, and people need paperwork.)

She has made her tour across the sky of the Impossible City, seeing such wonders and such marvels that she feels warm and satiated with the memory of it all, saturated with beauty. It will be weeks before she has access to the everything again, weeks before it's her turn to walk through the gate into the welcoming abyss, and so she doesn't hurry toward the gate. She allows herself to dawdle, to take her time.

She's still walking through the rainbow brilliance of the night she's had when something strikes the back of her head, hard enough that she feels bone giving way like the bark on a tree, feels skin splitting, feels the first hot wetness of blood working its way into her hair. She doesn't feel much more than that. She's already falling, tumbling toward the ground that suddenly seems so very, terribly, infinitely far away.

She isn't dead yet when hands grip her under the arms, dragging her deeper back along the rainbow road, back toward the window that looks out upon—

The City! is her last, despairing thought before consciousness winks out like an extinguished candle, leaving her to plummet down into a darkness where there are no rainbows, no gods, nothing but the infinite and echoing nothing that waits on the other side of the divine.

And there, in the far distance, a flicker of light, a lure for those beyond luring, an enticement for those who are beyond action, beyond agency, lost in the clouds that gather between one world and the next. She is no longer aware, but like a flower turning toward the sun, her face turns toward the light and there, inside and beyond it:

The City the City the City the City . . .

And she is no more.

Mare Crisium

Máni isn't back yet.

That's not entirely unusual: Máni isn't the most dependable god in the pantheon, never has been, and this latest incarnation is even more inclined than the last to lingering in the everything beyond the gate when it's his turn to shine. Chang'e, who was set to meet him upon his return, can't help thinking she'll be relieved when he retires, and hopes his general dislike of fruits and vegetables will hasten that retirement along. She feels a little guilty for thinking that way—they're supposed to be a pantheon, a team, and she doesn't want to be the villain of the piece—but he doesn't take his duties as seriously as he's supposed to, doesn't seem to really care about their sacred task, and without it, they might have faded the way so many other incarnations have.

She shouldn't judge. It's not like she was here in time for moonrise, when she should have escorted him to the gate with all proper pomp and circumstance. But she'd been distracted with a translation paper, and time had slipped away from her. She'd grabbed her things and raced for the gate, half-convinced she'd get there to either find him standing impatiently outside, or worse, to find Diana waiting to tell her that due to her negligence, the City had been forced to find another way, and their services were no longer needed. That would be the end of them all, if it were ever to come to pass.

After all, gods aren't natural forces, not like Summer and Winter; they're fractured reflections of natural forces. They don't necessarily endure. The ones who perform an essential service get to stick around, vestigial remainders of a time when belief had been bigger and easier, a time before the alchemists began tying everything down to a single system of understanding, turning people into weapons to wield against anything that wasn't the reality *they* wanted to control. The gods without an essential service . . .

Gods can be forgotten. Seasons can't. Oceans can't. But gods . . . gods are only ever here to go.

Maybe once there had been a true incarnation of the Moon, just one, singular and serene. But much as the Summer and Winter appear on every continent of the world, distinct from one another, shaped by the climate and conditions of the land they serve, the moon shines down everywhere, and people look up at it everywhere, and everywhere, those people looked at that moon and formed their own ideas about what it represented. Some of them saw men and some of them saw monsters and a surprising number of them saw rabbits. Incarnations are born from belief in the beginning and inertia in the end, and all over the world, the Moon fractured into smaller shards of itself, faces, and where there's a face, there will be someone to wear it.

And everywhere there were people, the moon continued to shine. The moon, celestial body that she was, didn't care how many little incarnations spoke for her, how many people were empowered in her name. She only needed to shine.

In the beginning, all the shards of the Moon served their own pantheons, walked among the people who truly believed in them. Chang'e would never have known Máni in those days, would never have been forced to deal with his casual refusal to take his job seriously. She would have been a part of the celestial bureaucracy, organized and occupied and, quite probably, completely miserable. She may not like how lackadaisical Máni is about things, but she doesn't like to be micromanaged; she's happier here.

But time passes, and gods fall out of fashion. Oh, everyone

remembers the Zeuses and the Odins, but she can't remember the last time she heard T'ou-Shen Niang-Niang invoked outside of a scholastic paper. Shitala has greater staying power, having diversified her portfolio. That didn't save her cognates. So far as Chang'e knows, only the lunar gods still have a fully intact company, a pantheon made up of refugees from dozens of others, and it's all because they have a job that transcends human belief, keeping the universe wedded to the idea of them as it isn't necessarily wedded to everything that calls itself divine.

Which Máni is screwing up.

Until he shows up for the handoff, she's stuck in her divine form, unable to step down without violating propriety, meaning she's the goddess of the moon and immortality and peach harvests before she's a linguistics major, and that's going to fuck her day eleven ways from Sunday if she doesn't get out of here soon. She's supposed to be meeting with her advisor in a little over three hours, and since her advisor doesn't really understand why she refuses to take classes with the best linguist in the world—most linguistics majors at Berkeley are here for Professor Middleton at this point, and while she can't blame them, she wants to attract his attention about as much as she wants a bad case of pubic lice—that's not going to be a fun meeting.

It gets even less fun if she shows up glowing pinkish gold and sprouting seeds wherever she walks. Academic advisors are primed to deal with a whole lot of weird as part of their daily lives, but they have their limits, just like she has hers. And one of those limits is never allowing herself to be alone in a room with Roger Middleton. It's a small thing. It's getting harder every year; he'll probably be head of the department before she's ready to graduate, and then she'll need to find an excuse to switch schools, which is going to be hard to do without sparking rumors of inappropriate behavior on *someone's* part. She's still at the beginning of her academic career, and she doesn't need "was inappropriate toward a professor" haunting her for the next twenty years. As for starting the rumor in the other direction . . .

She shudders, still watching the gate. The Moon always sets in the west; Máni should be coming from that direction once he gets his feet back under himself and gets reacclimated to the idea of *having* feet. That's one of the hardest parts of the adjustment, learning how to exist as a concept instead of a body, how to endure when there's no beginning or end to you, any more than there's a beginning or an end to moonlight. Still, he's been doing this job for six years now, and he knows the drill. He knows the drill, and he has the gate key, which he has to hand over before either one of them can stand down.

Chang'e has been doing this job for almost a decade, starting when she was sixteen and started hearing whispers from the moon at night, and probably continuing for the next hundred years. She's not ageless—no one ageless should incarnate before they turn twenty-five—but thanks to her peaches, she's the age she wants to be, and if not for her degree, she'd already have frozen herself in place, stopping where her joints are at their best and her bones can bend more than they break. Still, the need to graduate was drilled into her early and often by her parents, and while they're not with her anymore, she supposes she owes it to them to finish the task they gave her before they left.

Máni is one of the most frustrating people she's ever worked with, and if it were up to her, she'd knock him out of the rotation. And she knows he'd say it's because she's a man-hater—she's not—who doesn't want to work with any male Moons, as if at least half of the Moons she has to deal with weren't men. She wants him gone because he's bad at his job, plain and simple, and no one who's bad at their job should ever have access to the Impossible City.

The Impossible City isn't a place: it's a concept, an idea, an ideal at the center of all things. She supposes, on some level, that it's Heaven, the single Heaven that binds all pantheons that have ever existed, the perfect place to which they all aspire. It isn't a place, but the moon isn't a person, and so it's somewhere that can be gone to, a location that isn't a location, a contradiction wrought in masonry and glass. The Impossible City is the center of all things, the spoke around which their wheel spins, slow and stately and unstoppable. Alchemists, those humans who dream of controlling the universe when everyone who knows the universe knows it's the other way around, have tried a thousand ways to access the City, a thousand methods of breaching the walls and making it their own. They believe it will grant them godhood, give them power over everything, and the worst of it is that they may not be wrong. Take the City, take the concepts of creation. Control it all.

But as the City is and is not a place, there are certain rules around it. Chang'e knows people live there, walk its streets, breathe its air; she doesn't envy them. She likes cable television and delivery services and coffee from the cheap gas station near her apartment. She can't imagine they have those things in the City. She doesn't know where the residents come from, or how they live, or whether they can leave. There's a lot she doesn't know, but she knows this:

The City is a place that isn't a place, and that means day and night pass there, time melting hour after hour into days, weeks, months, years. The Impossible City changes. And when night comes to the Impossible City, the moon doesn't shine, because the moon can only find real places. So the Moon shines there instead. All the lunar deities who have ever become incarnate, taking their turn at crossing above those iridescent streets, those towering spires. They continue to appear in the real world, even when they lose all believers, even when they slip from the historical records, because the City needs a Moon.

Máni was the Moon last night. He missed his last two shifts, passing them off to another divinity with a smile and an easy promise to fill in for them one day, but this time, he wasn't swift enough to get out of it. She knows he went; if he hadn't, she'd know that too, by now. All she has now is waiting.

Máni is never happy to sail above the City, but he understands the importance, and he's always gone willingly enough. Chang'e begins to pace before the gate, checking her watch, watching time slip away, future becoming the past, plenty of time becoming incipient tardiness.

There's a shout from the other side of the gate. She stops pacing and steps closer, peering over the threshold into the everything. To someone who wasn't a Moon, it would look like nothing, like the void, but for her, it's a shaft of silver moonlight shot with rainbows, each textured with every possibility the universe is considering and rejecting, millions of sparks of color per second, most guttering out without even an echo. And there, in the middle of the corridor, is Máni, walking toward the gate.

He's moving slow, slower than he should be. He's a big guy, attending school on a football scholarship, fond of hitting the gym and hitting his teammates with almost equal enthusiasm; even when he's tired, he isn't slow.

Then he takes another step forward, and she sees why he's moving so slowly. He's carrying someone, body curled like a comma, limbs dangling limp and heavy. Another step, and she sees the long cascade of wheat-gold hair draped over his arm, tangled and, in one spot, matted with what looks like dried blood mixed with mercury. She shudders but doesn't step away. She's wondered, a few times, what would happen if one of them was hurt while they were fully incarnate, stepping into the space between human and abstract idea, creatures of light and belief capable of shining down on the Impossible City without being struck dead by the sight.

Apparently the answer is "the one who gets hurt bleeds moonlight along with the normal red stuff, and dies anyway." She's not sure she wanted to know that.

Máni stops just before he reaches the gate, putting his burden down on the shimmering silver-bright ground. The body that was Aske rolls a little, face turned upward, and her eyes are open, blue and blank and unseeing. She was a goddess. She had only just learned that she was a goddess. She should have had decades to shine, to discover the limits of her power, before she faded.

She shouldn't have *died*. But Chang'e can't look at her and pretend she's not gone. Her chest doesn't move; she doesn't blink; there's nothing left of Aske but meat.

"What . . . ?" Chang'e asks, looking away from the corpse, fixing her attention on Máni. "How?"

"I went to the City like I'm supposed to," he says. There's blood on his hands and smeared on the front of his shirt, still gleaming silver. It hurts to look at. "I went to shine. But when I got there, Aske was on the ground in front of the window, and the window was wrong. There was a . . . a trail, behind her, like she crawled there."

Chang'e swallows hard and looks at Aske's hands. True enough, the girl's fingernails are split and broken, her fingertips gleaming silver-red. She dragged herself to the window that allows them to enter the Impossible City somehow. How, Chang'e can't imagine.

"I didn't want to leave her there," says Máni. "I couldn't leave her there. But I had to shine. The light was building inside me, and it hurt. I had to leave her while I crossed the City sky." He looks at Chang'e, and there are tears in his eyes. Sweet Moon above, he looks like he's going to cry, and Chang'e doesn't know what to do with that. Maybe if she could step down into the mortal woman she is when she's not a Moon, she'd know, but the gate is open, and she's stuck as she is until it's closed. "I had to *leave* her."

"I'm so sorry," says Chang'e. "Come through the gate."

Máni looks at her like she's a monster of some sort. "I can't just walk through the door with a dead body, Judy," he snaps.

"Judy isn't here right now," says Chang'e. "She's in the waiting space until you come through the gate."

"Still a dead body," says Máni.

"Yes," says Chang'e. "I'm sorry, but if you can't carry her through the gate, you'll have to leave her where she is. Tomorrow's gate will be elsewhere, so she's not going to be in the way."

He stares at her. "That's . . . How can you even say that!"

"Very easily. I speak seventeen languages fluently, and I can say that in any of them." Chang'e looks at him calmly. "She's still stepped up into her incarnation. Even if you didn't worry about being seen carrying a dead white girl across campus, how would you explain a dead white girl who bleeds silver and glows in the dark?

Her divinity needs to pass before she can be moved through the gate."

"Can her divinity pass if it's not in the human world?"

"An interesting question, and one we should probably put before our elders," says Chang'e. "Please, come through, so the gate can close and the hour can pass."

Máni glares at her before he finally, belatedly, steps through the gate. The tunnel into everything on the other side trembles, shaking like a clothesline in a heavy wind, and then the gate is gone, and the place where it was is only the blank granite wall of the Campanile, the great bell tower that virtually dominates the campus. It was severely damaged in the earthquake almost ten years ago; the granite facing was only restored to the sides earlier this year, completing its long and intricate repair. The gate anchors here roughly once a month, which is convenient, if a bit more exposed than Chang'e prefers.

The gleaming silver blood on Máni's clothes and hands remains, a scrap of the incarnate world carried over into this one, and the sight of it is unnerving and exciting. This is something new.

The gate is gone, but the process isn't finished. Chang'e holds out her hand. "Key, please."

Máni looks at her with disgust but reaches into his pocket and produces the key, which is the same silver as Aske's blood. His fingers leave red smears on the metal, completing the likeness. Chang'e takes it and slides it into her pocket, bowing her head in acknowledgment. He doesn't return the gesture.

There is a shining light in the air around them, glitter dancing in the watery beams of the rising sun. As the key finds its place at the bottom of her pocket, the glitter fades, and the light fades with it, and they finally step down from their divinity, two shining figures becoming two twentysomething college students. Anyone who sees it happen will dismiss it as a trick of the morning air, a mirage, and it's both those things, but it's also a reality, as so many mirages are.

"The fuck, David?" asks Judy.

He raises his hands, showing her the blood on his fingers. It's visible against his dark skin in the dim light because there's still silver threaded through it, bright and impossible. "I can't believe you made me leave her there," he complains.

"Okay, as we've tried to make you understand, I didn't do that," says Judy. "Chang'e did that. We're not the same as our deities, we're more . . . the reflections they cast when they aren't using the energy to manifest."

He rolls his eyes. "I was here first."

"Debatable. But: if you saw a corpse, would you be able to bring yourself to pick it up and carry it back to your dorm? And even if you could, would you be able to go and do a full shift at your job first, knowing the body was there?"

David blanches. He's a dark enough man under normal circumstances that it doesn't show as much as it might, but he normally looks a lot healthier than that. How he avoids getting a tan when he spends half his time on the football field, Judy may never know.

"I don't know how I was able to just walk away from her like that." He looks over his shoulder at the wall, which shows no traces of the gate. "I just *left* her there."

"No, Máni did," says Judy. "You need to get a little distance between you. You'll be able to do this a lot longer if you can. We can't go around being gods all the time. Thank you for bringing back the key; I'll go talk to Diana this afternoon. Do you want to be there?"

"I have practice," he says, quickly. He's afraid of Diana. Most of the new incarnates are. She's the only one a lot of them have heard of before they encounter the whole pantheon, and while she's not the most powerful of them, her name gives her a certain reputation that Judy can't decide whether she wants to envy or be grateful she doesn't have to deal with.

"Okay," she says, shrugging. Then she looks at his hands again. "When you wash up, be sure to use bleach."

"I didn't kill her," he said.

"I know. This isn't about destroying the evidence. It's about making sure the alchemists can't use it."

"Oh. Right."

There aren't many alchemists on campus these days. New gods still need to learn good habits, like not washing traces of divinity down communal sinks. She sighs as she turns away.

Time to head for her advisor's office and begin dealing with the mortal, mundane day. God business can wait.

After all, what's the point of being a living face of the Moon if she still has to hurry?

Mare Cognitum

The alarm is going off again.

Kelpie doesn't look up from the reagent she's trying to mix. Several of the compounds she's using are dangerous ones, and on some level, she's incredibly proud that Margaret is willing to trust her with volatile chemicals, given the proof of past lab accidents that she sees every time she looks in a mirror. It wouldn't be unreasonable for management to restrict her to harmless tasks, like feeding the frogs in the bio lab or gathering the laundry. The alarm is a distraction, but it's not going to break her focus, oh, no. It's not going to make her mess up again.

Maybe if she'd been this focused *before* the accident, she wouldn't be in her current condition. But as Margaret likes to say, if wishes were horses, beggars would ride, and the only person who can bottle the past is a reality traitor who refuses to support the people who created her.

Kelpie doesn't understand that. Life is a gift. Constructs receive it as a burden, a task to complete to the best of their abilities, and cuckoos receive it as a treasure, a great and glorious miracle to be reveled in and revealed. For a cuckoo to reject the gift of their creation and go rogue is unthinkable. Yet two of them have, Reed's "perfect creations" choosing not only to flee the nest but to leave it burning behind them. It doesn't make sense. They should have been the most loyal of their kind, and instead they killed the man who made them and fled into the wider world, where they had yet to be recovered.

She wishes the damn alarm would stop. It's starting to make her head ache, and when she gets a bad enough headache, she sometimes has to lie down for days. Margaret says it's leftover trauma from the accident, buried memories of the explosion purging themselves from her psyche. Kelpie wants to believe her. She wants to believe this is something that might eventually get better. And to be fair, a lot of things have improved over the last year. She had to relearn how to walk, how to dress herself, all sorts of everyday tasks she's sure were easy once, before she forgot everything she knew and was forcibly demoted back to lab assistant for her own safety.

The alarm finally stops. She relaxes, reaching for the next flask on her list. Alarms are virtually an hourly occurrence when the lab is active, and this is a big season for them; there's a total solar eclipse approaching, and many of their projects will be able to mature or even come to full fruition while the sun is blocked by the moon. It's all about the sympathies, the greater universe singing to their work until a harmony can be established.

She doesn't remember the specifics anymore. She supposes that's one of the things Margaret has yet to teach her, but she's eager to relearn. The more she can recover of who she used to be, the better she'll be able to cope with who she currently is, and the easier it will be to see a path back to her true nature. Understanding is the key to evolution, after all.

Footsteps approach her station. She glances up, just for an instant, and then looks quickly back down, cheeks burning. Margaret is walking over. She's not alone.

The man beside her—because it's always a man when the Congress sends someone to inspect the lab; all these years, all these decades since the Asphodel incident, and they still continue to insist that only men can truly grasp the complexities of the alchemical world, as if rejecting Asphodel Baker wasn't the greatest mistake the American Alchemical Congress ever made—is thin enough that "bony" might be a better descriptor. His skin is pulled tight over his skeleton, until it looks as if it might rip in several spots, his cheekbones on the verge of wearing their way through, his collarbones a pair of commas visible even through the perfectly tailored fit of his suit. He's not as pale as many of the elder alchemists; this is someone who still leaves his lab on occasion, which is just shy of a miracle in the more powerful ones. His hair is the color of melted iron, dull silver and strangely unsettling, like it's something not meant to be looked at directly.

Margaret walks by his side, clearly anxious, a clipboard under one arm and her free hand fluttering beside her, nerves keeping it from stilling. Her hair is perfect, as always, a long, inky fall of black brushed to a mirror sheen—the one scrap of vanity the lab allows. Kelpie's seen her preparing to go out after work is finished, seen her dressed in lace and leather, kohl around her eyes and carmine on her lips, darling of the goth scene, perfect club princess. That's not the Margaret they have here. This Margaret wears sensible shoes and button-down blouses, perfectly pressed khaki pants and pristine lab coats. This Margaret is as much a creature of the lab environment as the white mice in their cages or the frogs in their purified water, as the constructs who work two levels down, or as Kelpie herself. And this Margaret is afraid.

Kelpie isn't at a particularly delicate point in the process, so she sets her flask aside, puts down her pipette, and straightens, trying to look eager to be helpful without looking like she expects the honor of an address from a visiting member of the Congress. It's a fine line to walk, and her balance isn't the best, but she tries, and sometimes trying is enough.

"And this is one of our assistants, Kelpie," says Margaret to the visiting alchemist. She shoots Kelpie a quick, quelling look, silently cautioning her not to speak unless spoken to. Kelpie's right ear flicks involuntarily back, but she gives no other acknowledgment that she's noticed, only stands in sentinel silence, watching the pair.

The man looks at her, frowns, and looks back to Margaret. "I was told this level of your operation was all naturals," he says. "No constructs or cuckoos."

"Kelpie's not a cuckoo," says Margaret, promptly. "She was in a lab accident last year, and there have been some . . . lasting effects."

Kelpie says nothing, doesn't acknowledge the fact that she's being talked about like she's not here. It's safer to be treated like a piece of lab equipment, especially when they have visitors. She's an interesting case, and there are plenty of people associated with the Congress who would be happy to take her apart and see how her organs are able to function, how the seemingly disparate aspects of her physical body can coexist without causing some sort of massive medical crisis. Better to seem serene and expensive than charismatic and expendable.

"Fascinating," says the alchemist. He looks more closely at Kelpie, who tries to hold as still as she can. "You're *sure* she's natural?"

"Absolutely," says Margaret, with just a flicker of discomfort in her eyes. That makes Kelpie blink, which seems to startle the man; even as close to her as he is, he had apparently done what so many do when confronted with her biological reality, and shunted it into a back corner of his mind where he could treat her like some sort of doll or sculpture, interesting, not alive.

"All right." The man turns to face Margaret, and Kelpie blinks again. He looks like he's about to start giving instructions, but they're in the middle of the lab, not in one of the closed offices. Instructions aren't given in the open, unless they're drastic ones.

"Master Davis is very impressed with the progress you've managed to make toward forcing the sub-incarnations into physical form, but disappointed that you haven't been able to intercept any of the more powerful Lunes. Your assignment was clear: the priority is the City."

"Many of the Lunars were historically known to travel in the company of their sub-incarnations," says Margaret. "You rarely saw Chang'e without the Rabbit, or Artemis without her Hind, or the Old Man without his Dog. If we can create their companions in a controlled setting, we can use those companions to attract them. They'll want to recover what they see as their property. We're close to a breakthrough—I think several of our prepared vessels have begun to accumulate the sympathy we're looking for."

"Master Davis received a report last year that implied you were close to the successful manifestation of Artemis's hind," says the stranger, not commenting on Margaret's use of the outdated term for the lunar incarnates. "Lunars" is seen as romanticizing a natural function of the universe, an inconveniently common and uncontrollable tendency of the moon to manifest human avatars who refuse to listen to the alchemists making perfectly reasonable requests.

Like requests for access to the Impossible City. It's not fair that a group of seemingly random nobodies should be empowered to enter that hallowed municipality nightly, while men of knowledge and education are barred. "Lune" is accurate, descriptive, and blunt. These people don't deserve to be romanticized. And they certainly don't deserve to have their pets returned.

"We were," says Margaret, voice carefully modulated, not looking at Kelpie. "But there were complications with the formulas we were using, and the project had to be restarted from scratch. We're currently much closer on the Rabbit and the Dog. I can take you to see them, if you'd like?"

"That won't be necessary." The man smiles. Given the tightness of his skin, he resembles nothing so much as a grinning cadaver, something that's been dead long enough to begin to dry and desiccate. "As I said before, Master Davis is very impressed by your progress. Your proposal was ambitious to begin with, and success was never a guarantee. He is, however, even more disappointed by your failure to produce concrete results, and by your refusal to disclose all projects to the Congress. Or did you think we wouldn't know about your little locked room?"

Margaret stiffens but otherwise gives no indication that his words have managed to strike home. Kelpie is less equipped to be subtle. She wraps her tail around her leg, squeezing tightly, and hopes he won't notice. Margaret has been working on a personal project for as long as Kelpie can remember, a human body growing in a vat, perfectly shaped, perfectly functional, and perfectly empty. It's a tailored suit made of meat, and on the days when she despairs of ever looking like a real person again, Kelpie dreams of slipping it on and doing up the buttons, of hiding her abnormalities under a veil of perfection.

She's always known Margaret was using Congressional resources for her work, but assumed she had received approval before starting. From the way the man is looking at her now, she guesses that was wrong.

She guesses Margaret's in real trouble.

The man nods as if Margaret's silence has confirmed everything he suspected. "Under the circumstances, you can't be surprised that Master Davis has elected to focus on a group with a more . . . practical approach to the situation."

Margaret stares at him. "You can't do that! We have Congressional approval through to the end of the year! It's four days to the eclipse!"

"As you say, but another research team has produced dramatic results in the past week, and may have achieved what you've been failing to do." The stranger stops smiling, now looking gravely at Margaret. The resemblance to something already dead doesn't fade. "Have faith in those who seek the City, and the light will guide you home."

"You sound like one of Reed's acolytes," says Margaret, tone sour. She doesn't seem to see the flicker of disappointment cross the man's face, or the way he turns to look at the equipment around him. He seems to be assessing it, charting its value, as if it were something he had the authority to liquidate.

"And you sound like an untrained amateur," he says, returning his attention to her. "One of those scruffy hedge witches who picked up a book in her school library and decided it made her powerful. They're like you, you know. Eager, ambitious, foolhardy. Unaccustomed to listening to authority. Master Davis *made* you and your little project. He has the authority to unmake you."

He gives Kelpie one last, dismissive look, says, "Lab accident," and walks away, shaking his head.

Margaret stays where she is, shoulders drooping as she clutches her clipboard to her chest and watches him go. Kelpie waits until he reaches the stairs, until he's well and truly gone, before she moves around her desk and puts a hand on Margaret's shoulder, offering what comfort she can.

"It'll be all right," she says.

"No, it won't," says Margaret. She reaches into the pocket of her lab coat, pulling out something small, which she slips into her mouth and beneath her tongue. "We're being shut down, Kelpie. That means they close the lab, liquidate its assets, and reassign our researchers. I worked for years to get this project approved, and it's working—it's *working*. We've been calling the incarnates more and more concretely into their vessels since last year's break-through, and we were going to have a usable one soon, I know we were."

"Why do we want a Lunar, anyway?"

The question is earnestly asked, and Margaret only sighs a little as she looks back at her. "I've told you this half a dozen times."

"My memory isn't what it used to be," says Kelpie. "That's why I'm not allowed to mix anything potentially explosive."

"Right. Right. Okay, do you remember the Impossible City?"

"I'd have to be a lot more scrambled than I am to forget *that*," says Kelpie. The Impossible City is Olympus, Avalon, Atlantis—the goal at the end of the long, winding, improbable alchemical road. Everything they do is in service of the City, of finding the way to get there before someone else can beat them to the gates. Before Reed's escaped, feral cuckoos can seize it as their own and refuse it to the decent, hard-working, *real* people who deserve to hold it.

"Just making sure," says Margaret. "Most people can't enter the City under normal circumstances. The Seasonals can, during a coronation, and we have reason to believe they become permanent residents after they finish serving their seasons. Some Elements can pass the borders, depending on their situations, and of course,

Reed's cuckoos have the authority to claim the Tower if they so choose."

"They can't *do* that," protests Kelpie. "The Tower belongs to the Queen of Wands!"

"And the Queen of Wands has been dead since before the turn of the century," says Margaret. "She made Reed, she set him to publishing her manuscripts and establishing her dogma, and she died. If she's going to come back, she needs to do it sooner than later, because those cuckoos could get tired of waiting any day now."

Kelpie looks at her sullenly. "I don't like that."

"None of us do. The Lunars are a special case. They go to the City nightly, to shine on the streets from above. They have some sort of system, one that lets them keep being ordinary people while they're also serving as the Moon over the Impossible City; when we've managed to get one under surveillance, we've never seen them go twice in a row. We don't know how they set their schedule. Just capturing one isn't going to be good enough, because what if this is something they do collectively, something they agree on and organize? Put a Lunar in a cage and maybe they never manifest again, or maybe they turn into moonlight and fade away. Either way, we don't get into the City, and they know we're hunting them, which puts us at a disadvantage."

"Which is why we're trying to force sub-incarnations to become manifest," says Kelpie, proud that she remembers this part. "If we can fully manifest a sub-incarnation, it should attract its primary, like a baby bird crying for its mother. And then we can use the sub-incarnation to convince the Lunar to do what we want."

"Which is let us into the Impossible City," says Margaret. She looks at Kelpie with uncharacteristic solemnity. "We *need* to access the City. Humans are so important that half the universe has rewritten itself to have the chance to experience humanity firsthand. Doesn't that mean we should be the ones in charge?"

"Sure," says Kelpie.

"Because, see, one thing we didn't consider when we started trying to do this is that even a sub-incarnation was likely to be a person in their own right. We thought since we were calling animals, at least according to the stories, we'd get *animals*. And maybe we would have, if we'd had any recipes that weren't based on Baker and Reed's work." Margaret refuses to refer to Asphodel by her first name, says it's not right that Reed always gets his surname when his creator was unquestionably the greater alchemist. She calls it a demonstration of casual misogyny, the way powerful men become surnames and powerful women never do.

Kelpie thinks she probably agrees with her, but she also thinks of the woman who crafted the first cuckoo as Asphodel, like she's a beloved family member or mentor. The name suits her better than either "Baker" or "Deborah," those being the other names she went by. Sometimes the shape of a name matters as much as the intent behind it.

She's sure she had a different name before the accident. It would be too on the nose for someone named after a shapeshifting water horse to have her shapeshifted against her will, much less wind up with hooves of her own. She's *sure*. She just can't imagine what it might have been, and none of the other names she's tried to wear have fit her.

"You mixed human into the vessels?" asks Kelpie, trying to make sure she understands what Margaret is trying to say. She's never been this forthcoming about the project before; every time Kelpie's tried to ask, Margaret has waved her off, saying she has better things to worry about than a bunch of silly science that she's never going to be asked to replicate.

Margaret nods. "Human, and material Reed harvested from a Lunar that somehow wound up in his keeping."

Kelpie has no idea what that means, but she doesn't want to interrupt again and ask, not when Margaret feels like talking. So she only nods, and listens.

"I think that's where we went wrong with our first batch. We wound up with *people* when we manifested the sub-incarnate aspects of the Moon. Yes, we made a Rabbit, and he had long ears and strong legs and looked like something out of a cartoon, but he was

also a person who liked to read and argue about sustainable farm-
ing techniques, and one of the other research teams snagged him to
work in their agricultural development lab, and we didn't have the
heart to tell them no, not when other approaches might still be successful. If we handed him over to the people who funded us, he'd be
used as bait to lure in Chang'e, assuming she's got an incarnation
on this continent, and then he'd be slaughtered like an animal. As
if that were all he was."

Margaret looks at Kelpie, very seriously, her face drawn.

"Essentially, we succeeded, and then we had to start over from
the beginning if we didn't want to become monsters in the process,"
she says. "The City is essential. No sacrifice is too great to achieve it.
But there's a difference between a sacrifice you make and a sacrifice
that's made. If the sub-incarnations are people, they need to understand what they're dying for, or the sympathies will be all wrong.
They need time to be people, and to live as people, and to not think
of themselves as anything *but* people. Do you understand?"

Kelpie is terribly afraid that she does. So she shakes her head and
says, "No. I don't."

That's not what Margaret was expecting. She blinks, mouth forming a round O of surprise for just a moment before she says, "You're
not that naïve, Kelp. You must have figured it out by now."

"There's nothing to figure out," says Kelpie. "I'm a researcher in
this lab. I came here after my alchemical studies reached a point
where I needed a group environment to progress any farther, and I
was in a bad accident a year ago that left me changed and missing
large pieces of my memory."

"Kelpie . . ."

"That's all I am," says Kelpie firmly. "For me to be anything else
would mean you'd been lying, and more, that you'd been lying for
my entire life, because I would never have known anything outside
this lab. And you wouldn't do that, because you're my friend. You
told me you were my friend. Friends don't tell lies like that, so I'm a
researcher who had an accident."

"All right," says Margaret, in a soothing tone. "That's what you are. But if the people who come to shut us down tell you you're something else, you need to be ready to run. You need to realize they're not going to see you the same way I do. Are you ready to die to reach the City?"

Kelpie recoils. She can't help it.

Margaret nods. "That's what I thought. You're going to have to run. I'm sorry we didn't have more time."

The alarm is going off again. Kelpie's really starting to hate that thing. She can't imagine what could have set it off this time, not when she and Margaret are alone in the lab. But the alarm is blaring, loud enough to make her head ring in sympathy. She claps her hands over her ears, looking around for some indication of what's wrong.

Something is coming out of the overhead vents. Something thick and gaseous and silvery gray. It sparkles in a way smoke should never sparkle, moves as thickly and viscously as a gel, but the way it hangs suspended in the air tells her it's not. Kelpie makes a wordless sound of displeasure and points.

Margaret follows her shaking finger and sighs. "That's about what I expected," she says.

"What is it?"

"Do you remember the way the inspector reacted when he saw you? How unhappy he was at the thought that there might be someone on this level who wasn't purely natural? This is the Alchemical Congress. Anyone who proposes a project to them understands that failure comes with consequences. You don't get the chance to fail twice, but there are always other ways someone can contribute to the pursuit of knowledge. You're not ready to die for the City, and that's fair and good and right. I knew when I was put in charge of this lab that I had to be ready, and I've *been* ready for a long, long time." Margaret sighs again, shrugs, and begins removing her lab coat, folding it neatly over her arm. "You might not want to stay for this next part, unless you need to see what happens in order to believe it."

"I don't . . . I don't understand."

"Lead really does block virtually everything," says Margaret, sounding oddly serene. Whatever it was she took before she decided to get unusually candid with Kelpie is working, taking the edges off what should have been a terrifying situation. "As long as we kept you down here, no one noticed your presence. Once you make it aboveground, she'll notice you soon enough."

"Who?"

"Artemis. She's probably been looking for you since you came manifest, even if she doesn't know what she's looking for. Oh, she's going to be happy to see you. I promise, she's going to love you."

The smoke has almost reached them. Kelpie grabs Margaret's arm, trying to pull her out of its path.

"You said they'd reassign the researchers," she says, frantically. "You're a researcher."

"I'm not," corrects Margaret. "I'm the project lead. I don't get reassigned. I get recycled. I get to be part of someone else's project, as raw materials, not as a contributor. Run, Kelpie. You don't want to watch."

Kelpie pulls on her arm one more time, but Margaret is heavier than she is, Margaret doesn't budge. Finally, Kelpie lets go and dances back, out of the path of the smoke. It continues to drop, finally reaching Margaret, who turns her face upward and closes her eyes, smiling like a child greeting the sun.

That pill must have been an incredibly potent painkiller, because the first thick tears that run out from beneath Margaret's eyelids are tinted the color of her eyes, and the ones that follow are red with blood. Margaret sighs, a shuddering sound that turns thick toward the end, burbling, like she's exhaling through mud. She's still smiling; she hasn't fallen. She tries to sigh again, and the sound turns into a cough, leaving her lips stained with a thin layer of blood. She raises her hand to catch the cough. Her skin is already beginning to bubble and drip, fizzing like it's been carbonated.

Kelpie can't watch any more of this. She turns and sprints away, scrambling for balance on the slick floor, and she doesn't stop running until she hits the stairwell. The stairs extend in two directions:

down to the safe familiarity of the lower labs, the hydroponics and the bio storage rooms, the kitchens and the residential quarters. There will be people down there, people who know her, who treat her like a junior alchemist who survived a terrible lab accident and had to relearn everything from scratch—people who have, if Margaret was telling the truth, been lying to her every single day, telling her one thing when they really mean another.

She believes Margaret. Margaret has always been good to her. Margaret has apparently been lying to her like everyone else, but there's no reason for her to have kept lying when she knew she was about to die. People tend to tell the truth when they can see death coming toward them. She doesn't *want* to believe Margaret. Believing Margaret means accepting everything she's ever known was a lie, and that comes with implications she won't be able to wrap her head around for quite a while, if ever. But she *does* believe Margaret. She can't go down.

Up leads to the higher levels of the lab, places she's never been, the personnel offices and classrooms, and eventually, at the very top of the stairs, the outside world. She's always wondered why she doesn't miss it more, the blue sky and fresh air and other things she's seen in pictures and always assumed were in the missing parts of her mind. Now she has her answer: she hasn't been grieving for the world beyond the lab because she's never been there. She doesn't know how she's going to survive out there, all things considered, but that's where she has to go, or the man with the skeleton smile is going to come back and find her, and what he does to her won't be nearly as merciful as what he did to Margaret.

Alkahest, when used in a gaseous mixture, is not a painless way to die, but it's a fast one, and Margaret had warning enough to take a painkiller before the alkahest began eating away at her nerves. As methods of execution go, this one came surprisingly close to kindness.

Kelpie's not very experienced. She's naïve but not unintelligent: she knows there's no possible way she was that close to Margaret when the alkahest reached her without also being exposed. The fact that she's not melting yet means Margaret was telling the truth. She's not natural. She's constructed. And if she was constructed using Baker and Reed's recipes, she's part of the subclass of constructs they call "cuckoos," and that means the man with the skeleton smile isn't going to be kind when he catches her. He's going to kill her, too, but he's going to take his time about it.

Cuckoos are dangerous. Cuckoos go feral and turn on their creators. Cuckoos seize the forces they were intended to embody and hoard them away from the alchemists who really deserve them. If she's a cuckoo, as long as she's alive, she's going to muddy the question of who owns her manifestation, whatever it's supposed to be.

Artemis's Hind, she supposes. It would explain the hooves, and the tail, and the other parts of her anatomy that never made much sense as the consequences of a simple lab accident. She's seen stranger—it wasn't outside the realm of possibility—but it was odd enough to make her wonder.

The Congress wants the Lunars. Margaret swore the companion aspects were the key to catching them, and Artemis is one of the ones whose name is still spoken with reasonable frequency; she's one of the more powerful Lunars walking the world, and that makes her desirable. Kelpie doesn't want to spend the rest of her probably short life as bait.

Up is the only possible direction.

So she climbs the steps, wincing every time her hoof hits the metal and sends the sound ringing through the stairwell, and she doesn't stop until she reaches the door at the top. She pushes it open and light floods in, so much light, light like she's never seen before. It's blinding. It's beautiful.

Kelpie steps out into the sun.

Lacus Timoris

TIMELINE: AUGUST 17, 2017.
FOUR DAYS TO THE ECLIPSE.

Judy's advisor is a smart man. He'd have to be, to hold his position for more than an afternoon; people who aren't clever tend to fail once they hit a certain level of academia. That's not a judgment—Judy's own parents couldn't understand half of what she said before they died, even when she was speaking one of their shared languages, and they were both brilliant. Their brilliance was just focused on other things, leaving matters like accreditation, thesis defense, and class planning to people with the mental room to care.

Judy cares. Judy cares a *lot*. The current record for most languages spoken fluently by a single person is forty-two, and she plans on beating that. Professor Middleton, who probably speaks languages numbered in the hundreds, doesn't count. He's never going to sit down with the people who maintain the Guinness Book and let them put him through his paces, because if he did, he'd be revealed as something more than human. Which means, given the way the scraps of magic still left in the world protect themselves, that he'd go through the whole process, only for the examiners to forget, if he was lucky. If he wasn't lucky, they'd turn out to be alchemists, or they'd be in a terrible accident before they could report their findings, and he'd have to carry the guilt over their deaths forever. Either way, he won't be appearing on any official lists.

Judy isn't like him, isn't the living incarnation of the concepts behind spoken and written language. She has a natural talent for languages, but she has to work at it, has to study and make an effort for every new sentence structure and scrap of syntax. Chang'e isn't a goddess of language, never has been so far as Judy can tell, and she's gone digging for every obscure myth and retelling she can find. Being able to read them in their original dialects helps a lot, and yet she's never found a mention of the goddess who maintains the peach orchards on the moon having a gift for Scrabble, much less the foundational blocks of language itself. That means she's not cheating when she goes for the record, and *that* means she needs to do things according to the rules. Which means degrees and advisors and so much homework that sometimes she wants to scream and start throwing things.

Dictionaries are heavy. They make surprisingly effective projectiles.

And because her advisor is a smart man, when she walked into his office this morning, emotionally loaded for bear and ready to pick a fight over basically anything, he had gone immediately into damage-control mode. He didn't agree to anything that was going to hurt her academically, but he also didn't bring up the increasingly sensitive subject of Professor Middleton's Language Acquisition course, which she needs to pass in order to continue with her current research focus.

(Judy chose Berkeley for her graduate work out of a list of possible colleges based on their linguistics department *before* it became common knowledge that one of their junior professors and rising stars was a cuckoo of Reed's creation. "Common knowledge" in this case meaning the Seasonals found out, and once the Seasonals knew, all the pantheons were quickly informed, since every group of gods worth knowing had at least one member associated in some way with the seasons. By the time she'd learned the unobtrusive man with the wire-framed glasses and the tendency to drink too much coffee before classes was also the metaphysical equivalent of a thermonuclear device without a safety, she'd been two years into her graduate program and well established within the local Lunar community. Starting over without a good, believable, mundane reason would be virtually impossible. ("I'm afraid I'll attract the attention of the man who just walked into a glass wall because he was so busy yelling at the baseball scores on his phone that he didn't realize it was there" isn't a reason.)

Thanks to her advisor's uncharacteristic sense of self-preservation, Judy leaves the meeting far calmer than she expected, ready to go and deal with Diana. Like Middleton, Diana is a teacher at the school, but as she teaches textile arts—the much-maligned "underwater basket weaving" course was one of hers, and she still defends it when people bring it up—she's at far less risk of attracting Middleton's terrifying regard than Judy is.

Some people have all the luck.

Judy lopes across campus with the quick, efficient stride of someone who's had someplace to be since five minutes before she was born and hasn't missed an appointment yet. She smiles and nods at other students as she passes them, endlessly pleasant, endlessly polite. It's easier that way. She's done the research; the amount of energy she expends being nice to people she'll never see again is far less than the amount expended if she has to deal with someone whose bad day explodes all over her when they decide she's being antisocial. Managing the feelings of others shouldn't be her job, and yet it's a job she's willing to do if it means she doesn't have to fight.

Many of them smile and wave back. She even knows a few of their names, the natural consequence of spending several years running across the same campus. She's never taken an art class here, never plans to—her main artistic activity is calligraphy, and while she's skilled, she doesn't feel the need to take it from hobby to profession, doesn't want to turn it into one more obligation—and still, she's a common sight around the department.

The reason why is just wrapping up a beginning weaver's course when Judy reaches her classroom door. Diana isn't currently stepped up into her divinity, which means she's just Professor Kira Williams, an ordinary middle-aged woman. She's tall and thickly built, ornately braided hair shot through with veins of incredibly pure white that started coming in when she first manifested as a facet of Diana, and look more appropriate to her age with every year that passes.

Most Lunars gray early. Judy herself started at sixteen. It's one of the only signs of aging the Peaches of Immortality can't conceal or erase, and in this case, it wouldn't matter if they could; Professor Williams believes divinity isn't the same as immortality, and that if it were, her aging would have stopped on its own, not because she drinks a few peach smoothies a week. She hasn't requested so much as a sip of peach juice since Judy came to campus, and it doesn't seem like she's going to start any time soon. She's aging the way everyone else does, and one day, when age catches up to her, she'll pass quietly into whatever waits for incarnate goddesses when they die.

Professor Williams wears jeans and a brightly colored smock, which means she probably has a painting class after this one. She sees Judy in the doorway and nods acknowledgement without stopping what she's doing, continuing to move among her students, nudging and helping them toward their desired results. She's old-fashioned and a little on the crunchy granola side of things, with her socks and sandals and office full of macramé she made herself, but her student assessments are always spectacular, and her graduates often go on to actual careers in the arts.

Judy retreats to the nearest bench to sit and absorb the sunlight while she can. It's been a long week. She'll be glad when it's over. Tonight is her turn to step into the sky above the Impossible City and shine down on a populace she's never known, one who doesn't care if she smiles and waves on her way to class.

Some people say that when Moons die, they get passports to the City. They can go there forever, if that's what they want to do. As long as it's not forced, Judy thinks that could be a pretty decent severance package. She wants to be the greatest natural linguist in the world (she's not natural, she's a moon goddess, but no one *made* her that way; her parents, Moon rest their souls, were ordinary people whose squalling, screaming infant daughter just happened to attract the attention of a cosmic force), and that means being *in* the world, for as long as it takes. It doesn't matter if Middleton will always outperform her. She'll know the truth, and that means she can win.

Shining over the City is the ultimate manifestation of what a Moon can be in this world. It's more relaxing than a week of good sleep or an orgasm so strong it takes your breath away. That's why they have to take turns, why there have to be so many of them passing the mantle around. It would be easy to get addicted to the sky above the City, to fall so deep into the pattern of waxing and waning in that psalm-bright air, that if one Moon had to do it alone for very long, they'd forget how to step down. They'd stop being human, and if they stopped being human, the Moon would leave them, because what's the point of having a mortal manifestation that refuses to be mortal?

No one knows what would happen to them after that. If it's ever happened, it was so long ago that it isn't even a cautionary tale anymore. Maybe one of the moon stories has the seed of that event tucked deep inside, wreathed in image and metaphor until it doesn't bear any resemblance to what actually occurred. Judy doesn't know.

Supposedly there's a Moon somewhere in Oregon who studies folklore for a living. Maybe she'd know. But that would require caring enough to ask, which would take energy, and right now, Judy doesn't have any. Right now, she has the sun, and the bench, and the sound of someone sitting down beside her.

Judy cracks open an eye, and there's Professor Williams, smiling kindly. There's a hard glint in the older woman's eyes, and Judy knows if she wastes her time, she's going to face the consequences. Professor Williams doesn't suffer fools easily.

"Are we alone?" she asks.

The professor nods. "For the moment."

"Is there somewhere we could go to make sure we *stay* alone?"

The hard glint softens, replaced by puzzlement. "Is there a reason you need to speak to me in private and couldn't wait for office hours, my dear?"

"Yes, and if I say it and we're not alone, we're both going to have issues. So is there somewhere we can go?"

Professor Williams stands with a sigh, offering Judy her hand and pulling the younger woman from the bench. Judy goes willingly—this is why she came, after all—and doesn't take offense when the professor drops her hand as quickly as she took it, not allowing the contact to linger. Moons don't like to touch each other when they can avoid it. They're all manifestations of different human ideas about the identity they share, but there's only one moon in the sky at night. There's a dissonance to the contact that the human nervous system isn't quite equipped to deal with.

Professor Williams starts to walk away and Judy follows, into the building and past classrooms both empty and occupied until they reach a large supply closet. Professor Williams gestures for Judy to follow her inside, then shuts the door and turns to face her. As she does, her dark eyes glint silver, and the air around her begins to sparkle with a pale, impossible light.

Diana.

"You didn't need to step up to speak to me," says Judy, without heat. She'd probably have done the same if one of *her* juniors had come to her and asked her to go somewhere alone with them, refusing to explain the reasons why. It's self-protection, and it only makes sense.

The Moons aren't like the Seasons. They cooperate. They get along. But there *are* old stories about times when one member of the pantheon decided they wanted more time above the City, and started taking people out of the rotation the old-fashioned way.

If she hadn't been there when Máni came through the gate with Aske's blood on his hands—if it hadn't been Máni, who clings to mortality like it's a lifeline—she might have suspected him of doing exactly that. Younger Lunars are more likely to be tempted by the sweet City air, even though they're less likely to have the power to do anything about it.

"I think I do," says Diana. Judy can hear Professor Williams under the voice of the goddess, but she's faint, an echo, like the woman is speaking down a long hallway. Diana's really nervous, then, if she stepped up that fast and that far. Judy has to fight the urge to step up to match her. Chang'e isn't as powerful as Diana. If Diana saw her natural reaction as a threat . . .

No. Better to stay as she is, and let the old image of the mortal petitioner kneeling before the divine placate Diana's anxieties. Judy takes a deep breath, pushing her own anxieties aside.

"Máni went to the City last night," she says. "He was late coming back by over an hour. I had to hold the gate open and wait for him to return with the key."

"That isn't my concern," says Diana. "I'm not the one who makes sure you come and go when you're supposed to."

Somehow, no one is, and somehow, that doesn't keep them all from sticking to the schedule like they're being managed. Even the ones like Máni, who'd rather not do anything that involves showing up for work, still know when it's their turn, and still show up. Maybe it's the actual moon, somehow, some intrinsic part of their shared identity reflecting down through the whole pantheon.

"I know," says Judy. "But I had to wait, and it's important you know I waited. I was at the gate before Máni came out. He didn't have a chance to hide anything from me. But he was late."

Diana frowns. Her irritation is starting to fade, replaced by concern. "All right."

"When he came back, he was carrying Aske's body. He found her dead on the ground inside the everything, right in front of the window. And Diana—she hadn't stepped down when she died. She was bleeding blood, yes. She was also bleeding moonlight. How could she be bleeding moonlight?"

Diana stares at her. When she speaks again, the voice of Professor Williams is stronger, more evident. "Judy, are you seriously saying we have a dead *student* on our hands?"

Judy shakes her head, quick and sharp. "No. I was able to convince Máni that being found with the body of a dead white girl from Minnesota would cause more problems than it solved, and she was still bleeding moonlight, so it wasn't like we could hand her over to the coroner. He left her in the corridor, just inside."

"Who shines tonight?"

"I do. Abuk is supposed to be there for the handoff. I was hoping you could tell her before it's time to go, so that if the body's still there, she won't be surprised."

"And if the body's not there anymore?"

"I think it will be. No one has access to the everything except for us." Judy looks at her gravely. "What could have done this? What could kill a Lunar inside the everything? Do we need to be worried about killers coming through the window from the City?"

"No," says Diana. She sighs, heavily, and Judy realizes she doesn't know how old Professor Williams is, how long she's been carrying the mantle of the goddess and splitting her existence between the mortal and the divine. "Thank you for telling me about this. It's important that I know. And that means I have something it's important for you to know, too."

"What's that?" asks Judy.

Lunars tend to cluster together. It makes it easier for them to manage the rotation, since the gate can only be opened with a special kind of key. Judy doesn't know how the keys are made, but she assumes they must be, since they're physical objects; they can be lost. That doesn't mean all the Lunars currently incarnate will be in the same place, or that it would be safe if they were. Berkeley is one of the larger current clusters—and she has some theories about why that might be—but it's not the only one.

So it's not entirely a surprise when Diana says, "I was speaking with Launsina, in Maine. One of her juniors died recently, the manifestation of Wu Gang. They found his body *outside* the gate, but he was bleeding as you describe, red mixed with silver, like he hadn't been given the chance to step down."

Judy never met the man, obviously, but she still feels a pang at the name of his manifestation. Wu Gang is one of the Lunars who supposedly shares her version of the celestial moon, chopping down an ever-growing olive tree forever as punishment for his crimes. None of the stories have him anywhere near her orchards, and so she supposes they're neutral toward each other, if not intended to be friends. Still, inside her, behind the wall she keeps to separate mortal from manifestation, she feels Chang'e begin to weep.

"Chandra reports much the same, only in her case, the fallen god was Wadd. Otherwise, the same pattern. Found outside the gate, dead but manifest."

"Ours is different," says Judy, trying to fight back the feeling of creeping dread. "Aske didn't make it out of the everything. Máni says he found her next to the window."

"Máni, or David?" asks Diana.

The difference is essential. Divine senses are sharper than mortal ones; if *David* found the body, he might have missed something. Judy shakes her head.

"Máni told Chang'e what happened before he stepped down."

"I would like to speak with her," says Diana.

Judy has been expecting that request since it became apparent they were looking at more than one death. Still, she catches her breath, steadying herself, before she says, "Of course," and lets the wall come down.

Chang'e is anxious. She doesn't like this any more than Judy does. No god likes to be reminded that they can die. She surges forward so hard and fast that Judy barely has a moment before she's washed away, banished into the depths of herself, and Chang'e is fully incarnate once more.

She understands that the Seasons, once they claim their crowns, exist as human and concept together always, the two beings sharing one body and one set of goals. The human can rise and fall within their season, allowing it to take however much control they feel is right, and in that regard, it's a lot like the divine stepping up and stepping down that Judy endures, but the human and the metaphysical are always present, always combined. For the Lunars, it's not quite like that.

Chang'e is always herself, distinct from Judy, the woman who carries her. They exist together, and they speak together when they choose, but which percentage of which is present varies from moment to moment. When Judy is fully stepped down, she's just a human, with nothing special about her save for a sharp tongue and a gift for languages. And when Chang'e is fully stepped up, she can grow a peach tree out of nothing with a brush of her fingers to the soil, and the fruit it bears will heal any ill, grant youth and even immortality to the one who consumes it.

"Wu Gang, truly?" asks Chang'e, as soon as she has sufficient control to choose her own words. "I didn't even know he was manifest in any of his aspects. How long ago did he find himself?"

"That matters less than his death," says Diana. "He was found outside the gate but was otherwise as your mortal half describes: human and divine at the same time, bleeding silver that didn't fade. His body was taken by Launsina; her portfolio includes the seas, and so when she asked the waters to rise and claim him, they did. His bones rest at the bottom of the Atlantic."

"Didn't his mortal aspect have a family?" asks Chang'e. "They'll miss him."

"He was a former felon who worked at an under-the-table mechanic's shop. No one will miss him," says Diana.

Inside Chang'e, Judy rages at the casual dismissal of a man's life, and Chang'e tries to soothe her without letting her own unhappiness show. She doesn't want to antagonize Diana.

There's a certain coldness that comes to the stronger gods, the ones who don't need to worry as much about their mortal halves. Diana has the power to make sure Professor Williams will never want for anything, to keep her safe and comfortable for as long as she serves as vessel to the goddess. So she forgets, sometimes, how fragile mortal lives and mortal relationships can be.

"Someone might," says Chang'e.

"That's their problem," says Diana. "He was still leaking divinity when he was consigned to the deeps. There was no way to give him to a human coroner without raising more questions than we have the ability to answer—or attracting the attention of the alchemists. Do you really think that would have been better for any human relations who might have come looking, to know the body of their cousin was stolen from the morgue? At least this way, he just disappeared. They may never know what happened, but that leaves them with the possibility of hope."

"I suppose," says Chang'e.

"I'm more concerned about the fact that Aske was found *inside* the gate. Who handled the hand-off when she went to shine over the City?"

"Um," says Chang'e. "It wasn't me. I don't . . . I don't actually know who escorted her to the gate. I'm sorry, Diana."

"You should know."

Should I? wonders Judy. She's not in charge of the Lunars of the area, has authority over them only in that she's a naturally pushy person and has organized them, to a degree, to her own liking. But she isn't responsible for them and can't actually tell them what to do. They listen because it's easier than arguing, not because she's their superior. *It sounds like she's trying to blame us for her responsibilities not getting handled. Don't let her put this on us.*

"You're right."

Coward.

Chang'e straightens, trying to ignore the small, angry voice of her mortal half. She wishes she could keep Judy pushed down as long as she needs to, give the woman time to calm . . . but it's hard to explain the glowing when she's not locked away with another goddess who glows even brighter than she does.

"Find out. We may have a traitor in our midst."

Chang'e stands a little straighter, eyes widening. "Are there any gods in common between the impacted communities?"

They don't discuss it often, but no single mortal manifestation can contain the full scope of a god. They would die for their hubris if they even attempted it. There are a dozen Dianas in the world right now, a dozen Artemises, and probably as many Chang'es. The big European gods may try to ignore her prominence, but the Mid-Autumn Festival in China celebrates her and the Chinese space program is named after her. She's an important goddess in her own right.

Manifestations of the same god tend to avoid each other when possible. There's a terrible dissonance inherent in sharing space with yourself, and the addition of their mortal aspects can make it endlessly confusing. Chang'e can probably get along with herself no matter what, but can Judy get along with whoever that other Chang'e also is? Dianas coexist better than most, in part because the core Greek myths they pull their belief from are so fragmented and varied. They're all different people, even as they're the same. That's one of the reasons they tend to wind up in charge of the regional groups, even when other, equally powerful manifestations are present.

Diana glances away, not immediately answering, and Chang'e frowns. It wasn't an inappropriate question. If there are concerns about traitors, looking for commonalities is what makes the most sense.

"No clear ones," says Diana. "You say Máni found the body? Is there any chance he moved it before he brought it to you?"

Chang'e's frown deepens as she sees the trap lurking below the question. Diana's asking whether Máni could have killed the other god, then moved her into the everything. She shakes her head. "No. I walked him to the gate. He already had the key from the previous night's hand-off . . ." She trails off. That's not possible if Aske never came out of the everything. Aske was the Moon over the Impossible City the night before, and if she died in the everything, Máni can't have had the key. It would have been with Aske.

Diana nods. "There, you see? He could have killed her as she stepped up, hidden the body, and come back later to move it into the everything."

"But that would have meant abandoning his post. The moonlight over the City would have faded or even failed, depending on how many gods were at their own windows, and we'd have heard about it by now."

"Would we? It's never happened in my knowledge. We all just assume that if something happened to interfere with the moonlight, the City would get us a message, but what does that look like, exactly?

Is there a newsletter we don't normally receive that you think would show up in our inboxes?"

Chang'e's cheeks burn red with embarrassment. "Then I suppose it's possible for him to have ducked away."

"Were you at the gate *all* night?"

"No. It's not part of the duty. You see the ascendant Moon to the gate, watch them walk into the everything, and close the gate from the human side of things. It disappears until the Moon begins their return journey across the City sky, and you can go do whatever you need to."

She doesn't mention that she didn't see him to the gate. In Judy's case, after missing the hand-off, "whatever she needed to do" had been asserting herself long enough to finish a paper that was due at the end of the week, drink two peach wine coolers, and flirt with brief, drunken abandon with a cute history major she'd run into on her way back to campus. Nothing special; nothing out of the ordinary or that Diana needed to know about.

Diana nods again, looking smugger. "Aske is dead, and that's a tragedy. Máni has some questions to answer, I think."

"He looked terrified."

"I would be too, if I had just betrayed the pantheon."

This doesn't feel right. Chang'e hasn't been a goddess as long as Diana has, doesn't know as many of the rules, but she doesn't feel like this is the time to argue, not with the air sparkling silver and Diana looking at her, so confident that she understands the situation better than Chang'e does. Still, she has to try one more time, and so she asks:

"Is there currently a Máni in either of the other communities?"

"I don't keep their memberships memorized. Go find him. Tell him I want to see him."

Something in her tone makes Chang'e shiver. But she nods, and says, "Yes, ma'am."

And then, to her surprise, Diana steps down, and it's Professor Williams looking at her wearily, not glowing at all. Just a woman like any other woman, soft and defenseless. She can move between states with incredible speed, and Chang'e knows that if she moved against Diana's mortal vessel, she'd be struck down before she could do any real damage. Still, it's a show of trust large enough to be confusing, and so she doesn't say anything, doesn't do anything, barely even dares to breathe.

"I appreciate you bringing this to me," says Professor Williams. "I know the girl was a friend of yours. I'm sorry for your loss."

She wasn't, rages Judy. *She was a junior goddess from Minnesota who barely had time to figure out how to shine before she died, and now her family is going to think all those stories about how dangerous California is are true. I don't even remember her name!*

In some ways, that's the worst of it. There's no point in mourning for Aske: gods are hermit crabs, and humans are the shells they wear. Even if Aske is too minor a goddess to have more than one mortal manifestation at a time, she'll be fine. She's already back in her personal pantheon's version of paradise, catching her breath before she finds a new mortal shell to nestle herself inside. She's lost a few decades of human existence, at the most. But the girl she wore on her back, the girl with the wheat-gold hair and the mild echolalia that made every conversation with her like conversing with a deeply genial parrot, that girl is gone, and Judy never bothered to learn her name.

Chang'e simply bows her head, a moment of private grief for what's been lost.

"You can step down now," says Professor Williams, a sharp note in her voice. Chang'e looks up again, startled. It's not standard for them to order one another between states like this, and even Diana, who is largely accepted as the last authority among the local Lunars, isn't normally this blunt.

Still, she pulls back and drops down, and Judy is there once again, allowing her frown free rein as she eyes the older woman. "I suppose you want me to fetch Máni before tonight's trip to the City?"

"Not necessarily," says Professor Williams. Judy blinks. Her confusion fades as the professor continues: "It's your turn to see the City, isn't it? You can check the supposed crime scene, and tell me whether you think anything's been disturbed, before I confront him. We're in this together, after all." She smiles, the small, conspiratorial smile of someone who knows they're going to get their way.

Judy didn't survive this long in academia without learning to recognize the signs of someone preparing to take advantage of her. So she smiles conspiratorially back and says, "That sounds good to me," and she doesn't mean a word of it, and she's just glad that Diana, for all her qualities, was never a goddess of the truth. She'd be in real trouble if she were.

Something's wrong. And before she brings anyone to talk to the professor, she's going to find out what it is.

Lacus Doloris

TIMELINE: AUGUST 17, 2017.
FOUR DAYS TO THE ECLIPSE.

The sun is hot.

Kelpie knew the sun was hot, honest she did. She knows the alchemical properties of the sun: it's used as a cleansing agent and is vital component in many complex workings, and of course, it's a giant ball of plasma that hangs high in the sky above the fragile world. It couldn't possibly be anything *but* hot. Still, knowing the sun is hot and *knowing* the sun is hot are two different things, and before just now, she only had the first one.

The sun is hot and the sun is bright, and the air smells like so many things she doesn't recognize, and some of them she wants to know more about and some of them she doesn't, but they're all fascinating. The door from the lab let her out in a brick courtyard surrounded by buildings two stories tall and hugged by walkways enclosed in wrought-iron rails, rows upon rows of doors facing the spot where she stands. Most of the rails are decked with hanging plants, giving the whole place a lush, green appearance that reminds her of the private offices below, but the ceiling is so high, and so blue, and so disorienting.

It's the sky, she *knows* it's the sky, but as with the sun, knowing and *knowing* aren't the same thing. This is the first time she can remember seeing the sky, meaning she's either been underground since her accident or—increasingly likely—she's never been outside at all, and this is the first time she's seen the sky.

It's vast and beautiful and *terrifying*. How do people go around with that sky hanging over them all the time, like a sword getting ready to fall? There are no wires up there. Anything *in* the sky could drop *out* of the sky at any moment, and there'd be no way to know it was coming down.

She's been working on a project about the moon for the last year, but she's never seen the moon. Somehow she always pictured it as the size it appears in pictures, as big as a quarter, something she could slip into her pocket if she needed to, small and manageable. Now, seeing how small the sun looks from here, while she can't help feeling its immensity, the thought of trying to do *anything* that affects the moon is barely shy of ridiculous.

The moon is huge and celestial and untouchably far away. The alchemists she works with act like it's a concept and a physical object at the same time, which made sense a few hours ago: change a concept, change the thing it conceptualizes. Simple, right? Sure, when you're talking about something the size of a quarter. Not when you're talking about something made on a scale that lets it radiate heat or light from a million miles away. No one should try to mess with the sun, or the moon. They should leave the moon alone.

At least the bright spots the sunlight left dancing in front of her eyes have started to fade; she can almost see normally at this point. She glances around, realizing just how exposed she is. She no longer knows how much of what she's been told she can actually trust—maybe she's a perfectly normal-looking person, outside the lab. Maybe hooves and tails and sunrise-orange skin are common things, and she's allowed herself to feel like something's wrong with her for no reason at all. She doesn't think so, though. Margaret was very blunt with her about her anatomical deviations from the human norm, and even after everything, she's inclined to believe Margaret.

They were trying to make a body that could appeal to Artemis's Hind, and in the legends, the Hind wasn't a human person. It was an actual deer. So maybe she should just feel lucky she has thumbs, and not fret too much about everything else she's got.

But if Margaret was telling the truth about how not-normal she is, then the first person who sees her is going to know that something's wrong with her, at least when they're comparing her to a human baseline. She doesn't so much care what strangers think about her. She cares that if they make enough of a ruckus, they could attract the attention of any Congressional representatives in the area, or even other researchers from the lab who weren't present for the liquidation. The alkahest won't have left any traces of what happened to Margaret. They could be naïve enough to believe Margaret is gone because she's been reassigned, and Kelpie should be collected and taken back below.

She was there for Margaret's dismissal. She should have died. That she didn't—that she's a successful, intentionally concealed construct, a cuckoo—is an affront to everything the Congress stands for. Their cleaners don't leave evidence behind. She won't survive an encounter with her former peers.

She looks around, half-frantic with the need to get out of the open. The buildings around her are adorned with dozens of doors, each accompanied by a large window. Thankfully, all the curtains she can see are drawn. She fishes deep in her memory for some idea of what these might be, and finds the word "apartments" to describe private living spaces larger than her own room on the dorm level (where is she going to sleep tonight? That's a question she hasn't dared ask before now, and one she probably should at some point). She pictures Margaret's office replicated again and again behind those windows, each iteration occupied by its own version of her friend. Her incipient panic draws closer. All it takes is for one of those doors to open and she'll be in more trouble than she's ever seen in her life.

There are green things around the edges of the courtyard, including a tall, rough-barked tree and several unfamiliar bushes. She hurries to the tree, stepping behind it, hopefully hiding herself from the people who live in these apartments—and more, from the window next to the door she came out of. She hadn't considered, as she'd been standing there gaping at the sky, that someone else could climb the same stairs she had, could emerge into the same sunlight.

But where is she supposed to go from here?

"Okay," she says, and is soothed by the sound of her own voice, which hasn't changed; that, at least, has managed to remain the same as she transitioned from the safe, sane, familiar world of the lab where she's spent her entire life into this open-aired wilderness of strange windows and unknown rules. "Okay," she says again, and relaxes, just a little.

"I need to go somewhere," she says. "Where can I go?"

If she stays here long enough, the sun will go down. She knows that, knows days don't last forever, knows they measure time the same way above *and* below the surface. Once the sun sets, her skin won't be as noticeable, and the rest of her little oddities might be dismissible as tricks of light and shadow. She shrinks deeper into the shade under the tree, trying to think of other things that might help her situation.

All right. Accept that Margaret was telling the truth. Horrible as it is to think, she's a cuckoo, not a natural-born human at all. She's an empty vessel, created through alchemical means to embody a concept that may or may not have any real interest in occupying a physical form. Or maybe it *does* want a physical form but not hers— she has thumbs, after all, and hands, and lips. She's more human than cervine, and it's possible the deer she was created to embody won't want anything to do with her. Either way, right now she's herself.

And "herself" is a construct, meaning she's almost purely alchemical in nature. That's good. Alchemy doesn't exist in the eyes of most people, not anymore. People outside the alchemical world often look right past the signs of it, unable to understand or accept what they're seeing. If she was what she'd always believed herself to be, she'd look horribly twisted away from what a person is supposed to be. If she is what Margaret says she is, she may not look like anything at all. The people who don't already know about the alchemical just . . . won't see her.

Either way, she's not going to risk anything more until the sun goes down. She leans against the tree, wrapping her arms around herself. It's a warm day, but she's shivering. Why is she shivering? Shivering is a response to cold.

Or to shock.

Her supervisor and friend is dead. She isn't what she thought she was, and she's going to have to live with that; even if the Congress catches her and takes her back without slaughtering her on the spot, she's going to have to live with the fact that she was made, not born, and everything she knows about her past was a fabrication. She wonders if Margaret was the one who wrote her supposed "history," who named her parents and her cousins and told her they were waiting for her in Florida, in a house overlooking the swamp. It's weird to mourn people who never existed, but she does. They were always abstract concepts to her, people she might never see again, depending on whether they were able to repair the damage done by the accident, but she'd been told she loved them, and so she has loved them for her entire life. Finding out they were never there to love her back feels like losing them.

She's in shock. She's been through a lot today. She needs a glass of water, or a hug, or somewhere she can sit and breathe and not be afraid. She doesn't have any of those things, and so she sinks slowly to the ground, letting the back of her head rest against the tree as she closes her eyes. She can't imagine falling asleep in this strange place, surrounded by these strange new scents and sounds, with no idea whether or not the man from the Congress is going to come up and find her at any moment. She's not worried about it, because there's no chance it's going to happen. No chance at all.

Silent and still trembling, Kelpie slides into sleep, and the hours pass around her, one into the next, handing down the chain of the day one link at a time.

*   *   *

It's not one specific thing that wakes her. It's everything put together—the change in the light, which has grown dim yet not truly dark, thanks to municipal and residential lights; the change in the air, which has cooled, dropping to a less-balmy temperature, although it's not quite cool enough to have become uncomfortable; the change in the ambient noise. Doors are starting to open and close nearby as people return to the apartments they left behind that morning. Her eyes are fluttering open when something cold jams into her half-curled hand, and she sits bolt upright with a squeak and a gasp.

A large, black-furred creature with a waving tail is sniffing her hand with curious intensity. Kelpie starts to pull away, and the creature licks her fingers, tongue soft and warm and painless. She squeaks again, and a gangly pre-teen boy rushes over.

"I'm sorry, miss!" he says, grabbing for the creature's neck. It's wearing a brown leather collar, she sees, almost invisible against its fur. "I didn't expect anyone to be sleeping here. You shouldn't be, you know. Apartment manager will be pissed if he catches you, and he enjoys calling the cops on people he thinks are loitering."

"I'm sorry," says Kelpie. She pushes herself to her feet. Her rump is numb from the position she fell asleep in, and there's a crick in her neck. She's fallen asleep at her desk before, but mostly she sleeps in a specially designed bed, one that accounts for the fact that she's a biped with a tail that doesn't like to be compressed against things for long periods of time. Oh, it's going to hurt when the blood flow to her ass returns to normal.

Not that it's going to matter if she's been fed to the creature that's currently straining to get to her. She presses her back against the tree, unable to retreat any farther, not sure where she would go if she could.

The boy smiles, genial and unafraid. "I don't mind so much. I used to fall asleep out here when I was a kid, 'til Dad said it wasn't safe to sleep so near the street."

Kelpie hasn't seen a street since she came aboveground—which means she hasn't seen a street probably ever in her life, and that's unnerving to think. How many concepts does she have in her head that are actually entirely new to her? And how many things is she missing? From the way the boy holds the beast, she can tell this is an ordinary creature, something she's expected to recognize and know, something she shouldn't be afraid of. That's good. That both probably means it's not going to eat her, and tells her not to ask what it is. If he hasn't noticed anything strange about her yet, better to wait and see if he does.

Then his expression sharpens, and he looks at her more closely. "I fell asleep here 'cause I live here. My family's lived here most of my whole life. You don't live here. I'd remember a white girl moving into the complex. Why are you sleeping here?"

He's younger than she assumed at first, twelve at most and tall for his age; her eyes were tricked by the shadows and by the fact that she's never actually *seen* a young person before, just read about them in books, which generally focused more on the reasons it was sometimes important to take a young person apart than the ways to identify them when you meet them. She doesn't want to take anyone apart. Especially not this friendly boy with his strange beast, which is still trying to reach her. Neither of them seems hostile. She probably shouldn't be hostile either.

"I ran away," she says, more bluntly than she intends to. "The people I've been living with, they . . . aren't very nice people, and the nicest of them warned me that they were probably going to do something really bad to me soon. So I ran away."

The boy blinks, eyes going wide. "Are they your family?"

"No. Not really."

"Where is your family?"

Kelpie pauses. "I don't know." Artemis is probably the closest thing she has to a family now, but she's never met her, and she doesn't know where she is. Where do moon goddesses spend their time? Finally, she just shrugs. "I'm not sure I have one."

"That's awful. I'm Luis. Do you want to come home with me? You can meet my mom. She always knows what to do."

Kelpie hesitates. The boy doesn't seem to see anything strange about her, and that both raises her hopes and breaks her heart. Margaret was telling the truth; people who aren't at least a little bit connected to the alchemical world will look at her and see someone entirely unremarkable. They won't even be able to describe her once she's out of sight. But that means no one's going to miss or mourn her, and she's not a part of the world, not really. She didn't manifest naturally: someone *made* her, built her like the science project she is. There's no family in Florida wondering if she's all right. There's no one left in the world who'll miss her if she disappears.

"Sure," she says, finally. "Are you sure your mom won't mind?"

"I bring home people for dinner all the time," he says, with the airy ease of someone who knows the world is a dangerous place, but has never actually faced that danger up close and personal, or else has seen that danger from a different angle than she has, one where it takes the form of things other than runaway girls in the flower-beds. "She's used to it. Dad might mind, but he won't be home for hours. Come on."

He waves for her to follow as he begins dragging his beast toward one of the doors. It's on the opposite side of the courtyard from the door to the lab, and so she follows, unsteady on her hooves in the grass, half-afraid of what she's agreed to, and half-exhilarated at the thought of interacting with real people, in the real world. Every step she takes is one step farther from the lab. Experience is its own alchemical agent, and it transforms the people it touches.

Thank you, Margaret, she thinks, and lets Luis lead her to the door, which looks just like every other door around it. Lush green plants in colorful pots hang from the balcony rail and sit on the air-conditioning unit; there's a red-and-yellow doormat outside.

"We have to wipe our feet before we can go in," he says, doing exactly that. His beast doesn't, too occupied with pulling against its collar, but he doesn't seem to notice.

It seems like a pointless ritual action, wiping their feet if the crea-ture is just going to track whatever covers its paws inside anyway, but Kelpie steps obligingly onto the mat, wiping the dirt and grass shards from her hooves. A surprising amount of mud caked there in the short time she spent wandering around the yard; it comes off in dark streaks, and she looks to Luis for approval.

He's staring at her hooves, a furrow between his brows. "Those are real weird shoes," he says. "Don't they pinch your feet?"

Kelpie, who has caused a few arguments and one borderline brawl in the cafeteria by asking whether she *has* feet in the classical sense, can only shrug. "Not really," she says.

"Oh." Luis's face relaxes. Now that he's not contending with some undeniable piece of evidence that not everything is as he expects it to be, she's normal to him again. She wonders, on some level, how he's coping with the horns. They're small, barely worth the name, but they're hers, and they're sort of hard to overlook. She's tried.

"Come on," he says, and waves for her to follow as he opens the door, releasing the beast's collar and allowing it to run inside as he does. Kelpie follows, close, and is unsurprised when the beast flips around and comes running back to jump up and put its paws on her shoulder. It makes a noise, sharp and loud and very close to her ear, and she suddenly knows what it is, memory and academic knowledge combining with reality.

A dog. This is a dog. They're real. The lab has been trying to incarnate the Man in the Moon's beloved Dog for as long as she can remember, but unlike the Rabbit—and, apparently, the Hind— they haven't had much success. Margaret used to say it was because people liked dogs too much, and it was hard for them to think of the creatures as components in an alchemical construct. Their personal desires got in the way of their art.

"Down, Bobby!" says Luis, and the dog stops jumping at her, sitting and staring up at her with large brown eyes, tail thumping an irregular beat across the floor.

Kelpie catches her breath. "I don't mind," she says, looking around the apartment.

It's small, and she supposes it's shabby—everything she can see has been mended at least once, including the couch, which is a mottled tan that looks like it's been stained and scrubbed dozens of times. The carpet is several shades darker, still brown. There's colorful art on the walls, and a blanket in a half dozen primary colors slung over the back of the couch, but everything else she sees is shades of black and brown. Bobby is as black in the light as he was outside in the shadows; Luis's skin is a shade of brown a little darker than the carpet. His eyes and hair are black. She's never seen anyone who looks like him. Maybe people come in more colors than she knows.

(One of the younger researchers had been slightly black-haired and black-eyed, with skin darker than the rest of them; her features didn't align with Luis's, and according to Margaret, she was from a research team in a place called Tokyo, assigned to their lab in order to help them better incarnate and embody the Asian Lunar divinities. Kelpie had heard her complaining about how white American alchemists tended to be, but since none of the people she could see were actually white, just different shades of peach and tan, she'd assumed it referred to some attribute that hadn't been included in her reeducation yet, and dismissed it as unimportant.)

If people come in colors, maybe Luis hasn't commented on her skin tone not because he can't see it, but because there's nothing strange about it. Although he did call her a white girl before, and she's anything but white.

Trying to make sense of things is making her head ache. The air in the apartment smells delicious, peppers she doesn't recognize, spices, some sort of frying meat, and it's all she can do not to follow the smells, leaving boy and dog behind in favor of feeding her suddenly aching stomach. When did she last eat?

Lunch, probably, but she doesn't know how long ago that was.

"Ma!" Luis turns to head deeper into the apartment, toward the source of the smell. Kelpie follows, not sure what else she's supposed to do, and the carpet under her hooves stops, replaced by linoleum. That's more familiar, and despite the slipperiness of the material, she immediately feels more stable, which helps as they turn a corner and another person appears.

This one is taller than Luis, with long black hair pulled into a ponytail, standing over a stove and stirring something with a wooden spoon. Luis runs to throw his arms around her waist, not seeming to care about the heat. Maybe human children are fireproof? The woman jerks slightly but doesn't flinch or yell or pull away, just pats him semi-awkwardly on one shoulder.

"What have I told you about surprising me at the stove?" she asks.

"Don't," he says. "That's why I didn't. I yelled *first*."

She laughs and says something in a language Kelpie doesn't know, and Luis lets her go, stepping away. "I brought a friend home," he says. "Can she stay for dinner?"

The woman pauses, turns. She's even darker than Luis, and her shirt is a bright red that Kelpie can't help but interpret as meaning "danger." Kelpie takes a half-step back, forcing herself to smile. Not everyone is going to be her enemy. Margaret wouldn't have sent her this way if everyone was going to be her enemy.

"Hi," she says, hesitantly. "I'm Kelpie. Luis found me in the yard. Whatever you're cooking smells amazing."

"Dirty rice to go with the enchiladas," says the woman, still eyeing Kelpie.

"Why is it dirty? Should we eat it if it's dirty?"

"We just call it dirty because of the color it turns when it's cooked," says the woman. "Luis found you in the yard? Really?"

"I, um, fell asleep under one of the trees."

"So my son brought you home for dinner, yes, that makes total sense, and isn't ridiculous at all," says the woman. She turns back to her rice. "Why were you under our trees?"

"I ran away."

"From home?"

"I suppose you could call it that."

The woman glances back again. Her eyes are very sharp. Kelpie feels like she's being seen, every inch of her, all her oddities, all her impossibilities. But if that's somehow the case, this woman doesn't seem to care about the parts of her that are other than precisely human, because she's more focused on her rice as she starts talking again.

"Can you go back there?"

The thought conjures the image of Margaret with her eyes closed, tears that aren't tears rolling down her cheeks, and Kelpie isn't hungry anymore. Hard to be hungry when she feels this sick to her stomach. "No," she says. "I don't think I can."

"All right, then. I guess you're staying for dinner. You like enchiladas?" The woman turns all the way around this time, offering Kelpie her free hand. "I'm Isabella. You're welcome in my home."

"Thank you," says Kelpie, and shakes her hand, and tries to focus on the bright, amazing smells in the kitchen, the light overhead, the people around her who don't see how strange she is, who don't want anything from her. She's enough.

This is enough. This has to be enough.

Mare Nubium

TIMELINE: AUGUST 17, 2017.
FOUR DAYS TO THE ECLIPSE.

It's almost time for the moon to rise.

Judy paces in front of where the gate will be, waiting for tomorrow night's Moon to come and see her through. They do it like this so someone on the mortal side of the gate will always know who's on the other side; they are each other's keepers. Plus, when two of them step up close together, it has a blurring effect for mortal eyes. They'll be able to achieve what needs to be done more easily and without fear of being watched if they do it in tandem.

A god alone is a curiosity and a marvel, something to be stared at. Two gods together is a sign of something coming, and is intended to be feared. It's why the gates can exist out in the open like this, while Judy would never dare step up in front of her advisor.

She just needs her partner for the night to get here. It won't be Máni. She tried to find him, so he could go and speak to Diana, but he wasn't in his dorm room; his roommate hadn't seen him all day. She left a note, and hopefully he has it by now, hopefully he's going to call, but either way, he won't be shining tomorrow. He's not coming to see her off. And it won't be Diana.

She's trying to remember who else is currently in the area, which manifestations might arrive to make sure things are done properly, when a dark-haired woman in athletic gear comes jogging across the open space between the clocktower and the brick wall where tonight's gate will open. She's not breathing hard, but her olive-toned cheeks are flushed; she's been rushing to get here on time.

"Sorry," she says, as she draws closer. "Sorry. I didn't mean to be late."

"You're not, quite," says Judy. "Have we met?"

"Last full moon," says the woman. "I'm Anna. Hi."

"Judy," says Judy. "Last full . . . You're here to see me off?"

"Someone has to keep the key," says the woman. "You know, it's bullshit that we can't just recognize each other on sight. It would be so much easier. Instead, it's all lurking and code words."

"Or introductions from the senior Lunars in the area," says Judy. "Diana should have made sure we knew each other. Are you new to town?" She must be, or Judy would have recognized her more quickly. All the established Lunars come to her, or to Chang'e, to get their peaches. No presence, no peaches. And everybody wants their peaches.

Anna's young enough that it may not have occurred to her yet that she needs them. She shrugs, easy and calm. "Not entirely new, but new enough," says Anna. "We gonna do this or what?"

"I guess we are." Judy pulls the key from her pocket, showing it to Anna in all its fresh-scrubbed glory, and reaches down into herself for the layer of divinity where Chang'e waits, and lets mortality fall away as the goddess catches hold and steps up into the evening air, which starts to sparkle around her.

Anna looks quietly amused.

"What?" asks Chang'e.

"You glow pink, is all," says Anna. "I didn't know that was an option."

"It's not," says Chang'e, with wounded dignity. "And I don't glow *pink*; I glow *peach*."

"Right! You're the immortality peddler." Anna bows her head, performing her own transition, and the air around her lights up with a sparkling, silvery glow. When she opens her eyes again, they've changed, deep brown becoming the impossible layered blue of the sea near Tuscany. "Losna," she says, by way of second introduction.

"Etruscan goddess of the moon and the sea, yes?" asks Chang'e.

She's known Losnas before, although not in this incarnation; what information she has is distant and fuzzy, and not entirely accessible to Judy.

Losna nods. "Got it in one. I'm an English major. I started here this semester." Her nose wrinkles. "I didn't realize there were so many Lunars in the area when I transferred in. Just wanted to run track and field with people who might be able to keep up with me."

"We do accumulate," says Chang'e.

She wants to say it's not their fault, that the Lunars aren't doing anything, because they're not. Professor Middleton, on the other hand . . . he's like a lead weight in the middle of a sheet. He presses it down, and gravity does the rest. The Doctrine of Ethos was never meant to exist in a material form; he can't help distorting things for the other metaphysicals, as much as for the naturals. And if he's ever removed . . .

She imagines the shock of the sheet bouncing back into its original position will scatter them across the continent, if it doesn't launch them all into the stratosphere. Even the Moon might not survive that.

She was one of two Lunars in the area when she showed up. Diana took a lot more shifts then, and both of them spent a lot more time in transit, heading for the location of the next gate. Now they can do an all-but-complete rotation without changing their calendars, and it would be wonderful if it weren't so worrisome. New Moons seem to show up almost every other week.

If something's hunting them, that just means a lot more targets to get out of the way. She doesn't like to think of it like that. She can't help it.

"What's your story?" asks Losna.

"Chang'e, Chinese goddess of the moon, keeper of the peaches of immortality," says Chang'e. "You'll come to me when you decide it's time to pick up the 'eternal youth' benefit package that comes with divinity. It's not intrinsic, you know."

"I do, but I haven't needed it yet," says Losna. "Next time I wrench my knee, I'll probably change my story. Ever been to China?"

"I was born there, millennia ago," says Chang'e.

"No, I meant the real you," says Losna.

Chang'e manages, barely, not to sigh. The new gods who think their mortal lives matter more than their divine ones are always frustrating. The goal is balance, which doesn't mean shutting off one side in favor of the other; it means finding a way to exist in two realities at the same time, even when those realities contradict. "Judy was born in Newark, New Jersey," she says. "Her father was from China. She's never been there. Maybe someday."

"You'd think we'd all manifest where we come from."

"There are Chang'es in China," says Chang'e. "At least four of me, at last count."

"And that doesn't bother you?"

"Would it matter if it did?" She shrugs, producing a peach pit from her pocket. It doesn't matter if Judy put it there. Any article of clothing Chang'e wears will have a peach pit in the pocket sooner or later. She just bent things so sooner would be "now," and later wouldn't matter. Holding it up for Losna to see, she continues, "If I put this in earth—any earth, however barren or shallow—I'll get a peach tree. One pit, one tree. And that tree will put out dozens of branches, and those branches will bear dozens of fruits. No single peach is the true peach that matters more than all the others. They all come from the same tree."

"You calling us peaches?"

"Maybe." Chang'e tucks the pit away again. "Chang'e, the original, was the peach pit. Now, every one of us who carries a fragment of her, we're peaches. Maybe Losna was a wave, and you're a tide pool. Doesn't make you any less a part of that first wave to break upon the beach."

"This is getting a little metaphysical for me," says Losna.

"Says one moon goddess to the other," says Chang'e. "I have the key. Will you witness my departure?"

"Sure," says Losna. "Then I stay for a while, and come back just before dawn, yeah?"

"Yes," says Chang'e. She turns to the wall, tapping the key against the brick.

The gate blossoms into existence, lines of bright moonlight spiraling out from the place the key touched, racing to reach each other and twine together, then rise up into the high arch of the frame. It's a beautiful, impossible display, and it takes Chang'e's breath away every time she sees it.

When it's finished, she tucks the key into her pocket and turns to Losna, offering the other goddess a small bow.

"The light is in the tower, and all's well," she says, formally. "I'll see you in the morning."

She straightens and, without waiting for a reaction or reply, steps into the everything.

The corridor of rainbow light forms around her, seconds flashing and dying in the abyss between all things. She looks, automatically, to her left, but Aske isn't there; this is where they left her body, but it seems something else has already taken it away. The thought of something scavenging in the everything is horrifying, and she'd rather not dwell on it. Not when she has to walk here alone, tonight and every other night she's called upon for the rest of her tenure in this world. Which will be quite long, if she has anything to say about it.

She looks back. Losna is on the other side of the gate, watching her go. Anyone not connected to the Moon will see her sparkling faintly, staring at a glitter-smeared wall. *Step down*, thinks Chang'e, fiercely. Losna has done her duty for the night; now she needs to focus on not attracting unnecessary attention.

Losna steps down, glitter fading, and the view through the gate turns opaque, as if a glass door in need of washing has been closed between the everything and the supposedly "real" world. Chang'e nods, satisfied, and begins to walk.

There's no rhyme or reason to how long it takes a Moon to travel between the gate and the window. The corridor is as long as it needs to be, night after night, and that need is determined by something greater than any single manifestation can know or understand. Chang'e walks, watching the rainbows flash by around her, and there's no sign of Aske, and there's no blood on the ground. The corridor is pristine.

She tries to breathe as she walks, forcing her anxiety away. All the times she's traveled this path, and she's never been this nervous, not even the first time, when she was still more Judy than Chang'e. She didn't know, then, how to let go, how to allow the mortal half of herself to slide completely down into the safe, sane stability of the depths. Now she knows, and still, she is afraid.

Chang'e is forever. Chang'e will endure after this mortal shell has been shuffled off and cast aside, and on some small level, Judy is forever too, because of Chang'e. The goddess will always have a fragment of her buried deep inside her psyche, a little reminder of the time when she was an orphaned half-Chinese linguistics major from New Jersey, small and fragile and human and afraid. But Judy, the essential core of who she is now, will be gone.

Judy isn't forever. Judy is as mortal as they come. She just shares her body with a goddess in a strange sort of timeshare rental agreement. Like the Disney Vacation Club embodied as a human being, trying desperately to keep it all together when the world is perpetually trying to crumble down around her. Judy isn't forever. Judy likes the things she likes, likes bad medical dramas and good horror movies and pop music and cheap sex and peach schnapps. She doesn't want to be a crumb on the plate of a goddess, and so she walks the spotless corridor with precise steps, unable to fully recede, present as she almost never is when the time comes to walk into the eternal like this.

Chang'e murmurs sweet, encouraging sounds without singular meanings, not words but the ideas that came before words, the concepts that eventually evolved into repeatable things. The prototypes of language. She's not used to Judy being this far forward on the divine side of the gate either, and while neither of them is exactly comfortable right now, they're both glad not to be alone. Being a hybrid entity means loneliness isn't a common occurrence anymore.

The rainbows of possibility flash and die around them, things that could have been but won't be, things that probably couldn't have been but definitely never will now that their moment has passed. They blacken when they die, unlike the possibilities that find themselves fulfilled. Those flash into eternity as definite things, flaring white before they fade away. There's no value judgment to the difference, not here; it's just that white is the color of *is*, while black is the color of *isn't*, fusion and the void bound in an endless balancing and unbalancing dance. Judy supposes they're a hybrid entity too, destruction and creation unable to exist apart from one another.

The length of the corridor varies depending on the phase of the actual, literal moon, metaphysical distance stretching out to match its real distance. They're not quite at perigee yet, won't reach it for almost another month, but they're well on their way, and so the route to the window is long. Chang'e keeps walking, even as the path below her feet begins sloping gently upward. She tries to focus on how fortunate she is to be here, how lucky she is to be manifest in this place and this time, how pleasant it is to share an incarnation with Judy, who has her flaws but is clever and tries her best to keep things working smoothly, even when she'd rather be living a more ordinary life. This stage of the journey is always better if she can focus on the things she likes about living in a mortal body, in a mortal age. The City is calling.

She can feel it, a hum under her skin, a thrilling frisson that calls her to walk faster, to hurry toward the moment when she can look out upon the glory of forever. It always seems to want her in this moment, to need her to answer it—her and only her. No other divinity will do. Even her mortal passenger is barely a distraction from the singing of the City.

But Judy *is* a distraction and the reason that, out of all the gods still standing, the Lunars are the ones who get this glorious duty as their own. There are Solar gods as well, she knows; she's encountered them across the centuries, big, bold, brave heroes, ready to fight the sky itself for the opportunity to shine above the City. The sun crosses the sky even as the moon does, and so the incarnate Sun is allowed a certain measure of access, even as the incarnate Moon must be. But they've never seemed the most pleasant or harmonious of people, these bright, shining scions of the sun, and she doesn't know what sort of systems they have in place, beyond the same cycle of manifestation and incarnation as the Lunars, every god combined with a mortal, someone who keeps them from surrendering entirely to the City's song.

Gods who can't anchor themselves to the material world can't come this close to the City, or they'd be lost to it. They wouldn't be able to resist. So she clings to Judy, her little distraction, her beloved other half, and walks farther and farther from the gate, closer and closer to the City, not rushing the moment, not hurrying toward her duty. She watches for signs of blood as she walks. She finds nothing of the sort.

Then, ahead of her in the everything, the window appears. It is a simple thing, a double window in a plain white frame, with a little latch meant to be opened by a single swipe of the thumb and a strong lip to make it easier to open. The first time this iteration of Chang'e walked along the corridor to the window, she lost her manifestation and fell back down as Judy came surging forth and started to cry, hands over her face, tears on her cheeks and snot running from her nose.

This window no longer exists outside the everything. It was the window of Judy's childhood room, the one that opened so easily when the fire started and she had to find a way outside. She'd woken up to the smell of smoke and fled before she could ask herself whether anyone else was awake, and even the firemen telling her later that it had been too late for them by the time she woke up had never been enough to ease her guilt over being the only one to make it out, the only one to have the time to run.

She wouldn't have had that if she'd been any younger. But she'd been sixteen, and the moon had been whispering to her for the better part of six months, transforming her into a light sleeper. A year before, Judy had slept like the dead, and she would have joined them, suffocating alongside the rest of her family. Instead, she'd woken up and made herself an orphan, and would never fully forgive herself for grabbing her notebooks and her laptop before she slipped outside, rather than screaming for her parents.

(It really *wouldn't* have done any good. Chang'e has spoken to other Lunars, has asked those who were nearby what they'd seen by moonlight; Judy's parents were dead before she woke up, suffocated in their beds by the absence of the air. Judy couldn't have saved them. She could only have lost herself. But such cruel logic is the province of the divine.)

The window was destroyed in the fire, and the window is here, and its appearance is part of why every Lunar makes this journey alone, aside from their eternal passenger. If one of the others were here with her, the window would try to conform to both of them at the same time, becoming the best-beloved window either of them had known during their current mortal incarnation. Some of those hybrid windows can't be opened. Some of them have no latches, or too many latches, or warped frames. It's better to come alone, even though none of them are ever truly alone, and to walk in their inherent contradiction to the point of connection.

Chang'e stops, catches her breath, and tries to sink deeper into the moment, to absorb it all the way to her core. There is nothing to show that Aske died here, no stain on the ground or blood spray on the window frame; the air smells as sweet and purified as ever, the atmospheric equivalent of those untouched mountain springs that have existed for millennia in secret, only to be found and pumped dry by some corporation eager to monetize the basic building blocks of life. No one's ever going to bottle *this* air. No one gets to breathe it unless they make it this far.

And even this is nothing compared to what waits on the other side of the window. Chang'e approaches, reverent, even as Judy finally releases her anxious hold and sinks down to where she belongs. It's dangerous for the human side of a god to be too ascendant when the window opens. The air in the everything is sweet and pure, but it's not addictive. The City air, on the other hand . . .

The City air is everything. Persephone's pomegranate seeds and the sweet allure of the fruit from the Goblin Market are pale imitations of the smallest whiff of City air. Chang'e can't imagine what it would be like to descend to the level of the streets, to eat the food or drink the water. Some nights it's so hard to stop shining that she thinks it would become impossible after a sip of City water. The heart only mourns what it knows to be true.

"Are you ready?" she asks aloud, and deep within her heart, she feels Judy give her answer, feels her assent. Aske is gone, and her dying left no trace; now is the time for them to shine. Chang'e steps forward, opening the window. Cool night air rushes through, clean and clear and intoxicating and

And

And

And everything is silver-bright and mercury burn, the color of moonlight on the water, the color of the City lights, the color of everything. The color of nothing.

*   *   *

Chang'e blinks and she's in the everything once again, her fingers resting on the window latch, ready to flip it closed. There are silver smudges on the heels of her hands, moondust etched upon her skin, and the inside of her mouth tastes like peaches. She reaches into herself until she brushes against Judy, who stirs and stretches, rising from a deep and dreamless sleep. She doesn't have a watch, and Judy's phone doesn't get reception in the everything, not even to keep the time, but she can tell it's been hours, and not only by the aching in her legs, which burn pleasantly with the aftermath of a long walk. She's been traveling that whole missing time, pushing back against the treacle-thick air of the high lunar roads, making her way across the sky above the City.

Now the moon is setting, and the Moon is allowed to rest. She shakes, reminding herself what it is to wear a skin, to have a body, to be a single concrete form and not an abstract idea projected onto something that will never truly know or care what people think of it. Judy rises up, not all the way but enough that she becomes they once again, plural and peaceful.

She begins to walk down the corridor, idly sucking the moondust from her fingers as she goes. It tastes, as it always does, of peaches. She's wondered, on occasion, what the other Lunars taste, the ones whose personal versions of the Moon surge with seas or grow green with grass, not a peach orchard in sight. She's never asked. Some things are too personal to speak aloud.

There is no blood on the ground, no sign that someone died here. Chang'e stops. Maybe because no one did. The Lunars walk the everything alone to avoid confusing the window, which would try to conform to more than one of them at the same time. Who's to say the whole of the everything isn't so malleable, or that they walk the same everything at all? Perhaps it's like an anthill, hundreds of routes to the City, all slightly different. She's always assumed there was only one window, that it changes shapes each night. What if that's not the case?

What if they each have their own window, their own path?

The thought is simple but staggering. If there are multiple paths through the everything, this isn't where Aske died. This is another route entirely. It explains why there's no sign of what happened, and why her body is missing. But it doesn't explain how Máni was able to find her, or even how he was able to be on the same path through the everything.

She frowns and starts walking again, trying to work her way through the impossible logic of it all. If they each have their own path, then she'll never see any signs of the murder. But that could mean Diana's right and Máni knows more than he's letting on.

The journey back is always faster than the journey out, the City glad to see them gone once they no longer have a task to perform. It isn't long before Chang'e sees the gate ahead of her, an opening onto another, more concrete world, one where symbols and ideas need flesh if they're going to walk among the mortal men. One where a woman can also be the Moon but the Moon can't also be a woman. She slows, thoughtful.

The view through the gate is still indistinct and cloudy, like she's looking through a thick pane of distorting glass. Lights flicker on the other side as cars pass in the dark beyond the campus, and there's a blurred shape she assumes is Losna. She starts moving again, and the shape becomes a little easier to see, although still indistinct. Yes. Losna. The other goddess is stepped down, attention on something in her hands, ignoring the actively flickering gate.

Chang'e stops, clearing her throat. Losna looks up, and a moment later, becomes suddenly crystal clear and crisp, the air around her glittering silver-blue as she steps up into divinity, leaving whatever had her distracted behind. She stuffs the object she was holding— her phone—into her pocket, and steps toward the gate.

"Have a good night?" she asks.

"I did," says Chang'e, distracted by Judy murmuring at the back of her head. She frowns, trying to understand, then says, "I'm sorry, forgive me a moment," and does the unthinkable.

She steps down inside the everything.

Not all the way down. Even if she *could* do that—even if she could step down so completely that she pulled herself from her host, dug herself out by the roots and left Judy alone in the rainbow corridor to eternity—she wouldn't, because no one knows what would happen to a normal human left in the everything. It's never happened. Not in all Chang'e's long, long memory. But she can pull back to such a point that Judy is essentially alone, mortal and breakable, abandoned in the everything.

Judy catches her breath, looking at the dying rainbows around her with wide eyes. They seem brighter than they did just a moment ago, like living things. They were warm before, gentle and welcoming, and now they're aggressively vivid, lights that never meant to shine for her. Sharing her body with a goddess is something she's had plenty of time to get used to, and most of the time, she can fool herself into thinking it doesn't matter which one of them is at the front; they're the same person, after all. Looking around at the vivid entropy of the everything disabuses her of that notion so completely that she may never get it back.

She doesn't belong here. She's Chang'e's baggage, and unattended bags are subject to search and seizure. Still, she asked for this, and so she shoves her fear down the same way she would shove *herself* down if she were trying to return control, looking toward the horrified form of Losna on the other side of the gate.

The other goddess is staring at her, eyes wide and glossy-bright. She hasn't stepped down, hasn't matched states with Judy. If anything, she seems more baffled by what just happened than anything else.

"Hey, can you come over here for a second?" Judy's voice is thin and washed-out by the everything, lacking the resonance it needs to fill the space, and for a moment, it seems like Losna doesn't hear her. Then she shakes off her shock and steps through the open gate, the two of them occupying the same space, the same iteration of the everything.

"Okay, lady, I've heard a lot of things about your incarnations in general, and this one in specific," says Losna, voice bright and a bit excited as she looks at Judy. *Her* voice still has the resonance of the divine, filling the space from top to bottom. "But you know what I've never heard before? I've never heard about how you have big brass ones. This is the ballsiest, *stupidest* thing I've ever seen somebody do! What the hell do you think you're trying to pull, standing in the everything just this side of mortality? You want to see if the stories about human hosts getting busted down into stardust are accurate or something?"

"Diana should have introduced us, if you're new," says Judy. "You're not new, are you?"

"New to the area, absolutely," says Losna. She blinks, and although she hasn't stepped down in the slightest, her eyes are brown again. "New to this incarnation, not so much. Diana doesn't know I'm here."

"I have to deal with a faculty advisor who doesn't understand why I refuse to study under one of 'the greatest minds of the generation'; I don't have time for some sort of Lunar power struggle," says Judy bluntly. "I've never encountered a Losna incarnate who'd managed to stay manifest long enough to accumulate any real power."

"Now you have," says Losna. "And you're standing in the every-thing with her, stepped down to the cusp of mortality. Your tide's out, little peach goddess, and I doubt you can call it back in faster than I can wash you away, if that's what I want. Fortunately, it's not. So what the hell is the point of this little stunt?"

Judy raises an eyebrow. It's a trick she spent a long time perfecting, and it normally makes people stop talking down to her and start listening to what she has to say. Thanks, Leonard Nimoy, for making people react to that expression like the person making it is the smartest in the room. Losna doesn't even blink.

"I needed to know if the everything would change when you were the only fully active divinity inside it," says Judy.

Losna frowns. "You risked getting vaporized for a *theory* question?"

"Yes, because it matters." She pauses. Diana doesn't know Losna is here, according to Losna, and they're alone in the everything. No one can find them here. Not with the key on this side of the gate. "How long have you been incarnate?"

"About thirty years. I'll give you the next one for free—I've been in Denver, and we have a Chang'e there. She's been feeding me grilled peaches since I was an undergrad."

"Have you been in college this whole time?"

"This isn't *Twilight*," says Losna. "Hell, no. I graduated and got a real job, where I could make real money and pay for a real apart-ment. And then the rumor mill started spinning up about the alchemists getting their knickers in a twist over something incom-prehensible and probably real, real stupid, since that's normally the sort of thing that really excites our alchemical brethren, so I started trying to find the epicenter of the chaos. Everything I could get my hands on seemed to indicate that whatever it was, it was probably out this way, California-ward."

"There's a lot of California," says Judy. "Why here and not some-place warmer?"

"I like redwood trees," says Losna.

"So you re-enrolled and came to Berkeley to find out why the alchemists were pissed off."

"And why time's been resetting itself for the past half-million years."

Losna says it so calmly that for a moment, everything seems to stop. The rainbow walls of the everything continue their scintillating flashing, but there is no other motion, no other sound. Judy swallows, takes a step back, and stares at her.

"What?"

"You heard me. Every thirty-five years or so, the universe resets itself. Always back to the same point, or very close to it. I'd like to know why. I've talked to all the gods who have their hands on time, and none of them are responsible, so I figure it's time to blame the alchemists. I've been trying to put together what they're up to, but those assholes don't make it easy." She smiles then, a little feral, and says, "That's what makes it fun. An easy hunt is no real game."

"You're not Losna, are you?" Judy manages not to take another step back. She reminds herself that Chang'e is a powerful goddess in her own right, even if her own upbringing in a Eurocentric culture means she sometimes doesn't think of herself that way. "Losna's not a hunter."

"No, but Artemis is." Losna blinks again, and once again her eyes are different when she opens them, green as young olives ripening on the branch. "I asked one of her current incarnations before I took on her mantle, just to be sure I wouldn't offend her somehow. She thought it was a quaint deceit, and gave her full permission. I can give you her number, if you want to double-check."

"I like that wording, because it implies I'm leaving here alive," says Judy. "But no, I think I'm good."

Artemis frowns sharply. "I would never kill another Lunar. Why would you jump so quickly to that conclusion?"

"I think the two of us need to take a little trip," says Judy. "I need to show you something. May I step back up?"

When Artemis nods, Judy lets go, and feels Chang'e resume her place of primacy, the goddess filling her from top to bottom, more intended for the light of the everything than Judy has ever been. Releasing the body is a relief, intoxicating in its power, and she's grateful to let go, even as she remains just below the surface to observe. She's not leaving Chang'e alone in this, even if she could.

Chang'e bows respectfully to the stronger goddess. "It is a pleasure to see you again, huntress. I know you say one of me has been attending to your immortality, but this one has not, and so I am reunited with an old companion."

"It's good to see you, too," says Artemis. "What did you need to show me?"

"It's a showing and a telling at once," says Chang'e, and turns. "Follow me."

Together, they walk deeper into the everything, and the gate is left unguarded.

Sinus Fidei

Isabella's enchiladas are like nothing Kelpie has ever tasted, and she wants to keep eating until there's no room left inside of her for anything but enchilada. They're sharp and spicy and sweet and savory all at the same time, striking flavors on her tongue she never imagined possible. She wants to wallow in them. She has to fight not to grab the serving platters and empty them onto her own plate, glutting herself in a way that would be entirely inappropriate for a guest.

She's never been a guest before, but Margaret was very insistent that she relearn proper manners after her accident, which Kelpie now supposes was Margaret making sure she was halfway civilized before risking her in the larger, if still limited, lab environment.

All her meals before this one were eaten in her room or the lab cafeteria, made in the same kitchen, nutritionally balanced and designed to flatter the humors of the researchers, keeping them in harmony with themselves. Maybe she never realized how limited the flavors of those "ideal" meals really were, but this is like discovering color after a lifetime of drawing in graphite alone. Graphite is a wonderful medium, and she's always going to have a deep-seated fondness for soy noodles and faux meat, but this . . .

This is cuisine as poetry.

She cleans her plate and, when Isabella asks if she wants seconds, barely remembers to ask if it's allowed before she accepts. Isabella laughs, and refills her glass of milk. She comments on how advanced

Kelpie's spice tolerance is in light of her unfamiliarity with the food, and it's not until Luis leaves the table to take the dog out that her expression sharpens and she focuses on Kelpie's face.

"You come from that lab they think we don't know about?"

Kelpie blinks. "I— What?"

"The alchemists. They think because they're the ones who wrote a rule book, they're the only ones who understand the way things work. Arrogant fucks. You one of their projects?" Her eyes, which were so soft and kind a moment ago, are sharp, shuttered; she's ready to defend her child and her home if she needs to, and Kelpie is the threat she's defending against.

Kelpie shrinks back in her seat. "I don't understand what you mean."

"But you do. That's the first lie you've told me. How about we do it this way: you don't tell me a second lie, and I might let you leave here still breathing."

Isabella is terrifying. Kelpie would never have expected Isabella to be terrifying. She seemed so sweet until the threats started, and to be fair, she still isn't reaching for a weapon—but that makes her more frightening, not less. All the people Kelpie knows, if they're reaching for weapons, it's because they feel like you're worth fighting. Isabella doesn't think she's enough of a threat to warrant a fight. That stings, a little.

"It's not a lie, because I really *don't* understand," says Kelpie. "I don't *think* I'm a project, even if they built me. I'm pretty sure I'm a person, and that means I *can't* be a project, not in the way you mean. I came through a door at the top of a very long series of stairs, and at the bottom of the stairs there's a lab, or there was, anyway. I ran because a man came and said he was going to shut us down. He killed . . ." Her breath catches. Saying it makes it real. That isn't even sympathetic magic: that's just common sense. Once you speak something into the world, it's true, in some way, even if it's a bald-faced lie. Once she speaks the truth of Margaret's death, it becomes true, and true things are real, and she doesn't want to say it.

Isabella is still watching her with hard, suspicious eyes, so Kelpie keeps talking, even though she doesn't want to. "He killed my supervisor because she worked on a failed project, and they don't reassign people who failed. He killed her right in front of me, and she told him lies that should have meant he was killing me, too."

"What lies?"

"She told him . . ." Another pause, another breath caught in her throat, like a stone she has to try to talk around. This one refuses to be dislodged, even when she forces herself to continue: "She told him I was a natural person who'd been in a bad accident, which is why I don't look altogether like a natural person to folks who know how to look at me. I guess she convinced him, because what he did to her would have killed me, too, if I'd been natural, and men from the Congress don't usually like to leave witnesses when they don't want to."

"Maybe he wanted to."

"What?"

"Maybe he knew she was lying, and didn't know whether *you* knew. Maybe he wanted to leave a witness, so he could see what you would do. Maybe he wasn't sure whether *you* knew."

"I didn't," says Kelpie, and it's so ridiculous that it sounds like a lie, even though it isn't. "I didn't," she repeats, more softly.

"Are you trying to convince me, or to convince yourself?" asks Isabella.

Kelpie looks sharply up, meets her eyes, and manages not to flinch away. Isabella sighs.

"You're cowering like a whipped dog, and I don't like that," she says. "Makes me feel mean. I fed you, girl, and that means right now you have a certain amount of leeway here; can't break bread with someone and then slaughter them in cold blood. Maybe that's a rule we got from the colonizers, but it doesn't matter when it's the sympathetic law of the land, and it's burrowed deep enough that it is now. I could have poisoned you when we sat down, if I'd wanted you dead and been willing to deal with the aftermath of Luis witnessing it. He's a young, impressionable boy; he doesn't need to see his beloved mother start killing people for what looks like no reason. His daddy's about as magical as a rock—and sure, some rocks are plenty magic, but way more aren't magic at all, and he falls into the second category. Luis hasn't shown us yet who he's going to take after."

"You're an alchemist?" asks Kelpie, mild fear flaring up into sudden terror.

Isabella looks offended beyond all words. "Please. Do I look like an old white man with a god complex? And if the answer to that would be yes, you have permission to tell a second lie after all, because I do *not* want to hear that."

"You don't," says Kelpie quickly. "You don't look like any of the alchemists I've ever met."

"Yeah, they talk a good talk about wanting to equalize the forces of the universe by giving humanity access to the power that should have belonged to us all along, but if you look closely, you see that their version of 'humanity' is always very, very pale."

Kelpie blinks at her.

"Now I know you're a construct."

"I don't . . ."

"You look a little freaked out by the idea."

"The lie my supervisor told the man who . . . who killed her, she told me that lie, too." Kelpie hunches her shoulders, looks down at the table. There are still a few smears of sauce on the plate in front of her, but her appetite has gone. She wouldn't have thought that was possible before this conversation started. "Until today, I really thought I was a natural person. That I was born, and grew up, and had a family waiting for me to come back when I finished working at the lab."

"No offense, honey, but have you seen you?"

"I didn't realize *you* could see me."

"That's fair, I suppose. Luis comes in from the yard with an orange girl, I'm not going to shout 'put her back, she has hooves' where he can hear me. Good to know I still have the best poker face in the neighborhood. But yes, girl, I can see you properly. You shouldn't be walking around with your face hanging out like that. Pull it back."

"I can't." Kelpie looks at her, pleadingly. "I used to beg Margaret to show me how, when she'd play the training videos about the natural manifestations. A manifest Winter can look more or less frozen, depending on how far forward their season is. And a manifest Lunar looks like a normal person unless they decide they want to look like their specific face of the moon. But she said it wasn't possible for me to look normal, because I wasn't representing anything but myself, and I wasn't embodying anything but me, and this was how I look."

She thinks, now, that Margaret was lying, or at least not telling the full truth. She's representing Artemis's Hind, a Lunar companion, and while she's not a divinity in her own right, she stands for something that was never meant to exist in this world. If she can't pull back on the parts of her that mark her as other than human, it's because the people who made her didn't want her to be able to. Someone made the conscious decision that she was going to be this way, all the time and always. They didn't ask her what she thought about it.

(The idea that someone designed her, *made* her, makes her wish she hadn't eaten quite so many enchiladas at dinner. How much of her did they design? Did they decide she was going to be curious and credulous, fond of asking questions and generally willing to accept the answers she was given? Did they make her like peanut butter and not honey? Is *anything* about her real?)

Isabella frowns. "They weren't ever going to let you out, were they?"

Miserable, Kelpie shakes her head.

"But you're out now. Why?"

"Margaret said when they made me, they realized I was a person, not just a vessel for them to fill with the concept they were trying to embody, and they couldn't go through with it, so they made me a lab assistant instead of telling the people who were in charge that they'd succeeded. They wanted to keep working." For the first time, Kelpie realizes that continuing to work meant Margaret's team had been hoping to embody the Hind again as something they felt less attached to. That would probably have killed her. Forced aspects don't like to be manifest more than once at a time. True Lunes can manifest in multiplicity, but the companions haven't been seen in so long that trying to make the universe support more than one of them really wouldn't be a good idea.

They had her working every day on her own demise, and they didn't see anything wrong with it. They were letting her live before she died, after all. Wasn't that good enough for her?

Up until today, up until she'd seen the sun, it had been. Now, though . . . now she doesn't think she could go back below even if Margaret were somehow miraculously returned to life. Below was fine when she didn't know any better. She knows better now.

"This doesn't make any sense," says Isabella. She eyes Kelpie. "You feel loyalty to those alchemists? You going to keep their secrets, go running back to them as soon as you have the chance?"

She remembers the face of the man from the Congress as he'd sentenced Margaret to death, the way he'd looked at her when he thought she was collateral damage. Kelpie shakes her head, reluctantly. "I want to, but I can't."

"Good. You mentioned Margaret. That the little goth girl?"

"Yeah. She liked the clubs around here. She said blowing off steam after hours helped keep her head straight, so she could manage the project during the day."

"Mmm-hmm. She was nice, for an alchemist. Used to come up the stairs sometimes, always had a friendly word and a smile for Luis. It's too bad they killed her. Alchemists would be less unbearable if they had more like that one. What was she doing for them?"

"They want to catch a Lunar."

"That's the second time you've used that word. You know about the Lunars?"

Kelpie nods, silently.

Isabella snorts. "It figures. They've been busy little bees lately. So the alchemists want to catch one. Haven't they done enough damage in the last few years?"

"I don't know about any damage, and I don't think my lab did it if there *was* damage," says Kelpie. "I know there was a coronation recently . . ."

"Mmm-hmmm. Last Summer Queen threw herself in front of a taxiing plane in order to take out her counterpart. Killed the bastard stone-cold dead. Wish I could've been there to see it. If there's anyone who deserved a nasty, ignoble death from someone else's suicide, it was William Monroe."

"How do you know that?"

"One of my cousins worked at the airfield where the accident happened. Said it was the damnedest thing. This lady in a white sheet came out of nowhere and just walked in front of the plane like it was nothing, and they couldn't turn in time. Flight never took off, of course, and by the time the authorities got there, Monroe was dead. Massive heart attack. They chalked it up to stress and being a general asshole, and no charges were levied against anyone. It's the funniest thing, though."

"What is?" Kelpie isn't actually sure she wants to know the answer, but the question is virtually unbidden, unavoidable.

Isabella shrugs. "Neither of the bodies made it to the county morgue. The woman was a Jane Doe, but Monroe, he was wealthy. He had connections, friends, patrons. Someone should have kicked up a fuss, but nobody did. Both of them just vanished en route, and not a trace of them has surfaced, not even in the night markets."

There's a ruckus then, and Luis comes surging back into the kitchen, Bobby beside him, the dog's tail waving wildly. "Can we go back outside? Bobby needs to use the bathroom again."

"Does Bobby really need to use the bathroom after you just took him out, or are you just tired of me monopolizing your friend's attention and looking for something to do?"

Luis grins a gamin grin, utterly unrepentant, and shrugs. "You don't normally steal my friends," he says. "I want her back when you're done."

"You'll have her, my prince of porchlights, I promise," says Isabella. She licks her thumb and leans over to wipe a smudge from his forehead. "Go out, but don't leave the courtyard, understand me? And take the potty bags! Maybe if Mr. Mendoza sees you carrying them, he won't blame us for the cat shit in his bushes. Not likely, though." She turns back to Kelpie, saying in an undertone, "Man can't tell the difference between cat shit and what comes out of a full-grown silver lab."

"Bobby isn't silver," says Kelpie, uncertainly.

"And American pit bull terriers aren't bad dogs, but until the people who make the rental rules get their heads out of their asses and stop trying to enforce unreasonable breed bans, Bobby gets to be a silver lab, and he still doesn't shit like a cat."

"Oh," says Kelpie. The world up here is much more complicated than she ever imagined it might be. She's studied in preparation for her supposed "return" to the world, and she thought she understood the complexities she was walking into, but she didn't know anything, not really. She doesn't even know what she shouldn't ask.

Isabella takes some pity. She leans across the table to pat Kelpie's hand. "It's all right. If you're not an alchemist, I can help you."

"I . . . used to work as a lab assistant," says Kelpie.

"You ever strip the fat off a baby, or break a crow down to its component parts?"

Kelpie stares at her, horrified.

"Didn't think so. You're not an alchemist. I'm not sure you *could* be, not when you're not a natural. Seems like that would be crossing the streams in a bad, bad way, if you could take the people who are more than just human and make them stronger. My coven, we don't have anyone with us who's not a straight-up human, no extra bits, no surprises at the bottom of the cereal box. Angeline says one of her cousins was tapped for the coronation, but they were never close, she and that cousin. She didn't even go to his funeral. I think being too close to a manifestation, even if you're not one yourself, can mess up your sympathy with the universe. So most likely, you would never have been good for anything beyond washing dishes and mixing chemicals together, even if you'd wanted to be."

"I don't think I want to be," mutters Kelpie.

"Good choice, really. And you say 'what damage,' and I say 'what damage *haven't* they done?' There used to be hundreds of different magical systems, all sorts of people doing things according to all different sets of rules. None of this 'my way is the right way and if you don't like it, you're not going to accomplish anything.' People could take a lot of paths to the same outcome."

"What happened?"

"The alchemists happened," says Isabella, darkly. "They started making rules, big rules, and when people didn't want to follow them, they started finding ways to enforce those rules. It got to where almost no one else could do anything, because the universe thought they were doing it wrong when they didn't follow the alchemists' rules. That's the problem with living in a world that wants to be a person. People tend to like rules. Even the ones who think they don't like rules, they like them. We enjoy having the same atmosphere every day, and knowing we're allergic to one thing but not another, and that we should drink water instead of hydrofluoric acid. We like gravity and thermodynamics, and even though we complain about it, we like time. We like the way it passes at a consistent rate for everyone and everything. We like *rules.* And when you turn the basic building blocks of reality into people, what you wind up with is a reality that likes rules just as much as people do. So they follow along. Even the rule-breakers acknowledge the rules, because if they didn't, they couldn't break them. You see?"

"Yes . . . no. Not really."

"The first horrible thing the alchemists did was convince the universe it needed rules to run smoothly. *Their* rules. They took a lot of chaos and they tamed it as much as they could. They weren't alone in those days—most people who had any pull with the universe wanted at least a *few* rules, to make things easier on themselves— but as time went on, more and more of the rules the alchemists made said 'and we're on top and everyone else is on the bottom, and that's the way things are meant to be.' The alchemists built the boxes, and shoved the rest of us inside, and then they got mad when we didn't want to stay where we'd been put."

"You're not an alchemist, then?"

Isabella laughs, loud and bright and genuinely amused. "If I were an alchemist, would I be so happy to talk shit about them? No, kid, I'm an hechicera. Unless you ask the ladies in my coven, then I'm a witch, although we have a couple of dabblers who keep trying to call me a bruja."

"What's the difference?" Kelpie's head is spinning. This is all so much, so fast and so out of order.

"An hechicera, that's like a sorcerer. We do big, deep magic—kind of like your alchemists do. We talk the universe into things. A witch, they stay shallow. They talk *people* into things. A bruja is a kind of witch, and there's nothing wrong with being one, unless you're Puerto Rican and a white lady keeps insisting that has to be what you are."

"Oh."

"So no, I'm not an alchemist. They might have been willing to have me when I was younger, if I'd been whiter or more male, but at this point I know so many rules they don't approve of that they wouldn't have me even if I was willing to have them. Which I'm not." Isabella leans forward, serious again. "Now. You were saying they wanted one of the Lunars. How does that drop a girl with hooves in my kitchen?"

"Oh. Um. Margaret was the head of a team that thought they could attract certain Lunars if they could force their traditional companions to incarnate. Like a dog, for the Man in the Moon? But most of those companions haven't been manifest in a long, long time, so they had to build the vessels themselves. I thought we were only working on animals, but I found out today that actually, they'd been using some material created for use in compelling nonstandard forces to manifest, and since it's human at its roots, they were getting humans with animalistic features."

"And you're one of those manifest companions?"

"I was supposed to be."

"Which one?"

Kelpie squirms. She doesn't like this line of questioning, doesn't like the way Isabella is looking at her now, like she's suddenly interesting for a whole different reason. Still, she's been truthful so far, and so she says, "Some of the stories have Artemis accompanied by a golden hind. I'm supposed to be the Hind."

"And you're intended to attract Artemis?"

Kelpie bites the inside of her mouth as she nods, watching Isabella. If the other woman moves toward a knife or anything else that could be used as a weapon, she's going to run. There isn't anything else she could possibly do at this point.

"Interesting. Why do they want her? If I was going to mess with the Lunars, she's not where I'd start."

"I don't think they want *her*. They just want one of the strong ones; I think they're just pretty confident they'd be able to handle any Lunar they could catch."

"Why do they want a strong one?"

Kelpie looks at her and exhales, slowly. Up until this point, everything she's admitted to being involved with has been innocent, in its own way. Nothing wrong with being a lab assistant, and it's not like she had a choice about being built in the same lab. This is where she admits to doing something that could probably be considered "bad."

"Lunars have access to the Impossible City," she says. "If we—if they—could catch a strong-enough Lunar, they'd be able to use it to get inside."

"And there it is," says Isabella, throwing up her hands. "It always comes back to that damn City. Has since Baker went and wrote her bizarre fantasies down and started shilling them to children, like the more kids she could get to dress up as Avery and Zib on Halloween, the easier it would be for her specific branch of alchemists to seize control of absolutely everything. Why did it have to be a city?"

Kelpie blinks. "What?"

"The center of everything, the summit of creation, the place where, if you have absolute domain, you can control the rest of the universe—why did it have to be a *city*? Why not a hidden grotto or an endless forest or, if you demand human control, a farm? Why would the universe be centered in something that had to be *built*?"

Kelpie has never heard anyone question the City itself before. It feels faintly blasphemous, like it shouldn't be allowed. "I— Every brick is a milestone in human accomplishment, every pane of glass is an achievement in enlightenment—"

"I believe that's what they told you, but that doesn't make it true. The City is. I can't object it into non-existence. But the City shouldn't *be,* and if it's going to be, we should stop trying to take it over. It exists just fine without anyone running the place. But okay, whatever. The Lunars have access, and the alchemists have decided that means they need a pet Lunar. Why now? Why the kind of urgency that puts a deer-woman in my kitchen, eating my enchiladas?"

"Um. Do you know who James Reed is?"

To Kelpie's surprise, Isabella clearly does. Some of the words she says are familiar, things Kelpie's heard when another of the techs cut themselves or hit their hands. Others are entirely new to her but said with the same intonation, making their position as profanity more than clear. Kelpie listens, wide-eyed, until Isabella winds down, panting slightly as she glares.

"That bastard," she says. "I hope he rots."

"That'll be easy, since he's dead," says Kelpie.

That takes Isabella aback, at least for a moment. She stares at Kelpie, then gets up and crosses to the counter, leaning up to open a cupboard and take down a bottle full of clear liquid. She returns to the table, removes the cap, and takes a long drink directly from the bottle before offering it to Kelpie.

"It's good luck to drink when a bastard dies," she says, by way of explanation.

Kelpie blinks. "I . . . Is that hygienic?"

"Of course. The alcohol kills the germs. Go ahead, have a bit." Isabella keeps offering the bottle, vehemently.

Kelpie isn't sure what this means, but she takes the bottle, hesitant and anxious, yet still afraid to offend this woman who can see her for what she is, and knows things about the alchemical world that Margaret never tried to explain. Watching Isabella warily, she raises it to her lips and sniffs.

The liquid smells astringent and herbal, sharp with something green and unfamiliar beneath a wash of a scent that is almost the absence of scent, so empty that it becomes a perfume entirely its own. She doesn't want to put that in her mouth. But it isn't poison, unless Isabella is one of those hedge witches who swallows a bezoar in order to pass tests from rivals, and she really, really doesn't want to get thrown out into the dark, complicated night.

Kelpie drinks.

The liquid burns like fire, but when she swallows, there is no pain; either the fire did no damage, or it did so much that the wound is already cauterized and she'll fall down dead as soon as her body realizes what just happened. She sets the bottle down with a surprisingly steady hand, looking across the table at Isabella.

"Good luck," she says.

"It's not a suggestion," says Isabella, reclaiming the bottle. "It's a fact. When a bastard dies, you drink in celebration, and the universe sees that you're *not* the same flavor of bastard, and it doesn't punish you for whatever the bastard did."

"But doesn't celebrating because someone's dead make you a bad person?"

"Not when the dead guy's James Reed. What happened to him?"

"He and his team managed to embody a universal concept called the Doctrine of Ethos. I don't all the way understand what that means, just that everyone thought it was very impressive that they could do that, and it might mean they could take control of the Impossible City. They used a lot of things to build a suitable vessel. All the things that usually go into crafting a vessel, and some more things, too—materials Reed had been saving for a long time."

Isabella's expression cools, eyes shuttering, like she's stepping back from the conversation without actually stepping away. "And what materials would those be?"

Kelpie feels as if the floor has suddenly fallen out from beneath her, and she needs to scramble to hold on to something or she'll fall too. "There are . . . recipes, standard components you use when you want to create a human life, and . . . some of them are human? I guess? Or were, once? They're not working with really . . . *raw* materials most of the time, once you get to Reed's level. They don't harvest the way really junior alchemists do."

Isabella makes a noncommittal noise, neither approving nor disapproving, and says, "Meaning they don't *usually* murder people for their science projects. I don't think that's the free pass you want it to be."

"I don't . . ." Kelpie stammers and stops, looking at her hands. Her throat doesn't burn anymore, and she can feel herself swallow, so she supposes the nerves weren't really cauterized, no matter what it felt like at the time. But her stomach, so full of those delicious enchiladas, is starting to feel unsettled, its contents roiling in a seasick way that makes her feel less orange than green. "I'm trying to answer your questions, but I don't know what you mean half the time, and if you keep looking at me like I did something wrong, I won't be able to tell you what you want to know."

"Sorry. I'll back off." Isabella sits, finally, and leans back in her chair, trying to look as harmless as possible. It's not working as well as it did before she got up to fetch the bottle, before Luis went away. "Why are the alchemists rushing for the City?"

"James Reed managed to successfully embody the Doctrine of Ethos in two constructed human creations. He called them his cuckoos, because they were placed in the nests of other birds. The early success of the cuckoo project led to multiple other attempted embodiments using the same base materials and rearing standards. The resultant cuckoo-children were raised in normal human families, exposed to conditions beyond those that could be easily synthesized in a laboratory setting. This was all before the Doctrine became manifest, you understand: once they manifested, that technique was abandoned, since it came with certain unanticipated complications."

"Meaning when you raise something to consider itself a person, it's going to act like a person even when that isn't what you want," she says, and laughs. "Oh, his little science project told him to go fuck himself, didn't it?"

"Yes," says Kelpie. "The Doctrine became manifest and came into its strength, and in the ensuing conflict, James Reed and Leigh Barrow were both killed. The cuckoo programs were discontinued, although some of the base materials are still in use."

"You keep saying 'base materials' like that means it's not human remains. If Reed started this project, you're talking about bits of Asphodel Baker, aren't you?"

Kelpie nods, that sick feeling in her stomach getting even stronger. She knows what she's supposed to think of Asphodel Baker—she may not be an alchemist in her own right, but no one works around alchemy for any length of time without knowing the woman who created James Reed, the one who betrayed the Alchemical Congress by releasing the Up-and-Under into the public consciousness without congressional oversight. When Baum rewrote and replaced as much of her creation as he could, *he* had worked with full approval and editorial review from the Congress. *He* had been able to understand that the City was to be taken for all of them, not only for himself.

Still, Asphodel touched the City, more than once, when she was alive. It was natural that her bone and tissues should remember the resonance of those streets, should encourage those they inhabited to strive to return. That was part of what made Reed's cuckoos so dangerous. Their power was immense, something that should never have been allowed to exist outside the proper hands. But their inherent need for the City, their almost-instinctive migration toward those hallowed streets . . . that was where the true risk came in.

"So the Congress is in disarray because Reed's cuckoos are trying to fly home to roost," says Isabella. "They can't stop something as big as the Doctrine. Those kids are probably unkillable through mortal means at this point. Unless they have a keyed-in weakness."

"If they do, Reed didn't document it where the rest of us could find the information."

"Okay. So you have two unstoppable, unkillable forces of the incarnate universe trying to find their way home to the City that Baker's people spent centuries establishing as, essentially, the control room of creation, and you're trying to catch a Lunar so you can get there before they do?"

"Basically."

"Oh, man." Isabella starts to laugh, clearly delighted. "You people are *fucked*."

Kelpie tries to smile, even as her stomach, filled by an unfamiliar mixture of spices and alcohol, gives a final lurch and she loses her dinner all over the table.

BOOK II

Waxing Crescent

The sun's a thief, and with his great attraction
Robs the vast sea; the moon's an arrant thief,
And her pale fire she snatches from the sun.
                    —William Shakespeare, *Timon of Athens*

Kneel at the water to witness the change
Know that the final result may be strange
Far stranger to dwell your whole life in one room
Than make your requests of the pale tarot moon.
                    —Talis Kimberley, "Tarot Moon"

"Avery!" She moved closer, until he had to bend his arm to keep from losing hold of her, and then she dropped abruptly away as she sat. He felt her hand grasp his ankle. "Where are we?"

"Still inside the mosasaur, I guess," he said glumly, and sat down beside her. She leaned, wrapping her arms around his shoulders in a brief but tight embrace before letting go and settling with her shoulder pressed to his, and the warmth of her skin just made him think about how cold he *wasn't*. The Saltwise Sea had been plenty cold, and when the improbable road had disappeared from underneath them, he'd been half-afraid he'd drown before he could swim, but here, it was warm and pleasant, even if they were still soaking wet. "It swallowed us, and it'll probably digest us down soon."

"I will do no such thing," said a deeply affronted voice, rich and warm and seeming to echo from absolutely everything around them. "Are you children *entirely* uncivilized? I am only here because my Lady of Salt and Sorrow asked that I should be, and while Seiche does not command the great beasts of the deep, we all love her well enough to listen when she calls for us, but I can go on my way easy as anything, and leave you to your previous destination."

There was a warning note in the voice that made Zib think she wouldn't have enjoyed whatever destination the mosasaur—because it simply *had* to be the mosasaur, they were inside the mosasaur, and the voice sounded like the one she heard in her head when she tried to talk without letting her teeth unclamp or moving her jaw—was talking about.

"No," she said hurriedly, before Avery could say anything. She adored him so, but sometimes his dedication to the logical way of doing things could result in his saying things that caused more problems than they solved. "We're very civilized. Why, we go to school and can do our sums and read books and everything!"

"Is that what you think it means to be civilized?" The mosasaur sounded genuinely curious. "That you could eat thinking people like sardines, but it would be all right, because you can do your *sums*?"

"Avery didn't mean it," said Zib. "It's just he's never seen a mosasaur before, and we didn't precisely have time for introductions before you were swallowing us, and it's only natural he should be a little bit confused. . . ."

—From *Into the Windwracked Wilds,* by A. Deborah Baker

Lacus Mortis

The everything flashes and dazzles exactly as it has always done, an unending rainbowed corridor into eternity. Chang'e and Artemis walk in companionable silence, new-met and old allies at the same time. It's strange sometimes, being a new incarnation of something so very old. The gods bring their own baggage to each manifestation, pieces of who they are layered over the humans they become, but they're forever starting over from the beginning. Chang'e has never met this Artemis before. Maybe they've been dear companions at some point in the past; that isn't enough to make them anything other than relative strangers now.

Which explains the disquiet with which Artemis looks at her and says, "I've seen the everything before, you know. You don't need to show me this."

"I know." Chang'e keeps walking, and finally, ahead of them, the window appears. It looks the way it always does, stolen from Judy's childhood bedroom, white frame with the single missing strip of paint on the lefthand side. She gestures toward it. "What do you see?"

"A window. Your window, I presume."

"Yours doesn't look like this?"

Artemis shakes her head. "My window is more Grecian. It changed about fifty years into this incarnation. Yours will change too, if you stick it out long enough. Does this conclude the show-and-tell?"

"Has another Lunar ever shown you their window?"

"No, you can't go near another Lunar's window, or it tries to change to suit you, and it can get confused."

"I don't know whether that's the truth," says Chang'e. She stops walking and gestures again, this time urging Artemis to continue forward without her. "I'm starting to think we don't share the everything like that. Why would the universe need to conserve space? It has all the space that's ever been. This is the everything. It can keep space open for both of us at once."

Artemis looks at her dubiously but keeps walking toward the window.

It doesn't change.

It's still a white frame from a suburban house when she reaches it, and when she reaches out to touch the latch, it still sticks just a little, the way that it's supposed to. She turns to look at Chang'e. "What is this supposed to prove?"

"I think that because I opened the everything and haven't left it yet, right now, it's catering to me," says Chang'e. "This is my window because the everything thinks I'm the one who's supposed to be here, and it's viewing you as my guest."

Artemis looks nonplussed. "No conflict?"

"Not unless we both tried to come in at the exact same time, and even then, I'm sure it would find a way to split the atom that tells it which one of us is ascendant at the moment of entry." Chang'e gestures Artemis back. "There's one more thing I want to try; come on."

"I do track and field because I like running. Running, not walking endlessly back and forth doing little science experiments."

"Uh-huh. Why did you come to Berkeley?"

Artemis blinks. "Excuse me?"

"You said it was because you wanted to join the track team, but you also said you were Losna. Then you said it was because you wanted to know why the alchemists were pissed off, but the alchemists are always pissed off about something. So clearly you had some other reason to want to be *here,* and to not want anyone to know who you were when you arrived. Why are you here?"

"You're the goddess of immortality, not simple detective work," says Artemis, tone gone mild and soft.

Chang'e pauses. The thought that this could be dangerous hasn't really occurred to her before just now: she's in the everything, baiting one of the big two moon gods, and betting on the fact that whatever brought Artemis out this way, she wasn't the one who killed Aske. If she's wrong about that . . .

A Lunar who passes themselves off as less powerful than they really are is a Lunar who's potentially up to no good. Aske is *dead*. Chang'e would prefer not to join her. Judy, who doesn't have the questionable immortality of another manifestation to come, would *very much* prefer not to join her. She's kicking and screaming at the back of Chang'e's mind, trying to claw her way back to the surface. They're so deep in the everything right now that Chang'e is pretty sure that would be ironically fatal, and probably a terrible way to die.

"You live forever, you start to pick up a few things," says Chang'e, voice carefully neutral.

And Artemis laughs.

"Right, right. We're allowed to have hobbies." She shakes her head. "I really did come to Berkeley to find out why the alchemists are so worked up, because you're right, they're always up their own asses about something, but they're not normally this kicked-hornet's-nest about their shit. And the whole 'time has been resetting' thing is a little disconcerting. I don't care for it. I only know because time doesn't reset inside the City, and I started to notice that things were happening out of synch with what I expected."

Chang'e blinks. "You started to *notice*?"

"Once you've been doing this for long enough, you'll be able to stay aware while you're crossing the sky. You'll remember things you see in the City. It's not always fun. I know one manifestation of Selene who fell in love with a resident of the City. They could never meet or touch; she just watched her from the sky every time she got to make the crossing. She said the woman she loved would always go out of her way to be outside while the moon was high, and they were happy together. Her love never married, and when she vanished from the City, Selene mourned until her mortal manifestation died from the grief. Observing lives you can't be a part of is hard on the heart." Artemis shrugs. "But yes, I started to notice. It's not right. Time is supposed to happen here and there at the same rate. Which, by the way, time is happening right now, and we need to get the gate closed before the sun comes up."

"All right. Follow me. There's something I still want to test." Chang'e starts walking quickly back toward the gate, and Artemis follows.

When they reach the exit from the everything—not the same as the end, because the everything never ends—Chang'e stops and pulls the peach pit out of her pocket, spinning it between her fingers. Then she turns, bends, and places it carefully on the ground. Artemis watches this, faintly perplexed. Her perplexity only deepens when Chang'e straightens and steps out of the gate, back onto the campus.

She steps down at the same time, sparkle in the air extinguishing like a blown-out candle, and Judy returns to her own body, her own life, with the burning desire to find a way to shake her divine copilot. Baiting more powerful gods is not a good way to live long enough to *become* a more powerful god.

But she understands what Chang'e was trying to do, and so she holds her hands out, gesturing for Artemis to stop.

"Is the peach pit still there?"

Artemis jerks to a halt, blinking at her. "What?"

"The peach pit I put on the ground. Is it still there?"

"Yeah. Where would it have gone?"

"Come out now."

Artemis steps out, the air around her bright with moonglow for the handful of seconds before she, too, steps down, and Anna—if that's her real name—is left, frowning at Judy.

The gate shivers, the tunnel on the other side shaking as it always does, and then it is gone, closed until the next time it's needed. Judy glances up at the still-dark sky. The sun has yet to make an appearance. They'll have to be quick, but there's time, if it's needed. She pulls the key out of her pocket and, as Anna watches, taps it against the stone, once to close the gate, and a second time, to open it again.

The gate spirals into being, exactly as it always does, appearing on the blank wall. Judy takes a breath and drops down, hard and silent as a stone. Chang'e turns to Anna. "Wait here," she instructs, and steps into the everything, looking down.

The peach pit is still there. First theory, proven. She emerges again, feeling heady with success, heart beating a little bit too hard. The gate closes with a tap, and remains closed as she offers the key to Anna.

"I need you to open the everything and go through," she says. "Find the peach pit."

"What?"

"Find the peach pit." She keeps holding out the key until Anna finally takes it.

Muttering, "Immortality gods are so *weird*," Anna drops down, and Artemis surges up. There's no pretense of being Losna this time; she just comes in silver moonlight, with eyes like the forest at night, looking at Judy like the woman is something unspeakable and inferior.

"Why am I doing this?" she asks.

"Because Aske died last night," says Judy, bluntly.

Artemis freezes. "What?"

"Or the night before last; it's hard to say. Anyway. Aske died, and we left her body in the everything, because she was still bleeding silver, but when I opened the gate to go through, she wasn't there. So either something took her body away, or every one of us opens our own channel through the everything."

"That can't be right," says Artemis. "We walk the same path."

"Then open the gate, and find the peach pit."

Artemis turns to the wall, uncertain for the first time, and taps the stone with the key. Once again, the gate appears, growing fainter as the dawn approaches, and Judy watches Artemis step through. The goddess stops just inside, distorted by the carnival glass-effect of the portal between them, and looks at the ground.

And keeps looking. Judy glances at the sky. The edge is getting lighter; they're running out of time.

"Artemis!" she calls. "Anna! Come back through!"

She won't step through the gate without an invitation. Even though they were just in her iteration of the everything together without coming to any harm, she doesn't trust it to support an uninvited visitor that easily.

Artemis glances up. "It's not here," she says. "It should be right . . ."

Her eyes widen as she notices how light the sky is getting, and she lunges through the gate, which is getting fainter all the time. For a moment, Judy thinks she's not going to make it out. What would that do, spending a whole day stranded inside the everything, without even the City to serve as a distraction? Can someone survive in there for that long?

Artemis emerges just as the outline of the gate becomes completely invisible, barely escaping the solidifying stone, and it seems almost like a formality as she taps the key against it to tell it that it can close for another day. If she hadn't, would it have closed on its own in the face of the unrelenting sun, or would the channel to the everything still have been "hers" when night fell again, set to whatever standards the everything has been using all along?

Judy suddenly feels very, very over her head, and only the fact that Chang'e is equally confused keeps her from going screaming for Diana.

"How did you know—?" asks Artemis.

Judy shakes her head as she turns to face the other Lunar, holding out the key for Artemis to take. "I didn't. I guessed."

"Explain." Artemis slips the key into her pocket.

"Aske was on duty two nights ago. She's new, so we were a little concerned when she didn't come back and stand down, but Máni had the key, and everything seemed fine. I don't think he killed her.

He's a sweet guy, for a football player, and that's not the sort of thing I'd expect from him."

"People can surprise you," says Artemis grimly, the silver glow beginning to fade from the air around her as she steps back down toward Anna.

"Tell me about it, *Losna*," says Judy. "But no, I don't think he hurt her. It just doesn't make sense. She was on duty, she opened the gate, she went through, she didn't come back. The next night, Máni opened the gate and went through, and when he came back, he had her body. We had to leave it in the everything."

"What? Why?"

"Because she was bleeding moonlight," says Judy grimly. "She was still stepped up into the divine when she died. And she stayed that way. Even if David had been willing to carry a dead white girl across campus, we couldn't have explained the way she was leaking divinity."

"I see."

"I expected to find her when I went through last night, or signs of what had happened to her, at least. Instead, there was no trace of anything. I think what happened is Aske *did* come back, and someone was waiting for her on this side of the gate. They attacked her as she was coming through, and she ran back inside without closing the gate. Her attacker followed, and they killed her in the everything, but it was *her* everything, not theirs. The gate never fully closed, just disappeared when the sun came up. That's not the same thing. When Máni opened it the other night to go through, he wasn't unlocking the door; he was . . . pushing open a door that had already been propped in that position."

"That's a pretty big jump to make from me not changing your window."

"Maybe. It was still an accurate one, though." Judy shrugs as she turns to start down the stairs.

Anna, as expected, follows. "What do you think this means?"

"I think I wish there was a way to test whether *my* everything is the same as the everything every other Chang'e gets," says Judy. "I'm sure we have different windows, because why would a girl from Beijing or Montreal have a window from a suburban house in New Jersey? But do we get the same tunnel to take us there? If we do, then we could find another Aske and ask her to take us to the place where our Aske died. If we don't, then as soon as we let the gate close with her on the other side, we lost her forever."

"If she wasn't stepping down after death, we already had," says Anna. "There's no way we could have told her family what happened without them seeing the divinity leaking out of her."

"I guess that's true," says Judy, somewhat glumly. She doesn't have a family. She's never considered that being what she is could mean she doesn't get a grave, either. "So when you were answering my questions back there, you never told me why you were pretending to be Losna."

"Ah." Anna shrugs. "I heard this region had a Diana running the place, pretty competently. Artemis got syncretized with Diana to such a degree that some people can't even remember which one of us came first."

"You're . . . grumpy because other people might assume another moon goddess came first?"

"No. I don't much care, and at this point, I've seen so many manifestations come and go that I realize it doesn't *matter* that much. We all shine in the same sky, we all do the same job, we all come to versions of you when we need peaches or else we all get old and die like anybody else. I'm pretty sanguine about it all. But when I was looking over the records for the area, trying to decide how I wanted to approach things, I found something that was really interesting, at least to me."

"What's that?"

"We're the big three." The statement is made bluntly, and without any real hint of ego. In a deadpan tone, she continues, "Go team Greek exceptionalism and Roman expansionism, I guess. And Chinese population growth. Colonialism wiped out too many followers of the North American Lunars for them to get the numbers they'd need to rival us; we ate most of the other Europeans. Hell, your Japanese counterpart barely even gets a footnote most of the time. Chandra and Khonsu try, and they probably have better traction in the places where people still worship them, but it's not belief that anchors us—it's *awareness*. How many people are aware we exist."

"Not explaining," says Judy. "Talking a lot about how cool you are, but not explaining."

"Ah. A region run by a Chang'e will usually have a Diana *and* an Artemis, and they'll get along, because no one wants to piss off the peach purveyor. A region run by an Artemis *may* have a Diana—we try to play nicely with the other incarnations, even when it's difficult, and we know we came first. The ego, she is soothed. But a region run by a Diana will very rarely have an Artemis. They tend to view us as unnecessarily repetitive, they don't want to deal with comparisons, and we remind them that they're not the oldest game in town. Technically I think Chang'e predates us both, but since there was never any real syncretization there, we can all get along with you."

"Thank you? I think?"

Anna shrugs. "Anyway. I came here to spy on the alchemists, and I came as a minor goddess that I know hasn't manifested in the region any time recently because the Losna in Denver said she was fine with it. Thought it was funny, even. And by telling people I was her, I could avoid attracting too much attention from your Diana, or making her all territorial before I knew what was going on."

"Timing sucks," says Judy. "Could have shown up being all undercover weirdo *before* people started getting murdered."

"I'll take that under advisement," says Anna dryly. "But your Aske isn't the first death I've heard about recently."

"Diana said something similar." Their walking has carried them halfway across the quad, still largely empty at this hour of the morning. Members of the campus homeless population who crept back after the final security sweep sleep under the tables and draped across the benches, their bodies wrapped in tattered blankets and layer upon layer of torn sweater. Some of them are also students.

They'll rise when the campus starts to wake for the day, heading off
to the gym for hot showers before they start their classes.

Judy hates that people have to choose between housing and tu-
ition. She wishes she were an actual god, something powerful and
cosmic enough to make this all go away. (Something like, perhaps,
the Doctrine of Ethos, which is by all reports more powerful than
a single manifestation of any given god. Maybe if she *were* Chang'e
and not just one more incarnation of a goddess who's scattered
herself across the globe in shining fragments, but she's not. She's a
timeshare manifestation, and she doesn't have the power to make
things better. One more reason to avoid Professor Middleton. It's
hard not to resent someone who *has* that kind of power and mostly
chooses not to use it.)

She continues to guide Anna toward the picnic tables outside the
drama department. They're mostly shaded by evergreens, constantly
a little damp and littered with fallen needles. No one much likes to
hang out here except for the drama students, and even they tend
not to linger, preferring to take their unrelenting chaos out into the
streets where it can get them the attention they so desperately crave.
She's never found anyone sleeping in the little picnic area, which
means no need to feel bad about waking people who actually need
to rest.

(One of the perks of being a manifest Moon: she barely needs to
sleep on the nights when she *isn't* assigned to the sky above the City,
and on the nights when she *is*, she doesn't sleep at all. The toxins
sleep would normally flush from her mind and body vanish during
her trip across the sky, and being able to get by on an hour a night
without long-term psychological harm has been a huge help in her
studies. Easy to get an edge over the competition when your day is
effectively six hours longer than theirs is.)

She brushes a layer of needles off the nearest damp picnic table
and sits atop it, resting her feet on the bench as she produces another peach pit from her pocket and spins it between her fingers like
a magician's coin.

"How many of those do you just carry around with you?" asks

Anna, looking with mild displeasure at the damp bench before echoing the brush-off-and-sit gesture. She lets Judy keep the table for herself.

Judy shrugs. "I don't know. Half a dozen or so, most days. More, during the high summer. I like to have them on hand. They keep me calm."

And they're the key to her only real magic trick. Without them, it would be far too easy to convince herself that she's just a very confused young linguist and not a god at all.

"There have been at least half a dozen," says Anna. "Your Aske is the first one I've heard of actually dying inside the everything; all the others were out in the real world when they had their accidents."

"Are we sure they were accidents?"

"The first couple, I was," says Anna. "By number four, I was a little more skeptical."

"Diana mentioned two, apart from Aske," says Judy.

"Which brings us up near double digits, and that's if it's *only* been half a dozen," says Anna, grimly. "I think it's been more than that. I just can't prove it. It's not like there's a directory of currently active moon gods."

"How . . . ?"

"They've all been minors," says Anna. "Not a single Diana, or Chang'e, or Artemis. Only Askes, and Losnas, and other gods who don't have a lot of punch in their pockets. They'd be easier to take than one of the big names. And they've all been the only representative of their Moon in an area. It's not unknown for more than one manifestation of the same god to come together. Makes it easier for them to set the transit schedule."

"That has to be confusing," says Judy. She's thought before about how nice it would be to have another Chang'e around, someone else who can tend the peaches, someone who understands her when she talks about the wind blowing through the orchards of immortality. She's never been to the moon herself, knows it's a lifeless chunk of rock floating in the void, but when she *does* sleep, she dreams Chang'e's Moon, which is lush and green and inviting, and *home* in a way no place in this world has been since the house in New Jersey burned down. She touches that Moon on her nights above the City, and she thinks she'd be willing to give up on her dreams of linguistic and academic success if it somehow meant she could stay there permanently.

What would it be like to be around someone else who knows that Moon? Someone who is, effectively, the same person as half of her but a stranger to the other half? It would be like a human centipede of the soul, and she's not sure that's something she wants to deal with, much less experience.

Anna shrugs. "Not as confusing as you might think. They always get along, anyway. Hard to really fight with someone who has a piece of you inside their head. Anyway, we have two Tsukuyomis in Denver right now, and they're both fine, even though another one of them just died in Austin three weeks ago. Bike accident. He was on his way to the gate to take his turn at crossing the sky. I heard about it because their Artemis was complaining afterward. She had to scramble to find someone who could fill in for him—she'd done the night before, and so she couldn't do it."

"Oh."

"I was already on my way here by then, which is why I was around to meet you on the last full moon, even if you were too distracted to pay attention to me."

"I'm sorry, I still don't remember you."

"Which is a genuine tragedy, or would be if we weren't in the sort of situation that makes flirting a little bit inappropriate." Anna sobers. "Look, it's like this. Every time one of us dies, the alchemists get all hyper for a few days, like they're working on something. I'm afraid they're involved with whatever's going on."

"So you came here undercover, pretending to be a minor Lunar who fits the profile for the victims, without telling our Diana who you were in case she got territorial, in hopes that what, you'll get murdered next?" Judy snorts. "Not a great plan there, sport."

"You have a better one?"

"Yeah. You just said you have two Tsukuyomis in Denver. We call and ask them to conduct our little test with the everything tomorrow morning, and then we'll know whether another Aske would let us retrieve our poor dead goddess. If we can get to her body, maybe we can learn more about what killed her." Judy spins her peach pit between her fingers, thoughtfully. "If someone's out there hunting Lunars, we should know about it. And what good would that do? Are we even useful to alchemists?"

"They have whole recipes built around harvesting 'materials' from the people they've had killed," says Anna, with exaggerated finger quotes to make her message excruciatingly clear. "They can get different metaphysical qualities out of corpses, depending on how they died. A really gruesome murder can give them all sorts of lovely toys."

Judy pauses, then scoots a little bit away from Anna, putting more of the damp table between them. Anna raises her eyebrows, questioning wordlessly.

"Sorry," says Judy. "It's just that you're a stranger who started out by lying to me, and who knows way too much about alchemical graverobbing to be a comfortable conversation partner."

"Ah, yeah. I can see where this might look bad," says Anna. "If you know any Lunars in the Denver area, they can vouch for me? Or I can give you the number for our Chang'e, and you can call her directly. I'm not sure she *can* lie to you. I've never seen a manifestation try to lie to another aspect of themselves. I feel like heads might explode if the effort were sincerely made."

"I don't really feel like exploding any heads," says Judy, and slides off the table. "Diana's going to find out eventually, you know. Especially if your Tsukuyomis can help us recover Aske's body." She's starting to feel bad, consistently referring to the dead woman by the name of the divinity that inhabited her. She needs to find out what her mortal name was, what the name of the grieving family was. They may never know their daughter died, may mark her down as one of the missing and spend the next twenty years hoping she'll come home, but at least Judy will know. At least Judy will be able to mourn her properly.

"For right now, let me be a Losna," says Anna. Her eyes flash green for a moment. "I don't want to show my hand until I have to."

"But you've been upfront with me."

"You showed me something new, and like I said before, I'd be flirting if it weren't currently inappropriate." Anna shrugs. "I like new things, and I like pretty girls."

Judy isn't quite sure how she's supposed to respond to that, and so she looks at the peach pit she's still spinning between her fingers. "How do you do that eye thing?" she asks.

"What eye thing?"

"When you were pretending to be Losna, they were blue, and when you're actually Artemis, they go green," says Judy. "I've never seen a Lunar who could do that before."

"Your eyes are always that funny hazel color," says Anna. "You can't tell me that's the color you were born with. I won't believe you."

"It's not," says Judy. "My dad was Chinese, and my mother was Scottish." She takes after her father's side of the family, almost entirely, except for a slightly more rounded figure and slightly sharper cheekbones. Her eyes were dark brown when she was born, just like his. It wasn't until the moon started talking in her dreams that they'd started to get lighter, until now, when they were clearly hazel—at least until she stepped up into divinity. Then, and only then, they turned the pink-yellow color of ripe peaches, something inhuman and startling.

She's never had any control over it. Certainly not the control Artemis has demonstrated, or the ability to choose between colors, like some sort of ocular mood ring.

"So you do it too."

"No. This is just the color my eyes are now, the same way my hair keeps turning silver," says Judy, defensively. "I can't make them change just because I want them to look like something else."

(She broke up with her last high school boyfriend over her eyes. He'd refused to believe that she wasn't wearing contacts, and accused her of trying to "look like a white girl," as if that would ever have been possible, as if the only barrier between her and white privilege was the color of her eyes, and not the shape of them, the shape of her face, the shape of *her*. She'd thrown her soda in his face and walked away, leaving him furious and dripping, while she stormed out of the movie theater where they'd been meant to be having a romantic outing. While she'd seen him at school after that, they had never spoken again, a fact that now seems melodramatic and disproportionate but at the time felt exactly right.)

"Ah." Anna leans closer, dropping her voice just a little, and smiles. "I can only change them right now because I'm hunting. As long as I'm hunting, I can disappear into the silence, and nothing will stop me from blending into my surroundings. I'm going to bring down my prey, one way or another."

Judy doesn't know what to say to that.

Lacus Odii

Mopping Margaret's remains off the floor of the lab had been the work of almost an hour. Not that Tristan had done it himself, oh, no; he'd taken great pleasure in instructing Margaret's former second-in-command to handle the unpleasant task, watching as the woman retched and gagged and tried, desperately, not to either drop her mop or add to the mess on the floor. The poor thing had been somewhat concerned that he would react badly if she made the mess worse, and possibly decide that she could be *added* to the mess, liquidated as her supervisor had been.

She hadn't been wrong about that, and even now he somewhat resents the fact that she was able to swallow her gorge before she gave him the excuse.

There had been no concealing the fact that the mess had begun its existence as a human being, assuming you could call a failed researcher that: even if any alchemist worth the name hadn't been well practiced in recognizing the various fluids the body could be rendered into, there had been the matter of her skeleton, polished white and glossy, with an opalescent sheen that could almost be attractive, if not for the fact that it had been lying in the midst of all the other awful, unspeakable things Margaret had been reduced to.

Tristan had reopened the lab two hours after the release of his improved alkahest, ordering the staff to get to cleaning preparatory to decommissioning the facility, even as he removed himself to Margaret's desk to begin going through her files. He had reason to suspect that she'd been more successful than she'd claimed, but if that was so, she'd been given the opportunity to repent: she could have told them at any time that she'd done what she set out to do but chosen to conceal it for some unknowable reason, hiding her light under a bushel while others pursued their own dead-end routes into the City. She could have told him, not stood there in front of that orange abomination, telling bald-faced lies about failure and lab accidents.

If she'd just been willing to be honest and admit that the girl was a construct, he might have allowed Margaret to live. The thought is a ridiculous one, and he pauses in his scanning of her files to look up and smile to himself, very slightly. One of the assistants currently occupied in wiping the last of Margaret off the floor catches that expression and pales, redoubling his efforts. He wants out of this house of horrors, which is so sterile, so clean, except for the horrifying mess still being scraped up off the floor.

(Every atom of Margaret will be preserved and repurposed. She may not have led a successful project during her time with the lab, but she'll be part of several, if her superiors have anything to say about it. And they have quite a lot to say.)

No, she was never going to survive the review of her work. She'd been too headstrong, too determined to do things her own way and in her own time. It was a weakness shared by a troubling number of James Reed's former students, most of whom had believed that because they'd once studied at the knee of a man foolish enough to allow Leigh Barrow unfettered access to his person, they were somehow touched by greatness. That James Reed's century-long reign of unfettered self-indulgence was their birthright, and all they had to do was continue pushing forward in his name.

Amateurs, every single one of them. Building Moreau-esque mockeries of humanity down here when they were meant to be finding a way to harness the minor aspects of the Moon. How was the Congress supposed to lure a major Lunar aspect if they didn't have a minor one under their control? Really, it was a miracle anything ever got accomplished. Tristan sighs, looks up again, and pauses as his eyes fall on the skeleton.

Skeleton, singular. Meaning the girl, the "lab accident," really was a construct, despite his explicit instructions about naturals only during his inspection. He snaps his fingers. One of the junior researchers appears almost instantly, scurrying to his side so quickly that he's amazed she doesn't leave tire marks on the clean linoleum.

He hates an ass-kisser. The only thing worse than an overly fawning lackey is one who doesn't know their place. Finding the balance between those two states is the best way to stay alive in his presence over the long term, and it's not his fault these people haven't had the time to study up on their own survival protocols yet.

He'll ask her to come see him after the review is finished. Yes. Removing her internal organs through her navel will be a pleasant way to relax after this frustratingly stressful day. He'd known before arriving that Margaret's project was a failure, of course—her status reports had made that perfectly clear—but he had never imagined she would be foolish enough to look him in the eye and lie to him.

"Yes, sir?" asks the junior researcher.

"When I came for the inspection earlier, Miss Margaret had a lab assistant with her," he says. "Orange skin. Hooves. Margaret claimed the girl was a natural result of a lab experiment when I reminded her that she'd promised me no constructs, but she must have been . . . mistaken, because if the girl had been natural, she'd have been downsized by the alkahest. There's only one skeleton on the floor."

The junior researcher is silent. He's glad he had already decided to kill her. If he'd still been thinking in terms of mercy, he would be very disappointed just now.

"Well?" he prompts, when the silence has grown long enough to be genuinely frustrating. He doesn't like waiting.

"I . . . erm, I think you mean Kelpie, sir. She was a private project of Margaret's. Never worked with anyone else."

"And why is that?" he asks. He looks at her, making no effort to hide his irritation. "Margaret should not have been wasting Congressional resources on private projects. She had a task to perform, and it sounds like you're telling me that she was never doing it properly. If you know something that might contradict that, now would be the proper time to tell me. Lives might be saved."

Not including her own, but she doesn't need to know that.

The woman swallows hard, throat working as she ponders his words. Finally, turning her face away, she says, "Because she was a success."

"A success at what?"

"Kelpie was our second successful minor manifestation." The woman looks back. Apparently, betrayal gets easier the longer it keeps going on. "We got the Rabbit first. Not the actual god, the one who hangs out with the peach farmer. We're still working on the two dogs, the Man's and Diana's, but they seem to be closely enough entangled with each other that getting just one of them to embody is difficult."

She doesn't mention the dangers of dual embodiments. After Reed's failure, no one who serves the Congress in even the least capacity needs the reminder.

Tristan makes a noncommittal noise.

This appears to spur the woman to deeper, more desperate levels of betrayal. "Kelpie was made using Congressional supplies, and we told Margaret it made her property of the Congress, we *told* her—"

"Even if your former supervisor had used only her own hand-gathered ingredients and materials, the girl would still have been created using knowledge which the Congress had supplied. She would have belonged to us no matter what." Tristan looks at her along the length of his nose, careful not to let her see his slow-building excitement. "She was always ours. Where is she now?"

"I . . . I don't know, sir."

He was already going to kill her. Now he's going to make it hurt. "You don't *know*?"

"I didn't know she was here when you did the inspection until you told me! If she was here, she was probably doing some menial task for Margaret, something too basic for the rest of us! We mostly used her for scut work. She had no alchemical talents at all, she didn't understand half of what we were doing, and even if she had, her own orientation would have skewed anything she tried to blend or brew! I have no idea where she would have gone! Are you certain she was here when you released the alkahest?"

She realizes her mistake a beat too late, breath catching as his pupils dilate and his gaze turns a little sharper than is strictly natural. He can hear her heart rate accelerate as he watches her fight not to back away. She's terrified.

Good.

"Did you genuinely just ask an accredited senior alchemist whether I was certain of my own actions?" he asks, and his voice is buttery smooth and velvety, pitched to soothe. "Was that a clever choice you made?"

"Sir. No, sir, it wasn't. I'm sorry, sir. I didn't mean to—"

"I should certainly hope you didn't mean to. Yes, the girl was here. I closed the doors and left them in this lab alone while the alkahest worked its way through the air. It would have cleared in ten or so minutes, but that doesn't explain where she would have gone. Is there anyone else who would have concealed her? You mentioned that she was the second. Could she have run to the first?"

"No, sir. They've never met."

"You're certain of that?"

"As certain as if my life depended on it," she says, and then winces, seeming to catch the inherent danger of her own working. "I mean, sir, Margaret kept her fairly strictly isolated. It was just this team that really knew she existed. Constructs, even odd-looking ones, aren't that unusual within a static research facility, and we've been able to push the boundaries more since Reed died."

Reed died and his cuckoos settled in Berkeley, the city where they'd come together after years of coming apart, the city where they'd determined who their adult selves were going to be. They had a little house together, according to the last reports, a little house no one could find or see unless the cuckoos allowed it, and they lived there with an assortment of people as strange as they were, people whose names were mysteriously missing from Congressional records.

Oh, the cuckoos hated the alchemists who'd made them, called them monsters, blamed them all for Reed's actions and the actions of his students; they didn't care that alchemy was a tool like any other, blameless without someone to hold it. They hated the alchemists and chose no sides, and that was part of why the Congress was willing to delay the inevitable call to open warfare. As long as the cuckoos were content to play house with each other and spurn all alchemy, they weren't supporting a challenger to the power of the Congress.

And having them stationary, so much of the guiding power of the universe, was making it easier to convince reality that it should allow alchemical innovation. As long as the cuckoos didn't fly away, labs like this one would be able to make incredible, world-changing discoveries with half the staff and a third of the funding that they would have needed anywhere else in the world. Of course they had been able to manifest two of the minor forces. Those facets of the Lunars had been manifest before, time and again, even if they'd been missing for centuries. If any lab was going to bring them back, it was this one.

Tristan rises, slow and deliberate, watching the researcher for signs that she's about to bolt. It would be the clever thing for her to do, even if it would be the last thing she ever did. Those two truths aren't mutually exclusive: both can exist at the same time.

She isn't clever, which he already knew, or maybe she's too clever, and still thinks she can somehow worm her way into survival, find a loophole to wiggle through while his guard is down. He's willing to let hope linger, at least for a moment.

"Show me where she was kept," he says. It's not a request.

The woman doesn't read it as one. She nods, sharp and obedient, and turns to walk out of the lab, away from the remaining mess that was Margaret, her heels clicking sharp and staccato against the floor. He follows, and neither of them looks back.

Slightly over half the lab assistants and junior researchers live in the building. It was necessary, if they were going to conceal the place in an urban area, that they minimize the number of people who were going to be seen coming and going on a regular basis. The Congress owns the apartment building at the top of the stairs, devotes several of the apartments to their staff, and still they have to be careful who goes up to the surface. In order to keep people from getting resentful of those who were allowed to see the sun, go to a movie, and generally live semi-normal lives during their time away from the lab, all junior staff and assistants were assigned residences down below, no exceptions.

That meant Kelpie never questioned the location of her room, which is down a hallway lined with identical doors, each painted white and marked with a small nameplate identifying the occupant and their position. One of those doors cracks briefly open at the sound of footsteps, then swiftly shuts again as the person inside sees who's walking down the hall. The air is still and a little stagnant, tasting of dust and silence.

"Here," says the researcher, indicating the appropriate door.

K. Hinde reads the nameplate, and Tristan actually snorts in suppressed amusement, earning himself a glance from the woman, who relaxes slightly, taking his show of humor as a good sign for her survival.

"So much of alchemy relies on the simplest of sympathies," he says, folding his hands behind his back.

"Sir?"

"Of all the fictional quadrupeds, how many have names suitable for a person to use on a daily basis?" he asks. "And that last name— old German for 'hind.' Really, your Margaret labeled the girl as clearly as she could without setting off alarms, and no doubt deepened her sympathy with her incarnation every day in the process."

The woman doesn't move.

He lifts an eyebrow. "Well?" he says. "The door?"

She moves then, sharp and uneasy, like a frightened child at the cusp of a horror movie. It's a delightful thing, to be able to inspire so much terror so easily. When he was an apprentice, he used to watch the senior alchemists and wonder how they could take such joy in frightening people less powerful than they were, how they could play at being monsters without seeming to care what it could cost them. He swore, then, that he would be different, and he is. He is.

He's so much better at it than they were. He doesn't need weapons or harsh words to put everyone around him into a state of delicious fear: he can do it with a look or an entirely innocuous question. Reputation does the rest.

As to why they did it, he got that answer quite some time ago, and has held to it ever since. They did it then, and he does it now, because it's *wonderful.* Alchemy is about transformation and power. Transforming the moods of everyone around him to suit his own is a form of both those things, and one he is gleeful in commanding.

The door opens smoothly, unlocked, and swings open on well-oiled hinges, revealing a small room all but free of personal touches. There are a few pieces of clothing discarded on the floor, a dresser cluttered with the small objects that accumulate, even in an underground lab, a narrow bed strewn with tangled bedding, a potted plant putting up cautious green leaves with spiky edges.

The air here is even cooler and more stationary than the air in the hall. He looks back to the researcher. He supposes she must have a name—people generally do—but as she won't be making use of it for much longer, he doesn't see much point in bothering to learn it now.

"She hasn't been here," he says. "Where else does she go?"

"As I said, sir, Margaret mostly kept her close. None of the rest of us were encouraged to get to know her very well."

"I didn't ask you who might be braiding her hair and singing her happy little campfire songs. I asked you where she *went.* Surely you're not incompetent enough that you don't know *that* much about the girl who, as you have so casually informed me, represents the greatest alchemical breakthrough this provincial little lab has managed to unlock." He takes a step toward her, standing straighter as he does, until he looms in a towering collection of angles and bones. "If you've lost her, you'll yearn for the death your superior was granted. I have much less pleasant tools at my disposal."

The woman swallows hard, all color draining from her face. She makes a pretty picture, rigid and barely breathing.

"Well?"

"The cafeteria and the biology lab," she blurts. "We let her feed the frogs. It kept her out of the way, and they seemed to like her—they responded well to her, at least, and who knows what a frog likes?"

"Another frog, I suppose." He stops looming quite so intentionally. "Was any amphibian material used in her construction?"

"No more than the amount needed to stabilize the genetic matrix. Margaret thought it might confuse the sympathies if we crossed clades too much while she was being put together. I'll take you to the cafeteria, sir."

"You do that."

Again, he follows her. She moves more quickly this time, clearly no longer entertaining childish fantasies of rescue and redemption. No one's coming to save her. It's time and past time that she admitted that, and he's faintly impressed that she's managed to reach that conclusion without any active threats. Too many people in her position think that as long as he's not twirling the mustache he doesn't have and cackling, they can still work their way out of the abyss. It's tiresome. People who get themselves into the position of being listed as "expendable" should have the good grace to understand that it's an irrevocable designation.

Of course, she might feel the reminder of how efficient alkahest is as a killer to have been an active threat rather than an alchemical fact. He'll have to ask her while she's still capable of speech.

He doesn't pay much attention to where they're going as she leads him down another set of halls, focusing instead on the architecture of the lab itself. They have subterranean fortifications like this one all over North America, the majority built since James Reed murdered much of the last American Alchemical Congress. Losing so many masters in one blow had been very nearly incapacitating for the continent's alchemical interests. But their apprentices had survived, in many cases, alongside the independent alchemists, the up-and-coming, the ones whose ways of thinking had been too innovative or iconoclastic for the hidebound structures of the old Congress. Out of destruction could blossom new growth . . . at least for a while.

The old Congressional holdings had been cleaned out, the bodies removed, the traps disarmed, and the research fairly distributed among the surviving students of the lost masters. Then it had been distributed again, among the survivors of the argument over that ownership, until the strong and the clever had been the true survivors, and the time of rebuilding could begin.

Most of the old lab facilities had been too small, too cramped, and too designed for use by people who had been extending their own lives since the American Revolution, reluctant to consider other ways of doing business. Half the demolished labs hadn't been connected to the phone system, much less equipped with modern internet, although a surprising number had been accidental Faraday cages, capable of blocking cellular signals with ease. Really, it was a miracle that some of those old masters had been convinced to wire their labs for electricity. Privately, Tristan suspected they wouldn't have been willing to *be* convinced, if not for the increasing difficulty in finding apprentices who were willing to work by candlelight, or who inherently understood the safety protocols of carrying an oil lamp in enclosed spaces or around flammable materials. Modernization had come in fits and starts, resisted with every step.

In a way, Reed had done the Congress a massive favor by clearing out the old masters. Oh, knowledge had been lost, but not as much as had been originally feared; even the most paranoid among them had kept reasonably detailed notes, which had proven incredibly helpful once decoded and translated into instructions others could apply to their own efforts. But removing them had opened holes in the power structure, in which new powers had been able to arise, and new work had been able to begin.

The City is still the goal. The City is the goal across the globe, and every Alchemical Congress knows there can only be one winner in the race for metaphysical dominance over the universe. But finally, America is free to pursue other routes toward breaching those hallowed walls, while the other continents and regions continue to labor under the weight of centuries. They aren't as nimble.

Facilities of the size a modern alchemical organization needed couldn't be constructed in the open. Not without attracting the sort of attention that rendered the idea of a "secret society" somewhat moot. It was one of the survivors of the old Congress who proposed their current structure, a senior apprentice of a man who'd been trying to recreate true Roman concrete for the better part of fifty years. His theory was that modern material engineers failed in what should have been a reasonably achievable undertaking because they were missing some intangible portion of the process, some magical imbuement that would make it possible again.

His apprentices had been fond of that lost alchemist, making him a rare beast among the dead seniors, many of whom had been unpleasant verging on abusive, and they had continued his work in his absence, with the apprentice who now led the lab-construction efforts making the final breakthrough after she was given access to a dead Lunar for her own studies. She'd extracted a sample of the creature's blood, taking it back to her own lab for further analysis, and upon spilling it into a batch of concrete in process had discovered the key:

Divinity. The Romans had bled their gods into their construction and been rewarded with a substance that could endure for millennia, that actively repaired itself when it was damaged, that would even grow back if it was chipped away. It was closer to living bone than to stone when looked at under the proper conditions, and all it had taken to mix enough to grow underground laboratories around the continent was ensnaring a few minor gods and trapping them in their ascended condition before bleeding them dry.

Lunar gods have the ability to move in and out of manifestation, much like the moon can wax and wane: one of them might seem perfectly normal and human, then turn around and begin to glow as they took on the aspect of their divine self. Still, there are ways of finding them even when they hide below the surface of their own mortality, and so many of them that it's child's play to pick off a few weaker members of the pack from around the edges. Best of all, they aren't like the Seasons: killing a Lunar won't cause an immediate search for their replacement. It's like even the universe understands that they're an archaic affectation, an oil lamp in a modern laboratory setting, but keeps making them out of habit.

To create a subterranean lab in a matter of days, all the alchemists need now is a dilute form of alkahest to chew tunnels into the earth, a suitable amount of concrete, a Lunar to bleed into their construction materials, and the bones of a dozen murdered innocents. Much like the Hand of Glory's use as a thief's best friend, the bones can be infused with slow-burning phosphorus and used to cloak the lab from all but the closest examination.

Alchemical labs have been seeded around North America like anthills or mushrooms after a rain, their entrances concealed beneath buildings secured by the Congress through one of a dozen shell companies, their utilities provided by local grids unaware that they've been parasitized, their foundations rendered safe and stable by the blood of the moon itself.

It's an elegant solution to a problem that's been looming larger and larger across the years: how are they supposed to transform the world when the world insists on leaving no place for them? Their art has been dismissed by the "proper" sciences, relegated to the sidelines and viewed as little more than another form of witchcraft, powerless and suitable only for sale at Hot Topic. They need space in which to work, shared labs in which to conduct their research, and the freedom to do these things away from prying eyes. Now, with the proper infrastructure finally in place and thriving in a modern setting, they can truly get down to the business of changing the world.

Best of the construction project's dividends is the wealth of knowledge it's forced them to acquire about the Lunars. Catching a reliable supply of the weak, often ineffectual creatures meant learning how they operated, where to find them and how to lure them away from their fellows. Some of them protested when they were grabbed, saying they couldn't be abducted, they couldn't be held prisoner, because they had an essential job to do.

That was how the alchemists came to learn something new and wonderful about the Impossible City. Tristan would have said there was nothing new for them to learn, not after centuries of studying the place, decades spent trying to break through the walls and take their birthright at the head of the universal powers. But it seemed the City still held her surprises and her secrets, and from the Lunars, they have learned that each night, all over the world, windows appear and incarnate moon gods slip through, becoming that which they embody as they make the slow trek across the sky. They shine on the Impossible City. These small, useless slices of divinity come closer to eternity than most creatures will ever even dream.

The alchemists have also learned—or, rather, confirmed—that Lunars are universally arrogant and self-important creatures, believing themselves somehow special just because they're touched by an archaic sort of divinity. Efforts have been made to use them to access the City, but even Lunars who know themselves to be on the verge of dying have refused to allow the alchemists access. No amount of cajoling or threatening breaks through their pompous dedication to their duty.

Margaret's project began as an attempt to get around that dedication. Many Lunars had been represented across the centuries with animal partners of one sort or another, beloved companions who might provide a lever to get that final, essential degree of cooperation. Those animals stopped embodying some centuries before, the universe deeming them unnecessary as people stopped believing in them. That didn't mean they'd never existed, or that the potential for their manifestation might not still be floating somewhere out there in the ether.

Alchemists could catch Lunars, easily. What they couldn't do was control them, and control was what they needed. It helped that most of the Lunars with animals worth chasing were on the stronger side—Diana, Artemis, Chang'e. The big gods of their pathetic pantheon. Get one of them to join the cause, and it would be child's play to either convince or remove the rest of the Lunars, and then? An open door into the City, and a guide to get them there.

The Lunars moved back and forth between states, now mortal, now divine. The recreated embodiments wouldn't need to do that. If they could be shaped successfully, they wouldn't be anything other than themselves, with no shifting between states. They couldn't retreat into themselves to become less of a lever against their primary. They could always be leaned upon.

Margaret's proposal was sound, and her early results were promising enough that this lab was planted and grown to her specification, hidden in the city with the largest growing concentration of Lunars, right under the nose of Reed's cuckoos. She was young, clever, and ambitious, and Tristan was honest enough to admit to himself that he'd been expecting the order to kill her because of her success, not because of her failure. The new rulers of the Alchemical Congress liked their positions, and they'd been young and hungry recently enough to not nurture their own replacements longer than they had to.

The long hall from the residential quarters to the cafeteria is carefully devoid of character, with blank white walls and concrete-gray floor and ceiling. When there was always a chance that any sort of accident would require sterilizing the place with an alkahest wash, there was no point in customizing it. Anything apart from the living concrete would dissolve.

Roman concrete, prepared with gods' blood, survives even alkahest. It's a fascinating contradiction, a substance the supposedly universal solvent can't destroy, but the stuff is too useful not to keep making, and if anything, its existence will motivate them to improve the alkahest, to make it what it was truly meant to be.

Like the rest of the lab, the cafeteria is empty, the air holding the faint aroma of scrambled egg and French-bread pizza. Somehow, every cafeteria winds up smelling like those things, even before they turn on the stove burners for the first time. Some quirk of universal sympathy too minor for anyone to look into too deeply, at least so far. Maybe after they understand all the other mysteries of the universe, that will be a question to set for the apprentices—why do group kitchen spaces always smell like eggs? Discuss.

"I'd expect to find her here, if she's not in the lab or her quarters," says the junior who's been escorting him around the lab. She continues a few feet deeper into the cafeteria, like her presence will somehow force the missing girl to appear.

As if they could miss her. Tristan didn't exactly take the time to study her when he'd seen her in the lab before, but his memory insists that she was rather extremely and distinctly bright orange. People don't normally come in that color. She should stand out like a flashlight in a graveyard, but there's nothing here, not a hint of color.

Slowly, he turns to the junior, expression blank. The blood drains from her cheeks and the muscles around her eyes tighten as she fully grasps both her situation and the fact that he's between her and the exit.

"She's not here," he says.

"There are other places we can—"

"Tell me the truth. I'll know if you lie." He hesitates just long enough to give her time to formulate that lie, then says, "Is the woman we are pursuing a successful embodiment of Artemis's Hind?"

She licks her lips, pupils dilating. "Yes," she says. "Yes, she is."

"That will be all. Your services are no longer needed." He waves a hand lazily.

She bolts.

Not for the door—that would be the easy way, and he gets the feeling this woman has never taken the easy way in her life. She runs for the kitchen. Smiling to himself, he languidly follows.

Perhaps this day will be interesting after all.

Sinus Honoris

TIMELINE: AUGUST 18, 2017.
THREE DAYS TO THE ECLIPSE.

Isabella's husband is a large man named Juan who looks startlingly like his son—startling because Kelpie would have sworn Luis was a tiny short-haired clone of Isabella until faced with his father. The boy is the best of both his parents, an alchemical marvel in his own strange right.

Juan came home as Kelpie was helping Isabella clean and disinfect the kitchen. Isabella had been pleasantly surprised by how skilled Kelpie was at cleaning up after herself, not apparently understanding what was involved in serving as an assistant in a large alchemical research lab. Still, he'd come in, and they'd been wiping up the last of the mess, and to his credit, he hadn't batted an eye when Isabella introduced Kelpie as "my cousin Marie's ex-husband's little sister's cousin, Kelly." Apparently, claiming a clear but distant relation instantly made her family and entirely welcome in Juan's home. He'd laughed at Isabella's skill at picking up strays and dished himself a plate, taking it to the living room while the ladies finished cleaning the kitchen.

"He's a sweet man," Isabella had confessed, somewhat conspiratorially. "Very straightforward. He says what he means, and he means what he says, and you never have to guess at anything. It would be awful if we didn't have friends, but we do. This isn't one of those households where we got married and decided we'd never need anyone else, ever again. Can you imagine?"

Kelpie, who has almost no frame of reference for a normal relationship, or a normal anything else, only blinked, and went back to wiping vomit off the floor. "No," she'd said, bluntly. "What happens now?"

"Now? It's late, and Luis has school in the morning. You'll sleep on the couch, of course." There didn't seem to be any question for Isabella: Kelpie was here, Kelpie didn't have anyplace else to go, Kelpie was staying. "Tomorrow, we'll start trying to figure out what to do with you. Maybe I can introduce you to the rest of my coven. Smita should be there, and she has more experience with alchemical constructs than the rest of us, even though she tries to pretend she doesn't. We're pretty sure she's dating one of them."

"What?"

"Smita never shows up on her own; she's always walked into our meetings by this high-strung blonde with the kind of eyes you don't get in real people, only engineered ones."

Kelpie had almost objected at that. She *was* a real person. Maybe she wasn't the kind of person she'd always thought she was, being built instead of born, but she *was* real. If she wasn't real, she wouldn't be so lost and scared, now, would she? But Isabella had been on a roll, and Kelpie had been so relieved to have a place to stay that she hadn't wanted to make too much of a fuss. Fusses could come tomorrow, when the sun was up and she could see more of this strange world she'd been released into.

"Blondie never stays for the coven meetings, and she's always waiting outside exactly when we adjourn for the day, even if *we* don't know when that's going to be," said Isabella. "It's like she's got a sixth sense for it. I'd bet you anything she's some alchemist's science project. Smita doesn't like to talk about her. I think she'll like to talk about you."

"Thank you? I think?" Kelpie had replied, and now, on the far side of midnight, she's lying awake on a surprisingly lump-free couch, under a hand-crocheted blanket in a whole rainbow of colors, wearing borrowed pajamas and staring at the ceiling.

Her eyes are burning. They have been for quite some time, tears pooling in the corners and refusing to fall. She doesn't want to cry. She *doesn't*. Margaret was her friend and now she's dead and that's good enough reason for tears, except Margaret *wasn't* her friend, because alchemists aren't friends with experiments. That's one of the first rules of working in that kind of lab, right after "wear protective eye gear" and "proper ventilation is essential." Alchemists don't befriend experiments, and they especially don't befriend experimental embodiments. Embodiments are either involuntary extrusions of a disorganized universe or intentional science projects, and either way, spending time with them on a social level would be weird and sort of gross.

She's the same person now that she was last night, when she was sleeping in her own bed, in her own room, secure in the idea that she was wearing her own skin, oddly colored but her own, and one day to be replaced by the skin she'd been born with, when Margaret finished unsnarling the complicated web of accident damage and chemical reactions that transformed her from a normal lab assistant to something bright and strange and all but impossible.

Kelpie rolls over as much as her anatomy allows and sniffles. She was made. She was made in a lab by someone who wanted to embody a celestial deer and didn't care who got hurt in the process. What is she even made of? Did someone die to give her a skeleton, a heart, her eyes? Is she cobbled together from a dozen corpses, each specially selected for the sympathies running through their veins, making her a perfect tuning rod for an energy that very sensibly chose to stop incarnating a long time ago?

And why didn't she ask these questions yesterday? She's always known the lab's ultimate goals. She never had a problem with it. She worked with pieces of people—people like Juan and Isabella, people who'd been alive and then weren't alive anymore, people who didn't always donate their bodies of their own free will—and she tried to convince them to harmonize with each other so they could be restored to life through alchemical means, transformed and transmuted into something that would serve.

She doesn't want to serve. So why was it all right that she was building other creatures to serve, that she was supporting a system she'd never realized was inevitably going to hurt her too?

She should have been asking these questions ages ago, even if she's only a year old, even if she's barely had time to figure out what the correct questions *are*. She should have known what she was doing was wrong.

She's still trying to figure out the ethics of her actions as her eyes drift closed, bathed in the moonlight through the window, which warms and soothes her as nothing else possibly could.

When she wakes up, it's to the sound of Luis talking loudly and excitedly about the upcoming school day while Bobby barks, claws scrabbling against the kitchen linoleum. Someone is frying eggs. She sniffs the air, not opening her eyes, and realizes the room is lighter; even through her eyelids, she can tell that much. The sun has risen. The sun has risen and the moon has gone, and that shouldn't feel like such a loss, but it does.

Slowly, she opens her eyes and sits up on the couch, the blanket falling to puddle in her lap as she tries to get her bearings back. On some level, she'd gone to sleep hoping that when she woke up, it would all have been a dream. She'd be safe in her bed, in her room deep below the ground, with Margaret waiting for her to get up and start on her tasks for the day. Nothing would have changed. Everything would still make sense.

Just to check, she pinches herself on the arm, swift and vicious, hard enough to hurt. She bites her lip to stop herself from squeaking, then sighs and pushes herself off the couch, rising with relative ease. New techs used to marvel at how good she was at standing on her hooves, like any creature won't learn how to use the appendages it has instead of yearning for the appendages it doesn't. Birds learn to fly just fine, even though they don't have thumbs.

Sure, she's occasionally looked with envy at the way people with proper feet can make themselves taller by leaning onto their tiptoes, or express uncertainty by rocking back on their heels, but that was when she thought her own hooves were temporary things. Now that she knows they're not, she's not going to waste any time wishing for something she's never going to have.

She finds Isabella and her family in the kitchen. Isabella's frying eggs and some sort of sausage on the stove. Luis is dressed for school, while Bobby sits beside him at attention, clearly eager for the scraps he's sure will soon be tumbling his way. Juan has a large ceramic mug in one hand; he gestures at Kelpie with it before taking a noisy slurp.

"There's the sleeping beauty," he says, blithely, and Kelpie wonders what he sees when he looks at her. Not what she actually is, that's absolutely certain. "Hope we didn't wake you."

"Oh, I needed to be up anyway," she demurs, smiling and hoping her anxiety doesn't show. "Is there anything I can do to help?"

"You're a guest, and guests don't make breakfast; guests get *fed* breakfast," says Isabella, waving her spatula. "One egg or two? Sausage? I know you're not a vegetarian; I saw you eating last night."

Kelpie has never considered whether she'd prefer to be a vegetarian, and the thought stops her for a moment. In the lab, they ate what the cafeteria provided, and while it varied from day to day, it was always bland, nutritionally balanced, and made of a supposedly ideal balance of proteins, fats, and carbohydrates. She doesn't think she's ever gone a full day without eating chicken.

"Sausage would be lovely, thank you," she says, with her very best manners, as she takes the open seat at the table.

Luis grins at her, sausage in his teeth and something suspiciously sticky pushing up the front of his hair. "Mom says you're a cousin now, sort of, and you're going to stay a while. Are you really?"

"I . . . guess so."

"That's good. Bobby likes you! I like you, too. It's nice to have company. Are you going to stay sleeping in the living room the whole time? I get up real early on Saturdays to watch cartoons. Do you care if I watch cartoons?"

Kelpie, who doesn't know what a cartoon is, can only blink at the unending torrent of words, trying to understand what's being asked of her. She's saved from the need to reply by Isabella setting a plate on the table in front of her, rumpling Luis's hair with one hand as she does, only to recoil.

"Ugh! Mijo, how are you sticky? We didn't even have waffles today! Did you forget that jam goes on toast, not in hair?"

Luis giggles, unrepentant. Isabella huffs, then points to the door.

"Go. Wash up, now. Jam out of hair, off face, off hands, and change your shirt if there's a speck of jam on it, anywhere. I won't have your teachers thinking I roll you in pectin before I ship you off to their care."

"Aw, Mom," he protests.

"Go!" she repeats, and giggling, he goes.

A beat later, Juan rises, taking his mug with him, and crosses the kitchen to kiss the crown of Isabella's head before he nods to Kelpie, says, "Have a lovely day, and I hope things at home improve for you soon. I'll see you both at dinner." Then he's gone, heading out of the kitchen with Bobby at his heels, the dog's tail waving wildly, as if he can't control his excitement over the moment and the chance that he might get to go outside again.

He doesn't. The door opens and closes, and the dog trots back to sit next to Kelpie's chair, silently begging for scraps of her breakfast. She laughs and moves her plate a bit away from him, shielding it with her arm. After last night, she didn't think she was ever going to be hungry again, but now she's ravenous, her stomach demanding satisfaction in loud and uncomfortable growls.

She watches Isabella carefully as she reaches for knife and fork, hoping the other woman will signal in some way if she's doing it wrong, but Isabella is busy studying her hair.

"How did you sleep?"

Kelpie shrugs. "Better than I expected to, since I've never slept in a room with a window before." Her eyes widen. "I don't have my toothbrush! Or my hairbrush. I left them in the lab, and I can't go back down to get them—"

"No, you can't," says Isabella firmly. "Last time Luis went to the dentist, they sent him home with a little goodie bag full of floss samples and flavored toothpastes, and a new brush we still haven't opened. With what we pay to have his teeth cleaned, they should have sent him home with a new bike."

As if summoned by the word "bike," Luis reappears in the doorway, the front of his hair now wetted down against his forehead. He holds out his hands for inspection, beaming at Kelpie and his mother.

Isabella crosses the kitchen to take his hands, turning them over for a cursory inspection. "Mmm . . . that will do," she says, finally. "Go get your things. You need to take Bobby out before you head for school."

"Dad already left?"

"If you wanted a ride, you shouldn't have let yourself get all sticky," she says, in a tone which makes it very clear she's teasing; this is a conversation they've had many times, in many settings, and while he may be playing it up a bit for the sake of his audience, there's no resentment here. This is just the way the morning goes.

Luis shrugs, still grinning. "I'll take Bobby out and then I'll go."

"Okay. You do that." Isabella watches as he scurries away, then finally picks up her own breakfast and sits down across from Kelpie. "Don't get the wrong idea. He's a good kid, but he likes to press the rules as much as any child does. If I gave him an inch, he'd take a mile. Fortunately, we only have one car, and Juan needs it for work."

"What does he do?"

"He's a mechanic. Works at a shop over in Oakland, comes home every night smelling like grease, with new calluses on his hands. It's wonderful. He enjoys his work, I enjoy not needing to worry about him, and his income is unpredictable enough that the government doesn't notice the money I bring in under the table."

Most of this makes no sense to Kelpie, so she just nods, hoping she looks like she understands, and cuts into her eggs with a quick swipe of her butter knife. The yolks rupture in a river of gold that seems oddly alchemical in nature, reminding her far too much of Margaret's eyes running down her cheeks, impossibly still pigmented in their original color. She pushes her chair back and drops her fork, abruptly no longer hungry.

"I'm sorry. I should have asked how you liked your eggs."

"It's not . . ." There's a lump in Kelpie's throat. She doesn't know how it got there, but it hurts. She swallows as hard as she can, forcing herself to speak around it, even as she wraps her tail around her leg and draws it tight, cutting off the circulation below the knee. "I guess I'm just not hungry. Sorry to waste food."

"I can put it in the fridge for later, but the eggs will congeal if I do that," says Isabella.

Congealed eggs won't run like liquefied human eyes. Kelpie nods immediately. "Yes please could you do that?" she asks.

Looking confused, Isabella rises, takes Kelpie's plate, and carries it to the counter, where she wraps a piece of tinfoil over it before putting it in the fridge. "This is here whenever you're ready," she says.

"Thank you," says Kelpie, meekly.

"But if you're going to be staying longer than a day, we need to talk about how much you actually eat when you're not traumatized."

Kelpie unwraps her tail before anything can go numb, flicking it out of the way, and blinks at Isabella. "Why?"

"Oh, for—because, hon, food isn't free when it's not being provided by the evil underground alchemy lab. I'm happy to feed you. You're a victim of those bastards as much as anyone else I've ever known, but if you eat like the age you look, we're going to need extra money, and there's no way you legally exist. Even if you could afford to take the risk of being behind the counter at 7-Eleven when an alchemist came in looking for bottled water and M&M's, they'd never hire you to begin with, because their computers will all say you're not real."

Kelpie's head is starting to spin. This is a lot, and she's been loose in the world for less than a day, and she doesn't know how she's going to handle any of it. Of course she exists! If she didn't exist, this would all be so much easier. But she's been called into being by alchemists whose educations outstripped their ethics by such a wide margin that they never stopped to ask themselves whether this, any of this, was acceptable. She *is*. How can a computer decide she's not?

"I don't know how much I eat," she says, in a small voice. "A normal amount."

"Was last night normal?"

"No. I was hungry and I'd been so scared and sometimes adrenaline can convert into hunger signals when the body comes down from the peak of panic, and the food was so good. I never had anything like that before."

"Sounds about white," says Isabella, and eyes her. "That stuff about adrenaline—why do you know that?"

"I helped with the animals in the bio lab sometimes," says Kelpie. "You'd have a rat so scared it was forgetting to breathe, and then five minutes later, it'd be trying to eat a chunk of bread bigger than its body. I know a lot about biology."

"And nothing about the cost of food. What a fun education you've had." Isabella sighs, but she's smiling; she's not mad. "Well, you can't get a job, and you can't go back to the alchemists, so that means you're going to have to learn how to do what an hechicera does, just a little. Maybe you're going to be amazing at talking the universe into things, since technically you're an incarnate piece of it walking around on two hooves—and don't think they were doing you any favors when they built you so far off the human norm, kiddo. Maybe most people won't see you for what you are, but enough will, and that's going to make you a target any time you go out in public."

Kelpie blinks. "Margaret always said I was a lab accident," she says, not fully aware that she's omitted the word "in" from that sentence; she's adjusting to the reality of what she is and how she came to be. "I don't know if they did it on purpose, or whether they could have made me any other way."

"You look kinda like a deer; maybe it's the Hind coming out in you. But by that logic, every Winter would look like Jack Frost, and every Summer would look like a harvest icon, so maybe it's just because they were working with something that didn't want to manifest. Who knows why alchemists do anything? They're like kids with a chemistry set way above their age level. Half the time, I don't think *they* know why they do the things they do."

"But I can go out?"

"Yes. As long as we stay out of crowds and avoid places where alchemists tend to congregate, you can go out. Which is good. You're coming to my coven meeting today, and then you and I are going to figure out what of my services you can help for. I do things for the local community. Luck charms, water-purification stones—with the plumbing around here, sometimes you don't have a choice—all the little forms of magic that the alchemists can't monitor or admit exist without showing their whole hand. If you can help me do my job faster, I can take more clients, and we'll be able to pay whatever increase you cause in the food bill. And we can start setting you up with funds for when you inevitably get tired of haunting my living room."

"Do you think that's going to happen?"

"Stranger things happen every day," says Isabella.

She's finished her breakfast while they were talking, and after a brief pause to rinse the dishes and load them into the dishwasher (which Isabella dismisses merrily as "a piece of crap" while still using it), she leads Kelpie to the bathroom and presents her with the available sanitary products: toothpaste and a fresh toothbrush, a hairbrush that looks like it might be up to the challenge of her hair, a washcloth, and a towel. She stays long enough to establish that they *did* have showers in the lab, then excuses herself, telling Kelpie to come out when she's ready, and leaves her alone.

The bathroom is small, square, and very, very white. It's the most familiar thing she's seen since leaving the lab. Kelpie looks at the brush and tube of paste in her hands, and decides to start with what she knows hasn't changed: oral hygiene doesn't care whether you're real or lab-grown. It's a constant. Her hair is more of a challenge. It's not curly so much as it's wavy and stubborn, with a tendency to tie itself into knots if she looks at it funny. Sleeping under a tree and then on a couch definitely qualifies as looking at it funny, and it takes the brush away from her several times before she feels like she can safely step into the shower.

The soap doesn't smell like anything she recognizes, and the bottle doesn't help as much as she'd like it to. Is "Summer Berry

Medley Dream" a kind of fruit? It's probably delicious, with a name like that, which explains why someone would want to smell that way. She lathers herself up and rinses twice, the way she always did down in the lab, and wishes she'd thought to go by her quarters for her nail kit. Normally, she files her nails every morning, and oils her hooves and horns to keep them from cracking. It's a tedious routine, and she never thought she could miss it.

"You drown in there?" calls Isabella from the hall, and she knows she's been in the bathroom long enough; the day here may not follow the ebb and flow of the days in the lab, but she still has duties to perform and marks to meet. That's almost comforting.

"I'll be right there!" she calls, and she means it. She has somewhere to be, with someone who wants her there, and she's not completely adrift in a world she doesn't understand, she's *not*. She's a part of something. Maybe it's not the something she always thought she was a part of, but it's something all the same, and that can be good enough for her.

That has to be.

She leaves the bathroom in a cloud of Summer Berry Medley Dream–scented fog, and Isabella wrinkles her nose at the sight of her. "I should have realized," she says. "Of course you don't have anything else to wear."

"I thought my clothes were better than your pajamas," says Kelpie apologetically. "I can't borrow any pants that button or zip. They don't have space for my tail."

"No, and it isn't the right weather for dresses." Isabella looks Kelpie frankly up and down. "Well, at least you don't look *too* abnormal."

Kelpie, who has worn a button-down white shirt and khaki pants every day of her life so far, is baffled by that examination but doesn't say anything about it. Some things are beyond all understanding. "Most people can't see my tail, you said."

"That's right."

"So what will they see if they look at me from behind? Will my pants just have a hole in them for no reason?"

That gives Isabella a momentary pause before she shakes her head and says, "When the coronation was on, we had potential monarchs slaughtering each other all across the continent, and it mostly didn't make the papers. People would remark on how strange it was, the way Miss Kinsey's boy died, and then they'd just move on, tragedy dismissed. No gossip, no evidence, no footprint on memory. The magical world knows how to conceal itself from people who don't want to see it. Will a hole in your pants count if it's there to allow for something most people won't realize or admit exists? I don't know. I suppose we're going to find out together." Isabella picks up a purse from the table at the end of the hall, brown leather in a shell of knotted beige twine, and slings the strap over her shoulder. "Isn't this going to be fun?"

"Yeah," says Kelpie, unenthusiastically. "Fun."

She follows Isabella out of the apartment, noting the way the woman stays between her and the decoy apartment, making it harder to see her from the windows. She doesn't think anyone's looking. If they were trying to find her, surely they would have done so already; surely there's something baked into the foundations of her that would lead them right to her location.

The thought is unexpected, and sends her stomach swooping toward her ankles, dropping hard and fast and brutal. She slept in Isabella's living room last night, only a closed door away from Luis and Bobby, and they could have come for her at any moment. She almost stops walking, but manages not to. Stopping here would leave her visible from the window. Stopping here would leave Isabella in danger.

She manages to hold her tongue until they've exited the apartment complex and made it down to the sidewalk, where true to Isabella's word, no one seems to notice her: the people continue to walk, the cars roll down the street, and no one stops to stare, no one runs into anyone else. Only then does she stop, grabbing the strap of Isabella's purse to make *her* stop as well. She turns to look at Kelpie, expression somewhere between irritated and amused.

"Penny dropped, eh?"

"They could have come in the middle of the night! You could all be dead right now! I know you're an hechicera, but that's not bigger than a master alchemist like the one who killed Margaret! You let me put you in danger!"

"All right, first off, keep your voice down, all right? Yes, most people can't *see* the magical world, but they can hear just fine, and if you go hurling certain words around, you might attract attention. Yeah, nine out of ten will think you're some college kid LARPing or whatever, but that tenth will tell a funny story about a yelling blonde woman, and that could reach the wrong ears before you know it. Part of why I'm happy to be an hechicera instead of a bruja is that almost no one in this country knows what that is, while 'bruja' is a word that makes them stop and take notice."

Kelpie blinks, then nods, looking down at the sidewalk. "I'm sorry," she says, voice much softer.

"Don't be sorry for wanting to protect my family, all right? If you need to be sorry, be sorry you didn't trust me to have thought things through. You're right. An hechicera, even a very, very good one, isn't a match for what you call a master alchemist. They cheat. They're not more powerful—they're as human as I am—but they have all the other alchemists in the world to borrow toys from, and they have no shame. They'll burn a whole building to ashes because they feel like one person inside it insulted them, and then they'll brag about how no one saw the fire until they wanted it to be seen. An hechicera doesn't cheat. We work within the world, not against it. That means I started to take precautions as soon as I realized what you were. By the time you went to sleep, that apartment was warded so tight that they could ring the bell and try to sell you cookies without realizing who you were, as long as you didn't go outside."

"So why bring me with you now? Wouldn't it be safer for me to stay in the apartment?"

"Call it a test." Isabella reaches out and gently tugs her purse strap out of Kelpie's hand before she starts walking again, letting Kelpie follow.

"For who?"

"Everyone, I suppose. We're testing whether I'm as good at hiding things as I think I am, and how good a job you can do of dealing with the world outside the lab. You're getting top marks so far, by the way. I thought you were going to see your first car and have a complete meltdown, but you're doing really well." Isabella's smile is wide and sincere. "And it's a way to see how many of the ladies in my coven are exaggerating their own sensitivity to the hidden world, since if they can't see how damn weird *you* are, they sure as hell can't see the auras they claim to find everywhere. You're my Karen detector."

Kelpie has no idea what that means, but she only shrugs as she keeps walking. "I know what a car is. Margaret showed me videos."

"Is that so?"

"Yeah. I didn't think they'd be this big, or this smelly, but the general concept, I get. Oh, do you think we might see a bus? I've always wanted to see a bus."

Isabella laughs. "You're delightful. It's like having a really big puppy that can talk. Yes, Kelpie, we'll probably see a bus. Probably more than one. You can learn to love and resent them the way the rest of us do." She turns sober as they walk on. "It's interesting that she showed you video of cars, though. It means she expected you to leave the lab someday."

"Well, yeah. She was working on a way to reverse the lab accident so I could go topside and rejoin the world. Or that's what she said, anyway. I guess maybe she was just looking for a way to make me look more normal so she could use me as an embodiment without the Alchemical Congress catching on. I don't know why she didn't like them. They gave her a lab, and all the assistants and materials she needed, and room to do her work. She couldn't have made me if not for them."

"People are complicated. I'm sure she had her reasons," says Isabella. "Love and hate are kissing cousins, after all."

Kelpie looks confused, and Isabella laughs again, and they walk on, following the sidewalk as it transitions from somewhat run-down residential neighborhood to a tree-lined street filled with small brick buildings, each one split between two or three stores with big glass windows displaying their wares to the world. True to

Isabella's word, no one looks at them twice. Kelpie is bright orange, and they don't seem to see her at all.

It's strange. It's impossible. It's ridiculous.

It's happening all the same.

They reach the end of a block defined by spreading maple trees and turn onto another residential street. This one has large houses instead of apartment buildings, each one with a set of stone steps leading up to its front door, most with small gardens or lawns in front, showing the world how wealthy the residents must be. The grass here is greener, healthier than the grass at the apartment complex, and Kelpie frowns.

Isabella catches her expression, and explains: "Water's expensive. California's experiencing a drought. So only the rich people can afford to water their lawns all the time."

"That's not fair," protests Kelpie. "The grass doesn't decide whether it gets planted by someone rich or poor. All the grass should have water."

"You're on the cusp of figuring something out there," says Isabella, stopping in front of one of the larger houses. "Come on. When they ask you to take your shoes off, mime it. No one's going to ask any questions."

"Why would they ask me to take my shoes off?" asks Kelpie, following her up the stairs.

"Because this house belongs to a very nice, very clueless, very New Age–y white woman who doesn't want us to scuff her bamboo parquet floors," says Isabella, ringing the bell. When Kelpie still looks confused, she sighs. "That means no shoes in the house. A lot of cultures do that for good reasons; she does it because she thinks it's spiritual, which is why I'm not actually being an asshole when I tease her lightly about it."

"But I'm not wearing shoes," says Kelpie, in case Isabella hadn't noticed.

"Their eyes will fill them in along with the feet when they try to see you as something perfectly normal, I promise," says Isabella. She steps back, putting a hand on Kelpie's shoulder. "Now smile."

The door opens.

Kelpie smiles.

The woman in the entryway smiles reflexively back before her eyes skitter to Isabella and her smile melts into an expression of petulant upset. "Isabella, there you are!" she says, a whining note in her voice that makes Kelpie's shoulders tighten and draw upward, toward her ears. "I tried to call the apartment this morning, the energy in the house is simply *dreadful,* I don't know how we're supposed to have a meeting here today!"

"I have salt spires; I can purify it very quickly," says Isabella, soothingly. "May I introduce you to my new apprentice, Kelly? She's a distant cousin of mine, and she has the family gift."

"Hello," says Kelpie.

The woman barely glances at her, too focused on Isabella. "Oh, I'm so glad you're going to have help; you overextend yourself so," she gushes, reaching out as if to pull her bodily inside. At the last moment, she thinks better of it and steps to the side, allowing Isabella and Kelpie to enter. "I was just saying yesterday, I was saying, Isabella burns the candle at both ends and in the middle, and she needs to stop if she wants to keep going! And we need you to keep going, we do, you're our spiritual leader, we would all be lost without you!" She does glance at Kelpie then, smile hardening and voice taking on the lilting quality of someone speaking to a child: "Take off your shoes, dear; this isn't a barn."

Barn comment aside, she doesn't seem to see anything strange when Kelpie lifts her hooves, one by one, and mimes the removal of the shoes she isn't wearing. The woman's only flicker of confusion comes when Kelpie puts her "shoes" down, since it's quite obvious that there's nothing there. Then she shrugs, dismissing it as nothing, and her attention swings back to Isabella.

"While you're looking at the humors of the house, can you check mine as well? I've been feeling faint in the mornings, you see . . ."

"I've told you before, Catrina, you can't cut salt entirely out of your diet, no matter how much of an internal toxin you've decided it is. Your body needs some salt to regulate itself."

The woman, who is tall and pale and not much older than Isabella herself, with silvery-gold hair pinned up in elaborate curls that look like they must have taken most of the morning, recoils, hands fluttering like she wants to brush Isabella's words out of the room. "Salt is like bug spray," she protests. "It's good for cleansing and purifying a space, but it's not meant to be taken internally! I don't know why you insist on buying into the lies told by Big Sodium the way that you do, Isabella; a smart woman like you ought to know better."

She begins to move deeper in the house, still chattering about the dangers of sodium. Isabella looks at Kelpie, smiling a little. "What did I tell you? She didn't notice anything was wrong about your foot situation, or anything else."

"Salt isn't poisonous to humans," says Kelpie, baffled. "They need it to live."

"I know that, and you know that, and Catrina's doctors know that, and I presume her in-home chef knows that and has been slipping salt into her food, since she hasn't dropped dead yet, but she's prone to crusading against things, and right now, it's salt," says Isabella. "At least she still lets us use it for ritual work. We could find another place to meet if we had to, but I'd very much prefer we didn't. This is a private home, which means we don't worry about rental fees or who might have been using it when we weren't around. We've been able to install and charge a permanent ritual circle, and those make certain things so much easier. Magic is magic as a natural force, while alchemy is magic as a domesticated beast. We're not doing science here."

She follows Catrina then, and Kelpie follows her, not sure what else she's meant to do. Her hooves tap against the bamboo floor with every step, and she can't help wondering whether whatever quirk of the universe keeps people from seeing her strangeness will also keep them from hearing it. No one barefoot sounds like she does when they walk.

The house, which seemed large from the outside, is clearly massive, almost as large as a level of the lab, and she glimpses a staircase winding up to another floor, implying the existence of yet more house beyond what she's already seen. She can't imagine needing this much house. There's no color, either, another thing that reminds her of the lab: the walls are white, only occasionally decorated with a tastefully framed, carefully placed piece of art, none of them in primary colors. It makes her yearn for the bright jewel tones and earth colors of Isabella's apartment. The air, which is almost as cool as the outside, smells of nothing, the sort of nothing that she knows comes only from constant cleaning and air purification. It's almost smothering. She had no idea people aboveground lived like this.

Maybe most of them don't. Based on what she's seen so far, lives like Isabella's are far more common than lives like this one. That's somewhat reassuring. She doesn't want to flee from one sterile environment into another.

Catrina vanishes through a doorway, and Isabella vanishes after her, and Kelpie pauses in the hall as she hears voices greeting both women, feeling suddenly shy. What if *none* of them can see her properly, and she has to spend the rest of her life feeling like she's lying to everyone around her by letting them believe she's something that she's not? Or what if one of them *does* see her properly and starts yelling about how she's some sort of freak?

Both options are almost equally terrifying, and so she stands frozen as she hears Isabella explaining, "I brought my new apprentice for you to all meet. She's a distant cousin of mine, and she's a little shy, but I hope you'll be friendly."

A murmur of agreement from the room.

"All right, if you promise. Kelly! You can come on in; no one's going to bite you."

Slowly, Kelpie steps around the doorframe and into the room, where half a dozen women have already gathered. They smile at the sight of her, with none of them so much as hesitating. She begins, cautiously, to relax.

"Cousin?" asks a woman. "She's *blonde*."

"Distant," repeats Isabella.

The woman laughs. "When I told you one of my cousins was in the running for Winter, you said that was proof we shouldn't work with family. What possessed you to take one as an apprentice?"

"I . . . I asked her to," says Kelpie, defensively.

"She know anything?" asks the woman who seems to have decided she's the one who makes the call on whether or not Kelpie is trustworthy. She looks her up and down, and Kelpie has the distinct feeling she's seeing something that's not there, some pale, unremarkable shadow of Kelpie herself. Finally, the stranger shrugs one shoulder and turns back to Isabella. "About the art, or about us?"

"She knows you're my coven, she knows you all practice in one form or another, and she knows I'm an hechicera, or I wouldn't be able to train her."

"You mean *bruja*, don't you, dear?" asks Catrina, who, for all the group's apparent deference to Isabella, has taken the largest and most comfortable-looking chair in the room as her own. "That's the word for witch."

"As I've told you several times now, I'm not a witch, and it would be dishonest of me to call myself one," says Isabella carefully. "I'm an hechicera, which is a different tradition, and works by different rules. I don't know how else I can explain it."

"We're a coven of witches," says Catrina. "We're women working with the sacred feminine and the divine energy of the goddess. You have to be a witch. You're our high priestess."

"I'm not your high priestess," says Isabella, with clearly fraying patience. "I'm your leader, yes, but that's not the same thing, and it never has been. If you want a Wiccan-style structure, with a high priestess telling you what to do and a deeply appropriative approach to ritual, you're more than welcome to find another coven to work with, or you can ask that I leave and do my workings elsewhere. You can't have me and the structure you're describing at the same time."

"I didn't mean that," objects Catrina. "Just that . . . we're supposed to be doing things the traditional way."

"There are many traditions," says Isabella staunchly.

There's a clatter from behind them as someone comes rushing down the hall, and a pretty, black-haired, dark-skinned woman in a diamond-patterned sweater containing all the colors the house doesn't appears in the doorway. She's barefoot, carrying a large canvas bag, and she looks like she's on the verge of panic.

"I'm sorry!" she says. "I'm sorry, I'm so sorry, I was at the lab and I lost track of time again, I didn't mean to be late!"

"I showed up five minutes after she was supposed to have left and she was still at her desk, looking at some diagram of acidic interactions that I couldn't explain if you paid me," says the woman who strolls calmly in after her, before she stops and stares at Kelpie.

Kelpie stares back. She feels like she knows this woman already, like she's known her all her life, like they're sisters and enemies and the best and worst of friends, all at the very same time. The stranger is shorter than her companion, more softly built, but the sort of softness that promises steel beneath: despite the layer of fat she carries, Kelpie can tell by the way she moves that she's physically the most powerful person in the room. Her hair is strawberry blonde, like she's been bleeding for years and never figured out how to wash it all out, and her eyes, as Isabella said, are impossible, blue on blue, like a butterfly's wing. They're eyes for a painting, not a person, and they're fixed on Kelpie with a sharpness that says, very clearly, that she can *see* her.

"Hello," she says. "Who's this?"

"Isabella's taken an apprentice," says Catrina, apparently happy to answer any question she can, even when those questions aren't for her.

"Hello, Erin," says Isabella. "I was hoping you'd swing through today, so I could introduce you. I think you're going to have a lot to talk about."

"Oh, yes," says Erin. "I think so, too."

Silence falls over the room, thick and heavy, smothering them all with its weight, and Kelpie resists the urge to turn and run.

Mare Ingenii

As a newly transferred student, Anna is in on-campus housing, sharing her room with three other girls, none of whom have ever heard the moon speaking through their bedroom windows, none of whom have any idea who they're living with. They look at Judy with the flat, disinterested eyes of junior predators who've already been fed well enough not to care when she enters the room on Anna's heels, feeling awkward and out of place and hating it.

She's used to being the second most powerful Lunar in Berkeley, coming directly after Diana in what passes for the local hierarchy. Not that it matters who's more powerful than who, unless it comes down to an outright brawl, and this isn't a comic book: they don't fight each other for access to the everything. That would be ridiculous. Still, it makes her a little uncomfortable to know that there's a new Lunar in town, one who's been embodied long enough to understand her powers and what they allow her to achieve. Chang'e probably has more active worshippers in the modern world, but Artemis has *stories*. Artemis has *Percy Jackson*. There's no denying the fact that those things feed into her manifestations, granting them a level of strength any Lunar would envy.

So yeah, she accompanied Anna when the other woman said she needed to grab something from her dorm, and now she's standing uncomfortably in the center of the room, watching the junior predators assess her potential as a future meal. She's unable to quash the relief when Anna returns, now carrying a backpack, and says, "Okay, Judy, let's go."

Judy doesn't need to be told twice. She falls into step alongside the taller girl, and together they exit the dorm, Anna taking every turn in the labyrinthine building with easy confidence. "How long did you say you'd been here?"

"Not that long. The place looks confusing, but it's really straightforward once you get the lay of the land. This used to be one of those houses too big for anyone sensible to maintain on their own. I don't mean like the bitchin' Victorians downtown, I mean like hello, Mr. Mansion. At some point, ownership passed to the university and they carved it up like a Christmas turkey, turned it into something they could stuff a couple hundred students into. That didn't leave the refurbishing architects a lot of internal wiggle room, and so if you keep going left, you always come to an elevator—assuming your building has one."

Judy last lived in student housing when she was getting her undergrad degree, and that was in a different state, in what sometimes felt like a different world. Berkeley's bewildering dorms aside, she understands the scarcity of elevators in supposedly accessible housing. "Is it legal for them to not have an elevator? In California?"

"Legalities and the speed with which they get applied are two different things," says Anna, as they step out of the dorm lobby and into the late morning air. The day is maturing beautifully, with clear skies and the sort of crisp, sharp chill that only flirts with the idea of becoming actually cold.

California won't be like this forever. It's gotten warmer even since Judy moved here, the crisp falls fading in a matter of weeks when they used to linger for months, the summers going from unpleasant to sweltering. But here and now, it's very close to perfect.

Anna glances at her as they start across the lawn. "Any idea where to start?"

"You're the hunter, not me," says Judy. "If I were a hunter, I think I'd want to start with someone who'd actually seen where the killing took place, though. I'd want to talk to Máni."

Anna looks at her again, eyes flashing green as she focuses on Judy. It's uncomfortably like having the full attention of some massive predator, and Chang'e stirs beneath the surface, very nearly stepping up to defend her avatar before Judy can nudge her back down.

"Do you know where to find him?"

The question is soft, mild, even, with nothing behind it to indicate that it might be a threat. Judy still feels her heart sink, pulse quickening at the harmonics in Anna's tone. The other woman hasn't stepped up, she knows that, but she feels as if maybe, when hunting, Artemis never really steps all the way down.

Anna is someone who would always bleed silver, if anyone could ever make her bleed.

"He's on the football team," says Judy. "I'd start with the locker rooms, if I really wanted to catch him. His daylight name is David."

"David," says Anna, rolling the name in her mouth like she can taste it. Maybe she can, somehow: maybe this is how she gets the scent of him. "Take me there."

"Sure," says Judy. "Not like I have classes to teach today or anything. Not like I was doing something with my time." But she's protesting out of habit as much as anything else. She's normally so reliable that an absence is unlikely to inspire anything but concern that something's happened; she has copious notes for the other TAs, who will cover all her classes for the day. She can always plead food poisoning, if she has to.

In fact, better to do that ahead of time. Pulling out her phone, she sends a quick message to her advisor, copying the department admin. She's not feeling well, she says; she needs to go back to bed and sleep it off. There's some risk there, since she's still going to be on campus, but the chances of either of them going out among the student body voluntarily are very slim, and a little risk is unavoidable.

She turns back to Anna, who's watched all this without comment. "You ready?" she asks.

Anna nods, and the pair strike off across campus.

"You're going to have to talk to Diana eventually," she comments, once they're safely alone on a bike trail, with no one close enough to overhear their conversation.

"Am I?" asks Anna.

"She's the senior Lunar in the area. It's polite, if nothing else."

"But there's no *rule.*"

"Well . . . no, there's not a rule," admits Judy. "But it's how things have always been done. You introduce yourself to the senior Lunar in the area."

"I did. I sent her an email."

Arguing further won't do any good; Judy can tell that already. So she sighs and shakes her head, asking, "Why are you so against meeting her?"

"Did she tell you to look into Aske's death?"

Did she? Of course she did. Judy tries to recall the specifics of her conversation with Diana, allowing Chang'e to rise just far enough to supply the fragments Judy wasn't present for, and realizes that technically, no, she didn't. She told Judy to find out who escorted Aske to the gate, but that was all. And she'd been oddly calm about the thought of needing to hide a body, hadn't she? Maybe it was already knowing about the other deaths, but it feels like more than that, suddenly.

It feels like a riddle. Unlike many lunar gods, Chang'e has never been particularly fond of riddles. They waste time, and while she's immortal, that doesn't mean time isn't precious, isn't worthy of being saved and savored whenever possible. Her avatars aren't immortal, after all. Take their peaches away, hurt them badly enough, and they die like anyone else does.

Chang'e isn't mortal. Judy *is,* and Judy very, very much doesn't want to die.

"She asked me to find out who escorted her to the gate before she died, but that was all," says Judy. "She also wanted me to warn Abuk when she came for the handoff—which, where's Abuk, by the way? I was so worried about finding a corpse hanging out in the everything that I didn't realize you weren't supposed to be my escort."

"Oh, I ran into Abuk yesterday morning and told her she didn't need to come," says Anna.

Judy eyes her dubiously. No Lunar passes up the chance to shine above the City, especially not in a field as crowded as this one. Their turns don't come up often enough to give one away. "How did you do that?"

"I told her I really, really needed to meet the peach lady before my next track meet, and she could have my next two shifts if she'd trade with me just this once," says Anna.

That's believable, at least. A new Lunar wanting to meet Chang'e made enough sense that Abuk wouldn't necessarily have questioned it—and she's an English major; she doesn't question anything that isn't written down—and two trips across the City for the price of one was a pretty good enticement.

"You really think you're sticking around for two full shifts?"

Anna shrugs. "If that's what I have to do in order to keep my word, that's what I'll do," she says. "Let's get back to Diana. She's your senior, but she didn't notice the substitution, she didn't notice when Aske went into the everything and didn't come back, and she didn't ask you to look into the death of one of her own. What *did* she do?"

"She told me there had been other deaths, and where some of them were," says Judy. "She wasn't surprised." That was probably the part that should have stood out from the beginning. Diana had been many things during their discussion. What she hadn't been was surprised. "Oh, and she wouldn't notice you trading shifts with Abuk. She doesn't pay attention to that sort of thing."

"So who does? Things function too smoothly around here for them to be decided by committee, no matter how into community management bullshit you people are."

"I do," says Judy, a little smugly.

Anna stops walking. Judy does the same, turning to face her.

"What?"

"You handle the admin?"

"Yes."

"Like some sort of glorified secretary?"

"Yes."

"You're a top three goddess! If Diana wants to be senior, she should be handling her own paperwork. Or she should be passing the position over to you, not leaving you to handle the City rota and grad school at the same time!" Anna sounds genuinely pissed off, which is a surprise and oddly gratifying all at once.

"I don't mind," says Judy. "I'm good at it. The Celestial Bureaucracy—"

"Belongs in the Chinese Heavens, and even if you're a Chinese moon goddess, you're not there right now! We're all supposed to pull our weight. It's part of why the City keeps us around. The senior for the area makes sure things are happening when they're meant to happen. We're creatures of the calendar, Judy! You really think the calendar isn't meant to be a responsibility? Being senior isn't just a title and a bunch of bowing. It's keeping the rest of us safe and moving." Anna sounds almost disgusted. She shakes her head, hard. "What the hell does your Diana even do?"

"I—" Judy pauses. When asked that bluntly, she doesn't know. It's not a matter of being unable to think of an answer; it's that the answer *isn't there*. There is no answer. "She teaches classes? She's good with the new gods, I guess . . ." When she takes notice of them at all, which mostly only happens when they cross her radar directly. Judy didn't meet her until she'd already been on campus for most of a semester and woke up one morning exhausted by the amount of time she'd spent away from the City. She'd gone looking for Diana then, and been put on the roster with a lot of smiling and platitudes about wanting it enough to work for it.

That wasn't how things had worked anywhere else she's ever been, even New Jersey, when she'd been newly divine and coping with the death of her parents. Even then, she'd had the local senior at her door in a matter of days, to tell her what was happening to her and what she was now going to be expected to do.

Maybe Diana *isn't* supporting the Lunars of Berkeley the way she's supposed to. Judy frowns.

"David first, then Diana," says Anna, apparently satisfied that she's going to get her way. "I'll leave the room while you tell her to start doing her own damn admin work."

"Yeah . . ." says Judy as she starts walking again, heading toward Piedmont Avenue.

While all of UC Berkeley is technically and legally a single campus, the school covers enough topics and requires enough specialized facilities that, when combined with the encroaching urban area, the need for student housing, and sporting events, there are large portions of campus that aren't remotely contiguous. Reaching them involves leaving the campus for surface streets or private land, which always feels a little unreal. Walking across the school to get somewhere shouldn't mean leaving the school, but it does, surprisingly often.

Judy and Anna walk quickly along Piedmont, students passing them in both directions, heading for other pieces of the school. Anna glances at Judy.

"Does this feel odd to you?" she asks.

"It does," admits Judy. "Like stepping up in a bathroom, or stepping down in the everything. Something that shouldn't be where it is."

"Getting naked in a movie theater."

"Walking your zebra to the grocery store."

They continue on, trading things that don't feel right back and forth, getting more outlandish with every exchange, until Anna breaks down laughing and claps Judy on the shoulder with one surprisingly strong hand.

"You're all right, peach lady," she says. "Most of you are sort of stodgy, but you're all right. I bet you aren't a snitch, either. You're not going to run to Diana as soon as I turn my back on you."

It's a warning wrapped in a compliment, and Judy understands the laws of language well enough to see it in an instant. She decides that in this case, she'd rather be warned. "She's been acting weird about this whole thing, and Aske deserves better," she says. "I'm not running to Diana. Although you *are* going to have to tell her that you're here."

"Before I leave, I promise." They're almost to the athletic building. The practice field is empty, and voices drift from inside, loud and jubilant in the way that usually signals too much testosterone shoved into too small of a space. Judy exhales, then takes a very deep breath, preparing herself to breathe through her mouth for as long as they're inside. Locker rooms always have a funk that she can't stand, body odor and a plethora of fluids barely contained by the smell of bleach and cheap imitation lemon.

They head inside, Judy slightly in the lead, and move toward the sound of voices. It's coming from the locker room, not the showers, which is a relief. Walking in on half-naked football players is rude at best, and sexual harassment at worst, but walking in on them in the shower is *definitely* grounds for some sort of disciplinary action.

She stops outside the locker-room door, looking to Anna. "I can go see which of the coaches is in the office," she says. "I know about half of them from around campus, and I'm sure they'll find David for me if I tell them it's an emergency. You wait—"

Anna is already walking into the locker room, ignoring her utterly. Judy stares at her back, wondering briefly whether it's worth the risk of following, then groans and pursues the other woman, only a few steps behind by the time Anna rounds the first bank of lockers and confronts the practice team.

"Hey, guys," she says, voice bright and airy, like a whole group of burly men aren't staring at her, half of them trying to step behind each other. She's keeping her eyes up, which is possibly the only reason Judy isn't trying to drag her physically out of the room. This is beyond inappropriate.

At least they all seem to be wearing pants, or at least underwear. That makes her feel a little better. They still shouldn't be here. It's rude and it's inappropriate and it feels like something out of a mid-eighties comedy, one where nudity is treated as a funny joke that's never harassment or cruel.

Anna is still beaming at them, seeming to share none of Judy's discomfort. She puts her hands on her hips, looking around at the team. "David here?" she asks.

The men shuffle around, none of them demanding to know what she thinks she's doing, although several of them clearly want to. Finally, two men are pushed to the front, one wearing sweatpants and a UC Berkeley hoodie, the other wearing nothing but jeans and the dark tattoos that circle his upper arms and spread across his chest in harsh, tangled shapes. Both men look at Anna, apparently waiting for her to narrow the field further than a fairly common masculine name.

Anna, for her part, turns to Judy, raising her eyebrows. "Well?" she asks. "Either one of these our boy?"

"Hey, David," says Judy to the shirtless man, keeping her eyes as firmly above shoulder level as she can. The temptation to look lower is as strong as it is inappropriate. "You done with practice?"

"What the living fuck are you doing here?"

"Looking for you, dude," says the other David, elbowing him lightly in the side, grinning like he, too, thinks he's fallen into one of those mid-eighties films, and feels much better about it than Judy does. "Didn't you hear her?"

"I heard her," admits David. He hunches his shoulders. "Yeah, we're done. Let me get my shirt on and I'll meet you outside?"

He doesn't directly tell them to leave, but then, he doesn't need to. The rest of the team is glaring and shuffling, viewing their presence as the intrusion that it is, and their patience is running out.

"Sounds good," says Judy, grabbing Anna's arm and dragging her away. Anna is taller and sturdier, arms ropy with muscle that Judy, as a linguist, has never needed to work on developing, but she's also not resisting, and Judy is able to pull her out of the locker room, back into the hall.

"What?" asks Anna, sounding baffled.

Judy stares at her. "You can*not* be that oblivious," she says.

"We needed to find David, we found David," says Anna. "He was our target, and our hunt was successful."

Judy eyes her for a moment. Anna blinks.

"What?"

"I'm just trying to figure out how serious you are, because

that's going to inform how annoyed *I* am," she says. "He was our target, yes. He's also a person, and ask yourself how you'd like it if he'd barged into the track-team locker room while you were all changing."

Anna frowns. "Oh."

"Yeah. Oh. If swapping the genders on something makes it creepy, then it was always creepy, and you just didn't want to admit it." She takes Anna's arm again. "Come on. We're going to wait outside, like he asked us to."

"He didn't ask."

"He said he'd meet us outside when he was trying to defuse an uncomfortable situation and keep it from getting even worse," says Judy. "He asked. Some forms of question aren't as direct as we might like them to be, much as there are forms of both consent and refusal that aren't always completely clear. Haven't you ever signaled yes or no at someone without saying the word? He asked. We're going outside."

Anna is quieter as they exit the building, more subdued, and Judy can't shake the feeling that the odd sensation of the other woman still being partially stepped up into Artemis has faded without going entirely away. With the immediate hunt concluded, the goddess is more willing to rest.

"I'm sorry," says Anna, once they're outside. "When I have an active hunt, if I can see what I'm trying to find . . . it can be overwhelming. I don't always have full control of myself."

"Are you stepped up right now?" asks Judy. "You need to tell me if you are."

Anna blinks, eyes flashing momentarily green again. "You can tell, huh?"

"I can tell." It's tempting to add some sort of boast, like "I can always tell," but she doesn't know yet whether that's true, and if she claims a skill she doesn't have, she's sure it'll come back to bite them in the ass. That's how lying usually works.

"I can't fully step down when I'm actively hunting," says Anna. "Artemis is always with me. And I don't sleep."

"I don't sleep much," says Judy. "I don't think any of us do."

"You don't understand: *I don't sleep.* At all. If I try to go to bed, if I close my eyes for too long, I can get stepped *on.* Artemis will just take over and push Anna all the way out of the equation. Artemis doesn't see anything wrong with busting into a room full of half-naked men; if they didn't want to be seen like that, they should have kept their clothes on, and besides, it's an honor to be beheld so by a goddess." Anna looks briefly haggard. "She isn't always a nice person, Judy. She doesn't have a problem killing people, as long as she thinks they deserve it, and so when she's this restless, when there's a hunt on, I have to stay awake. I have to keep myself as close to the surface as I can."

Judy stares at her, horrified. She hasn't always agreed with Chang'e; the goddess is old and set in her ways, and sometimes she likes to do things in ways Judy thinks are slow or inefficient or just plain wrong. But she's never been afraid her passenger was going to hijack her body and use her divine sense of justice to commit very real, very human crimes.

A Lunar imprisoned away from a Chang'e and her peaches will only have to suffer through a mortal lifespan, growing old and eventually dying of age, if nothing else comes to claim them. She has no idea what might happen to a Lunar with no way to reach the City.

"You need to stay close, because that was not okay, and that also wasn't quite a crime," says Judy. "It was inappropriate and rude, but it can be chalked up to enthusiasm, or to not knowing the social rules. You might get called in front of a disciplinary committee if someone makes an official complaint, but that's about as far as this goes. Artemis uses your body to steal something or stab somebody, that's a lot harder to get out from under."

"I know that," says Anna miserably. "I've known that since the first time she took over. She's hunting something, and I don't know what it is."

Judy pauses. "You didn't just come here because the alchemists are in a tizzy, did you?"

"Good word. 'Tizzy.' Gets the point across."

"Good attempt at deflection, but I will not be deflected this time."

Anna sighs. "The reason I *know* is the alchemists. The reason I *don't* know is something deeper. Artemis is carrying it so far down that she won't even share it with me, and I have no idea what it might be, only that it was vital we get here before any other Artemis could find the way."

Judy stares at her. "Are you telling me we're about to have an Artemis convention on our hands?"

"Not if we find what I'm hunting for fast enough," says Anna.

David emerges from the building. He's clothed now, sunlight lending a rich warmth to his dark brown skin, and catching silvered highlights off his still mostly black hair. He'll go gray soon enough, like all the rest of them, and Judy doesn't think it'll age him before his time; he's going to be one of those men who looks distinguished with silver hair. She has no idea if he's gay or straight or neither, but assuming he eventually goes looking for a partner, he's going to make somebody very happy.

Not Judy. She likes boys, but she doesn't like them nearly a foot taller than her, or occupied by other moon gods. When she hooks up with somebody, she wants them to be wholly human, or else aligned with another pantheon entirely, one where she won't have to compete with her partner for access to the City. Above all else, the City.

He scowls as he marches toward them, ire focused mostly on Anna, the stranger. Judy tries not to be pleased by that; some of the anger is for her too, she's sure.

"What the hell was that?" he asks.

Anna looks at him coolly. "Hello, Máni," she says, and stands straighter, eyes flashing green. She doesn't step up fully, but she moves far enough toward the divine to remind Judy that she's currently very mortal and thus very fragile.

She doesn't like the feeling, and steps up almost reflexively in answer. The sunlight is diffuse enough that the faint sparkle in the air will seem like a trick of the light; she's unable to cause herself any issues, uncomfortable as it is to be stepped up in full daylight.

David blinks, and then blinks again as Máni comes surging to the surface in answer to the obvious threat presented by the two goddesses in front of him. "Do I know you?" he asks.

Anna—Artemis—shakes her head. "Not this version of you. I've met many versions of you."

"Don't screw with his head," snaps Chang'e. "Máni, this is Losna. She wanted to ask you some questions about what happened with Aske."

Máni glances around, suddenly and clearly nervous in a way he wasn't even when presented with the goddesses. His shoulders hunch as he leans forward and asks, in a small voice, "Did you find her body?"

"No. It wasn't there when I went into the everything last night. Máni, I have a very important question for you. You're not in trouble, no matter what you say. All right?"

Judy waits until he nods understanding before she continues:

"Every morning, the next person to travel through the City meets the person who came before them at the gate, to get the key and make sure nothing happened during the transit. You were supposed to meet Aske. Did you?"

Máni jerks like she's stuck him with a pin. Chang'e sighs.

"You're not in trouble, no matter what you answer. We just need to know what happened. Did you see her before you went through the gate?"

"No. She never came out."

"So how did you get the key?" Because that's one of the major reasons they needed to talk to him: without the key, unless the gate remained open for a full day, he shouldn't have been able to get back into the everything. He certainly wouldn't have been able to pass the key along to Judy. So much hinges on a little piece of moonsilver metal, which looks, on its own, no more remarkable than any other key. A little old-fashioned, maybe, but not *unique*.

The keys are the reason they form communities, the reason they can keep a schedule, rather than giving in to their addicted urges to spend every night sailing across the City. Any one of them would give up a human life in an instant for another breath of that intoxicating air. Chang'e knows it, even as she knows Judy's human existence is important. Part of what keeps them anchored enough to the world that they can keep manifesting after so many others have faded and failed is their closeness to humanity.

Since the beginning of the world, humans have never stopped looking up at the midnight sky and dreaming of the moon. So long as there are keys, and gates, and reasons to linger in human form, not exhausting their incarnations in their eagerness to get back to the Impossible City, the moon is looking back on the world, and dreaming of it, too.

"She wasn't there," he says, slowly. "The sun came up and the gate disappeared, and I went home to steal an hour or so of sleep before I had class. When I got up, there was an envelope under the doormat with my name on it, and the key was inside. Why? Am I in trouble?"

If Aske hadn't come out of the gate, then someone must have gone in to get the key. But why drop it at Máni's doorstep rather than going inside and telling him Aske was dead? Why leave her body there? If Judy was right about the way the everything worked, whoever it was must have left the gate open, knowing Máni would step into Aske's passage when he went through again, unless . . .

"When you got to the gate, was it already open?" asks Chang'e, forcing her voice to stay gentle. Artemis is watching her as intently as a hawk. Any slip now could set the huntress on them both, and while she doesn't have the experience in this incarnation to know exactly how that would be a bad thing, still she knows all the way to the base of Judy's bones that it would be very, very bad.

"Yes," admits Máni. "I thought . . . You weren't there, and so I thought you'd come ahead and opened it for some reason."

"Even though you had the key?"

"I know you don't like me," he blurts. "You always look at me like I don't know what I'm talking about, and this is the most words you've ever said to me without snapping. You don't like that I play football, or that I like to have a drink every now and then, or that I hang out with pretty girls. But you don't have to talk to me like I'm *stupid*. Okay?"

"Okay," says Chang'e, startled into taking a half-step back. "I'm sorry, Máni. I didn't realize you felt that way."

"You mean you didn't realize I was smart enough to know *you* felt that way."

It's true, and so she doesn't argue, just rolls her shoulders in a shrug and says, "It doesn't matter whether I like you or not, right now. What matters is finding out what happened to Aske."

"Do you even know her name?"

"I—"

"I didn't," says Artemis, coming to her rescue by reminding Máni that she's there, he's not alone with Chang'e. He's being hunted, and he needs to stay aware of the predator in his vicinity, or the chase will end very badly for him.

"I— Who *are* you?"

"Now who doesn't know names, hmm?" Artemis smiles, thinly. "To you, I'm Losna. We'll see if that changes. You're Máni, known as David."

"Yeah," he says, clearly cowed, and looks back to Chang'e. "Her name was Eliza. She was majoring in early childhood education, and she liked strawberry ice cream and rare roast beef sandwiches and those little Beanie Baby knock-offs you get at the drug store. She was a real person. You only ever saw her as a face of the moon. You aren't even sad that she's gone."

"I . . ." Chang'e pauses. "You're right. I only saw her as a face of the Moon, as someone else I had to shove into the schedule and share the City passage with. She wasn't real to me the way she apparently was to you, and I'm sorry for your loss. And for Eliza. We should have been a better community to her."

"Yeah, you should have." Máni pauses, taking a deep breath. "I knew I had the key when I got there, and logically, that means you couldn't have opened the gate. But I was still confused by finding it the way I did, and I was running late, so I didn't dwell. I just threw myself into the everything and made for the window. Only when I got there, it was . . . wrong."

"Wrong how?" asks Artemis.

"It wasn't *my* window. It was *a* window, a perfectly good one, but I'd never seen it before. And Aske was on the ground in front of it. You know, I'd never thought of the everything as having a ground before? I mean, I had to be walking on *something,* but it looks so much like something out of a bad science fiction movie that I never really saw it as having a floor and a ceiling. But there was Aske, on the ground, bleeding red and silver. And when I looked around, there was more silver, making the ground more and more obvious, until I couldn't *not* see the ground. I had to stop seeing it. It was making the everything into *something,* and that hurt to see. I don't even know how to describe it. It was something that wasn't supposed to happen, a definition of a space that's supposed to remain undefined, and it hurt. I think if I'd looked at it for too long, it could have really hurt me. Maybe even killed me."

He shudders, glancing to the side. Chang'e finds nothing to indicate that he's lying; he seems entirely sincere, and genuine in his fear.

"I had to stop looking, but Aske was just *there,* and I could see she wasn't breathing, so I . . ." He stops, sighs, and looks at Chang'e, clearly regretful. "I went through the window. I went to the City. It wasn't the everything, and it meant I wasn't standing there watching the floor get harder and harder to ignore. I'm sorry. Maybe she wasn't dead! Maybe I could have *helped* her, but instead I just . . . I just ran away."

Chang'e steps closer, putting a hand on his arm. He shoots her a startled look.

"She was gone before you went into the everything, Máni," she says. "You only found her because no one had closed the gate between her transit and your arrival. You went into *her* everything, not your own. It wasn't your fault."

He blinks, several times, before he bursts noisily into tears.

Chang'e leaves her hand resting on his arm. He seems to need it, and she's failed the younger Lunars enough this week. As long as he needs her, she'll be here. She has a duty that she's been neglecting for far too long.

Máni keeps crying but wipes his eyes with the back of his hand, focusing on Chang'e. "I needed to hear that so much more than I realized I did. Thank you. Thank you so, so much."

"Don't worry about it."

"What do you mean, I went into her everything?"

"Chang'e has a theory, and so far, it's a good one," says Artemis. "Chang'e, you wanna explain?"

So they're continuing to put this on her? It makes sense, but it still annoys her a little, as she glances from Máni to Artemis and back again. "I don't think we enter the same everything," she says. "I think the reason we're told not to enter together isn't to avoid confusing the window; it's because each of us gets our *own* window, and if we entered together, we might get both, or neither, or something else entirely. When Aske died, she died in *her* everything, and that gate was never closed. You entered *her* channel through the everything that night, not your own, and that's why you found her body."

"But I left it there," says Máni, sounding horrified. "I left *her* there. Does that mean she's just going to . . . what, rot inside the everything forever?"

"Maybe if we found another Aske, we could get them to open the gate to her everything, somehow," says Artemis. "We're just now figuring out that the everything is divided, which seems like something we should probably have known before now, and I don't think we have any duplicated incarnations in Berkeley. So we can't test whether two iterations of Máni can open the gate to each other's versions of the everything, or whether they're locked into their own."

"If we can find a way to get her body, we will," says Chang'e, trying to sound soothing. "And if she's still bleeding divinity, we'll worry about it then. Right now, though, just to be perfectly clear: you went to the gate, Aske never came out to give you the key. You went home, and later found the key in an envelope with your name on it. David, or Máni?"

"David," he says, with certainty.

Chang'e nods. "All right. Did you save the envelope? Maybe we could identify the handwriting."

"You can do that?"

"Judy's a linguist," Chang'e says. "That doesn't make her a forensic handwriting analyst, but she's taken some courses. The way people write tells us a lot about how they interact with language, so she dabbles."

"I saved it, but it wasn't handwriting. They used a label maker." He sighs. "I guess that should have told me something was wrong, if the person leaving the key didn't want me to be able to figure out who they were."

"This is a college campus," says Chang'e. "Everyone has a label maker." Judy has three. One that prints in English, one that prints Standard Chinese, and one that prints Traditional Chinese. She's considered buying one of the big fancy ones that can print labels in dozens of languages; that's probably going to be a graduation gift to herself, when she finally gets her doctorate.

"I don't," says Artemis.

"You just got here," says Chang'e.

"I don't," says Máni, and Chang'e doesn't say anything at all. If he could tell she didn't like him, he'll probably take anything she says about his lack of a label maker as insulting his intelligence. Not the sort of atmosphere she wants to create.

"It's cool. We can borrow Judy's if we desperately need to label something," says Artemis.

Máni laughs, and the odd tension that had come with the label-maker conversation dissipates.

"Can we see it anyway?" asks Chang'e. "There are different brands of label maker. Maybe Judy will be able to tell which kind printed it, and then we just need to keep our eyes out for that brand."

"It'd be funny if we caught a murderer based on office supplies," says Máni. "But sure, you can see it. I'll bring it to the gate tonight?"

"I won't be there," says Chang'e. "It's not my turn."

"No, but it's mine," says Artemis. "I don't mind a little company, especially not when you're the one who understands the minutiae of label makers. You can come by."

"All right," says Chang'e. "It's not standard, but . . . all right."

They always do the escort and hand-off in pairs. The person who goes next meets the previous night's Lunar at the morning gate to receive the key, then is escorted to the gate in the evening by the next night's Lunar, who will either wait there until morning or come back just as the sun begins to rise. The chain is maintained, the key is passed, and nothing is lost.

Nothing is lost.

"So we have a plan, then," says Máni. "I'll bring the envelope, and Chang'e will take it and figure out who put my name on it?"

"Which will tell us who had the key when it should have been with either you or Aske," says Chang'e. "To get back to the sequence of events, you found the key in the envelope. You didn't go back to the gate to make sure that it was closed, yes?"

"Why would I have done that?" Máni sounds genuinely confused. "The gates don't appear during the day."

"But sometimes you can see the moon during the day," says Chang'e. "Maybe we've just always assumed the gates don't appear during the day, because we were never trying to use them. Maybe the key is less about being able to *open* the doorway into the everything, and more about being able to *close* it."

"Can people who aren't divine go into the everything?" asks Máni.

Chang'e looks to Artemis, who shrugs. She looks back to Máni. "I . . . I don't know," she admits. "I wish I did. It suddenly feels like something I really *should* know. But the person who taught me the system didn't mention it, and no one else has ever said anything, other than 'never open a gate where an alchemist can see you,' and they're not divine, so I guess if they're a danger, then it must be possible. I was able to step down inside the everything, and it didn't hurt Judy when I did it, but she's always at least a little divine, because I'm always with her, so I don't know if that proves anything. And it's not like we can test the theory. Either it works and we've just dragged someone normal into the everything, which is going to raise a *lot* of questions, or it doesn't work, and we've just killed somebody."

Chang'e is a giver of immortality, not a committer of manslaughter. She'd really rather not kill someone by mistake for the sake of testing a theory.

"What if we find ourselves an alchemist?" asks Artemis, as if this were the most reasonable suggestion in the world. "They're not divine. They're mostly not anything. From what I understand, if you're involved in alchemy and you start to display any signs of an affinity, even one of the really minor ones like the shoulder seasons, they kick you out of their little club. Usually in a very permanent manner."

Máni looks confused. Artemis drags her thumb across her throat. His eyes widen, confusion replaced by horror.

"They *kill* them? But it's not like you can decide to be affiliated with something! David didn't wake up one morning and volunteer to be connected to the moon! He and I get along pretty well, but it's definitely disrupted his life in some ways he couldn't have anticipated. Killing him because of me would have been pointless!"

"They think everything has a use and can be broken down for its component sympathies," says Artemis. Chang'e assumes the other goddess must have more experience with alchemists than she does, and stays silent. "To them, because you're connected to the Moon, you can be used to create a sympathetic link to the rest of us, or to the divine, or maybe to the Moon directly—they cut off your pinkie toe, they can convince the whole Lunar machinery to tilt into something that's more favorable to whatever horrifying alchemical thing they're trying to do this week. For them, having a student or an apprentice suddenly pop up as affiliated with a natural force has got to be like finding out that a box of generic mac and cheese is secretly filled with black truffles. You go from person to resource, like that." She snaps her fingers.

The sound is sharp and clean and somehow terrible, like a bone breaking, or ice giving way at the middle of a pond. Artemis, expression grim, shakes her head.

"It's not murder to throw an alchemist into the everything, whether or not they can survive it. It's pest control. Most people, normal people, they wouldn't notice if we never stepped down. We could stay manifest all the time, forever, and not have to worry. It's the alchemists who make us hide like prey animals in the underbrush."

And your hosts! shouts Judy, in the silence at the back of Chang'e's mind. She sounds truly furious, incandescent with rage over the very suggestion, and Chang'e really can't blame her. She turns to Artemis, frowning.

"This is getting off topic a bit, but if we never stepped down, would we be any better than they are? Right now, we have a partnership with the people who carry us. They lend us their skills and strengths, and we grant them ours. If we never stepped aside, we'd be stealing their lives. We'd be effectively killing them."

The ethics of the Lunar system were something she and Judy had debated many times, in the small hours of the morning, when there wasn't much else to do. People couldn't volunteer to become incarnate gods: it either happened or it didn't. And once the god was there, they couldn't be made to leave by any means that Chang'e knew of. What made them any better than parasites?

Artemis shrugs. "That's more philosophical than I like to get. And it doesn't matter if that would be wrong of us, because that's not the world we live in. We have this one. If we really want to test whether a pure human can survive in the everything, we need to find an alchemist."

Chang'e eyes her, uncomfortable with her casual dismissal of the issue, but unwilling to push it any further when Máni already looks like he's on the verge of bolting. "Aske never closed the gate; you received the key anonymously. When you went to the gate to step through, it was already open, and so you didn't open it a second time."

"I told you all of that!"

"Yes, and I'm making sure I didn't misunderstand at any point. It's easy to get things wrong when you only hear them once, especially in times of stress. I don't want to get anything wrong."

"You showed up after I went in, so you know what happened," he says, a little sullenly, like he's just been scolded. "And then I left her there."

"Because you didn't have a choice," says Chang'e, and touches his arm, very lightly. "I'm sorry. I didn't know she was your friend."

"She was sweet, for a girl who'd never been outside Minnesota before," he says. "She didn't know much about much when it comes to living away from home, or dealing with campus politics, but she wasn't afraid to ask for help, and she knew she could lean on me when she had to."

Which made it all the more terrible that he'd been the one to find her body. Chang'e shudders. "Thank you, Máni," she says. She glances at Artemis, keenly aware that the other goddess is a predator and she might be putting herself at risk with what she's about to do. Then, she steps back and down, and allows Judy to come back to the surface.

Máni sees the change instantly, and matches it with his own, letting David resume control as he steps back. Mortal, the presence of Artemis is terrifying. Judy feels like she's standing inside a tiger enclosure, or in one of those fantasy movies where the trees are full of predatory dinosaurs, ready to leap at any moment. She doesn't allow it to faze her, though, merely holds on to the feeling as she turns to Artemis.

"So now we know as much as we're going to know without finding a way into Aske's everything," Judy says. "Got any of her other incarnations in your contacts list?"

"Whoa, whoa," says Artemis. The air shifts as she steps back, becoming lighter, less oppressive. "You don't have to sound so angry about me trying to solve a *murder*."

"We're sure it was murder now?" asks David. "There's no way she . . . I don't know, slipped and fell and hit her head on the windowpane?"

"You were the one who found her," says Anna. "Did it look like an accident to you?"

David is quiet long enough to really think about it. Finally, in a soft voice, he says, "I didn't want to look too closely, and there was so much *blood,* but there were no injuries on her forehead. I guess she could have hit her temple if she fell, but there would probably have been a split in the skin, if nothing else. The back of her head was so bloody, I'd be comfortable saying that was where she was hit. I don't think she *could* have hit herself in the back of the head, even if she'd been trying to."

"Not an accident," says Anna, sounding satisfied. "Which makes it a murder, which means someone else was in the everything with her. Someone who knew how to get in and out again, who knew enough to bring the key out so we wouldn't have to find a new one. *Someone* did this."

"Is someone with that much information hunting Lunars?" asks Judy, horrified. Diana had been so casual about the deaths that it hadn't really occurred to her that this could be some sort of targeted hunt. At best, it had seemed like a series of bad coincidences. At worst, it could have been a few rogue alchemists, taking advantage of moments of distraction to harvest the sympathy they so desired.

That was before she'd thought through the implications of the everything. That, and a healthy spoonful of denial; she doesn't want this to be targeted. She's already juggling goddess-hood and graduate school. Adding "evading a killer" to the list is more than she's up for dealing with.

Not that she has a choice.

"I think so," says Anna. "I think that's exactly what's happening here. Aske is the latest, and your local alchemists are riled up. Time for me to hunt the hunters."

Palus Putredinis

The dark-skinned woman is Smita. She takes a seat at the front of the ring, where she can see everyone, resting her hands on her knees and leaning her bag against her ankles.

Erin—the unnerving Erin—doesn't take a seat at all. She finds a spot against the wall and leans there, still watching Kelpie.

"Erin?" asks Isabella. "Will you be staying for today's meeting?"

Erin jerks her chin upward instead of nodding, an almost-challenging gesture. "If that's not a problem, I will," she says. "You've invited me to stay before. I assumed the invitation was still open."

"Your new apprentice is good luck!" burbles Catrina. "We've been trying to entice the mysterious Erin to join us since Smita first started coming around."

"I'm not one of your little witches," says Erin. "Smita can do what she wants, and she knows I'll support her in whatever that is, even when it's coming here." She smiles at Smita, heart-meltingly gentle, and Smita smiles back, a little more reserved. "But that doesn't mean I'm in a hurry to sign up for your club. I'm just going to watch today's meeting, then have a chat with your 'cousin' when it's finished."

"All right then, I suppose we begin," says Isabella, with a clap of her hands. "Everyone, this is my cousin, Kelly. Kelly, this is everyone. She's going to be training under me as an hechicera, but as we all know, the hechicera's art is not incompatible with witchcraft, and so it seemed wise to bring her to today's meeting. Her mother sent her to stay with me because as she gets older, her potential gets stronger, and untrained, she could do serious damage."

Kelpie smiles hesitantly and waves to the room. It seems like the right thing to do. This accomplished, she flees to sit next to Isabella, who pats her on the shoulder and leans in close.

"You did well," she says, voice low. "Now try to look like I've just said something terribly important and wise."

Kelpie widens her eyes, turning her chin just a little, so that her head is tilted more toward Isabella.

"Very good. I'm going to start the meeting now, and afterward, you can chat with Erin and Smita. All right?"

Kelpie nods. Isabella begins.

The coven meeting opens with something they call "calling the quarters," which involves invoking four out of the five basic alchemical principles and asking them to become embodied in the room. Kelpie watches intently as this goes on, but none of the elements appear. These women, whatever they are or aren't doing, aren't somehow summoning manifestations out of nothing.

Which is probably for the best, since if they were, the alchemists would hound them to the ends of the earth for being able to accomplish such a vast and terrible working.

Each quarter is called by a different member of the group, with Isabella assigning the elements according to her "inner eye," which Kelpie assumes means "her whim." She closes her eyes and turns in a slow circle with one hand held out, then stops and points. When she opens her eyes, whoever she was pointing at is the one who calls that quarter.

Unsurprisingly, Catrina calls water. Smita calls fire. Angeline—the one whose cousin was tapped to serve the seasons—calls air, and a fourth woman calls earth, and Isabella declares the circle open. With her last word, candles around the edges of the room burst into flame, bright and dancing, filling the air with shadows. None of the coven members seem surprised, although Catrina slants a small, mean look over at Kelpie, clearly waiting to see surprise in *her* expression, and she appears disappointed when it isn't there. As if she needs to be part of such a marvelous thing that it inspires shock and awe in the unprepared.

She might have done better to watch Erin. The blonde's eyes widen when the candles start to burn, eyebrows raising toward her hairline, and while the moment of surprise doesn't last long, the calm that follows seems almost inhuman, more something suited to a praying mantis watching an insect's approach.

Each of the women of Isabella's coven has brought questions or concerns, workings they'd like to see performed. Workings for luck, or for money, or for love. Catrina's working is for power, which is a little bit surprising; she doesn't seem like the sort of person who'd be searching for power. Then Kelpie looks at the way she watches Isabella, the envy in her eyes, and she understands.

Isabella can see her for what she truly is, and she isn't surprised by Catrina's request for power. Whatever an hechicera is, it's something powerful enough to touch the scraps of wild magic that still linger in the world, free of alchemical control. Catrina doesn't have that. She knows it exists, she sees it in some of the women she invites into her home, and while Kelpie isn't any great student of human nature, she doesn't need to be if she's going to understand that some people will always want what they don't have. For someone like Catrina, who gets the biggest house and the most comfortable chair, knowing that magic is real when she's unable to touch it must be deeply frustrating.

Kelpie wonders, as the meeting and the castings continue, whether Isabella welcomes Catrina in her coven because the woman would be an easy recruit for the local alchemists, who aren't shy about offering power for nothing more than devotion, dedication, and money. She's spoken to the other lab assistants, the ones who view their time in Margaret's lab as training before they move on to their glorious and inevitable futures. Many of them have told essentially that same story. They brushed against something once that made them realize there was more to reality than they knew; they went chasing it; they found the alchemists, and it wasn't until they were in too deep to walk away that they realized any power they acquired would be on the other end of a long and arduous journey.

Not everyone who yearned for power could be recruited by the alchemists, or there would be a lot more of them, and probably a lot less of everyone else, given their tendency to dismantle what they didn't need.

Only the day before, she'd considered herself one of them, and had been able to justify all these things as necessary and even good. Kelpie frowns. How did she change her mind so quickly? She sinks into her own thoughts, trying to follow the thread of logic, trying to understand herself before she has to explain it to anyone else, and she finds an answer. Whether it's the right one or not doesn't matter as much as the fact that she has one.

In the lab, she had one source of input, and it came from the alchemists who trained and took care of her. It was always flat, always one-sided and absolutely sure of its moral convictions. There were no shades of gray, no complex questions. The only thing she's ever been asked to see in two lights at once was Asphodel Baker, and even that had been an accident.

Asphodel was the one who created the cuckoos, the one who pushed the bounds of alchemical knowledge in ways that have yet to be surpassed, even by her own student and creation.

True constructs, like Leigh Barrow, could become alchemists, could learn party tricks and simple rituals, but they could never truly innovate, could never become fully human, could never surpass their creators. Cuckoos, though . . . Asphodel Baker had been able to tap into the Promethean fire at the heart of all things, using it to shape a recipe that crafted life itself, true humanity, capable of innovation and exploration, even embodiment. All the world's alchemists working for all the world's centuries had never been able to tap into and capture natural forces, not before Asphodel came along and changed the game for everyone.

And the Congress reviles her. They hate her for being smarter than they were, for being a woman in a time when women weren't meant to be allowed anywhere near a lab, for refusing to let the second fact of her existence eclipse the first and send her discreetly and demurely into darkness. They use what she created, gladly and without hesitation, but they're more likely to credit it to Reed than to Asphodel, even though *he* was her creation to begin with. They make her out to be the villain, all because she refused to go away.

Kelpie first learned about her from some of the apprentices when they were talking in the cafeteria, casually trading theories and bits of their own work. Information was currency in the lab, and she didn't have any, so she'd always been reduced to eavesdropping, trying to understand the world without being able to barter her way into true enlightenment. The apprentices talked about Asphodel like she was a miracle, the woman who single-handedly dragged American alchemy into the modern age. Her death had been a tragedy; her life, a transcendence of all norms and standards.

So she asked Margaret about this Asphodel person, who sounded absolutely amazing, and had been baffled when Margaret replied with the official Congressional position on Asphodel: it was fine to use her research, because it had all been performed with stolen Congressional resources anyway, and she should have known her place. It was fine to claim her accomplishments. It was *not* fine to think well of her in any way.

That was Kelpie's first conflict, and it's one she still carries with her now, in this sun-soaked room, surrounded by women she barely knows. She wonders if any of them have heard of the Up-and-Under, or Asphodel, or anything else. She doesn't know how to ask.

It's easy to think the alchemists who were her sole companions until now may have lied to her, because she knows they lied to her.

They told her she was human.

Once she makes space in her mind for that lie, all the others become easy to believe.

The workings are drawing to a close, the air thick with herbs and dried flowers, some crushed and sprinkled, some added to small bowls of purified water, some burnt. Bowls of small, precious stones have appeared at some point, and more of the crushed-up flowers have been mixed in, meaning that all four of the invoked elements have been involved. Kelpie wonders if they know how close they tread to alchemy in the design of their workings. The four static elements, and then flowers to stand in for living things, which walk the ways of aether. Add a few more controls and some good warding seals, and this could have been a rite to purify glassware, or to return life to a dead beetle.

Maybe all magic is the same at the heart, and alchemical superiority is just another lie the alchemists told when they were afraid they might be losing control over the world as a whole. Kelpie has so much to unlearn.

Isabella stands. "Our time is done, our close is come; we bore our banners, and we won," she says. It's bad poetry, false rhymes and no internal structure, and yet the last of the candles burning around the edges of the room gutter and go out, somehow extinguished by her declaration. She smiles warmly at the women around her, then bows to them, deep and serious. When she straightens, she says, "I thank you, sisters, for your time in this circle. Go in peace, and know that you are powerful."

And then, perplexingly, the women begin to rise and leave, murmuring their own farewells as they turn to exit. Smita doesn't move. Catrina rises but lingers, watching the others, and then begins inching toward Isabella. "Isa, I was wondering—"

Isabella turns toward Catrina. "Go in peace," she repeats, but not the remainder of the phrase.

Catrina stops, jerking sharply into a tensely upright position. It's like watching a doll get lifted by its hair. She looks unsurprised but somehow affronted by Isabella's response, like *she's* not the one who gets dismissed. *She's* supposed to be the one who does the dismissal.

"We'll talk after," she says, voice clipped, and turns to follow the others out.

Isabella turns, not toward Smita but toward Erin, the woman who remained outside the circle the whole time. "The circle is open," she says. "It poses no dangers to the unaffiliated."

"I *am* the dangers, witchy lady," says Erin, pushing away from the wall. "I'm not afraid of you."

"Good, for I am not your enemy."

"Oh, you could be. You could be, really easily. These little circles of yours are basically chaos pits. You dig holes in the surface of the world and you fill them up with elemental energy. You know what happens when you dig a hole?"

"Erin, please," says Smita.

"Things fall into it," says Erin, unflagging. "If you scoop out all the elementalism by the time you're done, then maybe it heals, but if you don't, when it crusts over, you've made yourself a nice, ripe zit right on reality's chin. You're giving the universe acne."

"That's nice of you to say," says Isabella. "I suppose you've brought the acne treatment?"

"Me? Nah. That was my brother's gig. I just want you to know how much you hurt my eyes. You're doing things you shouldn't be doing. But you're not as bad as the people who made me, so I guess you're right, and you're not my enemy. Yet."

Smita sighs, leaning back in her chair. Kelpie sits up a bit straighter.

"Made you?" she asks.

Erin's gaze swivels around to Kelpie, and it's unnervingly heavy and direct, like a smothering sheet of cotton laid directly across her shoulders. "Yup. Made me. In a lab, deep underground. In Ohio, of all places, flatland at the center of the country. Oz territory. I think it amused Reed to know that he was pissing on Baum's grave with his work, after everything Baum had done to Baker, both before and after she was gone."

She leans forward, still watching Kelpie, measuring her reactions. "He didn't put me together himself. That was accomplished by Leigh Barrow, his right-hand woman and favorite monster. But he approved and adjusted the recipe that made me and my brother possible. He knew me completely, both inside and out, every bone, every organ. He wasn't my father. He was my doting uncle, and he killed my brother, and he owned me until the day he died. Got any more questions?"

Kelpie's heart is beating so hard it hurts, and she feels like she can barely breathe. Still, she manages to squeak out a faint "What *are* you?"

"I am something that should never have been, and will probably be forever now, because that's how the universe works, isn't it? It can go forever not incarnating a piece of itself, and then it trips and drops a concept into a human shell, and it's all over after that. It gets addicted, hooked to the possibilities inherent in mortal flesh, and it wants more, more, more all the time. Reality is greedy. It contains everything because it *wants* everything, and the greatest constraint on its hunger is the fact that in its natural state, it can't interact with half of what it has, any more than Smita here can interact with her own liver. Not directly, anyway. She can drink and bathe it in toxins, and interact with it that way, but she can't kiss and caress it, can't tell it everything's going to be all right after all. She's limited by the confines of her flesh, and the universe is limited by the confines of itself. Very sad, isn't it?"

"That's a lot of pretty words to not give an actual answer," says Isabella.

"Oh, I know you, hechicera," says Erin. "You've been sniffing around me for months."

Isabella shrugs. "I know a construct when I see one. You'll forgive me for being curious, I hope?"

"Ah, but you see, that's where you're wrong," says Erin. "I'm not a construct; I'm a cuckoo. The difference is the blood and body of Asphodel Baker, who has more descendants than she ever dreamed she might, thanks to the tireless efforts of her only son. He died childless, by the way. Every single one of us repudiated him, big-time. Over and over again, until it finally stuck and we decided we liked the timeline we were in well enough to let it continue."

"What?" asks Isabella.

Smita just sighs. She's clearly heard all this before, and while Erin might take pleasure from playing with people the way a cat plays with a bird, she doesn't. "Can we hurry this up?" she asks.

"Anything for you," says Erin. She focuses on Isabella again. "I am the living force of Order, forced to incarnate by Leigh Barrow as part of the run-up to James Reed's incarnation of the Doctrine of Ethos. They were experimenting with capturing what they saw as 'lesser forces' before they tackled the big one. My brother, Darren, was the living force of Chaos. They killed him when he ceased to be useful to them. So now here I am, alone in the madhouse, with no way to close my eyes to just how fucked everything around me really is."

Isabella blinks, eyebrows lifting. "I . . . see," she says. "That must be very hard. Does Smita help to center you in the chaos?"

"Nah. Smita's a friend from school."

Smita eyes Erin for a moment, looking faintly amused. "That is absolutely the most reductive description of our relationship that I have ever heard, Erin. You want to try again?"

"How open are we being?"

"Look at Isabella's 'cousin,'" says Smita. "I think it's more likely that she's a cousin of yours, and we're going to wind up taking her home with us, one way or another. So I'd say we're being pretty open, whether we came here intending to be or not."

"Are you a c-construct?" asks Kelpie, looking at Smita. She can feel a commonality with Erin, a certain recognition, even though they've never seen each other before. Cuckoos can, apparently, detect other cuckoos. Whether that extends to constructs isn't something she knows. Margaret never kept them around the labs. There was the one rabbity technician in the agricultural research department, but he was on a different team, and Kelpie had only ever glimpsed him at a distance.

And even if he was the Rabbit Margaret talked about before she died, that would make him a cuckoo, and being able to recognize him as like her wouldn't have told her whether she could spot constructs. Without the context of knowing that what she was spotting was another cuckoo, she might just have assumed he was like her: a normal person who'd been in a terrible lab accident.

Although now she wonders if that's something that actually happens, or just one more thing Margaret lied about. Maybe the story she's always believed belonged to her was impossible from the start.

Smita looks briefly taken aback. Then she laughs, bright and open and earnestly amused. "No, no, I'm not a construct," she says. "I'm naturally occurring. I'm a geneticist. I work at one of the biotech firms downtown, near the Vivarium. So I'm good for the cuckoos to have around, but I'm not one of them."

"You're also the only one other than me who ever remembers to buy toilet paper," says Erin. "We live in a house full of geniuses who wouldn't be able to wipe their own asses if they lost us, and you need to remember that whenever you start to question your worth."

"I wasn't!" says Smita.

"You were. You get this tone when you're appending the word 'only' to 'naturally,' like you should have been built in a lab, just so you'd fit in with the rest of the house. Trust me, it's not that much fun."

"Sure, Pinocchio," says Smita. "You know I think of you as a real girl. I don't need to be a cuckoo to understand the score. But—and I'm not trying to be rude; I know it's inappropriate to comment on aspects of someone's appearance that they didn't necessarily choose—but why is Kelly orange?"

"It's 'Kelpie,' actually," says Kelpie. "And I always thought I was orange because I'd been in a bad lab accident, but it seems I'm orange because the alchemists who made me made me this way. I don't know why."

"Visibility," says Erin.

The other three turn to look at her. She shrugs. "Reed made most of his projects in human skin tones. Usually white ones, because he liked to convince wealthy assholes to invest in his empty promises, and most of his investors were white. So when they looked at his science projects and saw their own children reflected back at them, they believed those children could be powerful."

"But not, it seems, as powerful as racism," interjects Smita.

"Yeah, well, what is?" asks Erin.

"You were explaining why I'm orange," says Kelpie.

"Ah, right. Thing is, when you're building a person from scratch, alchemically, you're not doing it according to the normal rules of biology and how things evolve in the real world. So you're not limited, as it were, to the things that reality has actually decided to put in a vote for. You can make anything if that's what you want to do, and you can make some gene expressions conditional on things that have nothing to do with genetics. With the Doctrine, for example, we couldn't decide ahead of time which half would be born first—and every incarnation of the Doctrine after the first was gestated as a set of twins. But the one who was born first always claimed dominion over Language, and the one born second would claim Math and have flashier, brighter coloring. Red hair, or white hair that didn't look quite natural, things people would be drawn to look at."

"To pull focus away from the elder twin," says Kelpie. "The Math children were supposed to draw fire?"

"Exactly. So tell me, how do you explain the second-born always having so much more dramatic coloring, if not for a gene expression that didn't happen until it reacted to the presence of the older child outside the womb?"

"Alchemists have no morals," says Isabella. "That's like building a time bomb into a child."

"Why, because maybe there's some unique medical situation where they're both born at once and the Math kid literally explodes? Or because you don't like the idea? Sometimes we don't like things," says Erin. "When alchemists are making fake people that they never intend to release into the general population, they get . . . creative. They make them with chromophores, or wings, or feathers for hair. They make them in every color of the rainbow. Sometimes they have the equivalent of dog shows with them, all these smug little alchemical innovators showing off their most impressive collections for the other monsters to ooh and aah over until one of them takes home Best in Show, and the rest get butchered. They made your girl here orange so she'd be visible, stand out in a crowd—can't run away. What are you?" Her focus shifts fully to Kelpie with the final question.

"I—I was a lab assistant until yesterday," says Kelpie. "Then a man from the Congress came and melted my supervisor, and I ran away. I don't think I can go back, even if I wanted to . . . and I don't think I want to. They were lying to me. They told me I was a normal human who'd been in a bad lab accident, and that was why I didn't remember anything before a year ago."

"And you believed them?" asks Smita.

"Maybe we should continue this elsewhere," says Isabella. She rises from her chair, beginning to gather the dishes left over from their ritual workings. The small stones and salt are tipped into plastic baggies, which vanish into the depths of her purse; the dishes are stacked, carefully, one atop the other. "Kelpie, can you get the ones with the water in them? We need to pour that onto the grass outside."

"Wouldn't the sink be closer?" asks Erin.

Isabella looks at her calmly. "Pouring it onto the grass lets it rejoin the natural world, and carries our intent into the universe. There's a reason for everything we're doing here."

"Including leaving?"

"This is Catrina's house, and while she's willing to respect that sometimes coven members want to hang back and speak with me after ritual is finished, she can get a little . . . needy if she's made to wait too long," says Isabella. "If we're here much longer, she'll join us."

"But why?" asks Kelpie. "She couldn't see my hooves, or anything else about me."

"No. But she saw that I took you as an apprentice, when I've been refusing to do the same for her since before the coven started officially meeting at her house. And she saw that Erin, who we've been inviting to stay for months now with no look at all, was willing to stay for the chance to talk with you after. She's going to be curious. We should join the others, briefly, and then get out."

"Join the others?" asks Kelpie, blankly. "They left."

"They left the *circle*," says Isabella. "Cleaning up the ritual supplies is my job, because I bring most of them to be sure they've been purified and treated correctly. Everyone's all still in the house."

"Oh." Kelpie had truly believed that once the other women left, they were gone, rejoining their own lives outside the influence of the coven.

"I have to deal with the granola brigade in a *social setting*?" asks Erin, sounding genuinely horrified.

Smita elbows her as she rises, lightly and with affection. "It won't hurt you. Come on, you might enjoy it."

"There are usually sandwiches," says Isabella, as if that changes things. She gathers a few more dishes, then gestures for Kelpie to get the ones filled with water. "You remember where the front door is?"

"Yes," says Kelpie uncertainly, picking up the dishes.

The group exits the room roughly together. Isabella smiles reassuringly at Kelpie. "Just follow the voices once you're done. We'll be waiting for you."

Indeed, the faint sound of unintelligible conversation drifts from the back of the house once they're in the hall, marking the location of the rest of the coven. Kelpie turns away from Isabella and the others, carrying the dishes of water to the door, careful not to spill any on the polished floor. Her hooves leave little scuffs as she walks; Catrina will be able to see *those,* even if she didn't see the hooves themselves. Kelpie wonders what the woman will blame for the marks. Will she decide someone must have kept their shoes on inside? Or will she find a way to justify it away?

It's a small thing to be concerned with, scuffs on a floor. But as she lets herself gingerly outside, dishes balanced on her arm to keep from spilling, it seems like the most important thing in the world. If she can just make sense of the small things, the big ones will unsnarl themselves.

One by one, she tips the dishes out onto the lawn, watching the water cascade onto the uniformly cut green strands. She's never seen a lawn by daylight before, and the smell of it is indescribable, bright and vibrant and *living*. Given her obvious cervine traits, she's briefly concerned that the smell will trigger some biological need and have her down on hands and knees, chewing on the landscaping.

To her great relief, that doesn't happen, and she straightens after tipping out the last of the water, taking a quick look around before she turns and flees for the front door, back into the safety of the house.

Once inside, she follows the sound of voices until she comes to the kitchen, which is nothing like Isabella's. It's as large as Isabella's whole apartment, or close to it, for one thing; the ceiling is higher than any other she's seen in this house, and one whole wall is windows, looking out onto a lush green backyard that's clearly been landscaped to within an inch of its life to look like a wild and carefree garden. One half of the space is taken up by appliances and cabinetry, while the other half is occupied by an oval table, a large hutch full of very fancy dishes, and a dark wood sideboard.

Kelpie lacks frame of reference for this room, but she can tell it must have been expensive. Everything is gleaming, wood, metal, and tile, all of it polished with the same intensity as the backyard landscaping. The appearance of perfection is the only thing that matters here. The reality is less compelling.

The women from the coven are mostly seated at the table, while Catrina holds court against the counter, next to a tall stainless steel urn which the other women visit, one by one, like supplicants coming to an altar. The smell of coffee fills the air. A tray of pastries has been set out on the table, next to a tray of tiny crustless sandwiches.

Catrina waves the mug in her hand when Kelpie enters the room. "Our guest!" she proclaims jubilantly, as if she'd been the one to invite the stranger into their midst. It's clear from the way the kitchen is laid out, the way people have positioned themselves, that she needs this moment to seem like the most important person in the room. This is where Catrina finds the power she was requesting during their circle, whether or not it's real.

Isabella is one of the women at the table, seated at the end along with Smita and Erin. Kelpie pauses long enough to flash Catrina an uncertain smile, then hurries over to the safe familiarity of the woman she came in with and the dangerous newness of the only other cuckoo she's ever knowingly met.

For her part, Erin seems to have noticed her the moment she stepped into the room. The other woman watches her every step, as silent as a snake. Kelpie stops next to Isabella, who looks up and smiles, reassuringly.

"Here, sit down, have a sandwich," she says. "You look like you must be hungry, and this is a part of the coven meeting. The cooldown afterward. We can go soon, and you and Erin can talk more."

"Or at all," says Erin. "I don't feel like we've even started scratching the surface."

"Oh that's so intriguing!" says Catrina, appearing at Kelpie's side as if by magic, mug in her hand and a curious expression on her face as she focuses in on Erin. "Do I hear the chirp of lovebirds in the air? Oh, dear, Smita, I'm so sorry it looks as if your love may have a wandering eye!"

If she was trying to cause trouble, she missed the mark fairly widely. Smita blinks, twice, then turns to Erin as she starts to giggle. Erin isn't that subtle. She begins to outright guffaw, laughing so hard all conversation in the kitchen stops, the other coven members turning to stare at her with suddenly focused fascination.

"You thought we were—" she manages to gasp, between peals of laughter.

Smita shakes her head, still more subdued in her amusement, and elbows Erin. "It's not *that* funny; I'm not *that* unfortunate to look at! I make good money, I'm clever, and I knit, which means I'm useful around the house. You'd be lucky to have me."

"I would," admits Erin, slowly getting herself back under control. "But it would be like dating my sister, and I'm not *that* kinky." She looks at Catrina, the last of the laughter slipping away, leaving her as reptile-calm as before. "Why does my wanting to talk to Isabella's cousin mean I must be romantically interested in her? She's at least ten years too young for me."

Catrina sputters, then focuses on Isabella, apparently not wanting to risk Erin's clear willingness to verbally draw blood. "We have a rule about guests at circle because you said we needed one. You said it could disrupt the energy in the room."

"Yes," says Isabella. "That's correct."

"Yet you brought two guests today."

"We all agreed months ago that Erin was welcome if she ever wanted to stay and enjoy our company," says Isabella. "And apprentices or initiates have never been considered guests. The rules allow them explicitly."

"But don't grant them membership."

"No, not at all. Kelly isn't a member, she's not an initiate, and she won't be attending every circle with me. But as my new apprentice, it was important for her to see what we do here, so she can understand it for herself. She may be running things for me one of these days, after all."

Catrina sputters, and the whole story comes clear in that reaction. She wants power; she's said as much. She expects to be able to control the world and people around her without too much difficulty. She offered up her home for the coven meetings; she supplies these pleasant refreshments, which Kelpie is sure are expensive or otherwise special in some way. She's their hostess. She's *important*. And here's Isabella, telling her without coming out and saying it, that she won't be the next coven leader, that she's going to be passed over for a quiet girl she just met, all because that girl has a familial relationship to Isabella.

Kelpie watches the way Catrina's eyes change, and wonders if Isabella is so used to her environment that she's no longer sensitive to its dangers. The lab didn't prepare her for a lot of things aboveground. It prepared her for egos, though, the way they could bruise, the way they could fester; the way they could get so large they pulled the air out of a room, leaving no space for anything but admiration of the ego's owner. Catrina isn't quite that bad, but she needs some fawning over or she's going to become dangerous.

"Did you make these sandwiches yourself? They look delicious," she says, trying to break the growing tension.

Catrina turns to blink at her, and the hostility that has been building in her expression falls away, replaced by a patronizing softness that Kelpie's seen before. It's the look the techs get when she asks them to explain something they consider blatantly obvious, and it means she's not seen as a threat in this moment—she's part of the furniture, almost an excuse to show off cleverness and very little more.

"Oh, no, dear, I don't do my own cooking," says Catrina. "That would be beneath me. I have a lady who makes these things on my behalf. I do set the menu, however, so everything you taste is a demonstration of my attention to detail."

Kelpie doesn't see how you can tell someone else to mix every step of your experiment and still claim the experiment shows your attention to detail, but she's trying to placate Catrina, not argue with her, so she only smiles and nods. "Well, she did an excellent job, and you have fabulous taste—and a beautiful home!"

Flattery does indeed appear to be the way into Catrina's good graces. The woman preens, standing a little straighter, gesturing to the kitchen with the mug in her hand. "I chose all the décor myself."

"It's very . . . harmonious," says Kelpie, who can't think of a better way to say "beige" without it turning into an insult.

Isabella stands, putting a hand on Kelpie's shoulder, and smiles at Catrina. "We're heading out. I have an afternoon appointment that Kelly has promised to accompany me on as an observer."

"Coven business?" asks Catrina, almost hungrily.

"Hechicera business," Isabella corrects. "It's not an exorcism—those are church territory—but it's asking an unquiet spirit to please move on and stop bothering the people who knew it in life. I wouldn't bring anyone at all with me, but Kelly is trained enough to protect herself, and she needs to understand this part of the business if she's going to take it over someday."

Kelpie tries to look brave and wise, although she doesn't really feel like either of those things.

Erin and Smita rise from their own seats and move to join the pair. Catrina's face falls and then falls further, as she sees all the people she was most hoping to make inroads with clearly preparing to leave.

"If you're sure," she says, and her tone manages to imply without stating that Isabella is making a terrible mistake, that taking Kelpie instead of Catrina is akin to attempting to remove a nail with a fork instead of the claw end of a hammer. But because she doesn't say it, Isabella doesn't have to answer it.

That seems to be the way people communicate outside the lab. Tones and looks and implications, things unsaid but inferred. Kelpie doesn't like it. They may have lied to her belowground, but they were blunt about it, not trying to tie her into knots with social signals she didn't have all the background to understand.

Isabella makes a quick circuit of the room, saying her individual goodbyes to all the members of the coven, and then the four of them head for the door, Catrina watching them go. Erin slouches along at Smita's side, hands in her pockets, walking like she's never rushed a day in her life and isn't intending to start now. Kelpie makes sure she stays on the other side of Isabella. She knows an apex predator when she sees one. There's so much she doesn't know, so much she still needs to learn, but she and Erin are both cuckoos, and she knows when she's in danger.

Once they're outside, Erin's affect changes. She stands straighter, moving so as to stand between Smita and Kelpie and the street, as if she can somehow block them both from view. Suddenly uncomfortable, she glances up and down the sidewalk, and mutters, "It's moments like this where I wish I hadn't gotten over my Hand of Glory addiction."

Smita elbows her in the ribs, and this time it's not so gentle. Erin jerks away, putting up her hands.

"Hey, kidding!" she says. "Do I look like I'm trying to find someone I can get away with murdering?"

"Not a funny joke," says Smita.

Kelpie looks between the two of them, baffled. Isabella is less subtle.

"What are you talking about?"

"Oh, in another timeline, I"—Erin gestures to herself, then to Smita—"stabbed her to death, chopped her hand off, and turned it into a Hand of Glory that I was going to need later. In *this* timeline, I chloroformed her, dragged her out of the lab before I torched the place, and let her keep both her hands. I didn't need the second Hand because I hadn't used the first hand completely on the night I was supposed to kill her. It was a whole thing."

"I don't remember this at all, but since all five of the people I live with insist it really happened, I'm inclined to believe them," says Smita.

"Anyway, this is where I tell the two of you that you're coming home with us," says Erin, frowning. "I need you to meet my housemates so we can figure out what we're going to do next. And this isn't something that's up for discussion, so I'm sorry if this isn't how you wanted to spend your afternoon. If you really need to be dealing with an unquiet spirit or whatever, just give me the address and I'll do it."

"That was just to get us out of there," says Isabella. "I don't do spirit removal."

"Pity," says Erin. "Could have been fun. Anyway, come on. We're going this way."

She waves for Isabella and Kelpie to follow, then starts down the street. Smita stays where she is until she can take up the rear of their little group.

None of them sees Catrina watching from the window as they walk away.

BOOK III

Half Moon

Thou sayest well, and it holds well too, for the fortune of us that are the moon's men doth ebb and flow like the sea, being governed, as the sea is, by the moon.

—William Shakespeare, *Henry IV, Part I*

Night, and the holy hunter rides:
And the stars stand still and the pale moon hides
And the brave deer run, but the King Stag knows
He will fall at the end to Ceinwen's Bow.

—Talis Kimberley, "Ceinwen's Bow"

"By now you know the Up-and-Under is in the service of the elements, and each of them belongs to a monarch," Niamh began. "The King of Cups owns the waters, for example, and the Page of Frozen Waters serves him, and the Lady of Salt and Sorrow was by his side. She may yet be again, if she decides to take him back, if the Page allows it.

Not every monarch has a consort. The ones who do tend to last longer."

"We know all this," said Avery crossly.

"Why should the Page have a say?" asked Zib. "She serves the King, doesn't she?"

"Yes, but she's never left his side, and the Lady has. If the Page objected loudly enough, the King might refuse to bring his consort home again."

"That doesn't make any sense," said Avery.

Niamh fixed him with a look. "There's no point to arguing with how much sense the truth does or doesn't make when we're all inside the same mosasaur—I like that word, it's much kinder than most of the things people from the land call the denizens of the deep depths, and it has a friendly sound to it. We'll get where we're going when we get there. If you want to hear the story of the sword, why I found it and why Zib has it, you'll be patient and let me tell it in my own way, and not whatever way you want me to."

Avery opened his mouth to say something else, and stopped as Zib slapped her hand over it, cutting him off before he could begin. "He won't interrupt anymore," she said. "I promise, even if he doesn't. I want to know. Please, tell me."

Niamh nodded, seemingly appeased. "All right. The consorts of the kings and queens are not kings or queens in their own right, because there can only be one crown to a quarter, and if they were to be crowned, we would have eight crowns, and that would be too many. But the Queen of Wands, who stands for fire and change and the bright burning lands of the Coalcatch Caverns, has never taken a consort, nor set one aside; she has only and ever ruled alone, singular and complete unto herself. And when she first took her place, the Lord of the previous queen was still in his place, and very angry to see a succession when he, himself, had never been in consideration for the crown. . . ."

—From *Into the Windwracked Wilds,* by A. Deborah Baker

Sinus Amoris

TIMELINE: AUGUST 18, 2017.
THREE DAYS TO THE ECLIPSE.

They have two possible directions at this point: Diana, or the alchemists. Judy is much more in favor of going to talk to Diana. She knows Diana. She's comfortable with Diana, or as comfortable as she can be with a powerful moon goddess who's been manifest for decades longer than she has. Best of all, she's reasonably confident that Diana isn't going to decide she's crossed some indefinable line and try to have her taken apart.

She's not sure she's ever spoken to an actual alchemist. But what she knows from stories and rumor doesn't exactly make her want to. Alchemists are the selfish, petty, terrifying monsters in every Lunar's closet, and she doesn't need to pull them into the open to understand that when you know where the monster is, you leave it there.

David's in favor of starting with Diana too . . . from a distance. He thinks that if she's involved with this, the best thing for them to do is leave school and go home, all of them, returning to their families and taking a leave of absence from their studies while all this works itself out.

Of the three of them, only Anna wants to start with the alchemists. Only Anna thinks hunting down and confronting the people who are most likely to be killing Lunars is a good idea. During the day, no less, when stepping up is more difficult and the Moon is slower to respond. Not that they have great cosmic powers at the best of times, but Judy *feels* a little sturdier at night, *feels* a little more equipped to deal with danger.

But Anna says the alchemists will be expecting them at night, and somehow this has become her show, even though David still thinks her other half is Losna, still believes she's a minor moon goddess with no real parlor tricks to speak of. Judy's trying not to be offended at that. She knows Artemis has always been charismatic; she's a hunt leader, and that means she needs to be able to convince people to listen when she wants them to take wild risks on her behalf. Chang'e does paperwork and gardens.

Maybe it's reductive, but watching David nod as Anna describes a plan that seems to center on them magically tripping over an alchemist in downtown Berkeley, it's how she feels. Judy produces a peach pit from her pocket to center herself, spinning it between her fingers. She doesn't want to be in charge. She's never wanted to be in charge, wouldn't have been so happy to let Diana continue playing the figurehead role while ignoring the duties *she* should have been performing as senior Lunar if Judy had *wanted* to be in charge. In charge is where the blame lies. In charge is where the responsibility is.

But someone's hunting Lunars, and someone knew enough to go into the everything and leave Aske's body there to rot, and someone knew how to find where Máni lives and leave the key for him without closing the gate to the everything. Were they trying to taunt or frighten the other Lunars? "Look, you're not safe even here, when you're outside the rules of normal reality"? Or was whoever left the key trying to send a warning? "They're hunting you, be cautious"? There are so many possibilities! None of them good.

Judy clears her throat. Anna and David turn to look at her. She sighs.

"This seems to rely a lot on things just happening to go the way we need them to go," she says. "Anna, you didn't answer before. Do you know another Aske we can call?"

Anna shakes her head. "Sadly, no. The last one I knew was years ago, in Chicago. Aske's not the most common manifestation, because not many people remember her. I think the universe spits us out less because the City needs us—the City could get by with a perfectly generic Moon, and that's what the Man is for, really.

Just make a few dozen Men in the Moon and let him handle the transit every night, none of these personalities or preferences or immortality-granting peaches—and more because the City somehow remembers that humans used to believe in us."

"We all know belief powers the manifestations," says Judy. "That's not news."

"No, but it explains why there are so damn many Dianas," says Anna.

"We should talk to the one we have," says Judy. "We should at the very least see what she has to say about the key situation."

"I'd really rather go looking for alchemists," says Anna.

They both turn to David, expressions questioning. He grimaces.

"Do I have to be the tie-breaker?" he asks.

"That's the nice thing about having three people," says Judy. "We can actually vote on things when it's a choice between two terrible options. Because let's be honest here, both of them really suck."

"Yeah, they do," he says wearily. "I don't like Diana. She makes me nervous. But both of you make me nervous too, and I have class in an hour. I'd rather go see the lady who makes me nervous already than some stranger who makes me nervous *and* might want to murder me. I'm with Judy. We go see Diana."

Judy resists the urge to punch the air, and instead turns to smile at Anna, choosing to be a gracious winner. "Come on," she says. "I know her schedule."

She starts walking and the others follow, a small, unremarkable cluster of students walking back across the tangled outline of the campus toward the art classes. No one gives them a second look, and why should they? The most noticeable thing about them is that they're all graying prematurely, and this is higher education: going gray before your time is nothing new. It would almost stand out more if they *weren't* showing signs of aging most often associated with stress.

They make it down Piedmont to the main campus without incident, and are almost to the building where Professor Williams teaches when disaster strikes. Judy walks straight into a tall brown-haired man in a tweed jacket—or maybe he walks into her, so distracted by the book he's reading that he doesn't see her until it's too late. It doesn't matter who's responsible for the impact; papers go flying everywhere as he loses his balance. Judy is knocked backward into David, who grabs her shoulders and steadies her before she can fall.

The man was walking by himself, and isn't quite as lucky. No one catches him. He staggers back, then falls as his knees buckle, dropping him onto his backside in the middle of the walkway. Judy gasps, clapping her hands over her mouth, and leans back against David, a show of fear and familiarity that clearly startles him, as he keeps hold of her shoulders, providing a steady backdrop.

Anna looks at the two of them, perplexed. "What? You knocked a guy down. It happens." She moves toward the man on the ground, already offering him her hand. "Sorry, sir. You probably shouldn't be reading and walking at the same time."

His hand closes on hers as he lifts his face to focus in her direction, and Anna gasps, trying to pull away. He doesn't let go.

"No," he says instead, and his voice is warm and kind, and filled with strange harmonics that scrape and itch against Judy's brain, all her linguistic training telling her that some of those sounds aren't *possible,* the human larynx can't *make* those sounds, and if it could, it would need more than two letters. She's hearing the words around the word, the unspoken shadows of the words that could have been, and she hates it as she has never hated anything in her life.

"I probably shouldn't," he continues, and pulls himself to his feet, still holding Anna's hand. He's shorter than David, taller than Judy; just tall enough to be unremarkable in the local population. Combine that with his hair, which is a brown so ordinary that it doesn't seem to want to catch the mind's eye, save for a pure white streak running from the crown to the front, which hangs slightly askew next to his face, and his generic "college professor from a romantic comedy" attire, and he's a man who could disappear in an instant if they look away.

Judy wishes, desperately, that he would do exactly that. Just disappear, fading away into the chaos of the campus and leaving them free of this ill-timed interruption.

Sadly, she's never gotten anything by wishing for it. He turns to look at her and David, and his eyebrows lift. Behind the wire frames of his glasses, his eyes are a pale, foggy gray, like the sky above campus in the morning, after the sun has risen but before its rays have burned the clouds away.

His eyes were made to hide the moon.

"I know you," he says, sounding just a little perplexed. The words around the words ask for explanation, for clarification, for detail piled upon detail. They want her life story, they *demand* everything she is, and Judy swallows bile and babble at the same time, forcing the words down her throat like stones to weigh her belly down. She meets those foggy eyes and steps up, just enough to feel her own eyes flash peach before she steps back down. If this were a normal man, she would never dare. If this were a normal man, she wouldn't feel like meeting his eyes risked dragging parts of her into the light that were never intended to be seen.

He smiles as if he's had something confirmed, and finally lets go of Anna's hand. "Thank you," he says. "I wondered why you always ran out of the room at department meetings when I came in, but I've never been able to get close enough to ask. Miss . . . Kong-Jones, isn't it?"

"Yes, Professor Middleton," says Judy, miserably.

"Are you going to introduce me to your friends?" he asks, and the words around the words whisper how easily that could be a command rather than a mild suggestion with the intonation of a request, so Judy takes a deep breath and begins.

"Anna, David, this is Professor Middleton, the chair of—"

He cuts her off before she can finish. "No, I mean *introduce* me to your friends."

It takes everything she has to swallow her words a second time, tilt her head, and say, "Not here. Not in public. There are too many people around."

He blinks, apparently taken aback by her refusal. "I . . . All right."

"Good. Thank you." Judy finally steps away from David, her attention staying fixed on Professor Middleton. It's like she's afraid that if she looks away he'll strike, and on some level, maybe she is;

on some level, he's the biggest predator she's ever seen, and he could wipe her from existence if he wanted to. It's always been a risk, staying on this campus with him around, but she's done her best to stay off his radar, and as long as she's here, one of the Lunars knows the threat he represents.

Diana knows too, of course. Diana has to know. Professor Middleton's manifestation had been the quiet talk of the undercampus as soon as it happened, everyone who had ever even brushed against the incarnate world making sure the news got around. But Judy's not sure the gossip has continued in the days since then. Anna and David don't look nearly worried enough about what they're standing in front of. David looks confused, and Anna seems wary, as if she got something when he touched her hand, but neither of them has reacted as much as they should.

"My office?" he suggests—and it *is* a suggestion. Nothing in the words around the words tries to say that it's an order, or even that it's a good idea.

"Too small," says Judy. "And I'm pretty well known in our department for avoiding your company. Someone would talk."

"Right," he says, and tilts his head back to look at the sky, smacking his lips thoughtfully for a moment before he looks back to her, and offers, almost offhandedly, "We could go to my house? My sister's probably there, so it's not like you'd be alone with me, and it's far enough off campus that no one's going to see."

Somehow, going with this man to an undisclosed second location seems like a safer plan than walking with him across campus. Judy doesn't know whether that's her own concern for her reputation speaking, or the strange harmonics that accompany his every word, but her mouth opens before she has a chance to think about it, and her answer is given:

"That works."

Anna scowls at her, less aware of the danger, more aware of the strangeness of refusing a public office for a private home. Judy can't understand how Anna can listen to him speak and not hear the strange harmonics wrapping around every single word, how she can look at him and not see the way space tries to distort around him, unable to make up its mind whether he should be more real than the rest of them or rejected entirely. He's more solid than they are, like something dropped in from another reality, one that makes this one look like tissue paper.

Anna is the huntress here.

She should recognize the greater predator.

Judy scrapes up an uneasy smile, flashing it first at Anna and then at David. "Professor Middleton is the chair of my department," she says.

"He's your advisor?" asks David.

"No," she says. "I've gone out of my way to stay out of his classes." She can stop herself from sharing information that shouldn't be thrown about in public, but she can't lie in his presence. She can tell, in an abstract sort of way, that he wouldn't like that, and part of her is more concerned about upsetting him than anything else.

"Why?"

"Because I terrify her," says Professor Middleton easily. "Come along, students. It looks like we're going to have an unscheduled class session at my place today." He gestures for them to accompany him as he begins walking, heading for the edge of campus. Judy wants to run. Judy wants to turn and bolt as fast as she can. She follows anyway. Running won't save her now, not when he knows her name, not when he's been wondering about her already. Not when she's caught his attention.

Maybe if she'd been more careful, if she'd watched where she was going, she might have been able to finish out her time at Berkeley without this happening, but she wasn't and she didn't, and now she'll have to pay the price for her mistakes on top of everything else.

Anna and David follow her, both perplexed by her seemingly meek obedience, neither of them saying anything or stepping up. They stay almost entirely themselves, as close to human as they ever get, and maybe that's part of why they can't tell how much danger they're in. David is still new to his divinity. Anna is less so, and she said before that when she's on a hunt, she's always partially stepped up, Artemis riding actively along with her human host. Her inability to sense the presence of a larger predator is confusing.

Maybe they'll find out why it's like this before they die. And if they don't . . . well. Hopefully someone else will start asking questions about Aske. She deserves some answers, and some peace, even if Eliza's family will never know what happened.

"You don't have to look like you're marching off to your own execution," says Professor Middleton, looking at Judy as he walks. "We're just going to my place to talk, because you didn't want to do it on campus."

"How far away do you live?"

"Not far," he says, turning down Bancroft and heading for Telegraph. That's the main street for the university's social scene: if you want cheap pizza or used books, you go to Telegraph. Judy's heard rumors of a happening nightlife that thrives there in upstairs and underground clubs after the sun goes down, but her evenings have been taken up by homework and Lunar duties for so long that the rumors have remained just that—rumors, things to eventually be proven by someone else, someone with more time to kill than she has.

Professor Middleton looks out of place here, weaving between the teenagers playing hooky and playing at being whatever version of alternative is currently speaking to their souls, brightly colored hair and denim jackets, patches of chainmail hung decoratively off recycled fashions from the Buffalo Exchange. Several of the street vendors smile as he passes, some pausing in their work or negotiations to raise their hands in greeting, and he smiles back, entirely at ease.

The feeling that he's out of his natural environment fades with the second. He's still too drab and too ordinary-looking for the color and chaos around him, but his posture seems to shift, adapting to his environment like an octopus changing color to blend into the bottom of a fishing boat. By the time they've gone a full block, he's entirely unremarkable once more, and their mismatched little student group is more likely to attract attention than he is.

It's a neat trick. Judy frowns, trying to figure out how he's been able to accomplish it. Professor Middleton smiles in answer.

"They call it body *language* for a reason," he says. "If you speak it fluently enough, you'll never stick out. I've heard good things about your work. You have a real gift for languages. I'm surprised you haven't spent more time studying this one."

"Kinesthetic linguistics is such a large field that I've never really had time to focus on it," says Judy, distracted into answering without a veil of terror between her thoughts and her voice. "Culture and environment play such a huge role, and it's always struck me as being almost on the border between linguistics and behavioral science. Maybe if I was planning to go into mental health care or social work. Being able to read the way people change their posture depending on threat assessment of their surroundings could be a huge help."

"Or if you just wanted to go anywhere in the world without attracting attention. One of my housemates is almost as good at it as I am, which is saying something, given that she doesn't really have a gift for languages. She's real good at physical stuff, though, so I guess she just came at it from the other side."

The thought of a professor having housemates—plural, apparently, and a sister who either lives with him or comes and goes at will—is a little jarring, a reminder that there's no benchmark in adulthood where capitalism ceases to apply. Judy frowns as she walks, glancing back at Anna and David. They don't appear to have noticed Professor Middleton's odd postural mimicry. Then again, they both move like college students, meaning they're still in their natural habitat this close to campus.

They reach the corner of Haste Street, and Professor Middleton turns. For a moment, just a moment, he can't see them, and once again, Judy sees the chance to run. Once again, she doesn't. If she runs, she'll have to keep running, maybe for the rest of her life, and as a goddess of immortality, that life could be very, very long. She doesn't know if the professor is the sort of man—or manifestation—who holds a grudge. She's gone out of her way not to know.

Haste is quieter than Telegraph, lined with private homes, gated apartment complexes, and the smaller, calmer sorts of business that a city center needs but the hectic social pyramid of Telegraph can't sustain—dentists and daycares and accountancy firms. They keep walking, and Judy watches carefully as Professor Middleton's posture shifts again, abandoning the veil of collegiate ease, becoming what she assumes is his natural stance. He walks like he's not afraid of anything, like he's seen the worst the world has to offer, shrugged, and decided to keep on going, unperturbed.

It's a terrifying walk, all the more because it offers no threats. As she watches him, she realizes she doesn't really know much about the man; she's read his published papers, which are meticulously researched, and precisely as petty as any other academic work, but she's worked so hard to avoid him that she's never risked attracting his attention by digging too much into who he is. She didn't even know he *had* a sister.

She knows he's an artificial person, built in a secret lab by alchemists who wanted to control the world, so the question of *how* he has a sister seems like a reasonable one. Either he was cloned from a naturally occurring person and they decided to adopt each other after he became the living force of universal control or—probably more likely, and way more frighteningly—his sister is an artificial person too. Judy can't fathom what she'd be the force of. Professor Middleton is the Doctrine of Ethos. There's only one of those. Right?

Her questions are all-consuming enough to keep her quiet as Haste turns into Shattuck—a main artery, yes, but more domesticated than Telegraph, farther from campus and commensurately more commercialized—and Shattuck turns into the warren of small residential streets. The houses here are old Victorians, imposing, meticulously maintained, and beautifully painted, some with that sort of decorative trim that people call "gingerbread" picked out in tastefully contrasting colors.

They're the kind of houses Judy dreams of owning one day, large enough to contain libraries and home offices and—

She stops dead. David and Anna do the same, all of them staring at a house so out of place that it might as well be a slap across the face of the neighborhood. Judy's supposed to be the one who's good with words, but she can't even convince her mouth to move for the first several stunned seconds—long enough for Anna to demand, loudly, "Okay, what the actual fuck is wrong with the people who live there? Did they lose a bet, or do they hate their neighbors?"

"I was colorblind until my sister and I killed our father and merged sufficiently to overcome our engineered shortcomings—and I mean true colorblindness, not the kind that normally occurs in the human population. There's nothing wrong with red-green colorblindness, or a lack of sensitivity to shades. I lived in a gray-scale world, and it's a miracle I didn't pancake myself across a highway or something before I figured out what colors were. Now I have them all, and they're still novel." Professor Middleton shrugs broadly. "I like 'em. We have all these colors, and all these words for colors. We should use them more."

Anna turns to stare at him. "There's using them more, and then there's painting your house to look like a prism fucked a rainbow."

"I didn't paint it," he says serenely, and starts walking again. Judy catches David's elbow before he can follow.

Leaning close and dropping her voice, she says, "Probably because he just asked the house to look like that and it couldn't figure out a reason not to."

He turns and blinks at her. "What are you talking about?"

"You need to *be careful* around him," she says. "He's dangerous."

"What?" David actually snickers at that. "He's built like a beanstalk. He's wearing *tweed*. I don't think he's dangerous, Judy. I think you're all freaked out by everything that's been happening, and you're jumping at nothing."

"You just dismissed Aske being *murdered* as 'everything that's been happening.' Doesn't that seem strange to you?"

Maybe David can't hear the words around every word Professor Middleton says, but he can react to them. The little subliminal eddies in the air telling them this is safe, this is fine, this is a good idea, they've been burrowing their way deeper and deeper into his thoughts, and now he can't see any reason why he shouldn't be happily following a strange professor into a house stolen from a children's television show.

Judy lets go of his arm. She can't fight this. Chang'e might be able to resist it better than she can, but for her to let the goddess take over is for her to admit that Judy's human life is coming to an end. If she runs, if she tries to break the other Lunars loose and take them with her, she'll make an enemy of the Doctrine. There's no coming back from that. Even if she abandons her hopes of linguistic success, she'll be on the run forever from the concept of language itself. As he so accurately pointed out, even movement is a language. She'll never escape.

None of them will.

Professor Middleton has reached the house, and is holding the gate in the fence open as he watches her talk to David. Anna is beside him, already too far away to reach. Shoulders slumped, Judy follows, and David trails along behind.

The garden is as much a marvel as the house is a monstrosity, unseasonable fruits and flowers warring for dominion. Like the house, it's a riot of chaotic color; unlike the house, it somehow manages to form something coherent and even beautiful. It's like a contrasting argument, like the house is in conversation with itself and its surroundings, and thinking about it too hard makes Judy's head hurt.

There's a peach tree near the fence line, branches heavy with flawlessly ripe fruit, and the sight of it makes Chang'e want to step up, to taste their sweetness and judge how close it is to her own. Judy has to fight her back down, to silently remind her that they don't want to make this situation any worse than it already is. If the professor takes her stepping up as a threat . . . No. The risk is too great.

He smiles as she approaches. "I was concerned you might have remembered another appointment," he says, like they're old friends and she's not here under unspoken duress.

"I think we need to talk this through," she says, and he nods, gray eyes grave.

"We do," he agrees. He waves them into the garden with a sweep of his free hand.

The porch steps are painted as garishly as the rest of the house, each board a different color, and as if that weren't enough, the windows are made of mismatched panes of leaded carnival glass, giving the whole edifice a funhouse air that simultaneously ties it all together and adds the final horrifying touch. Judy's surprised the neighbors haven't torched the place yet, their suburban sensibilities overwhelming the normal distaste for arson.

As for Professor Middleton, he heads up the stairs and opens the unlocked front door, revealing an ordinary hallway beyond, plain wood with doors to either side and a stairway about eight feet deeper in. He leans into the house, yelling an enthusiastic "Hey, Dodge, I brought home a bunch of stray moon gods, and if you don't get down here, I'm going to keep them!"

The house makes no reply. He turns back to the group, smiling more broadly this time. "All right, now that you know I know and we're not on campus anymore, come on in and you can explain who the hell you are and what you're doing at my school."

In he goes, and they follow, ducklings in a line with no other obvious options. Anna is the last one in, the huntress finally appearing to realize she's walking into a trap. The door swings shut behind her. She stops, turns, and tries to open it again. The knob won't budge, and there's no visible way to unlock it. Swallowing hard, she follows Judy and David, who are walking together through the narrow space.

Professor Middleton leads them to the kitchen, which is as oddly normal as the rest of the house, marble countertops and white walls and windows which, seen from this side, appear to be made of perfectly clear glass. If not for the bookshelves lining the walls of the breakfast nook, there would be nothing to distinguish it from any other middle class suburban kitchen. A round cat bed rests against the base of the central island, and the oldest orange cat Judy has ever seen is curled there, tail over its nose, sleeping soundly.

The bookshelves aren't a surprise. Their contents are. There isn't a single book on linguistics, not even one of Middleton's own, but there are several books on higher mathematics, some with titles so long and convoluted that Judy's not sure she could understand the credits page, much less the books themselves. The round wooden table in front of them is covered in papers and Post-It flags, again, exactly like similar tables in academic households around the world.

Anna doesn't seem to notice. Neither she nor David is really looking around, having just figured out how much trouble they might be in: they're watching Professor Middleton, Anna with predatory tenseness, David with something much closer to territorial irritation. Judy hangs back. She might know more about the situation than they do, but she doesn't know *enough*.

Professor Middleton heads for the coffee machine on one counter, picking up the half-full pot and decanting a cup. "Talk," he says.

It's a command. None of them are prepared to resist it, and they all begin talking at once, words tumbling over themselves as if they're trying to recreate the complex harmonics of the professor's own speech. Unlike his words, where the unspoken ones fade politely into the background and become harmonics, these words smother each other, becoming unintelligible.

He puts the pot down and pinches the bridge of his nose. "All right, stop talking," he says. They do, all of them. Judy's not sure she's ever going to be able to speak again, no matter how much she wants to. Awkward, for a linguist.

"I need you to go one at a time," he says, and indicates Judy with his coffee mug. "You, girl in my department who knows enough to avoid me. Who the hell are you, and who are your friends?"

"I'm Judith Kong-Jones, and I'm a linguistics grad student who was hoping to keep avoiding you until I graduated," says Judy. "Fucked that one up but good, since now I'm in your house. These are Anna and David. They're . . . I suppose 'work acquaintances' is the best way to explain our relationship."

"Mm-hmm. And what is it that you all do for work that has you acquainted?" he asks, sounding halfway amused by her attempt to dodge the undodgeable question.

"We're incarnate moon gods," she says, immediately, then claps her hands over her mouth, horrified by what just came out. "I didn't mean to . . . I'm so sorry, I didn't . . ."

"Calm down; you didn't have a choice," he says, and takes a

sip of his coffee. "Just so we're all equally exposed: Hi. I'm Roger, and I'm the living manifestation of the linguistic half of a universal concept normally referred to as the Doctrine of Ethos, when people remember that it's something they can refer to, which isn't very often outside of philosophy and music theory cl— Oh, thank God, Dodge!" The last appears to be a name, as it's accompanied by his eyes focusing on the kitchen doorway and him raising his mug in what appears to be a toast. "Get in here and save me from the student body."

"Which one? The one who looks like she's about to go for your throat, the tall guy, or the one who looks like a whole lot of missed alarms?"

"All three?"

"Sure, sure." The woman walks into the room, following the professor's path to the coffee machine. They have a certain facial similarity, but Judy wouldn't have pegged her for Professor Middleton's sister if she'd seen her on the street: her hair, for one thing. It's a shockingly bright shade of red, cut short and slightly feathered, like she's been hunting her whole life for the lowest-maintenance style possible, and has finally hit on this as the comfortable middle ground between "something I have to brush" and "something I have to take care of." Like the professor, there's a white streak at the front, running from the crown of her head down. It doesn't look like an affectation.

Unlike his traditionally professorial attire, she's wearing jeans and a Berkeley T-shirt, with a highlighter tucked behind one ear. She's also surrounded by a thin rainbow film of broken time. Not dead time—broken time, the kind that flashes in the walls of the everything, intangible and ever-shifting, dying even as it fully appears. Judy blinks, blinks again, and finally scrubs at her eyes, trying to make the afterimages disappear.

They don't oblige. "Who are you people, and why am I saving my brother from you?" the woman asks.

Her voice is genial and lacks the echoing subliminal commands of Professor Middleton's. That would be comforting, if not for those rainbows. Judy begins to open her mouth.

"And don't lie to her," says Professor Middleton sharply.

Judy tries to shut her mouth again. It refuses to oblige. She glares at the professor, then turns to the woman. "We're a group of incarnate moon gods currently attending the college where Professor Middleton teaches, and he picked us up and dragged us home as punishment for running into him on campus."

"Hey!" he protests. "This isn't a punishment. You're the one who didn't want to explain who you people were in public, and wouldn't go to my office with me."

"Poor baby. Are you terrifying the lesser incarnates again?" The woman pats him on the cheek. "Wow, sucks to be you. Anyway, which ones are you people? There are like ninety moon gods or something. You're like rats."

"Don't let her fool you," says the professor, as an aside to Anna. "She knows exactly how many moon gods there are, possible, currently incarnate, and no longer incarnating regularly. That's what she does. She knows the numbers of things."

"Oh fuck me the Doctrine has two halves, doesn't it?" says Judy, horrified.

The woman looks at her, amused. "You picked that up pretty quick, little Lunar. Yes, there are two halves to the Doctrine of Ethos. Most things have two halves, since that's what 'half' means. There should probably have been more, since it's also a means of describing musical modes, but that gets overly complicated, and then I have a headache, and you don't want me to have a headache. Hello, I'm Dodger Cheswich, call me 'Dodger,' and I'm basically the living concept of mathematics, which makes me fun at parties. You were going to tell me which moon gods you are."

"Chang'e, ma'am," says Judy.

Dodger nods, satisfied with this, and looks to David.

"Máni," he says.

Too late, Judy remembers that Anna's lie to David is still in effect—he thinks she's Losna, and she's about to tell the truth. Anna appears to remember at the same time. She pales slightly, mouth working like she's chewing on a fresh piece of gum.

She resists the command for a surprisingly long time before she spits out, "Artemis."

"Two of the big three, in our kitchen? My." Dodger sips her own coffee. "We should get out the nice dishes, Roger."

"They're not staying for dinner."

"Your strays always wind up staying for dinner, when they don't drop dead in the garden."

David, meanwhile, is staring at Anna in outright shock. Before Judy can tell him not to, he steps up, Máni shifting to the forefront as his eyes flash silver and the air around him takes on a sparkling, wintery air. Dodger lifts her eyebrows as she observes this, but doesn't comment, while Professor Middleton takes a deep, weary drink from his mug, leaning back against the counter.

"You told me you were Losna," says Máni. "Why would you lie to me?"

"I had my reasons," she says.

"We don't lie to each other."

"I just met you," she protests. "I don't owe you honesty."

Judy winces, and steps up to match Máni, Chang'e moving smoothly to the forefront. "Anna, please," she says. "There's no reason to antagonize your allies when you don't need to. Máni, I understand why you're upset."

"But you're not surprised," he snaps. "You knew, didn't you?"

More lies will only compound the damage already done. "I found out this morning. She was talking about hunting, and Losna's not a hunter. Artemis is."

"Hunters kill things."

That's an angle she hasn't considered yet. She looks to Anna, speculatively. Is it truly a coincidence that a minor Lunar died, and almost immediately after, she met Artemis pretending to be someone harmless? Could she have pulled that same ruse on Aske?

"I didn't kill her," says Anna. She's staying as she is, Artemis present but not dominant, making sure she doesn't look like the biggest threat in the room. It's a smart call on her part, since Máni looks like he's just about ready to start breaking things.

Chang'e doesn't think *that* would be nearly as much of a smart call, not with the Doctrine of Ethos—both halves, and how did she not know there were two of them? How did she never put it together?—standing right there, watching. If he starts something now, she's pretty sure Roger and Dodger will finish it, and that things they finish don't restart.

"We don't know that."

"Yes, you do, because I'm telling you the truth," says Anna. She glances to Roger. "You told us not to lie to your sister. Is that still in effect?"

"Yup," he says, and drinks more coffee.

"I want to know how you did that. Because I could feel it when it happened, like a net settling over a school of fish, and I knew I was caught, but now I don't feel it at all."

"Eh." He shrugs. "If you were always aware of your underwear, it would start to drive you up the wall before the end of the day."

"Spoken like a man who's been forced to understand why I hate thongs so much," says Dodger.

Roger shudders dramatically. "You are the *worst* sister. But yes, miss moon god, you are currently forbidden to lie to my sister."

"Cool." Anna turns away from Máni, stepping all the way up at the same time, so it's Artemis who finishes the motion, Artemis who faces the incarnate Doctrine, Artemis who says, in a voice as cool as running water, "Much appreciated. Can we agree that no matter where I'm looking, I'm addressing said sister?"

"Sure," says Dodger, sounding thoroughly amused.

Roger nods.

Artemis turns back to Máni. "I came to Berkeley because Lunars have been dying, and the alchemists have been in a tizzy all over the continent, but it's worse here than it is anywhere else. For some reason, the alchemists *here* are on the verge of bursting into flame from sheer nervous activity, and I want to know why. They must be doing something that has everyone worked up, and given that they're alchemists, it's not unreasonable to connect it to the deaths. I said I was Losna because you haven't had a Losna recently enough for anyone to know what her incarnations are supposed to be like, and I don't trust your Diana. I can't truthfully say I've never killed anyone—I *am* a huntress—but I can say that I have not killed a single person since arriving in this city, and the only other Lunar I ever killed was over a decade ago. He attacked me first. Unless you're planning to come at me with a knife, I'm no danger to you."

Máni blinks, taking a small step back, then looks to Chang'e. "You're okay with this?"

"I don't think it's up to me," says Chang'e. "She's telling the truth. She helped me search for Aske's body after I didn't find her inside the everything. She's a huntress, and there's something here to hunt, so she came here to go hunting."

"Is a Diana another kind of moon god?" asks Dodger.

"That is possibly the nicest thing you could have said," says Artemis. "Chang'e and I are as high in the pantheon as she is, but she goes around acting like she's the boss of everyone, even when she doesn't have a leg to stand on. And since she still has so many people who believe in her, you find her in almost every community of Lunars, which gives her a numerical advantage."

"Hold on, hold on." Roger pinches the bridge of his nose, pushing his glasses up at the same time. "Are you saying you people are composite entities? Some sort of distributed consciousness?"

"Not exactly," says Artemis. She glances to Chang'e. "You know this guy well enough to have been trying to avoid him. You want to explain?"

"Not particularly, but I'll do it," says Chang'e. It's easier if she avoids looking directly at either half of the Doctrine, if she just acts like she's talking to a particularly interesting bit of wall. "Lunar gods manifest on a regular basis all over the world. We grow in people who have enough of an affinity for our specific natures that they might eventually be able to hear us calling to them from the moonlight, and when they accept, we join them. We don't take them over, we don't replace them, we . . . share the space. We are them, and they are us; it's just that the personality travels with the power, so as we step up and down the ladder of divinity, either the god or the host will be more dominant. That means we all tend to begin our growth in the same sort of soil, and our hosts tend to have similar personalities. Any god you meet will have multiple manifestations at any given time. It's the only way we can be sure there's enough of us."

"Enough for what?" asks Roger. He sounds fascinated, and Chang'e isn't surprised. Judy finds this all fascinating too, even after as long as she's been living with it. Any place where the world of gods intersects with the world of men is likely to be enthralling: that's how myths are born, after all. Mortals like to feel like they're walking along the border of a myth.

Still, she hesitates, unsure how much she should say, how much she's *allowed* to say. They never discuss matters of divinity in front of people who aren't Lunars; their history is rich with cautionary tales about Lunars who made that exact mistake, who thought they could trust a lover or a friend and found themselves betrayed, committed to psychiatric care or, worse, handed over to the nearest group of alchemists to be "cured." There are reasons so many cultures yoke madness to the moon, and the Lunar tendency to slide into a person's mind and start speaking plays a large part.

She glances to Artemis and Máni, desperate for salvation that isn't coming. Máni refuses to meet her eyes, while Artemis nods, very slowly.

Returning her attention to Roger—or, more precisely, to the cabinets beside his head, which don't watch her with mild gray eyes and occasionally give commands that restructure the way the world is meant to work—Chang'e takes a deep breath.

"We have to be sure there's enough of us to shine above the Impossible City every night."

The front door slams open, all but punctuating her sentence, and Chang'e turns, eyes very wide, to see who dares intrude upon the Doctrine of Ethos.

Lacus Lenitatis

S mita is surprisingly chatty once they're away from Catrina's place, although she stays at the back of the group, watching as much as participating. Isabella allows herself to slow, drifting back until she paces Smita, matching her step for step.

"You've been with the coven for a while now," she says. "But you've never mentioned anything about living with the incarnate force of Order. I think I would have noticed if you had."

"Funny, I was just thinking I would have noticed if you'd ever said something about having an electric-orange cousin with hooves, but here we are," says Smita. "Looks like we've both been keeping some of our cards close to our chests, hmmm?"

"She's not actually my cousin," says Isabella.

"You don't say."

"She—" Isabella pauses, looking wearily at Smita. "You're not going to let this one go, are you?"

"Nope."

Erin looks back from where she's walking alongside Kelpie, pale eyebrows lifted high. "Everything all right back there?"

"We're great," says Smita sunnily. "Just working through a few things."

Erin looks dubious but faces front once more. Smita looks to Isabella and shrugs.

"I can forgive you for the little lie about your cousin, especially since it upset Catrina, if you can forgive me for not telling you I lived with an incarnate force of the universe. Also, how do you drop that one casually into conversation? 'Hi, I saw your signup sheet at the co-op, I've been trying to wrap my head around the idea that there's this whole magical world running in parallel to the one I've always known, and your nondenominational female-first coven seems like a decent way to ease myself into things, anyway, I'm not a witch or a Wiccan, I'm going to be primed for someone to say something bigoted or indicative of toxic views and might leave permanently at any time, and one of my roommates is the living embodiment of Order, but I try not to hold that against her'? Doesn't exactly flow, now, does it?"

"It does not," agrees Isabella. "Still, after you decided to stick around, it might have been nice to get a heads-up."

"I didn't even know if *you* knew magic was real and not just a way to fleece a rich white lady out of candles and coffee and a nice lunch once a week," says Smita. "It honestly could have gone either way, until today."

"You've been doing ritual work with us for two years, and you didn't know whether I knew magic was real? I think I'm offended."

"Doesn't change anything if you are."

They walk in silence for a few seconds before Isabella nods toward Erin and says, "I knew she was a construct."

"What?"

"That's why I wanted to bring the kid to a coven meeting. You have more experience than any of us with alchemical constructs, and I thought you might be able to help her. But then, I thought you were dating Erin, and that was why she always brought you to the meetings and picked you up after they were finished. I also thought she was a minor personification the alchemists had managed to force to manifest but didn't care enough about to keep track of—one of the Horae, maybe, or something even more intangible than the personification of a singular hour."

"You had that partially right," says Smita. "She's an alchemical construct, and when you compare her to what the alchemists who made her were actually fishing for, I guess you could call her a minor one. But they didn't lose track of her because they didn't care."

"They lost track of me because I broke confinement and went rogue," says Erin, turning to walk backward, facing them. She still manages to miss every crack and break in the sidewalk, her stride never varying. "I bet they say I went feral, since that's what you say about an animal, and they don't want to credit us with full humanity if they don't have to. Am I right?"

She glances at Kelpie, who flushes a deep red-orange and nods, looking almost ashamed of herself. "Yeah," she says, after a momentary pause. "All the c-cuckoos who escaped from Reed's lab are described as having gone feral and turned on their creators."

"Because we're not fully human to them, and that means we're not really people, either, not the way everyone else thinks of people." Erin elbows Kelpie, amiably. "At least Barrow was invested in making sure my brother and I could go to Disney World without causing some sort of a riot, huh? I don't have to deal with being Technicolor or wonder whether the people I meet will see something weird about me. Plenty of people see weird things about me without my needing to have hooves."

"Don't you find her existence a little, well, chaotic?" asks Smita carefully, gesturing to Kelpie.

Erin snorts. "Chaotic? Please. Not compared to you two. She's designed for a purpose, every gene exactly where it's supposed to be, every chromosome expressing itself just so. They made her this way because this was the way they needed her to be if they were going to catch the concept they were trying for. There's not a chaotic cell in her body. Now, you naturals . . ." She shudders. "All willy-nilly, genes combining on a whim, DNA sourced from two unvetted origins, all the mutations and recessive traits a body can hope for—nope. No, thank you. I'll take the orange girl any day of the week. She may be weird-looking, but it's a logical, linear weird-looking." She turns again, so that her back is to the pair. "Don't try to play the chaos card with me."

"Love you too," says Smita warmly. She glances at Isabella, watching the other woman fight to control her expression. "When someone grabs you, pulls you into the magical zone of invisibility cast by a severed hand, and says you have to pretend you're dead long enough for them to convince the people they work for that they're a killer, you listen. Erin did a lot more than that to convince me—"

"Because I'd had several trial runs before I found the argument you were willing to listen to," calls Erin, pitching her voice so it will carry, not turning a third time.

Kelpie looks nervous. Erin pats her reassuringly on the shoulder.

"Don't worry. People who don't see the orange girl aren't going to pay attention to a totally innocuous statement that only becomes ominous in context."

"Um. If you're sure."

"I am," says Erin, almost serenely.

"—than just light a Hand of Glory, but that went a long way," says Smita, as if a whole conversation hadn't just occurred in the middle of her sentence. "When that happens to you, you start believing in the alchemical world in a hurry. And also, you latch on to the person who was ordered to kill you and refused to do it, and you hang on to them for dear life, because no one else is ever going to take care of you the way that they will. Erin didn't kill me. That means I'm her problem now. Everyone else is just sort of collateral damage."

Erin seems to find this funny. She laughs, long and bright and absolutely delighted, the sound ringing off the buildings to either side.

They've been working their way deeper and deeper into the residential part of Berkeley as they walked, moving away from the part of the city where Isabella lives with her family, and even away from the overpriced modernity of Catrina's neighborhood, into something older and more settled. The houses here are as old as the city itself, and judging by the paint jobs and signs of renovation, many of their occupants are generational homeowners, people who could never afford a house in the modern market but who inherited one from a parent or grandparent and are holding on for dear life, refusing to be shaken off the moving back of the great beast that is the Bay Area real estate market.

All four women watch this change in their own way, and if they thought to share those ways with one another, they would understand so much that is currently unknown to them, but like most people, they aren't in the habit of sharing every thought that crosses their minds without filtration or consideration.

To Isabella, the houses around them now are a triumph and a tragedy. A triumph because she sees how many of them have the kind of herb garden that takes decades to establish, the kind of paint that hasn't been touched up in twice that long, because there's been no need; a little faded is more than good enough when you're never looking to sell. She sees the people who got in early and never let go, burrowing as deep as they could while the burrowing was still possible. And she sees the number of houses with freshly landscaped yards, newly repainted façades, and understands how quickly those legacy houses will be gone, how soon the inevitable march of progress will wear these small communities down, until only the lucky remain.

Erin sees much the same thing but tempered by the patterns that move through the neighborhoods, the little ways the established neighbors support each other and shun the newcomers, even when those new arrivals had nothing to do with the displacement of the previous residents. She sees the way this will foster resentment, how that resentment will fester and grow, until community collapses, broken past the point of any lasting repair. She sees the cracks through which not only light gets through but the twisting roots of weeds that will tear the whole edifice down. Erin, as always, sees the end of all things. In her view, no one is lucky.

Kelpie sees a whole new world of possibilities and potential, filled with things she's never seen before, things she never even dreamed. She sees marvels everywhere she looks, a world woven out of miracles, and she sees nothing but hope and glory. The world is beautiful. She sees none of the history, none of the chaos, none of the cracks in the foundation. For her, this is a perfect moment which may well last forever, and that's enough.

For Smita, the only one of them who still sees things mostly as a normal human would, who still walks through a mostly ordinary world, she sees a neighborhood. A little shabby compared to the ones a few blocks over, but still well outside the reach of most families. She'd feel bad about the fact that she lives very close to here, if not for the fact that she lives in someone else's house, and lives there in part because she's been legally dead for years, ever since Erin convinced her to fake her own murder for the sake of fooling the American Alchemical Congress. Dodger has run the numbers a hundred times, trying to find a way to narrow the gap between her first true synchronization with Roger and their inevitable ascension to claim the Doctrine. There isn't one. For them to have the time they need to settle and mature, Smita must spend a period among the lands of the dead, unable to reveal herself for fear of alchemical intervention.

Smita hasn't existed for slightly over a decade. She uses a dead woman's social security number; she works in a position well beneath her capabilities, using an assumed name and a fraudulent diploma. She never graduated college. Her original career path is outside her grasp, as is the comfort of her family, who mourned her long ago. But she has a supposedly rented room in a comfortable middle-class household, and that has to be enough, because she's not getting anything more. ("Supposedly" because Roger and Dodger own the house, and they sometimes forget to collect rent from her even when she's standing in front of them trying to press money into their hands.) She lives the closest thing a walking dead woman can to a charmed life, and so she sees a neighborhood, full of people living freely, living loudly, *living*. And she envies them, and she never sees how soon it all might end.

On they walk until the rainbow house with its wild glass windows comes into view. Isabella laughs. "We're going to the *clown house*?" she asks. "Oh, you never told me you lived in the *clown house*."

"Is that what people call it?" asks Smita, with real interest.

"Most call it the circus house, but my son Luis always calls it the clown house, and I like his name for it better," says Isabella. "You live there?"

"We do," says Erin.

"It's a little more . . . busy than I assumed your home would be," says Isabella, with a vain attempt at diplomacy.

"You mean 'chaotic,' don't you?" asks Erin.

"Is this going to be a thing?" asks Smita. "Because I *will* squirt you both with a spray bottle and put you in opposite corners like naughty cats, I swear. Yes, it's chaotic, but it's a purposeful chaos, and Erin does just fine. Yes, we both live there. Some friends of ours own the place."

"That's the nicest way I've ever heard you describe the wonder twins," says Erin dryly.

"They were my friends before you were," says Smita.

"Doesn't mean they're anybody's friends now," says Erin. "Remember the food chain."

Kelpie looks perplexed. Isabella goes past that, all the way to concern.

"Excuse me?" she says. "The food chain? What is that supposed to mean?"

"It means the same people who made me made *them*, and they're not as easily defined as I am." Erin looks to Kelpie. "Care to explain for your friend?"

Kelpie looks down at the ground, which only brings her hooves into view. She lifts her head again, tilting it back until she's looking at nothing but the seemingly endless sky overhead. In a monotone, she says, "James Reed was the heir, creation, and adopted son of Asphodel Baker, the greatest North American alchemist ever denied entry into the Alchemical Congress. He continued her work after she died, trying to achieve the one thing that had eluded her for her entire life: he believed, as she had, that if he could force the Doctrine of Ethos to personify and embody as other natural forces had already done he would be able to use it to seize control of the Impossible City."

"We've all read the Up-and-Under books," says Isabella, impatient. "Why are you explaining them to me?"

"I'm not," she says. "Asphodel Baker wrote those books to encode her theories into the public consciousness so they wouldn't die when she did. She wanted her ideas to live on forever. But everything I just said is real, from before she wrote the books. She made Reed, and no one knows how—if she kept notes, he burned them, because he wasn't as interested in sharing information as his creator had been. She made Reed, and she told him to seek the City, capture the Doctrine, and continue her work, and so for more than a century, that's what he did."

"That's not all he did," says Erin. "He knew whoever took the City would take the world, and he wanted to have as much of the universe under his control as possible when that happened. He obtained a more traditionally made construct, named Leigh Barrow, who had somehow managed to become an alchemist in her own right after killing her creator. With his aid, she was able to personify some of the minor forces—minor only in contrast to the Doctrine, which is major beyond all logic. My brother, Darren, and I were two of those forces. Darren died. I didn't."

"I'm sorry about your brother," says Isabella.

"So am I," says Erin. "No matter how many times we've gone back over things, we've never been able to find a way to save him. Not without losing everything else. Darren stays dead, or the timeline collapses."

"Which would be bad," interjects Smita.

"So this Reed fellow, he tried to embody some force so big it makes Order seem small, and he failed?" asks Isabella, and pales when Erin shakes her head and gestures for the others to follow her toward the house.

"No," she says. "That would be the easy way to have done this. He tried to embody some force that makes Order seem small, and he *succeeded*. Twice over, since it turns out the Doctrine is so big you can't stuff it into a single body and have room for that body to know how to be human."

Isabella doesn't say anything, and doesn't pale further, but does stumble as they approach the garden gate, tripping over a little irregularity in the sidewalk.

Erin is polite enough not to comment, just opens the gate and holds it for the rest of them.

"They're not that bad, really," says Smita. "The way Reed's protocol had them grow up means they thought they were normal people for a lot longer than most personifications do, and so they still have a lot of little normal-people habits and quirks that you don't necessarily see from the ones who grew up in a lab."

"You know, natural incarnations are more common than the artificial ones," says Isabella, finally sounding like she feels comfortable contributing to the discussion. Kelpie looks at her. "Summer, Winter, the various faces of the Moon, all of them personify without alchemical intervention."

"Maybe so, but that hasn't been my experience," says Smita. "People tell me natural incarnations are a thing, but they never seem to show up when I'm around. I met a very unpleasant lab-grown potential Winter once, if you can call 'refusing to let her into the garden while she practically frothed at the mouth' meeting someone. She went away when Erin came out and was terrifying at her." She gives the other woman a look of such adoring fondness that it seems hard to believe they're not together, or that Smita doesn't want them to be.

"Your experience is a unique one," says Isabella.

"Really? How many personifications have you met?" Smita sounds genuinely interested, and Kelpie looks to Isabella, eager to hear her answer.

It's Isabella's turn to redden faintly, blush appearing high on the arch of her cheekbones. "Before this week, two."

"I live with five," says Smita. "So even when we account for the people you've met, we're still leading with the artificial."

"We're losing the thread," says Erin. "Kelpie? Finish my story."

Kelpie ducks her head. "Reed continued Baker's work, striving for the Doctrine of Ethos and, by extension, for control of the Impossible

City. He was successful in 1986, when twin children were born to one of his incubators—"

"*Incubators?*" squeaks Isabella, sounding appalled.

"—and verified as potential vessels for the Doctrine. They were separated and placed in the mundane world to mature, one under the care of alchemists Reed had personally selected, one in the custody of a neutral family. As they grew, their connection became apparent and, after a certain point, unbreakable. Attempts were made to separate them, to no avail. They would re-entangle despite all efforts, making it impossible to isolate them, even though they hadn't physically met since birth."

Erin gestures for her to stop before digging her house keys out of her pocket and picking up the thread. "In 2008, shortly after the murder of Smita Mehta, the pair fully connected on the alchemical plane, manifesting their full potential in the physical world for the first time. The Berkeley Earthquake was the result, and it scared them back into separation. Eight years later, they would reunite and defeat their creator, finally ascending to their place as the incarnate Doctrine of Ethos. Long may they get on my fucking nerves, forget to buy milk, and generally drive me to distraction." She unlocks the door and shoves it open, so hard it slams against the opposing wall.

"I want to talk more about that 'incubators' comment," says Isabella, preparing to follow her inside.

"We use the language we're given," says Erin, and steps in, Isabella close behind. Smita moves to follow, then looks back at Kelpie, who hasn't moved. She seems to have become rooted to the porch, staring at the door like she's afraid it might snap shut and swallow her whole.

"You coming?" asks Smita.

"I should," says Kelpie. "Isabella says it's not safe for me to be alone."

And she doesn't move.

"Okay, so come on."

"I . . . can't."

Smita takes a step back, letting the door swing shut, and moves back toward Kelpie. "Why can't you?"

"I'm . . . I'm what they were talking about. I'm a fake person. I didn't know I was a fake person until just a few days ago, and I know how that sounds now that I'm out in the world where lab accidents don't turn people into monsters, and the shape you have is always basically the shape you were born with, but that was what they told me and I believed them, because I didn't know any better."

"That's all right," says Smita soothingly. "We don't use words like 'real' or 'fake' here—they're the kind of abstracts we don't need in this house—but even if we did, you wouldn't be the only one. Erin was made in a lab. So were Roger and Dodger, and the kids. I'm the only one who lives here who wasn't."

"But what if they're mad because I was helping the alchemists they ran away from try to find them? What if they look at me and go 'no, you aren't any tangible concept, the universe doesn't need to personify you, go away' and they make me be *not*? I know what Reed's cuckoos can do! I've seen the research!"

"They really did treat you like you were one of them, didn't they?" Smita sighs. "We don't do things the way the alchemists you're used to do them. We don't want to. If they look at you and think you're not supposed to exist, Erin and I will make sure they don't do anything unpleasant. And who cares if you're not a tangible concept? What *do* you embody, if that's not a rude question? Living with this lot hasn't really taught me much about dealing with other embodiments, or how they handle things among themselves."

"Not like I know, either," says Kelpie. "We were working on a project that was supposed to embody the adjuncts of the Lunars. Chang'e's Rabbit, the Old Man's Dog, that sort of thing. They used to appear on their own, but a few centuries ago, they stopped. If we could get one of them to manifest, we'd be able to summon and maybe even control the Lunar they belong with. And since the best-known companions go with some of the most powerful Lunars, that was a good goal to be working toward if . . ."

She stops then, looking guilty. Smita smiles, just a little.

"Do Lunars have some sort of access to the City?"

Kelpie nods, silent.

"Thought so. Come on. We need to join the others." Smita re-opens the door.

This time, Kelpie follows her inside.

The house is smaller and warmer than Catrina's, and while it isn't particularly cluttered or unkempt, it seems dirtier, in a vital, living sense, like dirt is *allowed* here, while it has been so thoroughly forbidden at Catrina's house that it would never dare enter. The walls have the well-scrubbed appearance of something that has *been* scrubbed, not merely wiped down, because at one point it needed to be.

Kelpie, who spent most of her life in sterile lab conditions, immediately decides she likes this much better. This house looks like people live in it, like it's happy to have people living in it, and that makes more of a difference than she could possibly have realized before it was placed in front of her. This is a good house.

This is a good house, but people are arguing very nearby, a multitude of overlapping voices. It sounds like a budget meeting in the lab, except that none of them are talking about resource allocation. Smita looks toward the noise, frowns, and takes Kelpie by the elbow.

"Come on," she says. "I have a few people you ought to meet while they take care of whatever all that's about."

Kelpie blinks but lets herself be pulled away from the sound of voices and up the stairs to the landing on the second floor.

Even more than the entry hall, the second-floor hall is filled with light, more than the windows can adequately explain, although the sun pours through them in honeyed sheets, illuminating the little motes of dust dancing in the air, turning them into a pale, phantom aura of gold around the pair as they move through. There are no artificial lights. The sun just seems to refract off of itself somehow, growing bigger and stronger within the enclosed space.

Tall bookshelves have been pushed up against the walls, and braided rugs in a wide variety of contrasting colors pepper the floor, almost like someone has been trying to replicate the experience of standing outside, looking at the house. One of the windows has a set of prisms hanging from it, adding tiny, glimmering rainbows to the scene.

The shouting is quieter here. Kelpie relaxes marginally, realizing how much tension she was carrying after their walk and conversation. Being out in the open is still new to her, and no matter how aware she is that most people won't see anything strange about her, it's difficult not to be afraid.

Smita watches, smiling a little as she sees Kelpie straighten.

"That's better," she says. "Did you know you wrap your tail around your leg when you're worried about something? You shouldn't do that. You'll cut off the circulation, and I don't know if even the most mundane doctor in the world could treat you without noticing you don't have feet."

"What do feet have to do with anything?"

"Normally, when people lose circulation to their leg, we worry about them possibly losing toes."

"Well, I already lost all of mine, so I guess I'm ahead of the game," says Kelpie, and giggles.

Smita's smile widens. "Good. I was afraid we'd traumatized you, and we still have so many opportunities to do that." She moves toward a closed door. Someone has placed a small whiteboard in the middle of it, and a complicated mathematical equation has been written there, the numbers surrounded by surprisingly well-drawn wildflowers in dry-erase marker. Smita knocks, lightly.

A feminine voice shouts, "Go *away.*"

"It's Smita," says Smita. "Dodger is downstairs making someone else's life more difficult than it technically needs to be, if the yelling is anything to judge by. I have a guest."

"You never have guests." There's the rattling sound of a chain being undone, and then the door is cracked open, and a face appears in the gap.

Kelpie blinks. So does the girl, whose eyes widen briefly at the sight of the orange woman in the hallway, before she opens the door wider.

"You can both come in," she says, in a tone that implies she's granting some impossible favor.

"Thank you," says Smita. "Kelpie, this is Kim. Kim, this is Kelpie."

"Nice to, um, meet you," says Kelpie, as she follows Smita into the room. She has to fight the urge to stare.

Kim isn't being nearly so careful. She closes the door behind the pair, turning to watch them.

"Your friend's orange," she says.

"Yes," says Smita.

"Your friend has a *tail*," she says.

Kelpie feels like she should contribute something at this point, so she says, "Your hair is green."

"No, it's not," says Kim.

"I mean, it looks white, mostly, but when the light hits it at the right angle, it's green," says Kelpie. "I didn't know human hair could look like that. It's really pretty, but if we're saying obvious things, it's the most obvious thing about you."

Kim starts to protest, then stops, and frowns at her. "It won't dye. I've tried, even though it makes me sick to my stomach to even think about dyeing it, but then the dye rolls right off as soon as it's dry. That's chemically impossible."

"'Impossible' is a thing people say when they want something not to have happened and don't have a good reason why it wouldn't," says Kelpie.

Kim stands up straighter, color leaving her cheeks. "Get out," she says, voice gone cold.

"What?" asks Kelpie.

"What?" echoes Smita.

"That's what Leigh used to say when—that's what the alchemist who raised me used to say, and I hated her, and I'm not going to sit here and listen to whatever one of her students has to say, even if you *are* orange."

"I wasn't one of Leigh Barrow's students," protests Kelpie. "I never even met her! The lab where I worked didn't open until after she was already dead! I'm pretty sure that's where I was made, since waking up there is the first thing I can remember. They told me it was because I'd been in a really bad accident that scrambled up my head, and since I already knew how to talk and do a lot of simple things, like dressing myself or running the autoclave, I never had a reason to think they were lying to me. But Leigh Barrow didn't teach me or create me or anything, and I can't know what of the things I've learned are bad to say if people chase me away as soon as I say one of them!"

Kim pauses. "You're artificial?"

"You didn't pick up on that just by looking at her?" asks Smita dryly.

Kim shoots her a sharp look. "She could have been a modified human. They came through the lab sometimes, people who'd decided two hands weren't enough, and given themselves prehensile tails, or feet like monkeys. The other alchemists scoffed at them behind their backs, called them 'Moreaus' and acted like they were fools for making themselves less than human. I always thought they were braver than the other alchemists."

"Braver? How?"

"A normal alchemist is so dangerous because they look just like everybody else. At least the ones who push themselves outside the bounds of what can be considered 'normal' give people a fighting chance to know they're in danger. And no, most people don't believe in magic anymore, so they wouldn't necessarily see those modifications before the alchemist attacked, but alchemists aren't wizards wandering around with nasty wands they can point at people and shoot spells out of. They need to get close enough to open a vial or throw something in your direction, or have the time to set runes and triggers for you to stumble over. But if an alchemist who'd modified themselves attacked somebody, and the person lived, they'd be able to find who hurt them. They'd be able to *see* it. Can't not believe in what hurts you."

"Meaning they lost deniability," says Smita, slowly.

Kim nods. "Yeah. So I thought she'd just been messing around with her own composition for fun, or because it was useful, or hell, because she thought orange skin made her tits look great! Who knows why an alchemist does anything?"

"I'm not an alchemist," says Kelpie, voice tight.

"Then what are you?"

"I'm . . ." She pauses. There are so many possible answers. None of them are good, or easy. Part of her hates the man who came to examine the lab, because he killed Margaret, but he didn't do it fast enough to stop Margaret from telling her the truth. The truth is complicated. The truth is oozing all over everything like alkahest, melting it away, turning it into something new. She was happy with the lies. She was happy believing she had a family missing her in faraway Florida, that one day she'd go back to them, that one day she'd be a normal human woman, and not have to worry all the time about someone seeing her on the street and knowing her for something made, not born. She knew who she was, and where she belonged, and she was *happy*.

And now she doesn't know any of that. Is she a lab technician? Is she Artemis's Hind? Is she a person who got hurt in an accident, or is she someone's science project? Even that question isn't as simple as it seems on the surface. Construct or cuckoo, manikin or monster, there are so many options for a made thing. She worked on the projects that apparently created her, she knows they used Baker's seed material at their root: she's a cuckoo, and the longer she stands near this girl with the cornsilk hair and the golden-brown eyes, the more she recognizes her as kin. They're vessels filled from the same well, not sisters, but . . . cousins, maybe. Distant relations spun on the same wheel and fired in the same kiln.

"I'm Kelpie," she says finally, and the words are flat on her tongue, like water that's been sitting out in the open air for too long, allowed to turn stagnant and stale. "That's all. They made me in the lab. I used to think I was one of them, and now I think I may be something they invented. The only thing I'm completely sure of is my name, because at this point, it's mine, and I'm not giving it back."

"She's a cuckoo, like you," says Smita.

Kim blinks several times, and then, to Kelpie's surprise and dismay, fat tears start rolling down her cheeks. They're not like Margaret's final tears: they're just water, not her eyes melting out of her head. Wiping them away, Kim turns to face the desk, no longer looking at Kelpie or Smita.

"There are no cuckoos like me, except my brother, and he's not enough," she says, voice gone dull.

"I don't understand," says Kelpie.

Kim sniffles—a thick, snotty sound—and turns back to Kelpie, still crying. "They made us to embody the Doctrine of Ethos, and we were supposed to be *perfect*," she says. "They used everything they learned from every failed pair, and they made us. We were going to manifest. We were going to catch the Doctrine. We were so close. We were going to be perfect, and we were going to be free, because as soon as we manifested, we were going to blow those bastards down. We had a *plan*." Her expression is pleading, desperate for Kelpie to understand. "All we had to do was survive long enough for them to give us what they made us to carry, and we could walk away, me and my brother, the living Doctrine. But instead, the last round of failures somehow overpowered the man who made us all, and they claimed the Doctrine, and then they wouldn't give it *back*."

She turns her face to the wall. "They took what we were made to carry, and they carried it away. Tim and I, we'd been entangled since before we could walk. I didn't know where he ended and I began. And suddenly we were two separate people, with two separate bodies, and it was so wrong it hurt, and there was nothing we could do about it. There's *still* nothing we can do about it. No one knows whether the Doctrine is going to get addicted to being human and stick around the way the other forces have. Maybe when Roger and Dodger die—*if* they die—it goes back to being nebulous and unconcerned with humanity. Or maybe it sticks around. Either way, it won't choose us. By the time they're dead, we'll be old. It'll want better hosts. Clean hosts. Hosts that didn't already fail."

"I'm sorry," says Kelpie, awkwardly. "I don't know much about the Doctrine, really. All Margaret ever liked to say was that the alchemists working for James Reed had managed to incarnate it, and then the cuckoos who were supposed to carry it went rogue and ran away before they could be properly put to use. They're real scared about it being out there in the wild."

"Why?" asks Kim, her tears finally stopping in the face of her confusion.

"They—the alchemists, I mean—are trying to get to a place called the Impossible City. The way Reed embodied the Doctrine of Ethos means the cuckoos who carry it have the authority to claim the Tower if they want to, and the alchemists want to get there first."

"But the Queen of Wands . . ." says Kim.

"The Queen of Wands is dead," says Kelpie. "Asphodel Baker claimed the crown before she wrote the Up-and-Under books, and since her death, the Tower has been standing empty, and there's no one in her parlor."

"The way you people treat those books like a religion baffles me sometimes," says Smita. "They're just kiddie books."

"They're a primer on modern alchemical reality," says Kim, somewhat stiffly.

"That's why Baker wrote them," says Kelpie. "She wanted to solidify her concepts about reality and spread them as wide as she could, because the person who got there first would win. Baum tried to unseat her with his Emerald City, but he made it too real. He spent too much time there. The Impossible City isn't real. It can't be. A thing that's real has been defined until it doesn't feel fully flexible the way something a little bit hazy does. The Impossible City is impossible in part because it has to encompass everything that everyone in the world can possibly ask it to be."

"So the alchemists want the Impossible City," says Smita. "We knew that. What does that have to do with Roger and Dodger being out on their own?"

"Baker proposed the idea of embodying the Doctrine because she believed it was the key to universal control, and hence to claiming the City itself," says Kelpie. "The City *is* the universe. Whoever controls it, controls everything. Reed continued her work because he wanted to control reality."

Kim wrinkles her nose. "Roger and Dodger can't control the universe. They're too weird."

"Alchemical constructs generally are," says Kelpie. She pauses and then, laughing nervously, adds, "Which includes me, I guess."

"I guess."

Kelpie looks to Smita. "Why did you want me to meet her? She's nice, but I don't understand."

"She's not terrifying, is she?" asks Smita. "She's just a teenage girl who was almost the human incarnation of Math, and now she isn't. But even if she never gets to be Math, she'll always be Kim. She'll always be a really real person, who also happens to be a cuckoo. How you're made doesn't matter. It's what you do once you exist that matters."

"Oh," says Kelpie. "I guess that . . . that makes sense." She looks back to Kim. "It was very nice to meet you. I'm sorry you didn't get to be what they made you to be."

"That makes two of us," says Kim, and smiles, expression at odds with her words. "It was nice to meet you, too. I hope you figure out what you're supposed to be, and that it's something you don't have to be if you don't want to."

"Ready to go downstairs?" asks Smita, almost gently.

Kelpie sighs, then nods.

"Ready as I'll ever be," she says.

Lacus Spei

TIMELINE: AUGUST 18, 2017.
THREE DAYS TO THE ECLIPSE.

Chang'e is still staring at the doorway when two women appear, one strawberry blonde with a peaches-and-cream complexion that looks like it would be personally offended by the suggestion that it might either freckle or tan, the other black-haired and brown-skinned, expression implying that she would rather be walking into a dentist's office in Hell than this simple residential kitchen. Behind them, Chang'e hears the door swing shut and then open again, more sedately this time. Footsteps ascend the stairs, the two women in the doorway blocking whoever they belong to from view.

The blonde folds her arms as she looks at the group, slowly taking their measure. The black-haired woman looks less self-assured. She's trying not to seem concerned, but she's clearly worried about being in the house, surrounded by people she has to know aren't entirely human. All three Lunars are stepped up, and the air around them sparkles like it's been filled with floating glitter. Roger and Dodger are less visibly inhuman, but their calm acceptance of the shimmer in the air has to mark them in some way as outside the norm.

Roger lifts his chin toward the new arrival. "Erin. 'S'up?"

"I feel like I should be the one asking you that, since you're apparently hosting a kitchen party without having warned your housemates." The blonde continues to eye the group, somewhat dubiously. "They're sparkly. Elementals or Lunars?"

"Lunars," says Roger. "Erin, meet Chang'e, Artemis, and I'm sorry, I forgot your name."

"Máni."

"Right, Máni. Two of the big three, and one of the Scandinavians, if I'm not mistaken." Roger phrases that like he *could* be mistaken, when everyone in the room knows he physically can't be.

Or at least Chang'e assumes he can't be mistaken. She doesn't actually know what the Doctrine is capable of, especially not now that she knows it's been divided between two bodies, Math distinct from Language and possessed of its own motivations and desires. This is all far more complicated than she was expecting, and she doesn't like it. Judy was right to do her best to stay away from the incarnate Doctrine, and all Chang'e can do now is wish her mortal aspect had been a little better at playing keep-away.

"Moon gods, fascinating," says Erin. She gestures to the woman next to her. "This is Isabella."

"Oh, the head of Smita's little coven," says Dodger. "She's told us about you."

Isabella lifts her chin, expression composed and stubborn. "I'm an hechicera," she says, almost like a challenge.

"I'm a mathematician," says Dodger. Roger rolls his eyes and drinks more coffee. She slants him a sideways look. "What? I thought we were making declarative statements. She's an hechicera, I'm a mathematician, we've presumably both trained and studied for our positions, why shouldn't they be on the same level?"

"Because she just confessed to being a sorceress, and you're being flippant."

"I'm not being flippant!"

Isabella frowns, deeper with every second that passes. She looks to Erin. "These are the housemates you wanted me to meet?" she asks.

"Some of them, yeah," says Erin. She puts her index fingers in her mouth and whistles shrilly, the sound incredibly loud in the enclosed space. Chang'e winces as she, along with the others, turns to focus fully on Erin, who drops her hands.

"Great, *thank* you," she says, sharply. "Isabella, these are Roger and Dodger, my housemates, who own the place. They're shitty roommates, decent landlords, and the incarnate Doctrine of Ethos."

"Hello," says Roger, lifting his coffee in greeting.

"Your names rhyme," says Isabella, sounding awe-struck.

"Alchemists have taken the concept of 'sympathetic magic' and twisted it until it started to scream for mercy," says Dodger. "The people who made us should never have been allowed near children. I sometimes think the universe decided we were the ones who were going to manifest because we had to grow up with the worst names. You want mean, drop a girl named 'Dodger' on an elementary school playground with an endless supply of dodgeball courts and a whole bunch of pre-teen assholes who believe in nominative determinism."

"You're an hechicera?" asks Roger. "How is that?"

"Like any other magical profession in the modern day: doesn't bring in much money, but I get to set my own hours and the people who come looking for my services really, really need me to help them," says Isabella, sounding a little less awed, a little more matter-of-fact. "I can't do as much as I'd like. Being an hechicera doesn't automatically give me a deep connection to the universe. I can nudge it along, but I can't work large-scale change."

"No earthquakes for her," says Dodger, and sips her coffee.

"No earthquakes for *anyone*," says Chang'e sternly. "Shaking the world to pieces does no one any good."

"Sometimes it makes things clearer," says Roger. "All right, Erin, I know why the kitchen's full of moon gods, but why did you bring us a sorceress? Is she hiding from the alchemists?"

"Only in the sense that everyone with sense is hiding from the alchemists, but that's not why she's here. She found a runaway cuckoo. The most minor one I've seen so far—they're apparently using Asphodel's remaining material for anything these days. And I figured if she's going to be dragging alchemical constructs to her coven meetings, it was probably time we sat down and had a serious talk with her about those little chaos pits she's been digging with her coven."

"Chaos pits?" asks Artemis blankly.

"She's an hechicera steering a coven of people with about as much magical skill as they have sense, which is to say, most of them don't have much to speak of, but they have enough to chant in tandem and try to force their will on the world," says Erin. "They've been using brute-force elementalism to gouge holes in the surface of reality, and they don't always remember to scoop all the elements they've called back out of the hole when they're finished. Which means it crusts over and curdles, and becomes a nasty little chaos pit, just waiting for someone to trip and fall into it. They're not big enough to do a lot of damage, but they can really ruin someone's day."

Isabella looks horrified. "I thought you were *kidding* before! None of our workings were intended to do anything like *that*," she says.

"When you grow a carrot, you've grown something delicious and nourishing, and that's great, but then when you pull it up to eat it, you leave a hole," says Erin. "Did you intend to grow a hole? No, you intended to grow a carrot. The hole was a natural consequence of the carrot. Does that make you a bad person for making a hole? No. Does it fill your lawn with burrowing crayfish taking advantage of the situation if you don't make sure to put dirt back in your holes when you're done harvesting your carrots? Possibly. Very, very possibly."

"That metaphor was a little tortured," says Roger.

Erin shrugs. "Never said I was good with words, now, did I."

Dodger cranes her neck, looking past Erin and Isabella. "So where's the cuckoo?"

"She went upstairs with Smita," says Erin. "Probably bothering one of the trouble teens to try and calm her down. She was raised by the alchemists who made her, and apparently she somehow thought she was a real girl until a day or so ago, when there was some sort of incident in their lab. Now she's here, she's all stressed out and spun up, she doesn't really understand anything that's going on, and she knows who the two of you are. They've told her stories about you. So I'm pretty sure the idea of actually meeting you has her terrified, and Smita wants to get her to chill out before she does the scary thing."

"We're not scary," says Roger. Dodger gives him a complicated look, some wordless exchange passing between them, and he sighs. "Okay. I guess if you were raised by alchemists who wanted you to think of us as the bogeymen under your bed, we'd be sort of scary. Or if you don't like being around people who're in active negotiations with the universe most of the time. Or— Dammit, Dodge, stop making sense."

"Or if you don't like telepaths," says Erin, dryly. Catching the bewildered looks from Isabella and the various Lunars, she explains, "Because of the way they were made, these two don't need to talk. They do it because they like the sound of their own voices, and because they're the kind of asshole that thinks it's funny to make the rest of us listen to them. They can't read your mind, thankfully, or I'd have to kill them while they slept, but they can read each other's minds. And that is just one of the many, many reasons Roger and I are no longer sleeping together."

"The main one being that you were only sleeping with me in the first place because Barrow ordered you to, and you needed a reason to stay close enough to keep an eye on me," says Roger without rancor.

Erin shrugs broadly. "We all do fucked-up shit when the alchemists get involved."

"Which is why I'm here," says Artemis, in the sort of tone used by kindergarten teachers trying to yank their class back onto the topic. "I'm not originally from this area. I transferred to Berkeley a month ago, because the alchemists around here have been all up in arms, enough so that people have noticed."

"Before you say you didn't notice," says Dodger peevishly to Roger, "please remember that you once didn't notice the kitchen was on fire for almost ten minutes, even though we were all yelling and trying to put it out. And then once you did, you just told it not to be on fire and it wasn't."

"Oh, yeah. I do remember that," says Roger.

Dodger sighs, looking to Artemis. "Please, continue."

"I . . ." Artemis glances to Isabella, clearly uncomfortable. Talking about Lunar matters in front of rogue alchemical constructs is one thing. Talking about them in front of an ordinary human woman is something else altogether. It's clear that she doesn't like it, but she pushes on, forcing herself to continue. "We know they figured out how many of us there were a few years ago, and started picking at our fringes. Minor Lunars began disappearing, especially the ones in areas where they didn't have a large pantheon to turn to for protection. The moon doesn't know whether you're urban or rural when it speaks to you. The moon knows whether or not you're in a position to listen. So some of us wind up pretty isolated, with no idea what's going on anywhere else. They orbit solo, and the moon tells them what to do, and either they break or they find a pantheon to belong to. Things began getting bad a little while after most of the alchemists' leadership died. We figure that cleared the board for some of the younger alchemists, the ones with big ideas who hadn't been able to put them into play before."

"Why hunt Lunars?" asks Roger. "No offense, but you're pretty minor as manifestations go. You've always seemed more like a habit of reality than a necessity in the modern world. Most of you can't even affect the world through your manifestations."

"Most?" asks Chang'e.

"There are exceptions, but I've never heard of a Lunar strong enough to shift the tides or build a bridge of birds between the Earth and the Moon." He slips so easily into stressing the words as the proper names they sometimes are. It would be impressive coming from almost anyone else.

Chang'e hears the echoes of all the things he isn't saying around every word he speaks, and she's not impressed.

"I don't know why," says Artemis.

"I think our guest upstairs gave us a large part of it," says Erin. "The alchemists are trying to take the City before you two assholes get around to it."

Dodger blinks.

Roger does the same.

For just a moment, the familial relationship between them is so obvious, it's almost glaring. Chang'e glances away.

"What the hell do we want with the Impossible City?" asks Dodger. "That place is getting by just fine without us. It probably has some sort of civic government that doesn't need a pair of untrained weirdoes bumbling in and trying to take over."

"The alchemists want the City so badly, they probably can't even conceive of someone who doesn't," says Erin.

Footsteps on the stairs herald the return of the people missing from this conversation. Erin steps to the side. Isabella does the same, and a moment later, Smita and an impossible girl appear in the doorway.

Smita is a familiar sight in this house, as comfortable and understood as the walls, if a stranger to the three newcomers. The girl beside her is not. The girl, whose skin is the color of the sky at sunrise, a bright and cheerful orange that has never appeared on anything mammalian, and was never meant to, is so clearly artificial that she barely needs her over-vivid complexion to tell them of her origins. She has the eyes of a prey animal, with horizontal pupils, their deep orange barely visible against the brighter orange of her irises. Instead of feet, she has hooves, and Chang'e shudders to think of how many small skeletal adjustments must have been needed to make that possible. Bipeds aren't made to be redesigned casually or on the fly. The human body is enough of a ridiculous miracle without starting to screw around with the way it fits together.

Something sways behind the orange girl, and looking more carefully, Chang'e realizes it's a tail, tufted at the end like a lion or a qilin. That's what this girl looks like—Chang'e can't quite think of her as a woman, not with her impossible anatomy and the wide-eyed expression on her face—she looks like an alchemist's attempt to make a qilin in the material world. She's close enough to human that she'll be visible to non-alchemists, but they'll see her as a normal person, someone who belongs in a normal setting. They won't see her as she is.

She's not the furthest thing from natural that Chang'e's ever seen, even in this specific incarnation. But she's pushing the limits in a way that bends the world around her, ever so slightly, making it seem thinner than it ought to be. Closer to the edges of the everything.

"This is Kelpie," says Erin, in a very slightly protective tone. She even shifts her position, putting herself slightly between the newcomer and the rest of the room. Interesting, that she'd be that protective so quickly. Chang'e wonders if that's normal for her, if she goes around finding lost puppies to adopt.

This is an odd puppy, if so.

"Hello, Kelpie," says Roger. "That's an interesting name. It comes from a Celtic water horse, a shapeshifter. Are you a shapeshifter?"

"If I'm supposed to be, I never figured out exactly how," says Kelpie. Her voice is soft and sweet, a little high, with no discernable accent. The hardest accent to hear is always the one rooted where you're standing, and so Chang'e supposes she grew up very near here. If she grew up at all. Maybe the alchemists made her at the age she is right now, setting her loose in an early, ill-defined adulthood. "I always wanted to be a shapeshifter, though. Just think hard and you won't be a color that's visible from space anymore."

"Kelpies also killed people," says Dodger. "Are you a killer?"

"I was a lab technician until yesterday," says Kelpie. "I never killed anybody, but I guess the things I prepared for other people to work with probably included bits of dead people. Alchemy does, a lot. Are you the missing cuckoos?"

"We are," says Roger.

"Oh. There are some people who really, really want to find you."

"That's not much of a surprise," says Roger. "Fortunately, we're not easy to find when we don't want to be found."

Chang'e snorts.

Roger looks toward her, eyebrows rising in mild curiosity. "Yes?" he asks.

"Sorry, it's just that I—that Judy—ran right into you. You weren't difficult to find at all."

"Ah," he says. "Well, most people wouldn't have recognized me for anything out of the ordinary. Not even most alchemists, if they didn't know me already—and I don't know whether any of the alchemists who would actually recognize me are still alive."

"Reed had pictures," says Erin. "Reed had so many pictures. And class transcripts, medical records, basically all the bullshit an absent but arrogant parent might want to collect. He had that stuff on both of you, even. I doubt it was all destroyed when you burned his lab down."

Dodger wrinkles her nose, looks down into her coffee cup, and says nothing. Chang'e is sure Roger is getting an earful none of the rest of them can hear. Telepathy is a two-edged sword.

"I learned all about the project that made you," says Kelpie. "A lot of people worked for a long time to get Baker's research to the point of having real-world applications. Even more people said it would never work, which is why Reed was considered sort of on the fringe right up until he succeeded."

"Fringe alchemy; I never thought I'd see the day," mutters Isabella.

Kelpie doesn't respond to her. She's still focused on Roger, trying to answer both the question he asked and the ones he hasn't fully voiced. She's responding to the harmonics. Chang'e wonders whether Roger even realizes he does that to people. He clearly knows he can give them direct commands. Does he also know he can push them toward the behaviors he wants with the things he *doesn't* say? It must be exhausting, either way, never knowing whether people are responding to him or to the Doctrine.

No wonder he lives in a carnival-colored house with a handful of other personified concepts. They may be the only people he stands half a chance of having a normal conversation with, ever.

"When Reed succeeded, I hadn't had my accident yet, which I guess means I didn't exist yet, since I was made, and that's going to take some time to work all the way into my thinking, but. When Reed succeeded, a lot of people got their minds really, really changed really fast. I guess it wasn't his success that did it, because that happened a while ago. It was when he and Barrow started taking out the people they saw as competition, and then when most of the Alchemical Congress got blown up and no one knows *how* that happened, but everybody knows it was somehow Reed. He got a bomb into the Congress, and he killed almost all the masters on the continent. It shouldn't have been possible, even for him."

"James Reed always did like to achieve the impossible," says Roger, quietly.

"Are you going running back to the alchemists who made you?" asks Erin.

Kelpie recoils. "The alchemist who made me—I think—was a woman named Margaret, and she's dead now, because it seems that's just what happens to alchemists. They die. They kill each other, and then they use the pieces for their rituals and experiments, and it's awful. If Margaret were still alive, I might be willing to go back even knowing I'm not who I always thought I was. With her being dead, I'm not going anywhere near those people. I didn't ask for any of this."

"None of us did," says Artemis. "Natural manifestation or constructed, we didn't ask for it. It just happened."

"Yeah," says Kelpie, sounding subdued.

"If you're not going back, I can confirm that yes, James Reed and Leigh Barrow were responsible for the alkahest-and-azoth bomb that destroyed the bulk of the North American Alchemical Congress," says Erin. "The old masters opposed Reed's theories, and had stated their intent to fight him for ownership of the City, even after he'd done the work to incarnate the Doctrine, see it to maturity, and guide it to the borders. A preemptive strike seemed cleaner than taking war to the Impossible City."

"Can you even *take* a war to the Impossible City?" asks Dodger, frowning sharply.

"You can take a war anywhere, if you're willing to do the work," says Erin. "They were going to fight him, he didn't want them to, he stopped them before they got the chance. That was what Reed did. He never considered himself the villain of the piece. He was a hero in his own mind, Asphodel's hero, and he was doing what he had to in order to achieve what he had been created to achieve. That was all. Everything he did was in her honor, all the way to the end."

"He was a horrible man who did horrible things, even to other horrible people, and I'm glad he's dead," says Dodger primly.

Kelpie, meanwhile, is nodding gravely. "I guess it's good to know he really *did* kill the old Congress. I wish someone would tell the alchemists, though. They spend a lot of time arguing over whether it was Reed or not, and I feel like some of them really, really want it *not* to have been, because they're trying so hard to pretend they were always on his side, they *always* thought he had the right idea about things, they were his disciples. And not knowing for sure that he did it makes it easier for them to say he was a great man who only ever did great things."

"People who want that badly to believe in his greatness are going to find a way to do it anyway," says Erin.

"I guess. So, um. After the Congress was wiped out, while the new Congress was being called, a bunch of new projects launched, people scrambling for space and people and resources. And several projects got approved using the remains of Reed's root stock, the material he used to make his cuckoos."

"Meaning the preserved bits and pieces of Asphodel he used to tote around with him," says Erin. "Because nothing says 'love' like keeping your dead mother in jars and using her genetic material to make new people."

"I love how you can always put things in the most disgusting way possible," says Dodger. "It makes me feel all warm and tingly inside, and not like an asshole's favorite toy."

"Don't flatter yourself, Dodger. You were never his favorite," says Erin, and laughs, as high and bright as a mockingbird, while Dodger glares at her.

"Do you want me to finish or not?" asks Kelpie, somewhat peevishly, and Erin stops laughing.

"Sorry," she says. "Please, tell us about the people who made you."

"They were trying to modify and adapt Reed's work, to make it less universally massive and prone to turning on its creators. They wanted controllable cuckoos. They've been trying all sorts of controls, including . . ." Kelpie pauses then, before she begins to laugh, borderline hysterically. Looking concerned, Smita moves to put a hand on her shoulder. Kelpie turns to look at her. "Controls like telling them they weren't cuckoos at all! Like telling them they were lab assistants who'd been in accidents!" She keeps laughing, harder and harder, until the "borderline" wears off the "hysterically" and she starts to sob, slumping forward until her face is pressed against Smita's chest, and she's just crying.

Smita strokes her hair with one hand, comfort offered on instinct more than anything else, and looks at Roger, Dodger, and the Lunars with her jaw set in a hard line. "Are we quite done torturing this poor girl?" she asks, voice as hard as her expression. "Because I think what she needs is to go and lay down for a little while, not to stand here and keep answering questions about where she came from. And don't try telling me it doesn't count when she volunteers the information. I know what it's like to have the pair of you looking at me, *wanting* answers. Even if you don't ask the question, sometimes telling you what you need to know is the only thing a person *can* do."

Roger looks faintly abashed. Dodger, however, only rolls her eyes.

"My kitchen," she says, "is full of moon gods, at least one of whom has come to town hunting alchemists, because the alchemists have gotten so worked up about something that a bunch of cosmic space cases who mostly check out on what life on Earth is doing have noticed. We now know, for sure, that those same alchemists have continued working with Reed's research and Asphodel's genetic material, which, believe me, is not making me feel any less like some asshole's science project. We're not harassing the kid. We're trying to figure out how bad the situation is."

"And how close they are to claiming the City," says Roger, rather more direly. "We don't *want* the Impossible City. I don't know much about the place, because I'm not supposed to. No one who exists in this world is supposed to know too much about *that* one. No one travels between them."

"No one but the Moon," says Erin, looking to Chang'e.

Feeling obscurely as if she's just been pulled from audience to actor after a welcome chance to catch her breath, Chang'e nods. "Every night," she says. "That's why there are so many of us. Every night, we go into the everything—the passage between this world and the outskirts of the Impossible City—and we take one more step up from our normal manifestation. We step into the sky, and we shine down on the City as we cross from one side to the other."

"That shouldn't need more than, what, thirty of you?" asks Roger.

"There are dozens of us shining at any given time," says Chang'e. "Moon gods from all around the world, coming together until we have the mass and power to form a proper Moon."

"A composite moon," says Dodger. "Fascinating."

"So you have nightly access to the City?" asks Roger, looking at the Lunars. When they nod, in ragged disharmony, he sips his coffee again. "All right. Could I access this 'everything'?"

"You? Probably," says Artemis. "Once you knew what it was and how to find it, I doubt it would be able to keep you out. If you're asking whether an alchemist could pull the same trick, I don't think they could."

"What if they were wearing one of us like a coat?" asks Máni. "Some real *Silence of the Lambs* bullshit."

"First person to say Thomas Harris is an alchemist is getting slapped," says Dodger, almost singsong.

"That's disgusting," says Artemis, to Máni. She pauses, then, considering. "But it just might work. If you could find the gate when you had managed to trick the universe into seeing you as a Lunar, you could probably enter the everything, and we've never had any indication that the windows would know the difference between a Lunar and a person playing pretend. Wrapping yourself in the skin of a wolf when you want to fool the deer into leaving you alone is an old hunter's trick. I think we have narrative weight behind it working here."

"Don't talk about us like we're stories," says Erin, and Artemis looks at her flatly. They stay that way for several seconds, two hunters sizing each other up and staring each other down. One born of science, one born of the human need to fictionalize the world around them. They aren't the same. They are exactly the same. In that contradiction waits their conflict, and their collaboration.

Erin looks away first. Artemis returns her attention to Dodger. "If you could fool the gate and get access to the everything, once you're in that deep, I don't think there are any defenses that would keep you from entering the sky above the City."

"And if there are multiple Moons up there every night, what's going to stop one from playing shooting star and dropping down into the streets?" Dodger looks to Smita. "In the books, didn't the returning Queen of Wands get access to the City by sneaking Zib in through an unguarded path and having her unlock the doors from the inside? We keep saying the Up-and-Under books were meant to be a roadmap for the alchemists to follow. What if that was the part where Asphodel told them how to get in?"

"They sent Zib along the graveyard path in one of the early books, but they didn't use the road of moonlight until what, book twelve? By that point, it didn't feel as much like Asphodel was teaching big lessons as like she was writing errata," says Smita.

Dodger nods. "Exactly. Reed focused all his attention on those first four books, the big elemental adventures, the ones with the most obvious alchemical applications. At this point, the people who are left are grasping at straws. Anything that gets them past the City walls is going to look like something worth trying."

"It always comes back to the damn City," says Roger. "Why do they want it so badly?"

Kelpie straightens, pulling slightly away from Smita as she turns to answer him. "The City is everything," she says. "The Tower is in the City, and whoever holds the Tower holds everything. The Tower controls the universe. It's the center of creation. If they can take the City, they can take the Tower. If they can take the Tower, it won't matter that you went rogue and destroyed your creator, or that I ran away, or anything. They won't need to follow the rules anymore, because they'll be *making* the rules."

Isabella laughs, a little uneasily. "You make it sound like whoever controls this Impossible City is some kind of God."

"Oh, no," says Kelpie. She gestures to the Lunars. "They're some kind of god."

"Moon gods, in specific," says Artemis.

"Whoever controls the Impossible City is just *God*. They get the whole mess. Mostly it runs on its own, and they don't have to do anything to keep it going. But they can make changes if they want to."

The idea of the alchemists who would commit the kind of atrocities they've all seen becoming God is horrifying enough that for a moment, the kitchen falls silent. Only Kelpie doesn't appear to share in the general malaise that has fallen over the rest of them. She looks from face to face, wide-eyed and curious, and pauses when she gets to Artemis, frowning just a little, like she recognizes her but doesn't understand entirely how. Pulling her gaze away, she looks to Chang'e and cocks her head.

"Your eyes are pink," she says. "I've never seen that before. Red, sure, in some of the mice, but never pink. It's pretty. More people should have pink eyes."

"They're not pink; they're peach," says Chang'e. "I'm Chang'e, the Chinese goddess of the moon and immortality. I tend the peach orchards that grow on my version of the moon, and that's where I go when it's my turn to shine down on the City."

"Were they always pink?"

"No. They changed when I took this form, and they change back to hazel when I step down to let my mortal host take care of things."

"That must be confusing, not always being the one in charge of being you."

"It can be. If I step too far down, Judy can do things without my being aware of her having done them, and if I step too far forward, I can do the same thing to her. Cruel Lunars can take advantage of the disconnect between our mortal and divine sides to abuse their hosts, shutting them out of their own lives and gradually isolating them from the world. I don't understand what would motivate someone to do that to something that is, at the end, a part of them, but I don't need to understand to disapprove. Judy and I are a partnership. We keep each other informed."

"Oh," says Kelpie, eyes wide and round. "Is she here now?"

"Judy? Yes. I'm not stepped so far forward that she can't see what's going on, and have her opinions about it. She's just . . . letting me drive right now, when it's better for us. Every Lunar has their own relationship with their hosts. Some choose to integrate, until there's only one person in the body; some choose to separate more than we have, making rules and drawing lines. And some go to war against themselves, as I mentioned before. The mortal hosts almost never win when that happens. They're not strong enough."

"That's awful," says Kelpie. "So you're all three the god of the same thing?"

"Sort of," says Chang'e. "I'm the only one of us who handles immortality. Máni is . . ."

"Máni is mostly vague, these days," says Máni. "No one's ever quite been able to tell me what I'm supposed to be the god of, but then, I haven't been doing this job for long. Maybe we'll eventually figure out what I'm supposed to be good for." He laughs then, large and without any real humor.

"Máni used to have companions," says Kelpie. "They would manifest and help him do his job. They were minor gods of the phases of the moon, and of harvest and healing. Bil and Hjúki. They were on the list the alchemists had for possible aspects to pursue, but rejected because Máni wasn't considered powerful enough to be worth catching."

"Catching?" he asks, with a dangerous note in his voice.

"That's what I was trying to explain, before everyone kept pulling things in different directions and asking questions," says Kelpie, a little desperately. "The alchemists who made me, they were trying really, really hard to incarnate the aspects of individual Lunar gods that have dropped away over the centuries, as belief waned. The Man in the Moon's dog, or Chang'e's rabbit. Not, um, Tu'er Ye, the rabbit god on the moon, but the rabbit that accompanied her in some earlier versions of her story. We have records that say she was seen on Earth with a celestial rabbit, a very long time ago, when people believed more in this sort of thing. But beliefs shifted, and the Moon stopped incarnating the supplementary aspects. Which means—"

"Which means the universe already has grooves worn into it where those aspects could go, but it stopped having enough belief to smooth the process and since they weren't strictly necessary, they got downsized," says Roger. "They still have the potential to manifest; they just need a little push."

"The alchemists have been trying to give that push by crafting perfect vessels for them, so there won't be any resistance when they try to manifest," says Kelpie. "That's what the project I was working with did."

"Mmm-hmm. And which one are you?"

Kelpie laughs a little, uncertainly. "I always thought I was working with the team that was trying to incarnate Artemis's Hind. A hind is another word for a female red deer, and Artemis used to appear with one. I always thought it was a little weird that a huntress appeared with a deer, and not with some of her dogs or something, but I didn't write the myths."

Artemis steps slightly forward, around Máni, who gives her a half-amused look. "In the myths, she would transform people into deer when she wanted to punish or protect them, and I guess the symbolism stuck."

Kelpie nods. "Yeah, that. So they thought if they could get the Hind to manifest, a manifestation of Artemis would be drawn to the lab, and they'd be able to catch and contain it, and force it to grant us access to the City."

"Why did they want a powerful Lunar?" asks Roger, gesturing Artemis to silence with a wave of one hand. "Wouldn't someone like Máni be easier for them to control? And wouldn't Chang'e have been a better choice than Artemis, by the same measure? I know if I were going to try to capture and control a powerful aspect of the incarnate moon, I'd go for the farmer before I tried to catch the huntress. Seems safer."

"These aren't people who focus on the safety of their work," says Erin. "Apprentices are expendable, and you can always get another one if you accidentally break the one you have. 'Slow down and come in second' might as well be the alchemist's creed."

"Right. So you go for the big gold ring right out the gate, on the theory that if you try for copper, you might catch it, but someone else will have managed to get there first. It makes sense, even if I don't like it."

"They tried for Artemis and Chang'e at the same time," says Kelpie, clearly choosing her words with care. "Chang'e is just as powerful, and she comes with the added bonus of her peaches—immortality is always an attractive offering to an alchemist. Even with access to a philosopher's stone and the ability to brew the elixir of life, the process is time-consuming and materially expensive. Growing a peach tree and living forever is a temptation no alchemist could ignore."

"It's not *that* simple," grumbles Chang'e. She wants to be flattered by the acknowledgment of her power, but she's slightly wounded at the same time. People always want to act as if it's the peaches themselves that have the divine gift, and not the one who grows them. Without her, all they'd get is fruit. Delicious fruit, to be sure, but fruit all the same. She's essential to the process of immortality. "You know the first alchemists got the idea for the elixir of life from my orchards? Mine and Iðunn's, although she grew apples. I haven't seen her in centuries. I don't even know if she's still around . . ." Her voice trails off, annoyance replaced by grief as she considers that yet another of them might have been lost.

They were friends once. Iðunn was never a Lunar god, but there was a time when more divinities regularly walked the world than happens anymore, and she was a sweet concept who incarnated in sweet hosts, always ready with a smile or a joke or a slice of hot baked apple pastry. The things that woman could do with a twist of dough and a sprinkle of sugar were virtually illegal. The idea that she might just not be considered necessary by the universe anymore is a little heartbreaking, like finding out that Tuesday has been canceled, or the sunrise has been deemed extraneous to needs. Something so constant and predictable that you never even considered it might be taken away.

Kelpie grimaces, sympathetic, and continues. "They want those peach trees, but not as badly as they want the City. The City is everything. We don't need peach trees if we can tell the Tower that humans live forever now."

"The *right* humans, I'm sure," says Erin. "We're talking about alchemists here. There's no way they take the City and bring about utopia."

"Probably not," admits Kelpie. "They always said it was good I couldn't leave the lab after my accident, because the people who weren't with us were the worst sort of people. They were dull and drab and not magical at all, and they didn't even know what they were missing. But Margaret would put on pretty clothes and go clubbing three nights a week, and sometimes she'd come back smelling like smoke and other people's perfume, with her lipstick all smudged, and she looked so *happy* when that happened, like nothing could ever go wrong again. And then I had to go out of the lab, and I met Isabella and her family, and Isabella's plenty magical, but her husband's not, and her son's not, and they're lovely people. They were nice to me, and I liked them lots when I met them. I don't think anyone should get to say who the right or wrong sorts of people are, because everyone's different."

"And thus do brand-new lab-grown people figure shit out faster than some of the ones who've been doing this the normal way for a hell of a lot longer," says Dodger, sounding disgusted. She moves to fill her coffee mug again.

"Should you really be having that much caffeine?" asks Artemis, somewhat delicately.

"It soothes my nerves," says Dodger.

"That isn't how—"

"I wouldn't argue with her," says Roger. "It's rarely a good idea, and I want Kelpie to finish telling us why the alchemists wanted a powerful Lunar, and not just any Lunar they could grab. There are so many of you, it would be easy to pick off a few around the fringes."

Chang'e relaxes slightly. These people aren't responsible for the deaths. She was fairly sure of that already, but now she's certain. That's good. She really doesn't want to deal with predators on all sides, especially not predators she can't either destroy or outrun. The Doctrine knows her face now—this one, anyway, and she wouldn't be surprised if that means the Doctrine can deduce all her other faces through some hand-wavy piece of mathematics. She can't run. She can't hide. She doesn't have to, and that's a relief almost too big to stand up against.

"They've already been doing that," says Kelpie, sounding bemused. "Pretty much since the Congress fell."

Everyone in the room looks at her with horrified dismay, even Isabella, who may be new to all this discussion of Lunar manifestations and alchemical plots, but can still tell that Kelpie just admitted to murder as casually as she might have mentioned making a grilled cheese sandwich. It's chilling, in its own way. Sweet as she seems, she was made and raised by people who saw the world as nothing more than an endless assortment of resources for them to harvest and bend to their own ends, and it would be unwise to forget that about her.

"What do you mean?" asks Artemis stiffly.

"Oh, an alchemist whose master died when the Congress fell started pursuing some new avenues of research, looking for better ways to shield against the alkahest and keep the other alchemists safe, and she found a use for Lunars. I think that's what put Margaret and her team on to the idea of catching one to get into the City. They'd mostly ignored the moon gods before that—I've seen the records, and there's a lot of mention of the overall uselessness of them. 'What good is a personification of the universe that does naught but smile and shine and fade away?' Plenty of really lousy poetry masquerading as research. But then she found a way for them to be useful."

"What would that be?" asks Artemis. She's getting stiffer by the second. Chang'e wonders if Kelpie can tell how much danger she's in, whether she's plunging merrily forward out of ignorance or out of foolhardy courage. Either way, it doesn't seem like a good idea.

"I'm not entirely sure. It had something to do with concrete. But whatever it was, it made the alchemists really notice the Lunars for the first time in a long time. They started picking off the minor ones, using them for what they needed and disposing of whatever was left at the end. I might be made partially from one of those minor gods." For the first time, she looks like she understands that she's saying something upsetting, like she knows this is wrong. It's a brief transition, but it's there. "But then Margaret—she was so smart, and so kind to me, and I'm going to miss her—Margaret thought hey, if the minor Lunars can be useful, maybe the major Lunars can be *really* useful. And she drew up the research plan for forcing one of their companions to manifest, because it seemed like the best way to lure them in. We'd make a perfect rabbit, or hind, or dog, and then we'd get a powerful Lunar who was willing to work with us, who didn't have to die to help us. Who could get an alchemist to the door they use to reach the City, and let them inside."

"But it didn't work," says Erin.

"Oh, no, it did," says Kelpie. "Margaret told me. They made the rabbit first, and he was everything he needed to be, and he should have attracted a Chang'e to us almost immediately."

Chang'e feels sick. She remembers Judy poring over the lists of colleges with good graduate programs in linguistics, looking for the perfect place to apply. She remembers nudging her host toward Berkeley, not knowing why she wanted to go there, only that it felt right. Had she been trying to move toward her Rabbit, unaware of his existence and drawn to him all the same?

"Then they made the hind, and she was perfect, too, she was properly manifest, but by then, Margaret had figured out something that alchemists aren't supposed to think about, and so she put the rabbit in the botanical research division, and she kept the hind for herself, and she kept working, trying to find a way to force a second manifestation without using the material from Reed's files."

"Wait—why?" asks Smita, sounding suddenly baffled.

"Because 'the material from Reed's files' is a nicely, needlessly euphemistic way of saying 'the remains of Asphodel Baker,'" says Dodger. "You use it when you're making cuckoos, like us. Even if they were trying to manifest animals, I bet they kept getting people because of the sympathies they were starting out with."

"I bet that's how they got you," says Roger, and sips his coffee, watching Kelpie closely. Watching the way she flinches, confirming his not-quite-guess: she's an escaped experiment with distinctly cervine features, talking about how the alchemists were trying to force a celestial deer to manifest for the first time in years. There was really nothing else she could have been.

He does glance away after her flinch, measuring the response from Artemis, who gave her name before Kelpie entered the kitchen, and hasn't repeated it since. She's staring at Kelpie now, eyes very wide and face very pale.

In a voice that shakes like a leaf in a stiff wind trying not to blow off its tree, she asks, "Hind? Are you—? Did they—?"

Kelpie says nothing, and for a moment, silence reigns.

Palus Somni

The door to the decoy apartment which connects to the stairway down to the lab opens, and a man steps out. He's thin, almost skeletally so, and he adjusts his tie with one hand as he turns his face up toward the afternoon sun, tightening the knot. Something must have gone terribly wrong for it to have been loosened in the first place; everything about him is pressed and proper, suit crisply ironed, creases arrayed just so, like a model of a man. A single splattered drop of something mars the toe of one perfectly shining shoe. No Avery here to sell the shine from his shoes for safety, no, sir!

Luis, who has returned home from school to find the apartment empty and a note on the counter reminding him to walk the dog before he watches cartoons, suddenly decides he would rather spend some time doing his homework before he walks the dog, delaying TV time even further (for he would never think to go against his mother when the welfare of his best friend is concerned; in other ways, certainly, but not this one). He grips Bobby's leash tighter as the dog whines, and stumbles backward through the still-open door, into the safety of the apartment.

Bobby's whining doesn't stop until the door is closed between them and the man in the pressed suit. He plasters himself against Luis's legs then, shaking hard, but determined to keep his body between his boy and the door. Luis can feel the growl radiating through the big dog's ribs, deep and almost inaudible, but strong enough to shake his bones.

He crouches, wrapping his arms around Bobby, and in doing so, he saves his own life, because crouching means he isn't visible through the window when the man turns his face toward the apartment. Isabella's wards are holding. The man did notice the boy and the dog, for an instant, but they dropped out of his mind as soon as they went inside, and he doesn't remember them as he turns a slow circle, assessing his surroundings for threats.

The man finds none, and so he lowers his face, straightens his spine, and pulls a piece of forked wood out of his pocket. Like all good dowsing rods, it grew in this shape, was whittled down but not truly carved, only refined. Unlike its naturally occurring kin, it *was* cultivated, trained into this shape while still on the branch. It grew on an impossible hybrid of willow and peach, fruiting and shade trees combined in a botanical lab whose research didn't quite follow the laws of nature. It is, by any measure, perfect, the points tipped in hardened ash where they were burned, the base capped with silver that rests cool against his palm as he turns a slow and easy circle, holding the rod at roughly waist-level.

When he is facing west, the rod twitches, ever so slightly, a small rise followed by a sharp fall, and he frowns in thought before he begins to walk, letting it guide him away from the apartment, out of the courtyard, onto the street. A brief, self-satisfied smile creases his lips as he leaves the apartments behind him.

Tristan Rapp has never been a patient man. Oh, he's capable of waiting—all alchemists are, and they have to be in order to succeed at their profession. Impatience does not help a solvent mature or bring a project more quickly to fruition. But waiting and patience are not the same thing. When he waits, he does so on a set timeline, knowing that in the end, the results will fit a very narrow band of possibilities. Patience involves trusting the universe, which is not something he has ever been inclined to do.

This lack of tolerance for wasting and wasted time has made him an excellent weapon in the arsenal of the new Alchemical Congress. He served under the prior masters, of course, has served for many years with distinction and with excellent results, but the prior

Congress was more conservative in many ways than these new, upstart children of the modern age. He takes orders from scholars eighty years his junior, and he smiles with all his teeth as he agrees to their inane demands, reminding himself in the silence that follows that he has seen better men than them hung by the chains of their own hubris.

He is an alchemist but not one of the serious researchers, the ones so invested in the Great Work of chasing and claiming the City that they lose track of life here in the world where all flesh begins and much of it will end. He makes his own philters and draughts, but he creates nothing new, pursues no innovations, crafts no cuckoos. There are those who think less of him for these choices, and others who think more, and he values both schools of thought precisely the same. None of them matter.

What he enjoys most is the sensation of a job properly and efficiently done, the sight of a body coming apart into its component elements, ready to be repurposed and put to better uses, the sound of an apprentice begging for the life they don't realize they've already lost. He knew Leigh Barrow, called her a colleague when others called her a monster, and respected her methods, even as he occasionally questioned the fervor with which she employed them. Barrow could never be truly great, for she allowed herself to be too easily distracted by vengeance and desire. He has no such issues.

Also unlike Barrow, he is a naturally occurring form of monster, born of flesh, and destined to die the same way if the City is not taken in his lifetime. He drinks his elixir of life, which tastes ever more of apples, and he endures, for his lifetime is a malleable thing, while the taking of the City is an inevitability.

The girl may have fled the lab while he was waiting for the filters to cleanse the alkahest from the air, but she didn't sanitize her quarters on her way out the door, and after the small matter of Margaret's assistant had been resolved—quite pleasantly so, at least for him—he had returned to the girl's room to locate her hairbrush, which had several strands tangled in the tines. One of them even still had the root ball attached.

Affixing them to the fork of his dowsing rod with a loop of ice-washed cobweb had been a matter of seconds, and now he will find her. Wherever she's hiding, unless it's behind protections she couldn't even imagine, he will find her.

The dowsing rod continues to twitch and tug as he makes his way along the sidewalk, ignoring the people who pass to either side. They are nothing more than mist and vapor to him, as inconsequential as a thought, and he pays them no mind. They go on their way, unaware of how lucky they are to be ignored, and he goes on his, passing storefronts and houses, attention reserved for the wooden rod in his hands.

Unlike Kelpie, he sees nothing of the newness or wonder of this world. Newness and wonder were worn away for him a long time ago, before this modern world was even born. All he sees now are disrepair and decay, all the places where this reality falls short of the shining perfection that waits within the City.

Tristan Rapp is many things. Man. Monster. Mutilator. Murderer. Destroyer of innocent lives and dreams.

But at the end, he is also a cautionary tale.

When he was a child in the faraway streets of London, his older sister, whom he loved beyond all reason, was called to the seasonal coronation. Summer sang in her soul, and over the course of her bid for the crown, he watched it blossom, until flowers sprouted where she stepped and fruit grew ripe and rounded at her touch, even when it had been rotted to the seed. He followed her through the trials and terrors of the coronation, until he had seen her walk into the maze that wavered on the edge between reality and unreality, fading into the pale liminal space reserved for creatures out of story.

All that, and she hadn't claimed the crown. She had come out broken and weeping, her hands cracked and black with frost, and she had died a week later in her own bed, wasting away to nothing in the absence of her season. But that hadn't been the worst of it.

Oh, no. For he had been a boy, young and quick and curious, in the way of young things everywhere, and when she had gone into the maze, he had followed. But for him, there was no clash of seasons, no Winter meeting Summer on equal ground and discussing the world that was yet to come, there were no tests or trials. There had been only blackness, the emptiness of the void outside all things, and then, in the dark, the endless rainbow flashing of instants passing to their deaths, of entropy made manifest. He had entered the everything, although he had no such name for it, and he had come to understand in an instant why so many human cultures saw the rainbow as a bridge between the heavens and the earth. The everything was no bridge, no Bifröst to lead him to Asgard, and yet it was something so far outside his experience that his mind had rejected it, refusing to accept what was happening around him.

Young Tristan had screamed into the abyss, and run deeper, unwittingly moving away from the exit that would have seen him restored to the world of men before he could damage himself permanently. Instead, he had traveled unhindered through the everything, until he had come to a window hanging in the air, perfectly suspended on nothing at all, and yet something concrete and comprehensible, something for his wounded mind to seize upon.

The window had been closed when he reached it, and he lacked the strength to pry it open, so he had been unable to climb through in his quest for solid ground. Instead, he had pressed his face against the glass and looked out upon a great and glorious city such as he had never seen before in his life.

It was as if his familiar, well-loved London had been somehow purified and transformed into the very ideal of what a city could be. The streets gleamed iridescent, as if they had been cut from the delicate whorls of a snail's shell. The storefronts were a riot of colorful delights, the produce stands boasted treasures such as even his sister's strange and growing powers could not dare to dream, and the buildings were flawless. It was the Platonic ideal of a city, and it struck him both silent and sightless in a matter of seconds, unable to perceive anything save for his memory of that city.

How he escaped the everything was a mystery to him then and remains a mystery to him now. He stumbled out of the maze where the potential kings and queens of summer and winter battled for their place, tears streaming from his unseeing eyes and his own breath a keening wail in his ears.

As his sister dwindled, severed from the Summer, his sight had gradually returned, and his voice had come back with it. Still, he did not weep when they gave her to the ground, she who he had once loved best in all the world, for whom he had stepped outside the bounds of the reality man was meant to know and trod the Bifröst as an unwanted intruder. He watched them pile earth atop her body, and could see no real change in her state, for everyone around him was decaying by the second, their bodies and bones slipping further and further from the ideals of that shining, impossible city he had seen.

Any alchemist or sorcerer could have warned his parents of what was going to happen next, but they were ordinary people who had intersected with the elemental world purely by chance, thanks to the nature of their much-mourned daughter. They had no one to warn them. No one to tell them *why* the City, so dazzling, so perfect, was forbidden to mortal eyes. Tristan started killing a month after his sister's burial.

He was clever and resourceful, even then, and carried out his first such acts with surprising skill, finding beauty in the arch of arteries and treasuring the last beating of each heart, the soft collapse of each lung. He sought the City in the broken bodies of those who moved too slowly to evade him, and he had nearly a year to hunt unhindered before he had come to the attention of the local alchemists. His latest victim had been a promising apprentice of theirs. With her death, he had passed from environmental hazard into figure of quiet interest, and shortly after that, he had been acquired.

Tristan's training with the British Alchemical Congress had taken several decades, as was the norm, but as his new masters had managed to capture a manifestation of Iðunn and keep her alive long enough to compel the planting of a healthy orchard, they had no need to focus on the purification of alkahest or the creation of a philosopher's stone. Their focus was, instead, on the search for a reliable passage into the City.

Then Baker's curious creation had begun gaining traction in the hearts and minds of children, causing them to map North America to her Up-and-Under, and when Baum had followed with his own imaginary world, reversing the elements, he left the concept of the City where she had placed it, right at the center of all things. It had become quickly apparent that if the City were to become manifest in this time, it would do so in North America. The alchemical heart of the world had been shifted by manipulation of children's dreams. Tristan hadn't even been able to resent that theft of power from the European Congresses. It had been done too elegantly, and too quickly to evade.

He had killed his masters on the same night the European Congress collectively admitted defeat, and he had left their bodies cooling in their own labs as he made for the shipyards and hence to the New World. With him he had carried his small store of personal possessions, the grimoires of the three men who had taken charge of the bulk of his education, and a small leather bag of apple seeds.

Iðunn herself had been long gone by then, and he might have been pleased to know that over a century later, a goddess of the moon would feel a pang of guilt over how long it had been since she'd last wondered after her peer in immortality.

It wasn't difficult for a man like him, even with such narrow and focused alchemical interests, to find the North American Congress. It had proven even less difficult for him to integrate himself within their ranks.

He had never joined Reed's wild attempt to harness aspects of the universe beyond those which incarnated naturally. Baker had been a genius, the sort that comes along once a generation at the absolute most, but that wasn't enough to have rendered her infallible. A candle is a controlled fire. Even a campfire can be used as a tool and a weapon, beneficial if somewhat riskier.

But forest fire is no one's tool. Perhaps it burns what you wanted to burn and perhaps not; the fire is burning either way. The fire doesn't care.

Tristan knows, perhaps better than most, that humanity owes everything they have today to the acquisition and "taming" of the flame, even though he also knows, deep in his soul, that no fire has ever been truly tamed. It is his unfashionable belief, which would limit his advancement through the Congressional ranks if he had any interest in advancing, that the manifestations of various universal constants are just another form of flame. Grasp a Winter or a Summer, you have a controlled fire. Net a minor god, a Lunar or a Harvest, and you have a tool or a weapon. Reach for something more than that . . .

Forest fire. The Doctrine of Ethos was always going to turn against the people who forced it into a single incarnation, because it blazes too big to be held. It doesn't warm. It devours. So when he heard of Reed's plans, inherited from Baker with her blood still wet on his hands, Tristan had turned away and busied himself serving other goals, other masters. He does that still.

He may be the oldest alchemist alive in North America, and he hasn't enjoyed a single full day of his existence since he saw the City. He subsists on the apples of Iðunn, which he has never shared—let the other alchemists think him more skilled than he actually is if they like, this strange, cadaverous man with his seemingly endless supply of the elixir of life. He lives on apples and the bitter, hateful knowledge that he may never see the City again. He will never walk those streets, he will never smell those flowers or taste those fruits.

He was not the one to propose the use of Lunars to gain access to the City, but he supports it. Slaughter them all. Not a one of them has earned what they have. Not a one of them deserves to cross that sky, to shine on those streets and spires, to have what he's denied. He'll see them all dead if given half the chance.

The dowsing rod in his hands shudders, guiding him onward. He'll have more than half a chance. He has the apples of immortality and all the time in the world to accomplish his goals.

Margaret had been clever enough, in her way. He's still not sure he supports the inclusion of women in the ranks of the Congress. There were always women who could serve as reasonably talented apprentices, who enjoyed the feeling of mercury running over their palms or viscera yielding before their blades, but they were the exception, not the rule. He's found women to be too sentimental in the main, too inclined to become attached to their subjects, to humanize what should never be humanized. To *care*.

Oh, men care also, but the men drawn to alchemy are usually the sort he's known all his life, the ones who can control themselves and retain their focus even in the face of temptation. Margaret's assistant had been very forthcoming once she realized she was never going to walk away from the lab. She told him everything about their concealed successes, about the conspiracy to hide cuckoos and resources from the eyes of the Congress.

None of those successes matter now, of course. The project has been canceled. Like all canceled projects, it will be stripped for parts, the pieces that work distributed among all the other, more deserving projects, while the pieces that don't will be recycled into anything that can still be of use. The "Rabbit" she and her team managed to incarnate had been in the botanical section when Tristan made his appearance, the creature wearing lab coat and goggles and behaving for all the world as if he had a right to be there. As if he were human.

Human or not, he'd died as easily as the rest of them. One more unnecessary incarnate, no longer walking around to complicate the alchemical transformation of the natural world. If only Tristan had been a little less willing to believe that Margaret was too smart to lie to him, if only he hadn't chalked her anxiousness up to a desperate need to save her own skin, this could all be over already. He could have killed her little runaway Hind and be on his way back to Maine to check in with his handlers.

Ah, well. It's too late now, and some things can't be helped. The dowsing rod is good; it will see him to his target, and he'll finish the matter tonight, wherever it is the girl has gone to ground.

The neighborhood has been changing around him as he walks, apartments giving way to larger single-family homes. He moves now in an atmosphere of wealth and plenty, the territory of the sort of people who never want for anything for more than a moment. The territory of alchemists.

There are methods of becoming rich that don't involve breaking the laws of nature, but those methods are far less fun than the methods practiced by the alchemically inclined. He continues to let the dowsing rod guide him, interpreting each twitch and tremor with the skill of someone who's been doing this for decades, and stays on its path even as he begins to detect traces of chaotic, semi-controlled working from one of the houses up ahead. Pure elementalism, performed with the enthusiasm of the amateur and the power of the professional.

The two make for uneasy bedfellows. He can feel the contradictions in the power as he draws closer. The professional has been fighting to control the enthusiasm, but not as hard as he might have expected. Efforts have been made to disperse the energy afterward, but they've only been partially successful—pools of elemental power are gathered on the ground and in the branches of the nearby trees, making him wonder whether there are any self-respecting alchemists left in this benighted city.

Margaret may have been a liar and a thief, but he'd always thought better of her work than this implies. She should have been aware someone was making such a mess in her territory. She should have stepped in. That she didn't speaks poorly to her training . . . or excellently to the shielding abilities of whoever made this mess. If someone has been actively hiding their activities, it's possible that Margaret wasn't *entirely* incompetent.

The dowsing rod leads him to the steps of a large house, and up them to the front door, where he rings the bell, listening to it echo. As the sound is fading, the padding of bare feet replaces it, and a blurry face swims into view on the other side of the leaded glass.

It's a woman. She peers through the glass for a moment before incorrectly assessing him as harmless and unlocking the door, one hand resting on the doorframe and the other on the door itself, blocking him from seeing too far inside while also telegraphing, none too subtly, that she can slam the door in an instant.

If she does, he'll come back later tonight with a Hand of Glory to guarantee no one responds too quickly to her screaming. She's not a target—yet—but he doesn't like to be denied.

She's tall, pale in the way of someone who never goes outside without cause, thin in the way of someone who can afford the high price of thinness, the delicate, delicious, calorie-light foods and the personal chef to prepare them nightly, the trainers and the surgeries and the endless pursuit of an impossible illusion of "perfection." As if "perfect" hasn't been as mutable as any other human ideal across the centuries. As if people didn't once pursue plumpness with all the vigor they now direct toward the opposite extreme.

Only three things in the universe are perfect: gold, alkahest, and the Impossible City. Everything else is flawed, and wasting time pretending otherwise has never served anyone well.

Her eyes flick to the rod in his hand, then back up to his face. A small crease forms between her eyebrows.

"Can I help you?" she asks. Her voice is pitched too high, a trained affectation intended to make her sound like something to be protected and cared for rather than pushed against. He pauses, giving her another look. Everything about her is designed to give that impression, to encourage underestimation, to nudge people toward the conclusion that she poses no threat, offers no obstacle to their own progress.

It's a fascinatingly constructed façade. She has no power. He can tell that as well, from the pools of elemental energy dotted around the property, some of which have started to curdle and turn septic. That will be a problem eventually, but the future is a room there's no guarantee either one of them will enter. Her, especially, with her measuring look and her hand on the door and her careful air of fragility.

Perhaps he can use that. He lowers the dowsing rod, taking in the perfect house, the elemental pools, the feigned fragility, and comes to a conclusion he hopes will be correct. It's not that he doesn't want to kill her—that would place too much importance on her one way or the other—it's that he wants this to be simple. And if he's correct, it still might be.

"No, but perhaps I can help you," he says, and smiles a skeleton smile as he tucks the dowsing rod into his jacket. "I can tell that you're a person of great power and connection within the local magical community." The word "magical" is sour on his lips. "Alchemical" is the correct term, the *scientific* term that treats the taming of a natural force as the art it is rather than some trick out of children's folklore. "Magical" is a word for people without training or safety rails, who believe the universe has no obligation to bow to humanity. It's a word for amateurs, and he hates it.

But from the way she lights up, he's alone in this. The line between her eyebrows disappears, replaced by a slight, smug tightening of the skin around her eyes, her puzzled look becoming a smile. "We took the flyers down months ago," she says, and the way she pronounces the word "we" tells him she had nothing to do with the manual labor of taking down flyers: that was all handled by hands that weren't as soft as hers, that were more accustomed to working. "How did you find me?"

"The sheer energy radiating from this location led me," he says, and while he's lying, he's also not. The dowsing rod picked up on *something*. The girl has been here.

"I'm sorry, but you've missed this week's meeting, and . . . forgive me for presuming, but we're an all-female coven. It keeps the energies cleaner when we're not pulling between the divine feminine and the divine masculine. I'm sure someone as learned as you clearly are will understand."

"Oh, I do, I do, but I'm not looking for your coven."

"No?" There's a glossiness in her eyes, a slightly husky catch in her voice, and he knows what she's hoping he'll say next.

Reed should never have tried to make his cuckoos mind readers. All he'd really needed to do was teach them to watch people, and the world would have been in the palm of their hands whether or not they became manifest.

"No," he echoes. "I'm looking for you. A coven has no power without its members, and even then, it accomplishes nothing without a strong hand at the wheel. A woman of your obvious position and potential . . . you must be that strong hand. I'm here because I need to speak to *you*."

She looks at him assessingly, showing her first flicker of true brilliance since she opened the door. All her masks and affectations may be enough to protect her from predators when she goes out into the world, but nothing will protect her if she asks the predators into her home. Tristan stands perfectly still, doing his best to look nonthreatening, and much as he wants to press the issue, he doesn't say a word, only waits. This is what she sees:

A man of average height who nevertheless holds himself like a tall man, like he expects to tower over the people around him and is perpetually surprised when it doesn't happen. His hair is a sandy shade of brown, cut short and slightly feathered at the top, clearly styled by someone who was paid well for their time; his suit is impeccably cut and pressed, and tailored to fit the skeletal angles of his form, not allowed to wrinkle or drape inappropriately. If not for the spot on one shoe, he would be perfectly groomed. His thinness is off-putting for some, but this woman has been trained not to criticize what cannot be changed in a minute's time, taught politeness like a weapon, and so she shunts that thought to the side as she continues her assessment.

He looks like the sort of man who moves in her social circles. He looks like money. Strangeness of the dowsing rod aside, he stands in her neighborhood like he belongs here, and she is thus inclined to trust him, to believe him when he speaks words of sweet flattery, to see him as one of her "own kind," whatever that means. Finally, she nods and steps to the side, the door opening as she does.

"I'd love to talk more about this," she says. "There's coffee in the kitchen, if you'd care to join me."

An alchemist is not a vampire: they don't need to be invited inside. A gentleman, on the other hand, is a sort of vampire, in that they do generally need the invitation. Tristan, who has considered himself a gentleman for quite some time, smiles his thanks as he steps past her into the conditioned air of the hall.

"Yes," he says. "I think we have a great deal to discuss."

Palus Nebularum

Artemis takes a step toward Kelpie, looking like she's been punched in the stomach hard enough to knock the air out of her and leave her reeling, no longer fully steady on her feet. Her hands have come up at some point, not reaching, not trying to grasp or grab, but just . . . hanging there, held in front of her like she no longer knows what to do with them.

Kelpie shies back, against Smita's side. She doesn't look afraid, exactly; she seems more resigned, as if this were something she knew would need to be dealt with eventually, but still held out hope it could be delayed a little longer, or possibly forever.

"Artemis," says Chang'e.

"I would have known if they'd managed—but I started watching Berkeley without a good reason, and that's how I saw how upset the alchemists here were. I only noticed because I was already looking. Did I start looking because of . . . Are you *really*?" There's a plea in her last word that defies all description. It's the sound of someone finding a lost lover or a pet they'd long since resigned themselves to never seeing again.

"I don't know," says Kelpie, voice peaking into a wail. "I don't know what I am! I was supposed to be a person, an alchemist, and Margaret was fixing me, she promised what she was doing was going to fix me, so I could be just like everybody else. I have . . . I have a family in Florida, and maybe they were always ever only lies, but she told me all about them, and they sent me letters sometimes, and so they feel real to me, no matter what the truth is. I don't *want* to be a cuckoo. I don't *want* to be a science project or a piece of the universe that stopped pretending it was a person because not enough people wanted it to be. I want to just be me, and I want being me to be totally normal, and not something that makes people look at me the way you're looking at me now. I want to go *home*."

"You can't go back to the people who made you," says Isabella. "Even if they weren't dead, they weren't treating you right. Whether you were supposed to be a person or not, you're a person now, and that means you deserve the chance to figure out what that means without people telling you lies."

"She's right," says Dodger, somewhat surprisingly; she hasn't exactly been the most generous or encouraging voice in this conversation. As she pushes herself away from the counter and steps up even with her brother, her eyes are on Kelpie. "You're a person now. You're as real as anybody else, because it doesn't matter how we're made, just that we exist. Those people lied to you, and they were planning to keep lying to you, and they didn't do you a favor by forcing you to manifest when you didn't want to. But then, no one asks to be born. Now you get to figure out who and what you want to be, and you get to go for it, no matter what. If you're a celestial hind, that's fine. Doesn't mean you *belong* to Artemis here, any more than you *belong* to the alchemists. I think we need to be focusing a little more on why Lunars are dying, and why the alchemists are in such a god-awful snit right now."

"The eclipse," says Chang'e.

Everyone else in the kitchen turns to look at her. Roger speaks first. "The which?"

"There's a total lunar eclipse coming in three days," she says. "The moon is going to be blocked out all the way across the contiguous United States. It's going to be obscured across an unusually large geographic area."

"Do they have eclipses in the Impossible City?" asks Smita.

Chang'e nods, very slowly. "They do," she says. "They mirror the mortal moon as closely as they can, and that means that on the nights when we see no moon here, they see no moon in the City sky. But since the moon is always visible somewhere in the world, there will still be Lunars going into the everything even when the ones here are staying home."

"Not nearly as many," says Máni. "If someone has access to the everything—enough access to have gotten in there and assaulted Aske while she was trying to complete her duties—they could presumably open a gate and get in without needing to worry about running into anyone else."

"But we determined that we each have our own path through the everything," argues Artemis. "Why would anyone need to worry about that?"

"We didn't really determine that," says Chang'e, slowly. "We determined that every Lunar has our own path through the everything, and they always lead us to the same place—to the windows in the sky above the City. We don't know whether another Artemis would use your path, or have their own."

"What do those windows look like to the residents, I wonder?" muses Roger.

"Stars," says Erin, in a tone that implies the answer is patently obvious to anyone who takes a moment to consider it.

The word spreads through the group, and then it *is* patently obvious. What else could the windows be, if not stars scattered across the glorious blackness above the City? Chang'e catches her breath as Judy stirs within her, glancing to Máni. "So the paths we take through the everything, they don't actually *close* when we shut the gate, do they. They stay where they are, so the light from the Moon can bounce off all the closed windows and turn them into stars."

"Yes," says Erin.

"I know how we can find Aske's body," she says, and turns the whole of her attention on Dodger, who blinks in brief surprise, and then in irritation. She's not used to being surprised anymore. She clearly doesn't like it.

"What do I have to do with this?" she asks.

"It's Artemis's night to cross the sky above the City," says Máni.

He hasn't contributed much up until now, but it's obvious he's excited by this new way of approaching the problem. "You could go into the everything with her, and while she's crossing, you could go from her window to Aske's."

"There are about eighty million problems with that idea, but the first one—the big one—is that I don't know which window you're talking about," says Dodger. "I'm not the most athletic person in the world—Roger, I swear if you laugh at me, I am going to tell the laws of thermodynamics, and your coffee will be cold for the next *month*—and I'm not super into the idea of climbing out a window and trying to jump across a void to something I don't know."

"You're Math, right?" asks Artemis. "If you went to Máni and Chang'e's windows with them before you came with me, couldn't you extrapolate where the next relevant window would be?"

"That's not math, that's divination," says Dodger. "Pseudoscience. There's also the question of whether the stars above the City move. Are you clustered together because you're here, or do your windows stay wherever it is they were when you became manifest? Or when you were incarnated?"

"You keep using all these different words like they're interchangeable, but they don't mean exactly the same thing, and I think I've earned a footnote," says Isabella. "What the hell is the difference between manifest and incarnated?"

"Sorry," says Roger. He doesn't sound sorry. "Sometimes we forget we're using the words the alchemists came up with for all these things, and not everyone knows what those words mean. Language is a shared consensus of concepts as much as it's anything else, and if we don't share the local definitions, we might as well be speaking a language you don't know."

Isabella blinks, then, and looks faintly mollified as she says, "Well, if you'll just explain yourselves now, we can get back to throwing people out of windows."

"Hey," says Dodger, dryly.

"A personification is a universal force that has been compelled to take on physical form," says Roger. "Normally human, or so human-adjacent as to make no difference, normally—despite the evidence of this kitchen—naturally occurring, brought about by patterns of myth and belief. People say the summer is a person enough times, they eventually get Summer, born into a human body and walking around doing things like a human might. Gods are just another form of personification. Most of them don't have any sort of cosmic powers or anything like that: they have what the stories gave them, and what we believe they're going to have."

Isabella looks, momentarily, horrified. "Wait, wait . . . if it's not just moon gods, are you saying that *the* God is wandering around all the time, wearing pants and eating sandwiches and looking like a normal human?"

"Erin, you want to field this one?"

"He's not," says Erin. "Any god more powerful than the strongest Lunars would take more belief than we have on the whole planet, and they'd be inherently limited by the shape they took. If you want omnipotence, you need the City. If any of the big-G *gods* currently has a physical form, that's where they'll be. Sitting in the control room of reality, keeping everything vaguely operational."

"Oh. Good."

"But little gods, like our Lunars here, gods that are closely tied to specific natural phenomenon or things, they personified a long time ago. And the universe is a creature of habit, just as much as the people who live inside of it are. Once it starts doing something, it needs a good reason to stop. So they keep incarnating, over and over again, probably forever. I would be willing to wager actual money that the gods we don't see anymore, the ones people have forgotten about, who don't have any believers to remind the universe about them, still incarnate. They just don't manifest."

"Because that's the difference," says Roger, stepping in and smoothly taking over. "An incarnation is someone who's been born who *might* manifest one day, who *might* become a living personification of a universal concept. Dodger and I were incarnate from the moment we were born. It took us a long time to realize we needed to become something more, and manifest. That was when we fully claimed the Doctrine of Ethos and *became* it, for all intents and purposes. As long as we're alive, we'll be the living manifestations of the personification of the Doctrine. Nothing gets to change that now."

"I met a girl upstairs," says Kelpie. "She had green hair, and she said she and her brother were almost the Doctrine. What is she?"

"Kim," says Dodger, with a flicker of regret. "She's an incarnation, like we were. She was made by the same alchemists, using the same material, and I guess on a purely merit-based level, she and her brother would have been better candidates for manifestation. We just got there first, and while a lot of incarnations can choose not to manifest if they don't want to, you can't really de-manifest. We couldn't give the Doctrine back if we wanted to."

"And we don't want to," says Roger. "We fought and bled and sacrificed a lot to be standing here, two manifest halves of a force without which the universe would collapse, watching you look at us like we're zoo exhibits. I'm sorry Kim didn't get what she was made to want. I'm not sorry my sister did."

Dodger bumps him with her shoulder, focusing on Isabella. "That's your answer, in the broadest terms possible. A personification is something that shouldn't be a person, but is. An incarnation is a person with the *potential* to represent that something, and a manifestation is someone who *does* represent it."

"Do we really need three separate words for that?" asks Isabella.

"*Yes*," says every incarnation currently in the kitchen, which is almost every other person there. Roger follows up with "We need thirty, for the gradations and subtle differences, and so people don't waste time asking what you meant. We need *more* words, not fewer of them, and these three are the ones that have managed to hang on for centuries, which means they're the best words available, even if they're still more limited than I would like them to be."

"So the moment we became incarnate is when this body"— Chang'e gestures to herself—"was born, and the moment we became manifest is when we agreed that we were willing to be gods.

For me, there was a sixteen-year gap between those two events. If my window is still where it was when I was born, it's nowhere near here. But I've always walked the same distance through the everything, and I can't say for sure, but I feel like there are so many stars above the City that they could absolutely move around if they wanted to. Lunars who shine from the same spot in the sky should have windows near each other."

"So it's settled," says Artemis. "She follows each of us into the everything so she can start charting out the location of our windows, and then either she swings over to the right window, or I do it. I'm probably a lot more athletic than she is. No offense."

"None taken. I'm a math nerd who manages to avoid spending eight hours at the gym every week solely because I'm also an immutable force of the universe."

"Not to point out the elephant in the room, but what are we going to do about the alchemists who lost her?" Erin hooks her thumb at Kelpie. "Alchemists aren't great about letting other people take their toys, and they're likely to be looking for this one."

"My apartment is warded," says Isabella. "My family is safe."

Roger starts shaking his head, and she blinks at him, bewildered. "No, that won't do," he says. "Dodge, how far are we going in adopting these people?"

"Erin likes them; I think we're keeping them."

"How do you know she likes us?" asks Kelpie.

"She hasn't murdered either one of you," says Smita, and Erin sticks her tongue out at her. Smita snickers.

"Okay, great. Dodge, start watching the listings."

"On it."

Isabella frowns. "I'm sorry, what's going on?"

"The kind of wards you can manage on an apartment are good, but they're going to erode fast as people come and go," explains Roger. "They'll collapse, and if you're not already in the process of setting whatever comes next, they'll leave your family exposed. Maybe only for a few seconds, but a few seconds is all these assholes need. You need a border that's entirely yours."

"So we're going to find you a house," says Dodger, like that's a perfectly reasonable thing for someone to say to somebody they've just met.

Isabella gapes at the two of them. "What?"

"House," says Roger. "That's what you need. Hey, moon people. When can we access this everything you keep talking about?"

"I feel like you can probably access it any time you want to," says Chang'e. "But more realistically, as soon as the moon shows up in the sky, we can open up the gate. It moves around every night, but the local version's been circling the clocktower, so we should probably check there first."

"Of course it is," says Dodger. "Guess we're going to campus at moonrise. Now if you'll all excuse me, this is about as much togetherness as I can handle before midnight, and I'm not going to get that much alone time. I'll be in my room when you're ready to go. Roger? Call me."

And she's gone, striding out of the kitchen like she's just remembered some incredibly vital appointment she needs to attend to *right now.*

"Huh," says Smita. "She lasted a *lot* longer than I expected her to."

"Not the most social person in the house," says Erin. "And given that we have two teenagers who mostly hide in their rooms, and also me, that's saying something pretty impressive. But if she says she'll help, she'll help, and that means she's with us for charting out your windows and hopefully figuring out which one you want. Why are we doing this?"

"One of our friends was murdered while she was in a place no one should be able to access without a Lunar," says Artemis. "We said we were looking for her body."

"That can have a lot of meanings," says Erin. "Sorry about your friend. And I'm sure you'll find the answers you're looking for now that you've got a little outside help. I'm going to go check on the kids, but I'll come along with you all when it's actually time to go out where the alchemists are." She gestures for Smita to follow her out of the kitchen, and the two of them make their exit, heading quickly up the stairs.

"I should get home," says Isabella, seeing the dissolution of their temporary gathering as an opportunity for escape. "My son will be home from school by now, and if there's any chance the wards might go down, I need to be there before it happens."

"Yes, you should be," says Kelpie solemnly. "The people who made me . . . they wouldn't think twice about killing him if they thought it would help them get whatever it is they want, and they'd use the pieces against you."

Isabella looks horrified for a moment, then says, briskly, "I'll look up moonrise online, and meet you all at the clocktower. Sir." She turns to Roger. "Can I bring my son and husband here while we're on campus? I can make something up to explain why, but I don't want them left alone."

Roger nods. "Tim and Kim won't be coming with us. If you say you're babysitting, they're highly unlikely to come downstairs and contradict you."

"Thank you," says Isabella. She gives Kelpie a brisk, one-armed hug, then flees for the door.

One by one, they're slipping away. Chang'e looks to Artemis, then to Kelpie. "Is there a place these two could go and talk, maybe? Without being listened to the whole time?"

"They can go out in the backyard," says Roger, and gestures to a door. "No one will bother them there."

"Wonderful," says Chang'e. "I want to go out front and check out that peach tree I saw before Judy shoves me out of the way and starts trying to interrogate you about linguistics."

Roger smiles toothily. "Having a little trouble keeping her suppressed?"

"You have no idea," says Chang'e. "Being at Berkeley with you and feeling like she couldn't talk to you has been wearing on her ever since we found out what you are. Máni, you want to come with me?"

"Going to leave me alone in the yard when she wins and jerks you back inside to yell at him, aren't you?"

"Oh, probably," she says, and he's laughing as they head back toward the front door, leaving Artemis and Kelpie to look at each other awkwardly. Roger sighs and puts his mug down on the counter.

"Door's right there if you ladies want to do this outside, or you can have the kitchen," he says. "I'll be in my office either way. It's the door at the end of the hall with the bronze sign that says 'Please, no,' in eleven languages. If you can read them all, you may knock. If you can't, unless the house is on fire, please leave me alone."

"Okay . . . ?" says Kelpie, and watches in bemusement as he picks up the coffee pot, refills his mug, and takes it with him out of the kitchen.

At last they are alone. Neither one of them looks particularly happy about it. Kelpie looks like she's going to be sick.

"I didn't—" she begins.

"I wasn't—" says Artemis, at the same time. She stops, catching her breath, and takes a step backward, putting some more distance between her and Kelpie, and at the same time, opening the path to the back door. "They're right, though. We should talk. Do you want to do it inside or out in the garden?"

"Outside is still really new to me," says Kelpie. "It's exciting. I've seen flowers before, but they were always in the hydroponics section, or part of someone's experiment."

Artemis frowns, biting the edge of one lip. "I don't . . . I don't like that for you."

"I didn't know anything different." Kelpie shrugs. "Margaret told me the accident had messed up my head just as much as my body, and I trusted her, so I thought she was telling the truth. I believed her when she said I could never risk going up to the surface, not until they finished fixing me."

"Fixing you?"

"I guess I was already too human when they made me for them to see me as the kind of tool they wanted me to be? Sometimes when new technicians came to the lab, they'd say I was in the 'uncanny valley,' and so funny-looking that I was cute. I didn't really understand what that meant, but they didn't seem to say it to be mean, and the ones who felt that way were almost always nice to me, so I figured it had to be a good thing."

"Okay . . ."

"Oh, um. Fixing me. Right. I looked a lot less . . . human? I guess? When I first woke up?" Kelpie waves her hands, encompassing the hooves, the tail, the complexion that not even the world's worst spray tan could explain. She doesn't look human. She looks bipedal but like a member of some other species entirely, something that was never intended to stand in this kitchen and talk about human things. "So they were working to change those parts of me so they'd be more normal. And give me back my memory from before the accident."

"Since now we know there was no 'before the accident,' what does that mean?"

"It means that Margaret would bring me papers she said I wrote, and my application to come and work in the lab, and pictures of my family in Florida. We'd do flash cards, with things on them that I needed to recognize so I'd be safe when I finally left the lab. Cars and buses and sidewalks and money. She worked really hard to get me ready." Kelpie sighs. "I know it's probably wrong, but my whole life, I've thought one day I was going to get to be something else, and even though I don't mind what I am that much—people should have tails, it's hard to tell what they're thinking when they don't, and toes are weird, I'm glad I don't have toes—it's hard to let go of what I thought I was meant to be."

"I get that," says Artemis. "I really do. I don't control where I incarnate, but when I introduced myself to Anna, she thought she was going to be a teacher. She grew up in a really strict family, and they had all these rules about what she could wear and who she could talk to and what careers she was allowed to even think about. 'Teacher' was one of the only ones that they said was suitable for a woman. And then I moved in, and told her it was okay to want to be happy, and she started pushing their limits." She pauses for a moment, expression turning somber.

"I think . . ." Artemis says finally. "I think it might be easier if we did things the way the alchemists do, when they make their perfect vessels. If we weren't sharing space. I'm Artemis, I know I'm Artemis, but I don't remember any of those things that people say about Olympus. I could hit a target dead-on from the moment I first picked up a bow, and anything that can be a projectile weapon is deadly in my hands, but I never trained. And sometimes the things I want and the things Anna wants aren't the same. I have to negotiate with myself all the time, forever, in order to stay on level ground. When I meet another Artemis, she's me, but she isn't, like a photograph that's been left out in the rain and gotten all distorted. But neither of us is a clearer picture than the other; we're just starting from someplace different. I've never seen a Hind before. They stopped incarnating a long time before this incarnation of me was born."

"Why?" asks Kelpie. "If the City needs the Lunars to satisfy its populace, and enough people believe in you that you keep getting born over and over again, why did the companions go away?"

"I think because the City didn't need you, and so it never pressed against the part of the universe that spends resources putting pieces of itself in living bodies," says Artemis. She finally moves to open the back door, gesturing toward it with an open hand, inviting. "You want to go outside?"

"Okay," says Kelpie, and crosses to exit, careful to keep as much distance between herself and Artemis as possible. It's like she fears something will change if they touch, and maybe something will; she was built to be a perfect companion to this woman, after all, and now that they're in the same place, the same time, she has no idea what that might actually mean for her. Right now, she still feels like she can walk away.

Or could, if she had anywhere to go. She's trying her hardest not to think about that. She can't go back to the lab, even if part of her wants to, yearns for the safety of familiar surroundings and routines. The man who killed Margaret would do the same to her without hesitation. She isn't even human. She's a failed project. There's no reason for him to let her roam free.

She can't go back to Isabella's apartment. What Roger said about the wards matches what she understands of such boundaries, which even the strongest alchemist can't render unbreakable without a lot more time and resources than Isabella has. Her presence puts that family in danger. She isn't sure if she's a danger to these people as well, but she feels like they would have said something if she were, like they would have pushed her out the door and told her to solve her own problems. More importantly, these people are as unnatural as she is. They understand in a way that Isabella can't.

But they haven't asked her to stay, and she can't invite herself. Out on the streets, on her own, she'll be a beacon for any alchemist who's looking to score points with the Congress by bringing the runaway back; she can't evade them forever. And from what she knows, having been on the companion incarnation project for as much of her life as she can remember, being Artemis's Hind isn't going to give her any of the strange abilities that some personifications get after they become manifest.

Is she even manifest? What if this is all the stage before that happens, and she's going to wind up like the Lunars, with someone else inside her head, telling her what to do and occasionally taking control of her body? They all seem comfortable with what they are and the way it works, but she's never considered needing to share the only thing that's really *hers*. She doesn't want to.

The existence of the steps up to the front porch should have made her realize how elevated the house is from the ground, but she's not familiar enough with standard architecture, and she didn't realize before. She steps onto the back porch and stops, hooves thudding dully against the weathered redwood surface. Another set of steps leads down to the backyard, which is a riot of color. Green dominates, of course, in the form of lush grass and surprisingly well-behaved blackberry vines, which have twisted and wrapped themselves around one another to form tidy mounds, turning the back half of the yard into a labyrinth of channels and paths. Their branches hang heavy with fruit. Much of the rest of the space is filled with vegetable beds, all as ripe and perfect as the ones out front, none seeming to care about the season or the weather.

This is a tiny slice of paradise, called into being behind a house in Berkeley. It's thriving, but Kelpie knows without asking that it's fragile; remove any of the pieces from this exact configuration, and the whole thing will come crashing down.

The door shuts as Artemis exits the house to stand behind her, still not closing the distance between them, still not touching her. Artemis may not share her specific concerns about what will happen when they inevitably make contact, but she's respecting Kelpie's clear concerns as best she can, even as she continues to lean toward the other woman like a flower leans toward the sun.

"I don't know why the City needs a Moon, or whether it's going to stop someday," she says. "I don't even know whether the people we see there are actually people, or if they're ideas, or ideals, or something else altogether. Maybe they're concepts that haven't personified yet, or maybe they're former manifestations that have gone to their reward for putting up with all this bullshit while they were alive. I think you'd have to go down into the City to find out for sure, and that's not allowed. We can't leave the sky while we're overhead."

Kelpie glances at her and nods, listening without interjecting.

"I think Lunars work the way we do because we have to be used to the idea of sharing space inside ourselves. When we go into the sky above the City, we're never alone. Every other Lunar who's come to shine that night emerges and shines with us, and when we come together, we make a Moon. But what I know about companions tells me they never do that. They don't combine to form one bigger than themselves. They stay in the everything, and they watch us pass, and then when we come back to the everything, they . . . help."

"Help how?"

"That's less clear. I think they're supposed to help us snap back into being ourselves, and not stay muddled up with all the other people we've been combined with for the whole night. Sort of like using a ground wire when you're working with electricity. They bleed off the extra energy. And that makes sense, when you consider that only the most powerful Lunars ever manifest companions."

"Máni," says Kelpie, dubiously.

"He used to be a lot more powerful than he is now," says Artemis. "Chang'e still has a *lot* of active worshippers, and the way the Holy Roman Empire fucked with European culture when they started expanding means that even though Diana and I don't have nearly as many worshippers as she does, just as many people know who we are, because they've read the books of Greek and Roman mythology. They know our names, and so we hold on to the power we should probably have lost centuries ago. Why us and not Máni, or Losna, or any of the others? It's all down to who managed to spread their stories farther and faster than anyone else, like dandelions going to seed and blanketing a whole meadow."

"Oh," says Kelpie, voice softer.

"So if you're worried that you're going to get swallowed up by something you never asked for, I don't think you need to be worried. Not the way a new Lunar does."

"What do you mean? You swallow them?"

Artemis looks momentarily guilty. "No. I mean, yes, but also no. We don't swallow our hosts; we share with them, and we make them stronger than they would have been without us. But at the end of the day, when we're manifesting our divinity, they're pushed way, way down. They become passengers in their own bodies, in their own lives. I have Anna's face and Anna's body, always. I can make a lot of trouble for her. If I break the law, her ID is the one they'll flag in the system. If I drop out of school or decide it would be fun to try some sort of really addictive drugs, she's eventually going to have to deal with that. And of course, when I have control, she doesn't. That's time that should have been hers, getting spent on being me. She can't get that time back. Not ever. And being Artemis means

I'm naturally manifest a lot of the time. I can't step all the way down when I'm on a hunt, even if I want to."

"Meaning . . . ?"

"Meaning right now, Anna is always sharing space with me in a way that means she doesn't have full control over her life—but she's still *here*. You have to remember that. She was here before I started speaking to her, and when she dies—because all mortal flesh will die, no matter how many peaches she steals from Chang'e's garden—Artemis will endure. This speck of the greater goddess will gutter out and fade away, forgotten like any other tiny variation on a familiar story, and somewhere in the world, someone else will wake up with the voice of a goddess ringing in their ears." Artemis sighs. "Gods die all the time. Especially tiny gods like us."

"Why do the gods have to be tiny?" asks Kelpie. "That's the part I don't quite get. If the universe has to use energy to make you manifest, wouldn't it be better to just make one of each of you at a time, and not spend all that extra energy?"

"The universe wants its personifications to be human," says Artemis. "That's the whole point of making us the way it does. It likes being able to experience things through a human lens, and so it casts some of its functions into human roles. But if all of me incarnated in one person . . ." She pauses, shivers. "I'm pretty sure that's the main reason the universe splits us up this way. Because we're small enough to share space with people, we don't completely destroy them. When a Summer or Winter becomes manifest, they're still the people they were before they were seasons, just with a sort of . . . overlay that never quite goes away. When a Lunar becomes manifest, they're still completely the person they were, just with a voice in their head nudging them along and occasionally asking for a turn at the wheel. But when an Element becomes manifest, when someone *is* Fire, or *is* Water, or whatever, the person they were before they manifested is gone. They're burnt out, drowned, blown away, buried. There's no going back. The Elements can't step down, because there's nothing left for them to step down *to*. If you put a whole god into a human body, you'd get a situation like those three

inside. There *is* no Professor Middleton. It's nice that he's pretending he's a person, and I guess he's not faking it entirely, because
he grew up already connected to the Doctrine through his sister—
breaking it into two bodies and tying them together means they
had to be a little bit manifest from birth—but really, there's nothing
there but Language. It's just Language with a name and a coffee
order at Starbucks."

Kelpie glances over her shoulder at the house. "I don't want that."

"That's what I'm trying to tell you," says Artemis, sounding frus-
trated. "I don't think you're *going* to have that. The companions
don't aggregate the way the gods do—and not even all the gods do
it, just the Lunars, although every kind of divinity I know of that
still incarnates does it the way we do, in little pieces. Everything I
know about the companions says they incarnate, and they incarnate intact. And then, if circumstances are right, eventually, they
manifest."

"I'm afraid I'll manifest if I touch you."

"So don't touch me."

"I think I have to." The admission is small. "I also think that if
I don't manifest, it's easier for the people who made me to catch
me and take me back again, and I don't want to be taken back. But
I don't want to be someone else, either. I want to be me, whatever
that means."

"Only one way to find out, but it's not something you can take
back if you don't like what happens."

"Really? There's no way for someone to say 'I don't like this, I don't
want it, I'll let it go'?"

Artemis hesitates. Finally, she says, "Some of the manifestations
can do that. I know the big Seasons can voluntarily step aside, and
since there's only one crown per season per continent, they sever
themselves from their seasons when they do that, and they die. But
if they're born with the potential to seize a season—incarnates—
and there's not a coronation during their lifetimes, they live their
whole lives and die without ever manifesting. They live human. It's
only if a coronation is called that they start to manifest, and after

that process begins, they can't live without the season that sustains them. If they refuse the crown, they die. If they don't win the crown, they die. There is no other way out."

"And for gods?"

"If I'd said to Anna 'I'm Artemis, goddess of the hunt and the moon, and I want you to be my mortal vessel and let me walk with you in the world,' and she'd said 'no, thank you,' I would have stayed a seed. I wouldn't have sprouted, and she would have lived her whole life with the potential to be me, but never *become* me. Now, she's stuck with me for the rest of her life. I couldn't leave if I wanted to."

"What about me?" There's a challenge in Kelpie's tongue. "I never invited anyone in."

"I don't think you had to."

Kelpie blinks, then turns her face away. "What do you mean?"

"I mean that, in your case, I don't think there was anyone for you to talk to. The alchemists made a perfect, empty vessel, and they made it so perfect that you couldn't stay out. They invited you into something you didn't have the capacity to refuse, and they put all the power into it that the universe wasn't offering. So you went in. You got comfortable. And when you woke up, they gave you a name and told you that you belonged to them. They invented a Kelpie for you to be. Or maybe she was real, once, and they used pieces of her when they made you. I don't know. I don't think anyone *can* know. But you never invited anyone in because you *are* the person knocking at the door. You *are* the seed, and you're already growing, whether or not you become manifest, whatever manifestation means for you. It's not like the stories we have ascribe a lot of powers to the Hind."

"She soothes Artemis when the hunt goes badly; she can enter sacred spaces without frightening the game already there, and allows all the hunt to follow without fear of failure. And she's supposed to be associated in some way with healing waters, but that always seemed a little weird to me, since Artemis isn't a healer."

"No, but you wash the wounds you incur while hunting, and if the Hind washes her wounds, it would make sense for it to gradually develop the ability to make the water more potent, or at least cleaner." Artemis looks at her carefully. "Are you really afraid there'll be a second voice in your head if you take my hand? Or are you afraid there won't be?"

"I want to be real," says Kelpie, a hitch in her voice. "I want to exist like everyone else exists, and to stay. Is it bad, that I want to be a real person?"

"You seem pretty real to me. You can talk, and say confusing things, and come with us tonight to access the everything and find out how Aske died. Does it really matter whether you have a person inside you even when you're not the Hind?"

"I don't know." Kelpie looks at Artemis's hands, hanging relaxed and nonthreatening at the other woman's sides. "I'm scared that I'll find out it matters a lot, and then it'll be too late to take it back."

"Be brave," says Artemis. "You were brave when you ran away from the alchemists, and you were brave when you came into that kitchen, and spoke to me. So be brave now. Be brave enough to find out who you really are."

Kelpie says nothing. Just steps a little closer, hooves thudding dully against the wood, and takes her hand.

Silence follows.

BOOK IV

Gibbous

Let us be Diana's foresters, gentlemen of the shade, minions of the moon; and let men say we be men of good government, being governed, as the sea is, by our noble and chaste mistress the moon, under whose countenance we steal.

—William Shakespeare, *Henry IV, Part I*

Sunlight wakes me
Warm and still
Moonlight moves me
Always will;
Firelight warms me
Starlight stirs me
No light at all makes me feel
Glad to be with you.

—Talis Kimberley, "Any Kind of Light"

The whittled-down Crow Girl was standing at the edge of the mesa, looking uneasily down, an expression on her face that implied she had never contemplated anything she liked less than the idea of jumping to join them.

"I'm too short to fall without hurting myself," she said, somewhat petulantly.

Zib blinked, then frowned. "Can't you be birds long enough to fly down?"

"I'm not sure being birds would be a good idea," said the Crow Girl, and hugged herself. "I think this is part of what it costs, eventually, to be a flock without a heart. The only way I get to be bigger again is if I make or steal more birds to join myself, and they won't have been part of whoever I was before I traded my name away. They won't know how to be *me*. I'm going to wind up turning into somebody else before this is all over, and I don't want it. So I don't want to be birds anymore, not unless I very much have to."

Avery, who had felt the loss of the shine from his shoes as a blow to his very identity, nodded slowly. Even if he assumed the Queen of Swords had told the Crow Girl all the consequences of getting what she wanted, even if he believed she had been honest and upfront, the Crow Girl had lost so many birds—and the memories that contained—at this point that she was no longer the person who had agreed to pay. She was, in many ways, caught in a bargain she hadn't made, just like any other child. And like any other child, she was afraid.

He stepped closer to the wall, so that he was right beneath her, and spread his arms.

"Sit and push yourself over the edge, and I'll catch you," he said solemnly. "I promise."

She looked at him gravely, as if assessing his honesty, then did as she was told, sitting and pushing herself away from the edge, eyes screwed tightly shut as she dropped toward him.

Avery caught her and staggered, more from the force of impact than from her weight, which was even slighter than he would have expected from the size of her. He remembered reading somewhere that birds had hollow bones, and supposed she must be proof of it. . . .

—From *Into the Windwracked Wilds,* by A. Deborah Baker

Mare Anguis

Isabella walks fast, purse clutched against her side, trying not to think about what may be waiting for her when she gets home, what she may have done by inviting a strange sunrise-skinned girl to stay for dinner. She's flirted with the magical world since she was a child and realized not everyone could see the spirits attending on their daily lives. She served her apprenticeship with the old auntie everyone had known was no relation of hers, who first taught her how to solicit the spirits for help, for the answers to impossible questions and the locations of hidden things.

It was when her auntie passed away that she had finally stepped forward and declared herself a proper hechicera, ready to convince the universe to do things her way through whatever means necessary. Even dead, her auntie had been there the whole time, supporting and egging her on, and when she'd followed up that declaration with the announcement that she was moving to America, the rest of her family had wept and cheered in the same breath, glad to see her following her own path—and, to a degree, even more glad that it was a path that would take her away from them. Hechiceras were nice things to have in the family, nice things to brag about or be able to call upon in times of emergency, but they were hazardous things to keep at home. If she was going to practice, it was better she do it far away from them, where there would be less chance of them getting caught in the backlash.

She *knew* those things, had known those things when she moved to California, when she allowed the whispering of the universe to guide her to a welcoming community and help her find her footing in a new land, and for years she had practiced the best ways of doing things. She had kept people carefully at arm's length, preventing them from getting close enough to be caught in the backlash when she inevitably pushed the universe too far and got slapped down for her troubles.

(For that moment, too, was an integral part of the hechicera's education. The moment when she pushed things too far and was knocked on her ass was a reminder of her place, telling her where the limits of her power were. Once she knew those limits, she could work to strengthen and expand upon them, growing the sphere of her influence until she was a properly powerful old hechicera and not a talented and ambitious young one.)

Only no one is really meant to be alone forever, however talented they are, however much the universe whispers to them in their dreams, and when a tall, handsome mechanic named Juan had walked into the occult shop where she'd been working, she'd been unable to resist making doe's eyes at him, standing just a little too close, bending just a little too far to give him glimpses of her cleavage. He'd been shopping for his sister's birthday that first time, and the time after, he'd been looking for a good luck charm for the shop where he worked.

The time after that, he'd been looking for Isabella, and the time after *that,* he'd found her. Their courtship hadn't been the stuff of fairy tales, but it had been the stuff of romance novels, all heated looks and sweat on skin, the taste of pheromones on their tongues making everything twice as delicious as it should have been, the sound of bodies against bodies. She's often believed that love begins with a look and grows to encompass every sense the body has. She had been lost from the moment she'd seen his soul.

Half her family had flown over from Puerto Rico for the wedding. Luis had paid for their tickets as a surprise to her, so she could be married with her Papa on her arm and her grandmother weeping in the front pew of the little church they'd rented for the occasion.

She wasn't going to pretend she'd gone chaste to her bridal bed, but she'd gone careful and well aware of the mathematics of the situation, and Luis had been born eleven months after the wedding, carefully timed so as to erase any chance of gossip.

He'd come into the world covered in blood and surrounded by spirits, wailing as the newly arrived always seemed to do, and she'd been exhausted and aching and instantly in love. Everything else had been forgotten in an instant, because now Luis was here, and Luis needed her to be a mother, and in those moments, she would have sworn she could give up her practice forever, could retire from being an hechicera and find absolute contentment in being a mother.

That stage had lasted for a little over a week before boredom had stolen in, between the feedings and the diaper changes, and she had found herself performing small cleansing rituals on the energy in the house, chasing out the negativity that had gathered in the corners, sweeping away the shades of fear for the uncertain future. Things were uncertain, sure. So what? Things were always uncertain. Being an hechicera didn't give her the power to see the future, only the ability to occasionally ask the world to bend that future to her benefit.

Luis grew older every day, settling into his existence in the world. He had ceased to be a piece of her long before he left her body, and once he was out in the world, he had quickly established himself as his own person, capable of incredible kindness, unexpected flashes of brilliance, and a stubbornness she recognized from herself. He was as solidly ordinary as his father, and he was perfect, and she was doing her best to make a perfect world for him. If that meant using her natural gifts to nudge the universe, what of it?

All she's done since the day her perfect son wailed his way into the world is work to make that world a better place for him, and now, through a simple act of kindness, she may have fucked it all up. Her thoughts are full of blood and worse as she hurries for home, crosses streets against the light, plows through crowds with little consideration for the people she bumps against and blunders into.

She has always lived her American life by the immigrant's credo: attract no unnecessary attention. What goes unseen goes unthreatened.

Well, they've been seen now. She let Kelpie into their lives and opened those lives to the eyes of people she never wanted anything to do with. She should have demanded they move as soon as she realized alchemists had purchased the other side of the courtyard, should have taken the approach of "the best place for an enemy is as far away from me as possible" rather than "keep them where you can see them." "Keep them where you can see them" was the attitude of a younger hechicera, one with less to lose.

Luis is everything to lose.

She's almost running by the time she reaches the corner of her street. When she turns that corner and sees her apartment building up ahead, looking exactly as it did when she left it this morning, she *starts* running, hell-bent for leather, feet pounding the pavement like an open assault, and she doesn't care who stares, and she doesn't care who sees. She's *running,* racing for home like she's never had any other destination in her heart or mind, running harder than she's ever run for anything before.

The apartment door is locked. Whether that means anything is hard to say. Isabella fumbles for her keys, glancing constantly over her shoulder. Is that motion in the bushes the wind, or an alchemist crouched down and watching? Did that curtain just twitch? Is she being watched, is she alone? There are so many questions. It would almost be easier if it was dark, but no, it's the middle of the afternoon, and the sounds of the city are complicating everything.

Bobby finally realizes there's someone at the door and starts barking as Isabella slides her key into the keyhole, a sound that becomes a whine as she undoes the lock and lets herself inside. She's never been afraid of the family dog. He's a very good boy they got from the shelter as a leggy, rambunctious puppy, all lolling tongue and flopping ears, and he's never had a mean bone in his body. But as she looks around the dark living room, she finds him backed into the corner behind the couch, pressed between the frame and the wall. His ears are flat, and his lips are drawn back from his teeth, which seem suddenly very sharp and very white.

A chill goes through her. Alchemists don't like big, flashy magic. They think it's beneath them. They think *magic* is beneath them: only their precious science is worth the honor of their attention. In that regard, they're closer to hechiceras than they are to witches: Isabella may sneer at them a bit for staying shallow, because they do, but a witch is more likely to be able to do the sort of tricks that people will recognize as magical. Flowers pulled out of nothing, flames lit with the snapping of a finger.

Dogs that have never known anything but love moved inexorably and irrevocably to rage.

Bobby snarls, taking a shaking step toward her, and Isabella's heart gives a lurch. She wants to turn and run into the kitchen, where the knives are, but turning her back on a dog that looks like that might be the last thing she ever does. So she stands her ground, trying to still the hammering of her heart, and breathes, slow and even.

"Bobby," she says, voice soft. "It's me."

He keeps snarling.

"Where is Luis? Where's our boy? Bobby, where is Luis?"

He stops advancing, cocking his head to the side, a puzzled light coming into his eyes. His ears prick forward slightly—not all the way, but enough for her to be reasonably sure he hears her. She slips a hand into her pocket, where the blend of herbs and salt she used to close the circle this morning still clings to the fabric. Rolling her fingers together, she scrapes up a pinch of the mixture, which is meant to encourage peace and harmony. Right now, a little peace and harmony can't hurt.

The wards are down. She feels it in her bones, would have realized it faster if she hadn't been distracted by fear and the barking dog, but the wards are down and the apartment is dark and Bobby is growling and it's reasonable that she's still too distracted to go investigating the reason. She can't exactly ask the dog to hold on a moment with his growls and clear agitation. That wouldn't work. So she tosses the pinch of salt and simples into the air, murmuring a quick plea to the spirits she's coaxed into watching over this house to come and attend upon her. She needs them. She needs them as she has never needed them before.

Much like an alchemist, she has never focused her talents on the big or the flashy. Those things can be faked with all manner of tricks and tools, and they tend to be the hallmark of an amateur, someone just dabbling in the invisible arts. Her focus has always been on protection and connection. She knows the small gods of this apartment complex as well as she knows her more physical neighbors. They're half the reason she didn't move out when the alchemists moved in. Yes, staying this close to an alchemical research station was a risk, but it was at least slightly balanced out by knowing that the local universal energies were inclined to like her and give her a hand when she asked.

Please, she thinks, as hard as she can, into the space where the quiet call of the universe has always existed for her. *Please, for the love of my son, whatever they've done, brush it aside. Calm this space. Calm this space, and I will reward you with sweet smoke and fresh cream, and all the offerings my hands can carry. Remove their influences here. Give me back my companion.*

There is a brief, intangible brightness in the air, indescribable but present, like the feeling of waking in the morning in a room already filled with sunlight. Not the light itself, but the sensations that accompany it, the golden brilliance of a day being born, of potential and possibility. A shadow flits through the air and is gone, burned out by that brightness, which fades as quickly as it came. Bobby stops growling. His ears come all the way up, and his tail thumps, once, before he's lunging at her.

This isn't the lunge she feared, the one that ends in teeth and tearing. This is the enthusiastic greeting of a dog who loves his people, who hasn't seen her in too many hours and missed her company. His tail wags wildly as he slams into her shins, and she bends forward, almost sick with relief, to run her hand along the bony crest of his skull, the silken fur of his ears.

"Where's Luis, buddy?" she asks. "Where's our boy?"

Bobby looks at her with infinite trust in his eyes, tail still wagging, and barks, once, then dances away in that playful way of dogs in familiar spaces, his wild bouncing bringing him coincidentally close to his food dish, which is, at this hour of the day, empty.

There are spirits among those she called upon to calm the air who take their offerings from the things she puts into Bobby's bowl, and so she lets him lead her to the kitchen, where she gives him a scoop of dry kibble and tops it with two slices of bacon left over from breakfast and a raw egg from the co-op. People who say you shouldn't give your dogs raw egg are worried about salmonella, and she avoids the risk by buying eggs from healthy chickens who can't pass the infection along. She gives the bowl's contents a rough stir before she sets it down and Bobby falls to crunching, ears going flat once more, this time with the blissful single-mindedness of a dog doing the hard work of eating.

Isabella leaves him.

The apartment isn't large; it's not like Luis can hide for long, even if he's actively hiding, which she hopes he isn't. Whatever ripped down the wards and antagonized the dog is gone now; she can feel it. So as she works her way down the hall toward the bedrooms, she calls, softly, "Luis? Are you home?"

A sniffling sound from the closet where she keeps the vacuum cleaner. Luis has never been a boy to seek safety in small spaces, but then, his dog has never turned mean for no clear reason; if he were afraid enough, he might well have chosen the securest place he could think of.

"Luis? Sweetheart? I'm going to open the closet door now."

She doesn't want this to be a gotcha or a scare loaded atop the scares he's clearly already experienced today; she wants this to be a gentle reminder that the world is still here, the world is still his to love and live in, and she's still here, ready to help him do both those things. So she eases the door open, unsurprised but relieved to find him tangled in the coats at the back of the closet, tear streaks on his cheeks and blood on his lips, chin, and hand.

Even expected, the sight of the blood is enough to make her stop and breathe sharply in. His eyes widen.

"No, Mama! He didn't bite me! I think . . ." He hesitates. He knows what happens to pit bulls who bite, even by mistake; he's heard the stories from the kids at his school, the ones who love to talk about killer dogs and how some animals are just bred bad. Isabella would shake them all if she could, demand to know who's pouring that poison into their ears, and why they feel the need to pour it onward into her son's. "I think he *would* have bit me, only I ran when he got all mad and started growling. I don't know why, I didn't *do* anything! But he growled and I ran and when I shut myself in the closet, I smacked my nose into the wall hard enough to make it bleed."

"And your hand?"

"Wiping the blood so it didn't go all over my clothes."

It's a believable-enough story that it doesn't matter whether or not it's true.

"All right, baby, well, Bobby's calm now, and having a little snack, so let's get you cleaned up and you can tell me what happened, all right?" She puts her hand on his shoulder, urging him out of the closet, and when he emerges, she wraps her arms around him in a tight hug, reveling in the warm closeness of him, the concrete reality. This is her boy. He's here, he's alive, he's lost a little blood, but boys are *full* of blood at this age; he has blood to spare, quick, vital creature that he is. He'll never notice its lack.

"I'm not a baby, Mama," he says, even as he burrows into the warmth of her.

"You'll always be *my* baby," she replies, and kisses the top of his head before she lets him go. "Now. What happened?"

"I came home from school and I was going to take Bobby for his walk, so he could do his business and then I could watch TV, but when I opened the door, a *man* came out of that apartment you told me to never go near."

"What kind of a man?"

"White man. Tall, really skinny, wearing a suit like he was going to go work in an office or something. He didn't look right."

"Not right how?"

"Not *right*," says Luis, and his voice peaks and breaks, like the ghost of puberty yet to come has dropped by for a brief visit, stealing away his childhood piping for an instant. Isabella fights the urge to clutch at him again. "I don't know how to say he wasn't right, only that he wasn't *right*. He stood like something that shouldn't be standing the way it is. Like he didn't belong here. Do you understand?"

She doesn't, and because of that, she does. Luis doesn't share her connection to the hidden world around them, but a person doesn't need to be connected to the hidden world to know when something is a threat. Not being able to see *why* someone is a threat would create a feeling of dissonant wrongness, indescribable and absolutely real.

"I do," she says. "I think what you saw was a very, very bad man. Did he see you?"

"I don't know. I thought he did, for just a second, but I shut the door and sat on the floor with Bobby, and he didn't come knocking or trying to look in the windows, so I figured he was gone. And then Bobby got all weird and mad, and everything turned scary, and I went and hid in case the man was coming back."

Isabella hesitates. If Luis is telling the truth, the man he saw may have pulled down the wards as casually as she brushes away cobwebs during her once-monthly dusting sessions, barely noticing the act even as she performs it. Removing the wards would have let whatever negativity he was pouring out of himself come flowing into the apartment, and while Luis has never been sensitive, Bobby *is*. It was part of what attracted her to him above all the other leggy, loving puppies in the shelter, any one of whom could have been a beloved member of their family. If that alchemist took down the wards without even knowing it, it's easy to believe Bobby could have been easily driven into a frenzy by the shadow of his passing, and not targeted at all.

Relief washes through her like bleach through a stain, washing her fears of intentional attack away. "All right, buddy. Thank you for telling me."

Luis sniffles. "I didn't ever take Bobby for his walk."

Meaning there might be a mess somewhere in the apartment, a little biological time bomb for one of them to find. "That's fine. You had good reason to hide, if a strange man was walking around and Bobby was all worked up about it. You didn't do anything wrong, I promise." She guides him to the kitchen, where Bobby has finished his snack and is now deeply immersed in licking his genitals, ignoring the humans. Luis still flinches away from him, and Isabella hates the alchemists even more than she did before. To make a boy fear his own dog . . .

She wets a paper towel and carefully, gently cleans the blood from his face, revealing no damage beyond a forming bruise around his upper lip that won't be bad enough to catch the attention of the school administration. Oh, how she hates the phrase "boys will be boys" and the way it leads to casual dismissal of violence between children, but she appreciates that in this case, it's going to work in her favor—no one call to child protective services because a boy got a bruise, as long as he's not showing any other signs of abuse.

She hopes this particular gap in the supervision doesn't lead to any children slipping between the cracks and being forgotten, even as she knows that it does, it must, it always has. Children are so sturdy and so fragile at the same time. It's easy to forget.

She's wetting a second paper towel when someone knocks on the front door. Bobby lifts his head and looks toward the sound, a low growl building in his throat as the hair on the back of his neck lifts up. Luis gasps, breath catching. He's never been scared of the dog before. He clearly is now.

Isabella feels almost bad as she straightens and says, "Wait here."

"I don't wanna," he says. "I want to stay with you."

"I know, love. But I need to get the door, and in case it's someone you don't want to talk to, I want to get it by myself."

He frowns deeply, clearly uncomfortable with the idea, but manages to force a nod and flatten himself against the counter, as far from Bobby as he can get in the confines of their small kitchen.

Isabella leaves them there, a boy and his dog. She's not worried Bobby will turn violent again; the growling this time has a different timbre, more frightened than furious. Carefully, she makes her way to the door.

"Hello?" she calls, not opening it.

"Oh, good, you're home," says Catrina's familiar, too-high voice. "I need to see you."

Isabella automatically reaches for the doorknob, which locked behind her when she came inside. She hesitates, hand hovering above the metal, and tries to pin down the question now itching at the edges of her mind, all sharp edges and urgency.

Without letting herself dwell too hard on why she's doing it, she pulls her hand away from the doorknob and reaches the deadbolt instead, flipping it home before she reaches higher up, for the chain.

"You saw me this morning," she says. "I'm tired now. This isn't a good time."

"Come now. Aren't we friends?" Catrina's voice drops, turns cajoling. "Didn't I open my home to your practice? And didn't you promise to keep me safe from the world I was only half-aware of?"

"I did do that, and so did you," says Isabella carefully. When she'd met Catrina, the other woman had been exactly as she'd remained up until this morning: smug and quietly superior, convinced of her own power and innate authority. She'd never once paused to ask herself whether the people she envied for their position had done anything to earn it; the accident of her birth was the only thing she considered to have been necessary to grant her whatever privileges she desired. Catrina was a lovely woman when you played to her ego and didn't contradict her in any way, and a remarkably fragile one when you didn't. Like many people whose social superiority had rarely if ever been challenged, she'd been unprepared to react quickly when people didn't do what she expected.

Isabella realizes, with a sick, sinking feeling, that she's started thinking of Catrina in the past tense: part of her has already written the woman off as lost. They're not *friends*. They've never been *friends*, not in any of the ways that truly matter. She and Catrina have never gone shopping, braided each other's hair, or shared secrets while giggling over ice cream, and she feels a pang for not having tried harder. Maybe the other woman had secret depths that Isabella has never bothered to go searching for. Maybe she could have been a bosom companion, a true friend to walk through life with.

Not anymore. There are strange harmonics in her sweet, familiar voice, things that sing to Isabella's sensitivities as black flags, warning signs of death come to the door.

"You made me promises, Isabella Diaz. You told me your coven would bring good things to my door, would light up my halls with power, would purge the shadows from the corners and the cobwebs from my dreams. You promised me wonders. Well, it wasn't wonders that came to me today."

"What did come?"

"Let me in, and I'll show you." There's a sour, cajoling note to Catrina's tone, beguiling and bitter. It blames, that note. It points fingers into nothingness, and says any crimes committed here belong to Isabella above all, no matter whose hands commit them.

Isabella's heart is hammering hard, a brutal pounding against the inside of her chest. "No," she says. "I don't think so."

"Mama?"

"Stay in the kitchen, Luis!" she snaps, and feels instantly bad about raising her voice to the boy, who has had such a long and terrible afternoon, and doesn't have the tools to understand any of it. She's always done her best to keep her home life separate from her work, and until today, it's seemed as if she could keep that up forever. Now she's wondering how long the tower of her deceptions has been teetering.

"Come on, Isabella, be a friend," cajoles Catrina.

"I *am* being a friend, Catrina," says Isabella, and the last, itching piece of information finally tumbles into place, bringing understanding in its wake.

She never told Catrina where she lives.

"Or I would be, if you were Catrina," she adds, a little slowly, a little sadly. She really did like the woman, frustrating and snooty as she could frequently be. This isn't the ending she deserved.

The woman outside her door hisses. The sound is inhuman. It belongs in the mouth of some great prehistoric reptile, something massive and scaled, slouching out of the depths of a primeval swamp with murder in its primitive mind. Isabella can't reconcile that sound with Catrina, not at all, and her confused curiosity is strong enough to lure her to the peephole, rising slightly onto her toes as she looks out onto the space outside her door.

A walkway runs along the side of the building, connecting the rowed apartments so the occupants won't have to walk on grass or wade through mud to get to their doors. The same runs along the second floor, overhanging the first. It's an earthquake hazard, but it's that or tier the building like a wedding cake, each floor losing a few square feet of living space as they try to keep things in balance. Each floor's hanging walkway supports the lower floor's exterior lighting, and so even as the sun is dipping lower, Isabella can see the figure outside her door with perfect clarity.

It's Catrina, and it isn't Catrina at the same time, and Isabella feels bile rise in her throat, hot and burning and difficult to swallow back down. The figure outside her door has Catrina's face, skin pulled tight across the shape of her skull, and Catrina's hair, silver-blonde and tied in a high ponytail that only serves to pull her face tighter. She has Catrina's body, familiar in its angles and its height. And that's where the familiarity ends.

The way she's standing isn't *human*. It's more like the stance of a large predatory insect that has somehow figured out how to take its natural gift for camouflage and elevate it to a whole new level of functionality. She stands like a praying mantis, almost, her hands tucked high against her chest in a way that might be comfortable or even natural for some but is entirely wrong for her. And it's not even that creating the impression that she's more something masquerading as human than actual human being—people carry their hands in all sorts of ways, and none of them radiate inhumanity the way Catrina is right now.

It's the strangeness of her posture, the subtle, almost indefinable little things about the way she moves, the slight sway as she stands staring at the door. People mock Lovecraft for his tendency to write things off as indescribable, but the truth is, the human mind isn't equipped to process every form of sensory input. There are colors humans can't see, sounds they can't hear, flavors they can't taste. The world is greater than the human form can comfortably encompass. Catrina has always moved solidly within the lines of what it means to be a human. Here and now, she doesn't, and it's that complicated, almost indescribable wrongness that keeps Isabella's eye glued to the peephole, trying to understand what she's looking at.

There are ways a person can be forced to share their skin with something *else,* something called and cajoled and finally imprisoned inside the structure of their skeleton. Alchemists usually don't practice those methods, but it's possible that if Erin was right about their ritual work leading to pits of raw chaos energy pooling around the house, Catrina might have reached for a reassuring calming chant or the like and managed to tap into something she shouldn't have been anywhere near.

There's no good reason for Isabella to be jumping straight to "an alchemist did this," except that everything about this day has primed her to place the blame on them. The alchemists are up in arms, they're nearby, and they have reason to be targeting ordinary people who might have crossed paths with their escaped creation.

Her stomach sinks. She warded her house like a vault door before she'd gone to the coven meeting in the morning, making it virtually impossible for anyone who wasn't already a resident to even notice the place existed. Hostile forces should have walked right by, never realizing the trail they were trying to follow went cold behind a door they didn't see. She protected her home and her family and . . .

And she didn't do the same for Catrina. She'd taken Kelpie, her little alchemical runaway, and she'd walked down the street as proud and exposed as anything, all the way to Catrina's house, and she hadn't been scattering salt and iron shavings behind them the whole way, she hadn't been squirting essence of St. John's wort into the air like a strange perfume. She'd been cocky and convinced the steps already taken would be enough, and now it seems Catrina has paid the price.

The thing inside Catrina's skin turns its face, focusing on the peephole, and smiles.

It's not a normal expression. Her lips draw back from her teeth and keep on drawing, smile growing wider and wider, until that smile must split the skin, must strain the muscles of her cheeks, until her teeth are exposed all the way to the rear molars, no secrets left in the caverns of Catrina's mouth, the corners of which are red with beaded blood. It doesn't fall, only pools there, thick and somehow sluggish—the blood of a thing that has died but not yet started to decay.

"Come out, Isabella," she croons. "Come out, little hechicera, and talk to your friend. I can tell you about my day. I'm sure you'll find it very interesting."

Isabella takes a step back from the door, self-preservation telling her not to stand so close.

"You're not Catrina," she says, voice strained but carrying. "She's never once called me an hechicera."

"If I'm not Catrina, it's because of *you*," says the creature outside. "It's because *you* led the danger to my door, *you* left me unprepared for what was yet to come. *You* did this. Not me. Not her, either. She was spoiled and indolent, but she was innocent. She believed magic was a trinket, a toy she could buy or bargain for. She thought the hidden world was hidden out of greed, and greed was something she knew well, so she thought it was destined to belong to her. You tried to warn her off, tried to tell her to stay shallow, stay within the bounds of what she could survive, but she was never going to listen. You know that. Women like her never, *never* listen to the help. And that's all you were to her. A different sort of cleaning service, a slightly more self-important version of the women she paid to make her life easier. Money is a kind of alchemy, you know. You can use it to turn other people's lives into your own, to steal their time and add it to what you already have. You knew what she was from the moment you met her, but she offered you the funding you needed to do the things you wanted to do, and so you ignored your reservations, and you pretended not to see her frailties, and now here we are, and if Catrina's gone, that's on you."

"Begone, foul spirit," snaps Isabella, all too aware of the boy in the kitchen behind her, the boy who is probably listening and wondering what all of this means, the boy she needs to protect at all costs. Catrina was an innocent, but the creature inside her skin is right about one thing: Catrina sought out the magical world on her own. No one had to push or lure her. She was just sensitive enough to know that there was something she didn't have, and that had driven her to desperation, willing to do anything for proof that she was right, and more than anything for access to the power she could feel just out of reach.

It was right about two things, actually, because Isabella *had* known what Catrina was from the moment they met, had seen the greedy desperation in Catrina's eyes. But she hadn't welcomed Catrina out of greed or self-interest. She had done it because that desperation had been the result of a lifetime of being overlooked as foolish or shallow, of being treated like a pretty piece of furniture rather than a person. Catrina's life had been one of immense privilege, absolutely, and she'd done things she should have atoned for, but she had also suffered, and suffering doesn't care how much a person has or how fortunate they should feel. It still hurts. Isabella had looked at Catrina and seen a desperately lonely woman aching for connection, and she had been in a position to extend a hand that could easily have become a lifeline. Catrina would have insisted that she never needed saving. Isabella had known better from the beginning.

Catrina was an innocent who chose not to be, in small, mincing steps that were always going to lead her deeper than she could possibly realize. Luis, though . . . Luis is a *true* innocent. He's done nothing to deserve this, nothing to put himself into the path of danger. If this creature makes it through the door, he'll never escape intact. Maybe not even alive. There are many things the shape standing in Catrina's skin could be, and none of them are good ones.

Isabella glances around the dim living room, familiar in the fading afternoon light as only a place you've been so many times that you cease to ever truly *see* it can be. Juan knows she has an interest in the occult—given where she was working when they met, how could he not know?—but she's always made an effort to keep her profession away from her family. An hechicera's bag of tricks may not be as gruesome or as immoral as an alchemist's, but it could still be difficult to explain if Luis found it and started waving it around. There aren't even candles.

She swears under her breath. There's salt in the kitchen, and a Tupperware of iron shavings in the junk drawer, but going back there means leaving the door unguarded and possibly dealing with questions from Luis, who is absolutely terrified by this point. She stands frozen, unable to decide what happens next.

Fingernails drag across the door, scraping the wood. It sounds like they might be leaving gouges in their wake, like they might be something more than "fingernails" at this point.

"Isa*bella*," says Catrina's voice. "Little hechi*cera,* let me in, or I'll let myself in, and you're already going to regret this. Don't regret it worse. I can do this quickly, or I can do it slowly, the way *he* did it for me."

"He who?" asks Isabella.

"The man who showed me everything you've been hiding, Isabella," says Catrina's voice. It's still horribly, brutally recognizable, even if it no longer belongs to her. "The man who sat me down and showed me the gates of the City. I always knew you were hiding things. I knew you were jealous of how much greater than you I had the potential to become. I never knew you were such a sneaky, slinky little liar."

Nails across the door again, but this time it's clear from the splintering sound that "claws" would be a more accurate word.

Isabella takes a step back, breath hitching in her chest. Even if she *had* her tools, this isn't the sort of thing she does or deals with; she has no recourse here. Once that creature breaks down the door, if it does, she and Luis will be helpless to escape.

This isn't what she does. This isn't what she trained for.

But it may be how she dies.

"I never lied to Catrina," she says, voice shaking. "I told her I would teach her to the limits of her power, help her hone her skills within the sphere she had the potential to control. I never promised her the entire elemental world. *That* would have been the lie. I didn't lie to her."

"To *me*, you mean," says the creature, voice filled with new, bubbling overtones, like the creature is speaking through a layer of silt. It's horrifying to hear. Isabella can't close her ears or turn away. "You say you didn't lie to *me*, but *he* said you did, and *he* unlocked more power in an afternoon than you've given me in years. Which of you should I believe? The woman who took my money and drank my coffee and elevated a *toy* above me in her estimation, or the man who showed me the Impossible City, who opened my eyes to the truth and my flesh to the splendor. The light will guide us home."

Isabella takes another big step backward, toward the kitchen. If she can't save her son, at least she can put her body between him and the thing that's coming to destroy him; she can die first and buy him a few more seconds. And if there's a cruelty to making a son watch his mother die, she can't imagine it outstrips the cruelty of making a mother watch her child die. One way or the other, they both suffer, and she's simply choosing the path her instincts order her to take.

The claws rake across the door again. Wood splinters and bows inward. This isn't a playful swipe; this is the beginning of a true assault. Isabella cries out, soft and strained, as she finally whirls and runs for the kitchen.

Luis is huddled on the floor, Bobby growling between him and the door. Luis's fear of the dog seems to have been overwhelmed by his fear of whatever's happening in the living room; he has his arms around Bobby's neck and his face pressed against the dog's soft, familiar fur, tears running down his face and leaving salted tracks behind.

"Oh, baby, baby," Isabella half-moans, hurrying to gather them both into her arms, a boy and his dog, a dog and his boy, and a woman who is not a witch but is something broadly similar, all huddled together on the kitchen floor as a terrible, impossible thing attacks their apartment door.

They can see the ending coming, each of them in their own way. Isabella knows Luis's thoughts won't be filled with the terrible economy of alchemists, who take the bodies of the dead apart and use them in a million different ways, refusing to let them rest.

Even dogs aren't safe. Bobby won't rest either, once they're taken. Isabella buries her face in her son's hair and breathes deeply, her own tears dripping down to mingle with the scent of his shampoo.

The clawing and tearing at the door continues for several seconds more, until it is replaced by a heart-rending silence. The wood hasn't given way; there would have been a final cracking sound if it had. Instead, the attacker has just . . . stopped. Isabella lifts her head and looks over her shoulder, frowning. Alchemical monsters don't just *stop*, especially not the ones who aren't built to look as human as possible for long periods of time, to blend in with the communities that unknowingly shelter them. The creature that stole Catrina's face and voice should still be trying to claw its way inside.

Then she hears a sound that would be welcome and wanted under any other circumstances, but is terrifying under these: a key, a simple key, sliding into a lock.

The key turns. The deadbolt disengages. A moment later, she hears the door open as far as the chain allows, only to draw up short when it hits the limits of that tether. Juan's voice, normally so beloved, asks, "Isabella? Luis? Are you here, are you all right? What happened to the door?"

"Juan?" Isabella hears no strange harmonics or bubbling undertones in his voice. She doesn't know what the alchemists did to Catrina, but that form of puppeteering must take longer than an instant, or there would be no question left of who ruled the world—the alchemists would have taken over long ago. As it stands, whatever they did to Catrina will have been expensive in terms of both resources and effort, and is probably not something they've done lightly.

Somehow, that doesn't make Isabella feel any better.

"What happened to the door? And why is the chain locked? Is Luis with you? Fuck, Isabella, tell me what's going on!"

He doesn't normally swear in front of Luis, but the fear has him now, too. He may not be sensitive, and the Catrina-thing may have made her retreat when she saw him coming, but he can see the damaged door, the shattered wood and splinters, and you don't need to be sensitive to the spiritual universe to understand that that's a bad thing.

Isabella unwraps herself from her boy and his dog, twisting to look toward what remains of the front door. "Juan? Is anyone else out there?"

"No, just me. Isa, what *happened*?"

She wants to be brave and she wants to be cautious as the same time. These are not impulses that can be mutually fulfilled. The dog has stopped growling, which decides her; his ears aren't up, but he no longer looks like he's going to attack at any moment. Moving with slow and agonizing care, she rises, taking a carving knife from the block on the counter, and holds it low to her thigh as she starts back toward the living room. Luis has his eyes squeezed shut and his face pressed against Bobby's neck.

"Mama will be right back, sweetheart," she says, softly. She's not sure he even hears her.

Knife against her leg, she makes her way to the front room.

It looks so *normal*. It shouldn't be allowed to look this *normal*, not with everything that's happening, but the Catrina-thing didn't quite break through the door before Juan somehow scared her off; from this side, it's perfectly intact, if open and stopped by the chain.

Isabella walks in a wide arc, so she can see out that propped-open door when she stops. There's Juan, normal, familiar, and beloved, protective coverall still zipped over his street clothes, a smear of oil on one cheek. He looks utterly baffled by the situation, which is more than reasonable. This is an utterly baffling thing to come home to.

"Isa?" he says when he sees her, relief radiating outward in a wave. Then he pauses, frowning. "Isa, why do you have a knife? What's going on?"

Something inside her snaps with a small shattering sensation, some safety wire giving way before the flood of relief that washes through her. "We have to leave," she says, rushing for the door. She drops the knife and fumbles for the chain, but he's still holding the door open, and she can't get the slack she needs to unlatch it. "Juan, let go of the door, and I can—"

But his eyes have gone glassy with shock. His mouth works in silence for a moment before he makes a thin, pained choking noise, and a bubble of blood forms at the corner of his lips, a terrible echo of the way the Catrina-thing's smile tore. He slumps forward, against the door, pulling the chain even tighter, and later, she'll understand that was a blessing: that was the only thing that saved their son.

In the moment, she isn't half that rational. Her husband is bleeding from the mouth and nonresponsive, limp against the door. "Juan? Juan?!" She grabs his shoulder, trying to keep him from slumping to the floor, trying to take some of his weight off the door. He's larger than she is, enough so that she can't do anything more than slow his descent, even when she grabs on with both hands. He's going to fall.

When he hits the ground, he's gone forever, she thinks nonsensically, as if holding on to his arm will somehow keep him from dying, something which is patently already an impossibility. He's going to die. He's going to die, or he's already dead—he's not making any more sounds, and the blood from his mouth is thick and dark.

Then the Catrina-thing appears behind him, her terrible wide smile a rictus slashed across her face, her eyes bright and manic behind a mask of skin that's started sagging around the edges, like she's coming to the end of the time she can spend in this form. Her arms are still her arms, but they're longer than they should be, and each ends in a spade-shaped claw, like something stolen from an armadillo. She still stands wrong, moves wrong, sways wrong in the breeze from behind her, and her claws are tipped with blood.

"I told you to let me in," she chides. "This didn't have to happen. This is *your* fault, Isabella. He could have come home to an empty apartment and walked away a grieving widower, convinced his beloved witchy wife had run off with another man. But no, you had to argue with me, and now he's dead, gone to take the graveyard path all the way to the Impossible City."

Her giggle is like glass breaking inside a trash compactor, is like rotten ice breaking on a stagnant lake, is like frozen waste being fed into a garbage disposal. It's the most terrible thing Isabella has ever heard.

"Now, then, shall we finish this?" asks the Catrina-thing, and slams into the door with all her weight, which seems to be much greater than her frame implies. The chain shudders in its socket, the metal bar at its base threatening to tear free of the wall. Isabella shrieks and spins to run back to the kitchen where Luis is waiting, intending to wrap herself around him once again. She hears the creature stepping back, hears it slam into the door a second time, and, worst of all, hears the chain give way.

There is a thundering gallop behind her, like something large has dropped onto all fours and is pursuing her into the apartment, and then there is a ripping, tearing sound, wet and awful, followed by the sound of a sack of concrete being dropped. Isabella stops, struggling to breathe, and turns to look back.

Mare Marginis

Part of Isabella is screaming that this is how teenage white girls die in the horror movies. She doesn't listen, because the rest of her is just screaming, screaming without end, and she's not sure it's ever going to stop again. She has to know. She has to *see*.

She finishes her turn.

The Catrina-thing is sprawled across the living room floor, only a few feet behind her. It looks . . . unraveled, somehow, like its seams have been unstitched. It looks more like a puppet whose puppeteer has cast it carelessly aside than anything real. Nothing about it seems like it could have been moving or speaking or attacking only a moment before.

Blood seeps from the splits in its skin, forming a pool around the body. From where Isabella stands, she can see that some of those splits are fresher than others, but she can't imagine what distinguishes them from one another. She's an hechicera, trained and skilled, and this is not her area of expertise; this is not what she wants to be doing right now, or ever.

The body of her husband blocks the doorway, and it's only a matter of time before one of the neighbors comes home or steps out of their apartment and sees him, a chaotic tumble of strong limbs rendered useless by the slaughter of the man who once controlled them. Tears burn in her eyes. She refuses to let them fall. Once she starts crying, she may never stop, and she should be dead right now, ripped apart by the thing that wore the face of her student and somewhat friend. The alchemists who made it and set it on her trail should have won.

So why didn't they?

There is a brightness in the air beside the door, one that her eyes shy away from, refusing to focus. She frowns and forces the issue, staring at the bright spot as hard as she can until her vision blurs and the brightness begins to look like a woman, olive-skinned and dark-haired, still dressed in UC Berkeley athletic gear even after a long day of breaking nature's laws and defying the constants of the universe. Even after she's isolated Artemis's outline from the brightness, the other woman is shaky and out of focus, illuminated from the inside, not quite solid and not quite real.

The hunting bow she holds gleams a sparkling moon-dark silver, and as Isabella watches, Artemis releases the string and lowers her hand, letting the bow go. It dissolves into glittering nothing, and the brightness fades, the blur around Artemis clearing like someone has wiped a window clean, revealing the person on the other side of the glass.

"I'm sorry," says Artemis. Her words are too big: she's not shouting, she's not even speaking particularly loudly, but they fall into the silence of the living room with a weight and importance that makes it feel like they've been brought in from some other scene, like she's been set up with a body mic and a hidden speaker. "I got here as quickly as I could."

"What did you do?" Isabella's voice shakes, and her words are small, the size words are meant to be, sliding easily into the spaces the world has made for them. No one should speak larger than this. No one should glisten and glow, either, or appear out of nowhere with a disappearing bow in hand.

"The woman had been subjected to some form of alchemical transmutation. I can't tell you precisely what it was, only that they used it to rip her out of this reality, show her the Impossible City, and then return her to this world. I don't know who did it, or what instructions they gave her, or how she found your apartment, but I promise you, that was not your friend anymore. By the time I let my arrow fly, your friend was gone."

Hysterical laughter bubbles up in Isabella's throat as her tears finally begin to fall. "She wasn't my friend. She was just . . . she was someone I knew. Juan, is he . . . ?"

"You don't want to see what she did to him." Artemis moves, putting herself between Isabella and Juan's body. "Get your son and a suitcase. We can't stay here."

"You don't understand," says Isabella, looking at Artemis, pleading with the younger woman to see what she's trying to say. "My husband—"

"Your husband is gone," says Artemis gently. "All you do now is harm yourself by trying to see the manner of his passage. Let him go, let him be gone, and save what can be saved."

"Mama?"

Isabella whips around, eyes seeking Luis. He's in the kitchen doorway, clutching Bobby's collar with one hand, staring at her in dazed bewilderment. The Catrina-thing is a product of the alchemical world, twisted and distorted away from anything that should be truly possible. He may not be able to see her. Whether he can see the body of his father is a question for greater minds than hers. He isn't screaming, which is either a good sign—he can't see what's really happening—or a terrible one—he's in shock. There is no middle ground.

Maybe there's never a middle ground. Maybe the middle ground is a pretty fiction people tell themselves to make the world seem a little bit less hostile.

"Baby." She rushes across the room, sweeping him into her arms. Bobby, released, trots over to sniff at Artemis before he wuffs a greeting, tail beginning to wave.

"Dogs like me," says Artemis. "Almost as much as deer do." She caresses Bobby's head and he stands up tall and proud, looking every inch the hunting hound, looking like he's ready to bring down the stars if it will please this woman he's just met. "If not for the Old

Man, they would probably have given me a dog. Do you need me to help you pack?"

"Pack?" asks Luis. "Are we going somewhere, Mama? Will Papa be there?"

Isabella gasps a small, choking laugh that turns halfway into a sob before she can swallow it back. Being unable to see the situation isn't entirely a blessing. Sure, he may avoid nightmares, but how is she supposed to make him understand?

"You're going to come stay with some friends of ours," says Artemis. "They're nice, but weird. They have too many cookies. You'll have to help us eat them all."

"I'm good at eating cookies," says Luis.

"I thought you might be. Go pack for a sleepover."

Luis looks to Isabella, waiting for her to tell him it's all right. When she nods, he grins, the afternoon's fears apparently forgotten, and runs down the hall to get his overnight bag. Isabella looks to Artemis, scowling.

"You better not go around bewitching my boy," she says. "I don't want you to do that."

"I'm not," says Artemis. "I'm just pumping as much moonlight as I can into the room, and hoping that between that and the alchemical nature of these deaths, he'll be able to make it out of here with his psyche in one piece. This isn't the sort of thing a child should see. Hell, this isn't the sort of thing an adult should see. I wish you hadn't seen it."

"Where did that bow go?"

"It went where the moonlight goes when the moon's behind a cloud. I couldn't have pulled it at all if I'd been outside; there's too much sunlight for the Moon to make her wishes known. Get your things. We're not coming back here."

Isabella knows enough about this sort of situation to know that the bodies will be moved or covered while she's out of the room packing a bag, adding one more layer of deniability to protect her and Luis. Just one more service the magical world has to offer when it's busy destroying your entire life. Her chest is too tight, and she's breathing too fast; she'll pass out soon if she doesn't get this under control. And yet . . .

That might be a mercy.

Juan was the man she chose to spend her life with. It's not possible for him to be gone, just like that. It's not something she can accept. He certainly can't be gone because their son wanted to help a strange girl he found sleeping in the garden. This is all too much, too fast, and she can't endure it.

She looks to Artemis and finds the other woman—the goddess—the girl watching her with open sympathy. Artemis doesn't say a word, only bows her head, then gestures toward the hall. The message couldn't be clearer.

Isabella scowls, then follows her son's path deeper into the apartment.

He's in his room when she glances through the open door, shoving clothes into a duffel bag almost mechanically. His teddy bear is missing from the bed, where it has remained stubbornly keeping watch even as its plushy peers were outgrown and pushed aside. She can't see anything else that isn't where it ought to be. Briefly, she considers going in and making sure he's bringing enough underwear, the necessities like his hairbrush and deodorant, but in the end, she continues onward. Those are things that can be replaced, and they may not return here. He's younger than she is; he has less to lose. Let him pack the things he'd miss if they were gone.

The bedroom she shares—shared—with Juan is dark, curtains drawn to keep nosy neighbors from "just looking" as they walk by outside. This is their private space, always has been, and even Luis asks before he comes inside, into the cocoon of his parents' presence. The air smells of candle wax and sweat, the blood from the living room not yet having drifted this far back. Isabella stops and breathes in deeply, unable to fight a feeling of unreality. This smell will fade, soon enough, and one more piece of Juan will be lost forever.

But the most essential part—his son—will remain, and she has to protect Luis. She holds to that thought as she moves toward the closet, taking out the suitcase she uses when she flies back to Puerto Rico to see her family. For the first time, she wishes it were bigger, that she hadn't consciously chosen something small to keep the weight down and prevent her parents from sending her home with too many unwanted gifts every time she came to visit. She'll be able to save so little of the life she's just lost.

First, her jewelry box, and Juan's small selection of precious things—his father's watch, his mother's earrings, the things he kept in his nightstand. The money from the cookie jar on top of the dresser, her small makeup case, and finally clothing to fill the gaps. Her wedding dress she leaves behind, too large and awkward to waste space on packing; their wedding album, she takes, and the precious family photo album that contains the best pictures of their life together. That's what Luis will have to remember his father by, more than anything else.

Finally, the basket that keeps her working tools, the accessories of her art; she hates it right now, that art and practice, wishes she had never flirted with the spirit world or heard the universe speaking to her. If she had been as unattuned as most people, she would have looked at the gangly woman her son brought in from the garden and seen nothing worth sheltering, nothing worth being curious about. Kelpie would have been sent on her way, and Juan would be alive. More than that, she would never have formed a coven to help her with her practice, and Catrina would never have come to the alchemist's attention. Two lives would have been saved, if she weren't an hechicera.

Oh, how she loathes the things she has gathered with such loving care, the things that allow her to perform the small wonders and necessary miracles she was made for! And still she takes them, granting them their share of the scant space inside her suitcase, because leaving them behind is not an option.

She hesitates. She doesn't know what happens next. This was a murder committed in the shadow lands that skirt normal reality, and she knows how the universe glosses those over, obscures the clues, dulls the interest of the people who stumble across them.

Juan's death will be written off as a home invasion gone wrong, and the only real question is whether Catrina's body will be something the coroners recognize as human. If it is, they may actually find something worth sensationalizing, and Catrina will finally have the fame she craved so deeply. "White woman murdered" is probably not the headline she would have wanted, but any port in a storm, as the sages say.

Isabella smiles slightly at the thought of Catrina's rage upon being reported as a victim. Oh, she would be so mad. That would have been something to see. But if the dead walk, she's never seen it; the spirits who speak to her are spirits of place and prayer, embodied aspects of the universe without the strength or weight to move all the way to incarnation. If all ideas incarnated, there would be no lares or pentates. No people, either, just small gods and natural forces walking around, all playing at being human, all convinced they were the only ones.

She starts to close the suitcase, hesitates, and grabs one of Juan's T-shirts from the hamper, putting it in on top of her own clothes. The smell of him won't linger forever. It will linger long enough that she might remember how to sleep before it fades. There's nothing else.

There are so many things she'd love to take, if she had the time to box it all and consider every piece. But time is a luxury she doesn't have, and so she shuts the suitcase on the memories she *can* carry, hoists it, weighing it out with her arm and her heart at the same time—this is the weight of a life; can you balance it against a feather?—and turns her back on the bed she'll never sleep in again.

Nostrils full of the scent of Juan, she goes to retrieve their son. He has finished his packing; he's staring at the wall. He looks around when she enters the room.

"Something bad is happening, isn't it?" he asks.

Isabella pauses. "Yes, sweetheart. Something bad *is* happening. I'm sorry."

But he doesn't want her apologies. She's his mother. He wants her strength and support, wants her to have all the answers he doesn't.

His face screws up, just a little, as he thinks. Finally, he says, "It sounded bad. But I don't remember why it sounded bad. If it's so bad, I should remember it, shouldn't I?"

"Sometimes your mind doesn't want to remember the bad things," says Isabella. "If it's important enough, you'll remember it later."

"Oh." He picks up his duffel bag, looks to the suitcase in her hand. "Are we going somewhere?"

"Yes, we are. Your friend Kelpie from last night, she'll be there, too."

"Oh!" He brightens, just for a moment, then asks, with heart-breaking wariness, "Is she why a bad thing happened?"

That answer is huge and complex. Isabella goes for the shorter, simpler one: "No, and neither are you. This is no one's fault."

No one but the alchemists, may they rot for what they've done to her family. All of them, everywhere in the world, may they rot where they stand. She sees no purpose to them, no reason for the universe to continue their appearance or allow their education. They are nothing but parasites attaching themselves to the spiritual skin of the universe, taking and taking and giving nothing back, and she hates them as she has never hated anything in all her life, as she did not know she *could* hate. It doesn't seem possible that she could hate this much, but she does, as she takes her son by his free hand and leads him back to the living room.

The shattered shape of the Catrina-thing is still sprawled across the floor, difficult to look upon or truly comprehend; Isabella is deep enough into the elemental world that she *should* be able to see it more clearly than this, or at least feels like she should. The back of the woman's clothing appears to have been sliced through and stitched back together, the seam visible due to the otherwise seam-less slickness of the fabric. The back of the creature's neck and arms makes it clear that the seams go all the way to the bone, that what was cut into was more than merely fabric.

Once she comes to understand that, Isabella looks no deeper, sud-denly grateful that Luis doesn't seem to see the body at all. Instead, he focuses on Artemis, and Bobby, who is standing rigidly at heel beside her, posture tight and perfect, ready for the hunt. He looks like a sighthound, like something bred to follow prey through ancient, endless forests. Bobby has never seemed *noble* before, but in this moment, in this light, he does.

"That's my dog," says Luis, almost petulantly. "Who are you?"

Artemis looks at him and smiles, sweet and gentle, like she's trying not to upset him. "My name's Anna, but my friends call me 'Artemis,'" she says.

"You mean like from *Percy Jackson*?" asks Luis, brightening.

"Yes. Just like from *Percy Jackson*," says Artemis. "I'm a friend of your mother's. I'm here to walk you to where you'll be staying tonight."

Isabella remembers that in the old stories, Artemis is also the goddess responsible for child care, and feels a vast surge of sudden relief. Artemis will make sure Luis is safe, even if Isabella can't protect him herself.

"Now," Artemis continues. "I like taking walks, especially walks with a dog as good as Bobby here, but I like it even better when we can play a game at the same time. Do you want to play a game with me?"

Luis nods, enthusiastically

"Wonderful. For this game, I need you to close your eyes and follow the sound of my voice, and don't open them until I say you can. Do you think you can do that?"

"I can," says Luis, and screws his eyes obediently closed. Curious, he asks, "What game is this?"

"Um . . . I call it Bats! Because we're traveling by echolocation, see, and you need to trust your ears since you can't trust your eyes when they're closed. Real bats don't fly with their eyes closed, but their eyes are very small, and they do almost all of their hunting in the dark, which means they have to find their food by sending out sounds and following them."

"Okay," says Luis.

Artemis looks at Isabella and winks broadly, before taking several steps back and saying, "Okay, walk toward me."

Bobby follows her, and Luis walks toward the sound of her voice, Artemis calling out directions and corrections to lead him where he needs to be. She manages, somehow, to steer him out of the apartment without stepping on the body of his father, which has fallen to halfway block the exit; Isabella can't understand quite how that worked out but, now that she's looking, can see that it's true.

"Juan, I am so sorry," she says to the empty apartment once the others are gone. She keeps her voice low, to avoid attracting Luis's attention. Artemis has him outside without understanding what's happened. She doesn't want to change that. "I had no idea this could happen. I swear, if I'd even suspected, I would never have let her in, I would never have let you go to work today, I would have done so many things so very differently. I will never stop wishing this had gone differently, and I will never stop loving you. I'll keep our boy safe. You have my word."

There is no reply. There so rarely is, when talking to the dead. She sighs, feeling as emptied-out as the husk that was Catrina, and follows her son and the goddess of the moon out of the apartment.

She doesn't even try to shut the shattered door. She just keeps walking.

Artemis has managed to guide Luis all the way to the end of the courtyard. The two of them are waiting there, giving her the space and time she needs to catch up. She hurries to join them. Her husband is dead but her son is alive, and the alchemist who transformed her not-quite-friend into something monstrous and sent it hunting for their escaped lab project is still out there. They need to get Luis to safety.

That means the house of the Doctrine, and Isabella is relieved when Artemis waves and starts walking in that direction, destination already set and verified. Luis keeps his eyes shut as he follows; he hasn't realized yet that they're never going back. Isabella's heart aches for the moment when he'll understand, which is coming faster than either of them would like and will change absolutely everything.

Still, she falls into step, and they walk without speaking to each other. Artemis continues to call out instructions to Luis, keeping him on the sidewalk, distracting anyone who sees them from the oddness of two women, one with a suitcase and the other with an unleashed dog, cutting through the neighborhood at this hour of the day. Not that Isabella is truly worried about being seen: they might not all have the preternatural camouflage the universe affords to incarnations like Kelpie, but for the most part, people see what they want to see, and they ignore the rest. She and Artemis are safe, as long as they're not covered in blood and actively discussing murder.

The last thing she wants to talk about right now is her husband's murder. She knows she's not going to have a choice soon: it's going to matter to the people she hopes will shelter them, and if the alchemists have moved to turning innocents into weapons and setting them against their enemies, that's going to make a difference. That's going to be the sort of thing the Doctrine, at the very least, should know about. But she's had a long day. She's tired. Her husband is dead, her home is effectively lost, and she's not sure either one of them thought to grab dog food.

The thought summons the immediate, burning desire to turn and go back. It's not an excuse; it's an actual need to go get something the dog requires. And she knows she can't give in. Even if, by some miracle, no one has noticed the smashed-in door or the body yet, giving in now will mean she never finds the strength to leave again. Let her son grow up in the care of the gods of the moon; she'll stay with her love, who needs her now as much as ever.

She fights the urge and looks to Artemis, who is watching her with sympathy. She wonders what the other woman sees when she looks at her, whether she thinks Isabella brought this on herself by getting involved with forces beyond her comprehension, whether she's angry. None of those questions lead anywhere good, and so she leaves them all unasked, instead asking, "How did you know to come?"

"Erin," says Artemis. "She came outside and said there was a lot of disorganization rising from your area, and that if I wanted to stop some serious chaos, I should head over. Kelpie didn't want to come, so she's waiting back at the house. Unless she's taken this as an opportunity to run for the hills."

"What will you do if she has?"

Artemis shrugs. "Grieve, I guess. We both know the people who made her aren't going to stop looking, and she doesn't seem to have any natural defenses. I'm . . . *more,* when she's with me, and echoes of it last a little while, or seem to. I couldn't normally pull my bow even in a dark apartment with the sun still this high in the sky, but it came easily today, and I feel like I could pull it again if I needed to, although it wouldn't last long. Maybe that's what the companions are for. They make us *more.*"

"I'm glad you came. Luis doesn't know it yet, but he's glad too."

"Yeah, well." Artemis raises her voice. "Three big steps forward, and then stop."

Luis does as he's told, coming to a quivering halt on the corner, only about a foot and a half from the street. He stays frozen until the adults catch up to him, when Artemis gives the next instruction and he starts walking again, clearly enjoying this break from his usual routine, even if he doesn't understand it.

"What *was* that back at the apartment?"

"Do you really want to have this conversation now?" asks Artemis, and nods her head toward Luis.

Isabella sighs, very slightly. "No, I suppose not. Soon."

"Oh, absolutely." Artemis pauses, then laughs, almost under her breath. "This has been a fun game, but he shouldn't miss this. Open your eyes now!"

Luis stops and opens his eyes, then gasps at the sight of the carnival-bright house in front of him. He looks over his shoulder at the adults, a question in his eyes.

"Yes, that's where we're going," says Isabella.

"The clown house?"

"Yes, please tell the nice people who live there that that's what you and your friends call the house," says Artemis, deadpan. "I'm sure that won't upset them at all."

Luis looks between her and his mother, uncertain. Isabella sighs again.

"No, buddy, she's not being serious. You can go ahead and go into the yard, and even up the steps, but you wait for us there, you understand?"

Luis beams. "Okay, Mama!" He unhooks the gate and bounces into the unseasonably green yard, delighted as only a young boy on an adventure can be.

Isabella takes a great, shuddering breath, trying to grapple with the enormity of it all. She flinches when a hand settles on her shoulder, then turns to find Artemis watching her with sympathy.

"He's safe," she says. "That house isn't even *there* when they don't want it to be. No one's going to find him or hurt him while they have him in their care, and they said you could come here for shelter. I don't know how long-term that's going to be, but for right now, he's safe. I swear. Now let's get you safe, too."

Artemis leads her to the garden gate. Isabella steps through, and she's paying attention this time, she feels the moment when the air changes, turning into something timeless and out-of-season, like the house runs on its own chronology. And maybe it does. It would be no stranger than anything else that's happened today.

Luis is waiting at the top of the steps, eagerly looking at the glorious wonders around him, and Isabella can't help being grateful that if this all had to happen, it happened now, while he's young enough to be delighted by the adventure and not dwell on the reasons it would be happening. There's time for grief later—and it will come, she knows.

Grief is the ultimate ambush predator. If it fails to catch its prey in the moment, it will retreat and lurk until its time arrives. And its time always arrives. It is the price we pay for having loved something, the misery that pours in to fill the holes that are left behind when it departs.

Isabella is already at the start of her grieving. She'll do what she can to keep Luis from starting his before he's ready.

Artemis flashes him a smile as bright as summer and rings the doorbell, the sound echoing through the house and not quite fading before the door opens and Erin is standing there, looking starkly unsurprised by the assembly on the porch.

"Guest room's down the hall, last door on the left before the bathroom," she says. "Just ignore the books, and the boxes. Dodger shoves anything she doesn't want left out in the open in there, says it's unrealistic for us to have a basement in this part of California, and since I live in the attic, she's trying to respect my privacy."

"How many rooms does this place *have*?" asks Isabella, stepping inside and gesturing for Luis to follow.

"How many does it need?" asks Erin philosophically. She looks to Luis as he crosses the threshold, her gaze startlingly like a hawk's. It's sharp, and predatory, and pins him in place. "Who are you?"

"This is my—" begins Isabella.

Erin shifts that sharp, predatory look over to her. "Did I ask you?"

"No," says Isabella.

Erin looks back to Luis. "Just checking. Who are you?"

Luis swallows hard. "I'm, um. I'm Luis Diaz? Anna and my mom said we had to come here for a while. I'm in sixth grade and your eyes are really blue. I've never seen eyes like yours. Are you wearing anime contacts?"

"No," says Erin. "These are just my eyes. But that's a good question, and it's always a good idea to look at people's eyes. You can tell a lot of things from eyes. Are you going to be okay sharing a room with your mother for a few days?"

Isabella holds her breath as she awaits the answer. She's sure if he says "no," Erin will nod and casually mention another guest room, keeping to her promise that they have as many rooms as they need. But she doesn't want him in a different room. She's a widow so recent that she doesn't even have a death certificate yet, and she doesn't want to be alone.

"Oh, yeah," says Luis. "We share a hotel room when we drive to LA to see my grandparents. It's fun. Like sleepaway camp, only my parents are there."

"Very well, then," says Erin. "Enter freely, and be not afraid."

Luis giggles. "You're funny," he says, and heads down the hall. Isabella follows.

Artemis is the last of the three to step inside. She waits until Isabella and Luis pass out of earshot, then sighs heavily and shakes her head.

"You were right," she says. "I needed to be there. I just needed to be there a little sooner than I was, that's all."

"Her husband's not going to join them, is he?" asks Erin, as she looks at Bobby, who has settled at Artemis's feet, sitting as politely as any long-trained show dog.

Artemis shakes her head.

"Well, shit."

"Yes, that sums it up nicely." Artemis sighs. "I need to go check on my—on Kelpie. Can you handle them from here?"

"Can she tell me what happened? Because I'd like to know before you go if you're not sure she can."

"One of the alchemists who's been sniffing around the place recently got hold of someone Isabella knew, and used them as the basis for making an auf. Then they set it loose, and it followed Kelpie's trail back to Isabella's apartment complex."

Erin frowns. "She said she'd put up wards."

"Well, something took them down." Artemis shrugs. "The creature was in the process of breaking down the apartment door when Isabella's husband came home and interrupted. The auf backed off to let him undo the locks, and then ripped out most of his internal organs through his back."

Erin's frown becomes a grimace. "Oof. That's a nasty way to die."

"At least it's a fast one. He went down, the auf broke the door open as I was getting there, and I shot it before it could get to Isabella." Artemis pauses, looking at Erin. "I pulled my bow before moonrise. I pulled it, and it was solid and real and when I shot the auf, the auf went *down*. During the day. I've never been able to do that before."

"It's almost the eclipse, and you found your Hind," says Erin. "Both those things turn your power up. She's out back, by the way. Máni is out there with her. Chang'e came inside when she finished checking out the peach tree, thanked me for letting her look, and then she did that funky trick you people do, where she stepped back and let someone else take over. The human chick she's time-sharing with. Judy? She's in Roger's office now, probably quizzing him on verb tenses or something."

"I hope they're having a nice time?" says Artemis uncertainly, glancing toward the kitchen door. "Do you mind if I . . . ?"

"No, go ahead. I'll stay here and deal with the sad human and her son."

Artemis smiles before she flees for the kitchen with the dog at her heels, running away from the relative complexity of ordinary people trapped in extraordinary circumstances, returning to the comforting familiarity of the divine. Erin watches her go and sighs. It must be nice to be able to move between two worlds as easily as breathing, to slide from one into the other when either becomes too difficult to withstand. She's never had that option. None of the people living in this semi-coherent, unreasonably malleable house have. Even Smita, who could technically still return to the world of the living if she wanted to put in the time and effort, has slipped too far into the alchemical mire to go back to what she was.

Turning, Erin wanders down the hall toward the guest room she half-identified, half-conjured for their unwilling houseguests. The door is open; from inside, she hears Isabella trying to explain to Luis that his father isn't coming to join them. The boy doesn't understand yet, based on the querulous noises he's making. He will, and Erin doesn't want to be here for that. She keeps walking, heading for the door with the PLEASE, NO sign advising her to stay away.

She can't read all the languages on the sign, but she knows what they say, and she figures that's close enough for government work. Raising one hand, she knocks briskly.

There's a pause before Roger calls, "Is the house on fire?"

"If the house were on fire, Dodger would be in your head demanding you tell it to *stop*," says Erin reasonably. "It's me."

The door opens, and Roger is there, hair slightly mussed in the way that means he's been running his hands through it. It's strangely appealing. She hasn't seen him looking like that in a while—not since he became the living Doctrine and stopped being strictly human. It's a nervous habit that comes out when he's confronted with an interesting linguistic problem, something he has to think about, not just snap his fingers and solve. Manifesting as the living incarnation of language has made it harder for him to find things that intellectually excite him.

Erin's always been a little sorry about that, although not sorry enough to recommend they try another reset and pass the Doctrine to Kim and Tim. There's a reality where they survive and one where they don't, and she prefers to stay in the one where they do.

"What?" he asks, eyes bright and cheeks flushed with what could be irritation—or arousal. He used to look at her like that.

Doctrine's gonna bag a moon goddess, she thinks, and it's a sufficiently amusing concept to take the sting out of the idea. "Isabella's back. She brought her kid."

"She told us she was going to." He moves to shut the door.

Erin grabs hold of it before he can. "She didn't bring her husband, and she's not going to. The alchemists found her before we could get her back here."

"What?" He lets go of the door and stares at her. Behind him, Erin hears someone moving around. Judy, coming to listen.

"They made an auf—a sort of flesh-puppet thing that replaces a real person, like splitting the difference between a construct and a clone; they're fast and dirty work, starting with coring out the person you want to replace—and sent it to track Kelpie's steps. It found Isabella, and it killed her husband. Artemis got there before it could kill her and the kid, and she brought them back here for safety's sake."

"And now we have houseguests," concludes Roger grimly. "You get them situated?"

"Yeah. They're sharing a room downstairs. Kid's as normal as normal comes. I'm not sure he'll notice anything weird the whole time he's here."

"Oh, he'll notice plenty that's weird," says Roger. "It'll just be all the normal sort of weird, like Kim making breakfast-cereal sandwiches, or Dodger doing differential equations on the window in Sharpie. Still, it's good to know we'll need to pull back around him."

"Unless you want to make his future therapy bills even higher," says Erin.

Roger, who has more experience with traumatized teens than he ever expected he would, sighs. "And they'll already be high enough."

Erin nods. "They will, and this isn't over yet. We have some additional tasks to complete."

"Make sure Isabella isn't being held responsible for her husband's murder, get rid of the alchemists that attacked her, find her that house we promised, get her out of our guest room," says Roger, rapid-fire.

Erin nods again. "And deal with the infestation of moon gods we seem to have developed."

"I don't know," says Roger. "I like a few of them."

"Mm-hmm. I can see that. You two have fun. We've got about an hour before we'll need to head for campus." Erin grins, sudden and sharp. "Don't do anything I wouldn't do."

She turns and walks away before Roger can answer her. Some statements don't need replies.

Mare Undarum

Máni and Kelpie are exploring the blackberry maze. Kelpie's hands are filled with fruit, the orange skin around her mouth stained with streaks of purple like delicate bruises. Máni is more familiar with blackberries; he's clearly been picking them as well, but more carefully, and his hands are nearly clean. Both of them look around as Artemis comes clattering down the porch steps, Máni relaxing at the sight of her, while Kelpie tenses.

Artemis hopes the other woman will eventually be able to look at her without seeing a loss of autonomy and an unasked-for future full of gods and monsters. Desired or not, that future is coming for them both, and this will be easier if they can accept it. Máni waves.

"Artemis!" he calls. "Any trouble?"

"The man was dead when I got there, but I saved Isabella and the boy." Bobby sees Kelpie and bounds across the yard to greet her, tail wagging wildly.

She pales, even as she shoves her handful of blackberries into her mouth and bends to pat the dog almost robotically on the head. Swallowing her mouth of half-chewed fruit, she manages to squeak, "Dead?"

"The alchemists who made you somehow tracked Isabella's footsteps back to the apartment," says Artemis. "They made an auf, and set it to catch her."

"She told me she'd warded the apartment. She swore!"

"I think she was telling the truth." Artemis pauses briefly, expression sorrowful. "The boy and dog were both inside when she got there, or they'd be dead too. There must have been *something* preventing the auf from just ripping its way inside."

"What's an auf?" asks Máni.

Kelpie has a more pressing question: "Who . . . who was it?" she asks.

"A woman. Blonde. Isabella knew her. She didn't tell me what her name had been, but . . . she knew her before this happened."

Kelpie wobbles, looking momentarily like she's going to throw up. "Catrina," she says. "Her name was Catrina. The coven met at her house. Isabella took me there. Oh, they were looking for me, and they found Catrina."

"Which gave them a destination they could backtrack from," says Artemis. "Smart. Primitive, as hunting techniques go, but . . . smart, all the same."

"You're *praising* them?" asks Kelpie.

"Not in the sense of admiring what they've done, but refusing to acknowledge the skills of your enemies doesn't take those skills away. It just leaves you more vulnerable to having those skills used against you." Artemis shrugs. "It wasn't a stroke of tactical brilliance. Like I said, it was primitive. But if they wanted to find Kelpie and Isabella had wards keeping them from perceiving the apartment, hollowing out someone Isabella knew and using them as a hunting dog was clever, especially for alchemists. It's so simple and so gruesome that modern alchemists don't usually think of that sort of thing."

"But you recognized it right away," says Máni, eyeing her warily.

"I'm a hunter. I know hunting techniques," says Artemis. To her relief, he lets it go with that.

She focuses on Kelpie, who's still bent over, petting the dog. Bobby, for his part, is in ecstasy at all the attention. "How are you feeling?"

"The same as I've felt all afternoon. Lost. A little confused. But still like myself, if that's what you're really asking."

"You're the one who was worried," says Artemis. "I drew my

bow. At the apartment. It's the reason Isabella and the boy are alive. I shouldn't have been able to draw my bow before the moon was out, but I needed it, and when I reached, it was there. I saved them because I could do something that shouldn't have been possible. I saved them because you were here."

"They were in danger because I was here," says Kelpie, and Artemis can't argue. She sighs as Kelpie straightens and storms back into the house, Bobby following. He stops halfway, looking uncertainly back at Artemis. "Go with her," she says, and he goes, bounding after Kelpie, vanishing.

Artemis turns to Máni. "I don't know how to help."

"I don't know if you can help. She's trying to cope with the idea that she was made, not born, and it's tearing her up inside. I think she's more embarrassed and frightened than anything else."

"Fear I get, but embarrassment?"

"Look at her." He shrugs. "It doesn't seem quite realistic that she would have thought she was anything other than constructed, does it? Especially in a lab where everyone else was a natural human. If she'd been thinking clearly, she would have looked at them, looked at herself, and known the truth without anyone needing to tell her. But she couldn't think clearly, because she didn't have all the information. She did the best she could under the circumstances. And now she's in the real world, where all those pretty lies are falling down, and she can't fool herself anymore. She feels bad about that. She's afraid spending too much time with you will wipe out who she is as a person, and she's also afraid that might not be the worst thing ever, because who she is as a person let herself be lied to for so long."

"Ah," says Artemis, softly.

Máni shrugs again, smiling. "I just want us to finish this, and figure out what the hell is going on. Blackberry?" He holds out a hand filled with fruit, and Artemis takes one delicately, popping it into her mouth.

It explodes on her tongue in a perfect cascade of sweet and sour. It tastes like the height of summer, like the harvest in its most platonic form, and she swallows almost eagerly. "Fuck, that's good."

"Guess when the Doctrine of Ethos orders a garden to grow, it listens."

"Guess so."

They're quiet for a moment after that before Máni asks, slowly, "Were you telling the truth before? About why you're here in Berkeley?"

"I was." Artemis looks at him. "That's not really what you want to ask, is it?"

"Why were you pretending to be Losna?"

"Because I knew there wasn't a Losna here to contradict me, and if your Diana heard an Artemis had come into the area, she'd start trying to make me leave." Artemis looks at him calmly, trying to make her point without forcing him to see things her way. "She doesn't like other Lunars who might rival her for power. She only puts up with Chang'e because she needs the peaches, and every Chang'e I've met who's been around more than a few decades knows better than to go near Berkeley. This Diana likes her territory to be *hers,* and she doesn't like to share."

"How old *are* you?"

That's a question she doesn't want to answer. Grimacing, she sidesteps. "Old enough to know that I didn't want to start a fight with an established Diana in her own territory. That's the danger of Dianas. For all that they're syncretic with Artemis, they're a lot more territorial than we tend to be. We follow the hunt where it leads us; they find a forest and claim it as their own. So even though we're generally comparable in power, most of us won't go into a Diana's den and start poking them in the ribs. The ones who think that's funny don't make it long enough to understand why it's not."

"And Losna . . . ?"

"Isn't a threat to Diana's authority the same way an Artemis is."

"What are you planning to do if Diana shows up at the gate tonight?"

"Has she ever done that before? Just decided to drop by and see whether things are going the way they're supposed to?"

"Well, no, but she could."

"And if she does, we'll deal with it." Artemis's expression hardens. Máni has to make an effort not to look away. That look doesn't make it seem like "dealing with it" would be something temporary.

The back door swings open, and Chang'e is there, back at the forefront, Judy once more tucked neatly out of the way. "It's time," she calls to the other Lunars, glancing up at the sky, where the pale disc of the moon's daylight face has appeared through the clouds. "We can open the gate now."

"And we're sure this is the best way?" asks Máni.

Artemis glances at him. "You're full of questions today, aren't you?"

He shrugs. "I want to understand what's going on before I wind up joining Aske in the everything."

"A noble desire. Come on." She starts for Chang'e, looking her up and down, taking in the disheveled state of her hair and the new wrinkles in her shirt. "Mmm."

Chang'e flushes red. "Just because you're a virgin goddess, that doesn't mean the rest of us feel the same way."

"Isn't he the head of your department or something?"

"He's not my advisor." Chang'e shrugs. "He speaks languages I've never even heard of. It's a nice change from all the monolingual assholes I have to deal with on a daily basis."

"Right. Is Kelpie coming?"

"She is." Chang'e sighs. "She doesn't want to, and she's pretty upset about what happened to Isabella's apartment and husband, but if her being there ups your effectiveness, it's worth it. It means she might be able to give us the edge against anyone who thinks they know what we're capable of."

"I wish she felt better about all this, but coming along grudgingly is better than not coming along at all," says Artemis, climbing the stairs to the back door, Máni close behind her. The three Lunars proceed into the kitchen.

Dodger and Erin are already there, the one making a fresh pot of coffee, the other making sandwiches. Dodger looks over her shoulder as the door swings shut, giving a short nod of acknowledgment.

"We're leaving the civilian and her son here," she says. "I know she was planning to come to campus, but that was before she got widowed. Tim and Kim are fine with it; they're not planning to come downstairs anyway. And the wards on the house will keep the alchemists from finding her again. She'll be safe here until we can get that house set up and establish some protections."

"You say 'wards,' I say 'negotiations with the universe on a scale that few people can perceive, much less match," says Erin. "Anybody want a sandwich?"

"I want a vocabulary sheet," grumbles Máni.

Erin laughs, and keeps slapping sandwiches together. It's a good use of her time; manifest or not, being incarnate means being at least partially human, and humans need to eat. They'll be on campus right around when they should be eating dinner, and not many of them have had lunch today. Personified concepts underpinning the universe do not survive on coffee and spite alone.

In short order, the five of them are on the front porch, waiting for Roger and Kelpie to join them. The orange woman emerges first, wearing a borrowed cardigan over her dress, the sleeves too long and the neckline too low, the knit fabric swamping her like a canvas draped over a piece of furniture. It makes her look smaller than she is, more fragile, and her tail is wrapped around her leg, tightly enough that if she had toes, Artemis would be worried about her cutting off her own circulation and losing a few of them.

People with hooves should probably still worry about blood flow, but this doesn't seem like the time to point that out. They collect on the porch, a ragged group of seven, and the afternoon air is cool. The pale face of the moon above them is a small comfort.

"This is the plan," says Chang'e. "Just so there's no confusion. We proceed to the Campanile, verify the gate is anchoring there, and open the everything in a rotating order. Tonight is Artemis's night to cross the City, so we'll start with me, then open for Máni, and finally open Artemis. Once we open the first passage, we'll take Dodger inside, and she'll start doing the charts to establish which window belongs to Aske."

"Can we back up to where you said 'verify'?" asks Erin. "Is there a chance we get there and the gate *isn't* there?"

"It moves," says Máni. "Not every night, thankfully, or we'd spend all our time chasing the thing, and not nearly enough time doing our actual jobs. It felt stable enough last time I was there."

"I'm expecting it to move tomorrow, probably to the back hall of the old UC Theatre. It's been there about once a month for the last year. But right now, it should be on the Campanile. I don't know whether the everything has preferences, but it definitely has patterns, and it didn't like being unable to open on the Campanile while the repairs were going on. So it tends to show up there reliably."

"Okay," says Dodger. "What happens if I can't go into this 'everything' of yours?"

"I was able to go in while stepped all the way down," says Artemis.

"Yeah, but you were still a Lunar, stepped down or not," says Dodger. "I am still the Doctrine of Ethos, irritated by a system I don't understand or not. There's a difference."

"As if you can't convince reality to view you as anything you want," says Erin, sounding halfway amused.

"Not the point," says Dodger. "If we need to be able to get you, or Roger, or even Kelpie inside to avoid splitting the party, we need to know what happens if I can't get in."

"Not sure I follow, but let's go with that," says Erin. "Chang'e?"

"Dodger's right: we haven't technically tested this with someone who isn't tied to the Moon in some way," says Chang'e. "If nothing else, we should hopefully be able to pull you through by holding on to your hands until we're safely into the everything, and then we just take you to the window. Honestly, my bigger concern is what happens to someone who's not a Lunar if they're present when we open the window? City air is . . . intoxicating, even for us, and we're basically designed to endure it. I don't know what happens to you."

"Reed created us to take the City," says Roger. "I'm not worried about getting drunk or passing out. If anything, I'm worried we'll get one whiff and decide it's time to fulfill our purpose."

"Nope," says Dodger, easily enough. "I just joined another think tank in Australia, and we're going to figure out the necessary calculations for creating perpetual motion."

"Isn't that engineering? Or physics?" asks Máni.

Dodger shrugs. "It's all math when you dig deep enough. Pretending otherwise wastes everyone's time."

"Let's not stand here and start a philosophical debate when we have things we need to be doing, all right?" asks Roger, mildly. "Erin, you ready?"

"Ready," she confirms, and starts down the stairs.

Artemis frowns. "I know why the two of you are coming, and we couldn't do this without you, so I'm not complaining. But why are we bringing her?"

"She's our best killer," says Roger. "If something goes wrong, or we lose control of the situation, Erin will take care of it."

"Love to be useful," says Erin, deadpan. "But yes, I'm capable of murder, and I'm not squeamish when we're talking about killing alchemists. Some people need killing."

"That's a very soothing and reassuring attitude, and not at all alarming," mutters Chang'e.

Erin shrugs, unrepentant. "If it's us or them, you'll be happy to be on team 'us.'"

"Right," says Chang'e. "We access the everything, and Dodger determines which window belongs to Aske. Then we find a way to get to her window, and we break in. That should get us into her version of the everything, and let us try to figure out what happened to her. There's a good chance her body is still there, since Máni left her inside to avoid uncomfortable questions."

"And once we know? What does that do to solve things? We have dead Lunars, we have agitated alchemists, we have no *proof* they're connected—"

"Except that they're happening at the same time, and it seems like a pretty extreme coincidence if they're not."

"When you put this many nonhuman people in the same place, we have to start distorting the laws of causality at least a little," says

Roger. "I would be shocked if we didn't. That would actually be more of a stretch than the idea that we *do*."

"You do," says Kelpie. "I mean, we do. It's part of why there's a lab here. Setting up under your noses meant taking advantage of the strain on the laws of reality, and being able to turn those little improbabilities to nobler uses."

Silence falls, uncomfortable and awkward. Kelpie grimaces as she realizes what she just said.

"Or, um. To use them to hurt people, I guess. Sorry."

Artemis pats her on the shoulder, stopping when she sees how Kelpie shies away. "It's all right," she says. "You're still adjusting."

"They killed someone," says Kelpie, sounding miserable. "Two someones I knew, and maybe more than that. I shouldn't need any more time to adjust. I should be able to just know they're the bad guys. But even if I don't know for sure that your dead Lunars and the alchemists being all upset are connected, I do know it for sure, because the eclipse is coming. Margaret was in a tizzy for weeks, trying to push everyone to find the answers she needed, and when they didn't, the man from the Congress showed up to investigate the lab, and that's when she . . ." She pauses, swallowing hard, and looks away from the group, staring at the house. "That's when she told me what I was, and told me to run, and died. When the Congress came. The only thing that changed was how close we are to the eclipse. So that's what's going on."

"If they've been trying to find a way to trick their way into the City, could killing enough Lunars let you fake being one for long enough to get into this everything you keep mentioning?" asks Erin, thoughtfully. "Just lie to the world, get to the window, and slither into the Impossible City. Once you're inside, you can open the gates to anyone you want. We know that from the books."

"Earlier, Smita mentioned Zib getting into the City via the grave-yard path," says Dodger slowly. "She assumed we would be looking for someone who was trying to use the road of moonlight to get inside, but what if we're wrong about that?"

"My sister, the literary analyst," says Roger, sounding almost entertained. "What are you thinking, Dodger?"

"I'm thinking Artemis told us the alchemists who're looking for Kelpie made an auf," she says. "They're not alive, not really, but they're not dead either. They're in-between, unresolved integers, and they could probably use the graveyard path, if you could get them access."

"How do you open these gates?" asks Roger.

"We have keys," says Chang'e. The conversation leaps from place to place like a rabbit on hot cement, never staying still long enough for her to feel like she has her bearings. "We use them to tell the gate who's coming."

"Uh-huh. Does everyone have their own key?"

"No. We share them around."

"So where do they come from?"

"Hecate," says Artemis. "She doesn't manifest often—she's associated with the moon, but for some reason she's not generally considered a goddess *of* the moon, and I guess that keeps most of the people who still believe in her from lumping her in with the rest of us. But when she does manifest, she's the goddess of entries and of keys. She makes the keys we use to open the gates, and then we pass them around, because they're physical things, and when they're lost, they're gone."

"Could the alchemists be killing Lunars to try and get one of these keys?"

"Wouldn't work," says Chang'e. "There are only two keys in Berkeley right now. The one I brought with me when I moved here, and the one that was already here when I arrived."

"How did you get one?" asks Máni. "Why didn't I know you had your own key? Shouldn't someone have told me?"

"First, no one told you because most people don't know. I play it pretty close to the vest," says Chang'e. "I think most people who have their own key do it that way, for the sake of not having people get careless about the gates. As to how I got it, it was given to me by a Chang'e who was tired of doing her job. She'd been incarnate for so long that she'd buried her husband and all three of their children, and the youngest of her grandchildren was about a year away from going into assisted living. She was tired of crossing the sky. She was ready to go home to her version of the Moon and walk in the peach orchards forever."

"And where did she get it?"

"Hecate, I presume," says Artemis. She reaches into her pocket and produces a perfectly normal-looking key that gleams like mercury, surface glittering like it's been infused with pearlescent glitter. It's a solid object, but something about it looks like liquid, like it could burst and flow away at any moment. "That's where I got mine."

"How old *are* you?" asks Máni again.

Artemis shrugs. "Older than I like to admit. Old enough that I probably knew the Chang'e you're talking about. Was her human host's name Grace?"

When Chang'e nods, looking stricken, Artemis smiles.

"I always liked Grace. She was friendly; even welcoming, and she never objected to new people washing up on her patch. She used to make this spiced peach jam that was absolutely to die for, except for the part where if you ate it, you'd live forever." She looks to Roger. "We get the keys from Hecate, and then we pass them along until she comes back again."

"Who owns the other key here in Berkeley? The one you all use?"

"I think you know the answer to that one."

Roger sighs, deeply. "Yeah," he says. "I guess I probably do."

Mare Vaporum

TIMELINE: AUGUST 18, 2017.
THREE DAYS TO THE ECLIPSE.

They walk in a silent line along the sidewalks between the house and campus, a mismatched group that has no business moving in concert but moves in concert all the same. Roger and Dodger take the lead, the professor and the disappearing genius, cutting through the late-afternoon crowds like an arrow through air. Chang'e and Kelpie come after them, the Lunar and the cuckoo walking in uneasy time. They are followed by Máni and Erin, and at the back walks Artemis, a few feet behind the rest of them, giving Kelpie her space as best as she can without putting too much space between herself and the group.

The sky is still bright, the sun riding high, even as the moon shows her face through the clouds, a pale disk hanging in the afternoon sky. Chang'e hesitates as they reach the campus, grimacing.

"There are going to be so many people around this time of day," she says. "There's no way we can open a gate without being seen."

"Will people even notice us walking into a wall?" asks Erin. "They generally ignore that sort of thing unless you go out of your way to draw attention to it."

"Yes, and I generally help that happen by not drawing attention to it," says Chang'e. "Walking into a wall in *broad daylight* is the definition of drawing attention."

"If you give the actual definition, I will stab you," says Erin pleasantly to Roger, who sulks exaggeratedly.

"It doesn't matter," says Artemis.

"We're not killing people just because they see something they shouldn't," says Chang'e.

"We don't have to," says Artemis. "The gate's not here. Can't you feel that? There's no gate on campus right now."

Chang'e hesitates. "Maybe it just hasn't appeared yet."

"No. It's not anchored here right now."

"So where *is* it anchored?"

"I don't have magic-gate-detecting powers!"

"Can't you make it a hunt? I thought you said you could hunt anything."

Artemis shoots her a wounded look. "That's not what I meant, and you know it. I can't just *find* things. And hunting for a door isn't the same as hunting prey, or hunting an enemy. Unless the door was my enemy somehow, but that's just silly."

"I can find it," says Kelpie.

The rest of them stop and turn to look at her. Artemis speaks first. "You can what?"

"That key you have feels fizzy, like the way some things feel when they get too close to me. I think because I was made to be attuned to unclaimed Lunar energy, I can feel things that are connected to the Moon but aren't preoccupied with being people. I don't know how it works. I don't know how anything works, really. But I feel like if you want me to find the gate, I can find it."

"Why didn't you say something before?"

Kelpie shrugs. "You knew where it was. You were so sure of it. I didn't think I could say anything that would help if you already knew where it was."

"Can't hurt," says Roger. "Which way?"

Kelpie turns a slow circle, face screwing up with concentration. Then she stops and points away from campus, back the way they'd come. "There," she says.

"You heard the woman," says Roger. "This way."

They start to walk again, initially backtracking, then quickly passing the house, heading down Telegraph Avenue until they reach Bancroft, then turning and walking onward to Shattuck Avenue.

Kelpie doesn't speak, all her attention focused on the journey, and the rest are quiet as well, letting her set the pace and lead the way. She continues until they're approaching a neighborhood only Artemis seems to recognize. She hesitates.

"Kelpie?"

Kelpie keeps walking.

"Kelpie, are we going back to Isabella's apartment?"

"Is that a problem?" asks Erin.

"Gates don't normally anchor in private homes," says Artemis. "It would make it too difficult for us to be sure of getting the access we need. Can't exactly knock on someone's door and ask to come inside to make the journey to the moon, now, can you?"

Kelpie turns in to the apartment complex, and the others follow, having no better options immediately at hand. On she goes, passing the broken-down door to Isabella's apartment. It's sealed with police tape, garishly yellow and glaring. Juan's body is gone. Groups of neighbors litter the walkway, talking in quiet voices, clearly gossiping about the day's events. The police have been and gone, taking their notes and, one presumes, taking the victims.

It's hard not to wonder what conclusions they'll be able to draw, or how hard they'll even try. Crimes committed on the fringe of the alchemical world have a way of slipping through the cracks, investigations forgotten or dismissed, evidence misplaced. As long as Isabella doesn't push too hard for answers—unlikely, since she already has more answers than she could ever ask for—the authorities will forget this happened within the week. The neighbors, even more quickly. There already aren't as many of them out here as there should be, given the lurid nature of the situation.

It's a blessing, in its own way. It'll be easier for Isabella and Luis to start over without the fear of being charged with Catrina and Juan's murders hanging over their heads. It's also an abomination. Justice will never be served.

Kelpie seems to notice none of this. She's almost in a trance now, walking without seeing, without varying her pace at all. She approaches a door that looks like all the others.

"The gate won't be inside a private home," Artemis says again, a little louder this time.

Kelpie opens the door. It isn't locked. That's odd. Unlocked doors aren't safe. No matter how much you trust your neighbors, unlocked doors are a bad idea.

Inside, the room is square and empty, the walls painted white, the floor lacking any sort of carpet or padding. Kelpie walks straight to the door on the far wall, opening it in turn.

This door reveals a stairwell, descending down into the dark. Motion-sensitive lights come on as she steps onto the landing, illuminating the space in artificial brightness. Artemis surges forward, catching Kelpie by the elbow before she can step onto the stairs.

"This is the *lab*," she hisses, in case Kelpie somehow doesn't know, in case she's led them here with no real idea where she was going.

That thought isn't too far off. There's a glazed, absent look in Kelpie's eyes, like wherever she is mentally, it's very far away. She looks at Artemis's hand on her elbow, then back up to her face, her own eyes very wide and guileless.

"We have to go down," she says. "The gate is down."

"Why would the gate anchor here?" asks Chang'e.

"Because maybe the Moon is tired of something picking you off one by one, and wants you to finish this?" suggests Erin. "I mean, that, or it's trying to get you all slaughtered so it can start over with smarter moon gods. I don't know. I'm not the folklore expert here."

"We don't have one of those," says Roger. He steps into the stairwell, nose wrinkling. "It smells like alkahest."

Dodger follows, slow and unhappy. "I don't like labs."

"I know," he says, reassuringly.

"They can't keep us here. If they try—"

"They'll regret it."

He speaks with such absolute authority that Dodger calms, and the rest of them follow her lead. Artemis lets Kelpie go. The orange-skinned woman shakes her head, rolls her shoulders, and begins to descend into the light, tail twitching and hooves making little ringing sounds on the metal steps.

They follow. There's not much else to do at this point, not when she's supposedly leading them to the gate, not when the gate is so far below. Down and down they go, so far beneath the Earth that it shouldn't be possible, not in earthquake-prone California. Erin winces several times, picking up on the instabilities in the walls around them, but calms incredibly quickly; none of those faults are severe enough to set off her chaos radar for long. That seems to make her tenser rather than soothing her, and by the time they reach the third flight down, she's tight-shouldered and scowling, glancing around like she expects to be attacked at any moment.

The Lunars stay clustered together as they walk, and halfway down that third flight, something changes in the air around them, like a camera filter has been removed, a layer of soft-focus glitter stripped away. Chang'e makes a small, soft sound of dismay, glancing over her shoulder at Roger, and the way he meets her eyes somehow makes it clear that he's looking at Judy. The gods have gone. Only their human hosts remain.

Anna stumbles, nearly falling, only to catch herself on the stair rail at the last possible moment. Blinking rapidly, she turns to the others, searching their faces in desperation. There's no recognition in her expression. "Where are we?" she asks, and her voice has changed, dry, almost generic tones replaced by something closer to the American Mid-Atlantic accent, which sounds at once completely wrong and completely right coming out of her mouth. She's too young to sound like that.

But she's not as young as she seems; she's made that more than clear. Judy hesitates, remembering Artemis saying that she never steps all the way down when there's a hunt happening, and wonders how long it's been since Anna—actually Anna, not a pretense of her put on to make people feel more comfortable with the situation—has seen the surface.

"We're in a stairwell, beneath the city of Berkeley," says Judy gingerly. "We're heading down into an alchemist's stronghold, to find the gate that hopefully lets us access the Impossible City."

"Children's stories and nonsense," says Anna. "I don't know what

I expected from a dancehall girl. Why are we *here*?" She looks to Roger, apparently flagging him as the leader of their little group, and waits for a reply.

"Was that racist?" asks David. "I feel like that was racist."

"Almost certainly," says Dodger. She's looking at the air above Anna's head, eyes unfocused, visibly working her way through some sort of incomprehensible equation. "I'd say she's standing roughly a hundred years ago right now. Nineteen twenty-something. Of course, that's just a guess. Keep her talking and I'll be able to narrow the field considerably."

David looks at her blankly. "I thought your brother was the linguist."

"He is. He speaks all the languages that are, or ever have been, spoken upon the Earth."

"So how can you narrow down a time period from her accent?"

"I'm not going by her accent," says Dodger. "I speak English and just enough Spanish to order lunch at the taquerias downtown without being a total asshole. This isn't about language."

"Then what . . . ?"

"Roger speaks languages, but Dodger speaks time," says Erin, eyeing Anna with distaste. "This isn't a form of time travel I'm familiar with, and I'm not going to pretend I like it very much. This one came the slow way, in a box at the bottom of a deep well, where no one would mess with her or try to draw her out. Artemis put her there, whether she intended to or not. I thought you people practiced coexistence."

"We do," says Judy, sounding disturbed. "The gods can't suppress us like that."

But maybe the rules are different for Artemis when she's on the hunt. Maybe she can do things the rest of them can't, or wouldn't, do.

Anna looks alarmed, taking a step backward and down the stairs, her hands held out in front of her in a useless warding gesture. She's outnumbered, even before you account for the fact that with or without the moon, half of them are more than purely human.

"You're with *them*," she accuses. "The voices from the moon!

You're part of that great delusion! Well, I'll not have any part of it, do you hear me? I refuse the idea that I'm to share my inner space with someone I never asked for and never invited in!"

"So she wasn't a willing host, then," says Erin quietly. "That's an interesting variation."

"Calm down," says Roger, with the force of a direct command. His eyes are on Anna, and his words are clearly meant for her; she catches her breath as if she's going to object, then sags, objection dying in the force of an order she can't refuse. Her shoulders relax, her hands lower, and her face goes slack.

"Now, tell us who you are and what you know."

Judy frowns, reviewing the conversations she's had with Roger. He doesn't give orders. He asks for things. He makes his wishes clear. But for a man with all of language at his fingertips, he speaks with remarkable care, never quite demanding when there's any other choice. She wonders how he figured out he had to be so careful with the world, and how difficult it is for him to navigate when the slightest misspoken word can render everyone around him incapable of saying "no."

His weirdly codependent relationship with his sister makes more sense all the time, and the wisdom of voluntarily entangling herself with this man fades a little deeper into the mists of confusion, but she can already tell she's going to do it anyway. He's charming, in his own eccentric way, and he can skip language to language in the middle of a sentence in a way that appeals endlessly, and is so difficult to find out in the real world. She's a part-time goddess of the moon. She was never that infatuated with the real world anyway.

Anna sighs, shoulders sagging in what looks almost like relief. "My name is Annabelle Austin, and I'm the daughter of Charles Austin, who owns the Austin Continental Rail Company. My father's a very important man, which is why he was very alarmed when his oldest daughter started hearing voices. I was meant to be making my debut into society, and instead I was arguing with the moonlight. I had to be seen to."

"Seen *to*?" asks Roger.

Anna nods. "Seen to. He found a lovely man who promised he could heal my instabilities and set me back on the path to becoming a functional member of society. Dr. Reed was quite skilled with the art of the mind. He took me into his care, and under his tutelage, the voices stopped. I no longer heard a woman calling to me from the moon, as was only right and proper; there are no women in the moon, and if there were, they wouldn't use the moonlight as radio waves, beaming themselves into my dreams."

Erin steps forward, expression going sharp. "Ask her what Reed ordered her to do. There must have been *something*, or she wouldn't have let Artemis in. The Lunars have to be allowed to take root and grow inside their hosts. For some reason, she allowed it."

Judy frowns. Artemis's avoidance of Diana makes more sense now, as does her insistence that the other woman had to be doing something wrong. Diana is more hands-off than she should be as a senior Lunar, more distracted by the human side of her existence, but she's never shown any signs of being an alchemical puppet.

"What did Reed ask of you?" asks Roger, obediently. "You have to answer truly. I need to know."

Anna's face screws up with momentary discomfort before she says, in a sharper tone, "He was embarking on a great project, one he had started with his mother's assistance, before her passing. He was going to have children of his own, a boy and a girl, and he was going to raise them to be the most perfect people who ever existed."

Dodger scoffs. Roger glances at her, expression sharp.

"He may have intended to do things that way in the beginning," he says. "She's not lying if that's what he told her he was doing. One of the dangers of asking someone to tell the truth is that they can only tell you the truth as they understand it, and not necessarily the truth as it actually is."

Anna nods. "He was very determined to be a parent. He called them his cuckoos, and said one day they would fly. And he might not be there to see it, but I would be. He was quite sure of it. He said I was a fascinating subject, useful and useless at the same time. I don't care to be called useless. It seems impolite at best, and insufferably rude at worst. But he told me I had access to a place he dearly wished to enter and feared he might be banned from. He prepared me to serve as needed."

"And Artemis?"

Anna's face screws up in sudden disdain, so pure and absolute that Judy winces. She can't imagine sharing her life with someone she dislikes as much as it seems Anna dislikes Artemis. She and Chang'e may not always be in perfect agreement, but they're always friends, and they navigate the complexities of their shared life with relative grace.

"He said I had to let her in. He said he needed to talk to her. So I let her in. So he talked to her. And then . . . I don't remember much after that. The taste of peaches, frequently. Flashes of my father's funeral, my mother saying I had some nerve showing my face there after the way I'd broken his heart. And then it was all a dark room, with a window that let in the moonlight."

"Quiet now," says Roger. "Go to sleep."

Anna closes her eyes and bows her head, swaying as she appears to fall asleep on her feet. Erin moves to steady her, keeping her from falling down.

"Great," she says. "So Reed was fishing for Lunars before any of the rest of us were born. What was he planning to do with them?"

"I think he must have been afraid we'd do exactly what we did, and break away after we claimed the Doctrine," says Roger. "So he creates his cuckoos and then they don't hand him the City—what then?"

"Then he'd start planning another way to get inside, since us existing makes the City more concrete than it was before," says Dodger. "Us being here, on Earth, as material creatures that need things like air and gravity, means the City has to appear the same way. It has to be solid so we can enter it. In a way, forcing us to manifest forces the City to manifest. Cause and effect don't have to go in that order, not for this equation."

"So Reed incarnates the Doctrine, and that lures the City close enough to become solid, and then, what, it echoes backward?"

"Maybe." Dodger shrugs. "Causality is squishy where we're concerned. You know that. Baker made the City a place when she wrote the Up-and-Under—except it was already a place, because we already had stories about Olympus, and Avalon. Even the Christian Bible says, in so many words, that Heaven is a city. Baker redefined it to fit what she wanted it to be, to fit *us,* or the idea that was eventually going to become us. Do you think the Lunar system worked the same way before that happened, or do you think it adapted after she changed the way reality works?"

"This is giving me a headache," mutters David.

"Welcome to my world," says Erin. "Much as I hate to break up philosophy club, we're standing in the stairwell leading to an alchemical research center owned and operated by people who don't like us much and have already demonstrated that they're more than happy to commit murder to get what they want."

"And, um, what they want is at least partially me, but I bet they'd be happy to take us all," says Kelpie, sounding anxious. She sounds anxious perpetually enough that it's not setting off alarm bells yet, but Judy can see where they might eventually learn the flavors of her anxiety, come to understand them as individual and distinct things, and be able to calibrate their panic accordingly.

Of course, first, they have to live that long.

"Anna," says Roger. "You can wake up now, and take a breath, and then you'll go back to sleep, and let Artemis come forth again. I know the moon isn't shining this far underground, but the gate is here, and we need Artemis right now."

Anna opens her eyes, giving him a spiteful look. "You want to put me away again," she accuses. "You're just like Dr. Reed. When he'd had enough of me, he sent me away, and for you to do the same, sir, proves only that you are no gentleman at all, only a pale mockery of same."

"That's fair enough, and you're not wrong. But now you need to go."

"You're just like your *father,*" spits Anna. Roger reels back as if he's been struck, and maybe he has been, maybe some forms of assault have nothing to do with the physical. Then Anna's eyes glaze over, and between one blink and the next she's gone. Artemis is back.

Artemis stands differently than Anna does. She has a greater tension in her limbs, a certain assurance that she knows precisely where she belongs and will have no trouble getting there. At the same time, an arrogance is missing, one that Kelpie recognizes only because she's seen it in so many alchemists, and in Catrina as well: the belief that the universe has been arranged for your benefit, even if it harms everyone else around you. Artemis has a different flavor of arrogance to her, the kind that says she knows exactly what she's capable of, and has no question of her worth. She's proven it, time and time again.

She has nothing left to prove.

She also, for the moment, looks totally baffled. "What just happened?" she asks.

"We'll explain in a few minutes," says Erin. "For right now, we move."

Suddenly concerned, Judy reaches for Chang'e as they resume their descent toward the bottom of the stairs, and is relieved to find the goddess, reduced and somewhat pushed aside, but present at the bottom of her psyche, lurking.

What? asks Chang'e.

Just wanted to know that you were here, replies Judy, feeling a little foolish. *Did you see what happened to Artemis?*

I did. Chang'e sounds regretful, almost ashamed. *There's a reason we coexist rather than taking over entirely. That sort of behavior is shameful and unkind. We must never push our hosts from the chambers of their own hearts. We owe you coexistence.*

Anna and Artemis haven't been coexisting.

No. Not for a long time.

Kelpie pulls them up short as they come to the bottom of the stairs, sticking one arm out to prevent them from going any farther. She gestures to the door. "That's the way to the main lab," she says. "That's where I was when . . . That's where I was. In there."

"So that's where we'll find the alchemists?" asks Dodger. "Great. I have a few things I'd like to say to those assholes." She pushes Kelpie's arm aside and makes for the door, wrenching it open without further hesitation.

On the other side is a lab, gleaming chrome, glass, and glaring white light . . . and an utter absence of people. Half the equipment has been covered in plain cotton sheets; the exposed half is as clean and shining as the rest, but clearly only because it's been maintained, not because it's new and top of the line. This is a lab in the process of being decommissioned.

Kelpie blinks, then steps forward, almost knocking into Dodger. Roger thinks, only half-rationally, that her hooves make more sense now; for a science project that can walk and talk and think for itself, living in a facility where all the floors are linoleum or tile is the equivalent of belling the cat. She's never been able to sneak up on anyone in her life.

"Where are they?" she asks, breathless, voice tight with sudden concern. She can't stop herself from looking at the drain in the center of the floor, as polished as the rest of the metal in the room, a channel through which mortal remains can pour and be collected. "He can't have killed them *all*."

"I think you'll find I can," says a voice, mild, cultured, and calm. The whole group looks around.

A door has opened on the far wall, partially obscured by a rack of jars and vessels, most of which look too old-fashioned for the lab around them, all of which are spotless. A man is in the process of stepping through. He is tall and almost skeletally thin, with the air of unreality about him that Roger has noticed most alchemists seem to possess, as if he's looked at the laws governing the rest of the world and decided that no, he doesn't need to abide by those after all. Those are the restrictions of something lesser than himself.

His eyes are dead. If not for the fact that he's standing, moving toward them, speaking, Roger would be perfectly willing to call the man a corpse.

"They were a failed research team that wasted Congressional time and resources on a doomed project," he continues, studying the fingernails of his left hand like he thinks there might be something fascinating beneath them. "Contributing their personal resources to our stores is a kinder outcome than many would have offered them, and those who understood their place were properly grateful for the opportunity."

"I don't believe that," says Kelpie, voice wavering.

He looks away from his nails, finally focusing on her. "It was kind of you to return here of your own volition," he says, lowering his hand. "You, yourself, are a Congressional resource, and you had no right to remove yourself from the premises."

"I am not a Congressional resource, I'm a person," she counters.

"You're a construct, a cuckoo, and the purpose you were built for is almost upon us," he says. "You'll pry open the gates of the City if it kills you." From the tone of his voice, he'd be perfectly happy with that outcome. One more loose end tied off, one more aberration removed from the world.

"No, I don't think she will," says Artemis, stepping between Kelpie and the man with the graveyard eyes. She glares, her own eyes flashing olive green and dangerous.

The man smirks. "Reed's little double agent. I knew they'd signaled you when the project seemed to be nearing completion; Margaret's notes were sloppy and quite unprofessional, but they were thorough. I did hope we'd have the opportunity to meet, Miss Austin. You've long been one of my favorite examples of the lack of inevitability even in predestination."

Artemis glares at him. "I don't work for you."

"Don't you?" He snaps his fingers, then hums the first six notes of an orchestral fugue.

Artemis stiffens. Dodger inhales sharply.

"That was the theme for the 1907 stage musical of *Over the Woodward Wall*," says Dodger. "The sheet music was supposedly lost after the theater burned down. How . . . ?"

"How can *you*?" counters the man. Artemis's expression, meanwhile, has gone slack, all animation draining away. The man frowns. "Miss Austin," he says. "You should be here now."

"She can't," says Roger. "I gave her strict instructions to sleep, and you don't have the authority to overrule me."

"As to how *I* can, music is sort of like math, and time is absolutely a form of math, and music that time took is one hundred percent in my wheelhouse," says Dodger. "You're not going to get control of her."

Kelpie turns to Artemis, losing interest in the man, at least for the moment, and grabs hold of the other woman's shoulders. "We don't need Anna," she says firmly. "We need Artemis. We need to get to the gate."

Artemis blinks, then shakes her head, clearing away the fog. "Hey," she says, focusing on Kelpie. "Where is it?"

"Behind him."

"Of course it is," says Erin, sounding disgusted. She steps forward. "Hello. Judging by the fact that you look like you've been embalmed, I'm going to guess you're the local Congressional representative. Am I warm?"

"I serve the Congress; I don't belong to the Congress," he says, sounding almost amused. "But yes, you're quite close to the reality of the situation. Can I help you in some fashion?"

"You can let us pass."

He taps his chin with one finger, expression turning thoughtful. "Mmm . . . no, I don't think I'll be doing that."

"Then you can make your peace with whatever divinity you serve."

"I don't think I'll be doing that, either," he says, producing a flask from inside his pocket. Kelpie, who recognizes it all too well, makes a wordless sound of dismay and recoils. He holds it up for Erin's inspection. "You seem too well educated to be a part of this little mob. Who did you study under?"

"Barrow, primarily," says Erin.

For the first time, his composure flickers. Only for a moment, but long enough for the whole group to see it happen. "You're one of . . ."

"One of Reed's, yes," she says. "I'm the one who handled his cleanup when he didn't want to do it himself. You can drop that flask, but you'll have to ask yourself which is faster: airborne alkahest or an angry construct with nothing left to lose."

"I'll bet on the alkahest," he says, and tosses the flask, a bare moment before he retreats through the door, slamming it closed behind him.

The glass shatters when it hits the floor, a thick, silver-gray gas beginning to billow forth. It's too much to have been contained in that flask at any point; even the most generous of reagents would have overflowed the available space.

There isn't time to dwell on the impossibility of the moment. He knew his targets when he prepared his poisons. This isn't like before, when he thought he only needed to kill a human. If this alkahest touches them, they'll die, divinity and cuckoo alike; flesh is not immune to consumption, no matter how it was created.

Kelpie shies back, pressing herself into Artemis, who puts her arms around her and drags her several feet back, while Judy and David try their best to step behind Roger and Dodger, neither of whom look particularly disturbed.

Dodger rolls her eyes. "Gravity is a mathematical concept, did you know?" she asks.

Roger nods. "You do love reminding me," he says.

"Well, it seems important," she says, and looks at the cloud of foggy gas that's pooling by the door. She begins to recite a string of numbers so complicated it sounds more like a witch's incantation than a math problem, and the gas falls out of the air, splatting on the floor with a wet sound. Dodger nods, apparently satisfied. "Go tell it that it's impossible now, okay?"

"Cleanup crew again," says Roger, and moves to stand at the edge of the puddle of alkahest. "You don't exist," he informs it. "Alchemists struggled for centuries to create you, and failed over and over again, because you don't exist. You're a literal impossibility. For you to exist, a dozen laws of nature would have to be violated or rewritten, and that hasn't happened, so you're not real. You're just fancy colored water."

He crouches and reaches for the pool. Kelpie's eyes widen in terror.

"No!" she yelps, just before he touches the surface of the liquid. It ripples, and nothing else happens.

He pulls back his hand, showing her his wet fingertips, then wipes them against the side of his leg. "All I had to do was make it understand that it's not real," he says. "I could have gone for more of a sledgehammer approach, told it that it wasn't there, but that's rude. I don't figure the universe likes having itself ripped apart just because it's convenient, so if I can do things the subtle way, I generally will."

Kelpie continues to stare at him with wide eyes, clearly waiting for the moment when he starts to melt. It doesn't come. Roger straightens.

"You said the gate's through there?" He gestures to the door the man from the Congress retreated through. "Are we all feeling good about following him?"

"No," says Erin. "These people love to set traps almost as much as a *Scooby-Doo* villain does. We open that door, we could set off all kinds of nastiness."

"Which is why you go first, since you'll pick up on anything that's not where it's supposed to be."

Erin gives him a blankly unhappy look, expression going flat. "I wish that didn't make sense."

"I know."

Erin sighs, then turns toward the door. She blinks, once, and the world changes focus, going from a series of solid forms and sharp edges to what looks almost like a series of values. She's not seeing the physical world anymore. She's seeing the chaos all around her, the energy that's always there, running along the edge of her awareness whether she wants it to be or not. She's seeing the entropy and the decay that the alchemists fight so hard to control, even at the expense of the natural integrity of the world they inhabit.

She knows now, why they can dig so deep, why the walls don't crumble inward at the slightest shake. The knowledge comes as easy as catching her breath, bringing with it a hundred unwanted connections. She manages, barely, not to look at any of the Lunars. They might see the understanding in her eyes, and know that they walk through a necropolis, a foundation built upon the bodies of their own dead.

The alchemists may or may not be responsible for all the dead or missing Lunars, but they're certainly responsible for some of them. She can't tell, from this surface glance at the situation, how many people were bled out to make this much concrete, how many gods and goddesses of the moon gave everything they had for someone else's dream. She isn't sure she'd want to know.

But with all the chaos of the world firmly in her mind's eye, she moves toward the door, Roger close behind her. If she can spot the traps without triggering them, or even if she does trigger them, if she can do it without putting herself in direct danger, he'll be able to tell the traps why they aren't real and thus can't hurt any of them. It's an oddly efficient way of clearing space, as long as they go in the right order.

(It's also remarkably *in*efficient if looked at with a critical eye. The Lunars are living incarnations of moon gods, but Roger and Dodger are living gods, literally. They can negotiate with reality to a degree that no one else has been able to accomplish, ever, the peak of natural manifestation combined with alchemical personification. They could snap their fingers and bring this all to an end, opening the paths ahead of them without making any real effort. But that's *why* they make an effort, why they're so exquisitely careful in everything they do. They could easily shatter reality without intending to, making everyone else's needs secondary to their own. That they don't is a testament to how much care they take every single day. But sometimes that determination to be careful translates into moments like this one, where there's an easier way, rendered unavailable by their own standards.)

She tries the knob. It's locked, of course, and so she glances over her shoulder to Roger, nodding once. He looks at the doorknob.

"It's a real pity, these modern latch mechanisms, the way they never hold up against even the slightest amount of pressure," he says. "You'd think that by now, we'd be better at making locks you can't knock loose with a hit in the right place."

"You'd think," agrees Erin, and smacks the heel of her hand into the door just above the lock plate.

There's a *click* from somewhere deep inside the mechanism, and when she tries the knob again, the door swings open, revealing a narrow hall.

It looks like a continuation of the lab, white and chrome and sterile. The signs of shabbiness are creeping in here as well, the blank patches on the bulletin boards, the scuffs on the floor, but for now, it's almost as pristine as it was the day that it was made. The seven of them ease through, Erin at the lead, Roger and Kelpie close behind, Dodger following them, looking unhappy to be separated from her brother even by such a short distance. The three moon gods bring up the rear, Judy and David keeping a close eye on Artemis, who moves a little jerkily, like she's still not sure what happened back there.

She may not know, even now, what Reed did to Anna, and Erin hates that this is just one more life—or pair of lives, more properly—that the man managed to destroy. He's dead and gone and still ruining things, and sometimes it feels like he's going to be ruining things forever. He's never going to go away and leave them alone.

Or maybe it's not right to blame Reed. Maybe they should be blaming Asphodel, who started this whole obsession in the first place, and left them walking her improbable road whether they wanted to be or not. Erin walks down the hall, steps slow and measured, neither hurrying nor creeping along, but content to travel at the speed her body sets and let it bring her to her destination. Nothing explodes or triggers or comes bursting out to harm them. That's not as reassuring as it could be.

Alchemists are, by and large, reasonably smart people. This doesn't make them tactical geniuses, or equip them for a siege; they're as likely to let death in through the front door as anyone else is. But they think about their own safety, about their legacies, all but constantly, and for the man who appears to have killed everyone in this facility to just let them walk in the way he has says one of two things: either he's so bone-confident in his alkahest that he can't imagine any of them are still alive, which is hubris bordering on foolishness, or he's got another way out, and has already fled the lab complex for the world above.

Even surrounded by divinely infused, self-repairing concrete, Erin can see a hundred ways to bring the apartment that houses the laboratory entrance crashing down, blocking off the door. Sure, Roger could whisper the stones into vapor, or Dodger could find the equation that lets them dig their way out in no time flat with nothing harmed but their schedule, but both those things would strain the limits the cuckoos place on themselves. Others could be hurt, civilian lives lost, and all because they let him get away.

It's a distressing-enough thought that she doesn't hear Kelpie call for her to stop at first, but keeps walking, trying to reach the end of the hall. Once they reach the end of the hall, they'll find their answers. She's sure of that. She really is.

And then Kelpie's voice breaks through her fugue, and she stops, looking up at the ceiling as she tries to organize her thoughts. There, worked into the pattern of perforations in the ceiling tiles, she finds a series of sigils designed to encourage focus and single-mindedness among lab technicians. They're tuned highly enough that they're effectively weaponized. Anyone who walks down this hall will find themselves unable to deviate from their assigned course, which means she wants to keep going, no matter how important it is for her to stop.

There are many downsides to being a living chaos detector. One of the more pressing, which never seems to occur to anyone unprompted, is that while she can spot things like tripwires and explosive devices designed to cause chaos, she won't see orderly dangers until it's too late. She's missing a full half of the threats, because they're orderly and thus don't register.

Erin sighs and looks down again, then turns and backtracks to where Kelpie and the others are gathered, their attention on a particular section of wall.

"You're sure?" asks Roger dubiously.

"It's here," says Kelpie.

"She's right," says Judy, moving to the front of the group and reaching out with one hand, brushing her fingertips against the wall. "I don't know how it can be down this deep. The gates are only meant to appear where there's moonlight. But it's here."

"There's moonlight everywhere around us," says Artemis. "It's been severed from the moon itself, but it's still moonlight. It comes out of the walls. It's so strong I bet the place glows in the dark."

"It does," says Kelpie, sounding almost serene.

"Can you open it?" asks Roger.

That is the important question, after all; they've found the gate, but can they open it? Erin watches, holding her breath, as Judy dips her hand into her pocket and produces the key, which she taps against the wall like she's trying to ring a bell. Then she scowls.

"Nothing," she says.

"Let me try," says Artemis. She reaches into her own pocket, producing a second key. It's not quite identical to the first, and neither has the mass-manufactured sheen of a key from Home Depot or some other big-box hardware store; they're hand-worked, these keys, antique and gleaming. They've never been given time to tarnish, for all that Erin's fairly sure they're the oldest things in this hallway.

Artemis taps her key against the wall, parallel to Judy's, and the gate appears.

It looks like something a computer generated for a movie about fantasy worlds hidden beyond impossible doors, all curls and gentle arches spiraling out from the two points of contact, braiding themselves together to form the arched structure of the gate itself, which gleams silver and brilliantly white, like someone has covered the wall in a thin layer of embossing glitter.

Judy takes a deep breath and drops away, her eyes changing tones as Chang'e rises to the surface. "We're so far from the moon, but I feel it all around us," she says, glancing to Artemis. "Whose everything is this? Which of us opened the door?"

"I don't know," says Artemis. "I guess go through and see?"

Chang'e nods before walking calmly into what was previously solid white-painted concrete. There's no resistance; she's just through, appearing on the other side of the glittering veil. She looks around, then turns back to the others. "It's solid," she says. "I don't know whether it's mine—I suppose the window will answer that. Dodger, try to come through."

The living force of mathematics steps forward, and scowls as she bumps her nose against the wall. "Ow," she says. Then she looks more closely at the shimmering veil. "I could force it, but I don't think that would be a good idea. The equations that comprise this thing are—woof. They're complicated. And that's putting it really, really lightly. I guess this was a bust. So now we find the asshole alchemist and get the hell out of here."

David steps forward, his own eyes gleaming with an icy sheen for a moment as Máni steps up to the forefront. He takes Dodger's hand in his, ignoring the way she half-recoils, and walks into the wall. Walks *through* the wall, pulling Dodger with him, into the black-and-rainbow tunnel beyond the gate.

Dodger yelps as they pass through the gate, then yanks her hand from his and glares at him. "Don't touch me," she snaps. "I didn't say you could touch me."

For Kelpie and Artemis, every word is clear as day. For Erin and Roger, her mouth moves, but no sound emerges. She's somewhere else, somewhere beyond their ken.

Roger's eyes abruptly widen, and he lunges for the gate. Erin is quick enough on the uptake to realize what must have just happened; she catches his arm before he can slam into the wall, as incapable of passing through on his own as his sister is.

"The two of you got by just fine for *years* without playing cranial roommate; you can stand being separated for five minutes," she says, pulling him back, away from the transparent patch on the wall. Artemis looks at her, puzzled.

Erin sighs. "There's only one Doctrine of Ethos," she says. "Fitting it into a single human body was impossible—it's too big, and that's saying something, given some of the concepts they *can* cram into a human skin—so they had to give the Wonder Twins here two bodies to work with. Doesn't actually make them distinct from each other. They grew up enough apart to develop individuality, and they're separate enough to be considered different people, but as soon as they became manifest, they moved into each other's heads, and they haven't been apart since then. If Dodger's on a different plane of reality, I'm betting they can't hear each other's thoughts. I'd think he'd see this as a good thing, especially if he's planning to get frisky with a moon goddess."

Artemis lifts her eyebrows. "Oh? Which one?"

"The one whose host loves languages almost as much as he does, if that's even possible," says Erin. "Not *you*."

"I mean, no, not me," agrees Artemis. She looks at the gate, through which the trio remains visible. Máni is holding Dodger back; she's trying to get to the gate, apparently as distressed by the separation from her brother as he is by his separation from her. "I'm definitely not his type."

"Not linguistic enough?"

"Too gay. Hang on."

She steps through into the familiar rainbow black of the everything, clapping her hands together. "Dodger! Look at me!"

Dodger stops pulling against Máni and looks. Artemis smiles, trying to look reassuring.

"Cool. Glad you can listen. Erin says you probably don't have your brother in your head right now, and that's why you're freaking out. Can you still do the necessary calculations while you're distracted by the quiet?"

"I can," says Dodger, sullenly. "There used to be a little door in the back of my head, and when I closed it, I couldn't hear him. So I know I can work when it's quiet."

"Good. Chang'e?"

"Yes?"

"Take her to the window. I'm going to stay here with the others, make sure I can defend them if that alchemist comes back while we're waiting on you."

She steps out of the everything there, leaving the three of them to start their journey.

Outside, Roger is still staring raptly at the gate. Erin and Kelpie are watching him, both looking profoundly uncomfortable with the situation, with splitting the party. Artemis moves to stand next to the trio, watching as the others move away into the dark.

"That's the everything?" asks Erin.

Artemis nods.

"It hurts my eyes."

"Why?"

"Because there's nothing chaotic about it, and absolutely *every-thing* about it is chaotic, at the same time."

"Ah. I guess that makes sense. It's the passage between this world and the City. I always sort of figured the rainbows were a function of entropy, and entropy is chaotic, isn't it?"

"Yes, but it's a perfect manifestation of order at the same time." Erin shrugs broadly. "I'm not the one who made the rules. Sometimes I sort of wish I were, because a lot of them would be very, very different."

"It's so *quiet*," complains Roger.

"Only because you're too used to having someone in your head all the damn time. I liked it better before that happened." Erin gives Kelpie a sidelong look, then says, in a tone that implies she's imparting a great and profound secret, "Dodger used to talk more. Not in conversations about serious shit, just like, in passing. She'd comment on the weather or ask about dinner. Normal people talking to each other things. Now she can go *days* without saying a word, and neither of them notice, because they're so busy carrying on a conversation none of the rest of us can hear."

Roger blinks at her. "You didn't tell me it bothered you that much."

"So there's something in the world you don't know? Be still my heart."

"You okay?" Artemis asks, looking at Kelpie.

Kelpie hesitates, then shakes her head. "No," she says. "I don't want to be here. I was never going to be here again. I'm only here because we had to get to the gate. Why is it down here?"

"Maybe we needed to be down here, or maybe that alchemist we saw figured out a way to force the gates to manifest where he wants them to be."

The door at the end of the hall slams open, then, and two figures in white lab coats lurch into the room. There's something wrong with their faces, some indefinable lack of tension, some inaccuracy in the way their skin fits over their bones. Kelpie stiffens.

"You know them?" asks Artemis.

"I did," says Kelpie.

"What does that mean?"

"It means they're dead," says Erin, moving in front of Roger and falling into a fighting stance. She tilts her head, smiling sunnily at the pair. "Hi. I'm the one who's about to ruin your entire day."

"Auf," says Artemis with disgust, stepping to the side, putting herself next to Erin. She reaches behind herself, gripping something that isn't there, and when she brings her hand around, she's holding a bow, long and curved and gleaming like the gate.

"Why is this asshole so enamored with the things?" asks Erin. "They fell out of fashion *centuries* ago, right around the time you stopped being able to swap somebody's kid out for one of them without getting caught."

"What's an auf?" asks Kelpie.

"Used to be an interchangeable term for 'changeling,'" says Roger, eyes on the pair. They're slowly advancing down the hall, walking without difficulty, their heads occasionally twitching as if they're not quite sure what's in front of them. "Of course, they're not the same thing."

"Nothing ever is," says Kelpie.

"Alchemists make them out of dead people," says Erin. "They're different from constructs because they're not as durable. An auf will fall apart in a matter of weeks unless you put a lot more care into it than most alchemists do. And you don't want to know why they might take that kind of care. It's almost always a sex thing."

"Ew," says Kelpie.

"Precisely."

The two auf are continuing to head down the hall, not moving with any real urgency. They feel more like an environmental hazard than a real threat, or possibly a psychological attack: Kelpie is getting paler and paler as they approach, clearly recognizing the people they used to be. Artemis pulls her bowstring back. There's no arrow notched. Maybe there doesn't need to be, not when the bow and the arrows are made of the same textured moonlight.

"This isn't a sex thing," says Kelpie. "This is a message."

"What's the message?"

She pauses, swallowing hard. "Everyone I've ever cared about is dead," she says, after a long moment has trickled by, unremarked. "These two worked in hydroponics. That's where Margaret said they put the Rabbit they'd managed to manifest before they got me. So he's probably dead too. The Congress is cleaning house."

"Cleaning house and making it personal," says Erin grimly. "All right, Artemis, you've dealt with aufs before. Anything I need to know?"

"Haven't you?" asks Artemis.

"Yes, but not from the 'killing them a second time' side of things. It was more that I was around when they were being put together," says Erin. "I even helped with a couple. Leigh called them her little craft projects. She never liked making her monsters out of mud or iron or other inanimate materials, and constructs like us were too much trouble. We got ideas in our heads, we rebelled against our makers. A good auf will never do that. A good auf is a tool, always and forever."

"I don't think there's any such thing as a 'good' auf," says Artemis. She pulls her bowstring back a little farther, and looks to Kelpie. "Can we kill them?"

Kelpie blinks. "Why are you asking me?"

"Because they were your friends. They're going to reach us in a minute, and then they're not going to give us a choice, but it might be easier on you if you actually saw them attack us before we start cutting them down."

Kelpie looks at her for a moment, wide-eyed. "You care that much about whether you upset me?"

Artemis shrugs. "Well, yeah. I've been looking for you for a long, long time. I don't want you to hate me. But if I have to make you hate me to keep you safe, that's what I'll do."

"Fine. I just can't watch." Kelpie turns her face resolutely to the gate, and doesn't look, not even when she hears the bowstring snap back into place, when she hears the dull thud of the first arrow striking home. There's a second thud as the auf Artemis shot collapses to the hallway floor, all without making a single sound.

"Efficient," says Erin approvingly.

"Can you do better?" asks Artemis.

"Watch."

Roger sighs. "Please don't show off."

"Someone has to." The sound of running follows, footsteps light, ending in the scuff and tap of a leap. Flesh tears a moment later, strangely dry, like someone is slicing through a dinner roast and not a moving person. There's not a single thud after whatever Erin has done. There's a series of them, sharper than the first had been, like whatever she's dropped has the momentum to bounce.

"Okay, that's impressive," says Artemis. "Nice technique."

"I learned from the best."

"I thought you learned from Leigh Barrow."

"She was a monster and a horrible person and I hate her, I genuinely do, but she was also my maker and my mother, and she was genuinely good at what she did. I'm sorry she made me. I'm sorry she hurt so many people. I'm not going to pretend she wasn't a master of her craft, or that I never loved her. It's tempting to behave that way. I want to. But it would be a lie, and that kind of lie absolves me of a lot of terrible things, so I'm holding on to what she was to me, and who I was to her, and who I am now."

"Look!" Kelpie's exclamation is tinged with bright relief. The others turn, following her gaze to the gate. There, on the other side, their companions are returning through the everything. Dodger looks annoyed and a little wan, but otherwise normal; she's taken no damage from her current situation. Chang'e and Máni walk to either side of her, an escort through eternity, and neither of them looks like their mortal selves at all. They're stepped so far forward that they may as well be truly divine, with nothing of humanity remaining.

They reach the gate and step out, Dodger first. She stumbles as she transitions back into the hall, then flings herself across the distance between her and Roger, wrapping her arms around him and holding on like they've been apart for a hundred years instead of fifteen minutes. Roger wraps his arms around her in turn, clasping her like he thinks he's unlocked the secret to undoing what the alchemists have done to them, of rendering them a single body once more.

"Dodge," he says, not letting go or loosening his grip in the slightest. "Slow *down*. You're going too fast, you need to slow *down*."

"She's not saying anything," says Kelpie blankly.

"Not so the rest of us can hear it, maybe," says Erin.

Chang'e and Máni step down as they emerge from the everything, letting Judy and David take their places. Judy's breathing hard, like she just hiked up a very steep hill. David gives her an almost-fond look, smirking to himself.

"This is why even English majors should take a general fitness course," he says.

Judy smacks him on the arm. "Never call me an English major again, you Western centrist."

He laughs, and the sound is somehow profane in this chamber below the earth, surrounded by walls of stone and cut off from natural moonlight. Artemis looks at him.

"Aren't you going to ask about the bodies?" she asks.

"I'll be honest. I was hoping if I just ignored them long enough, they'd be one more thing that goes away as soon as I stop looking." He does look, though, frowning as he turns to study the corpses on the floor. "What's wrong with their skins?"

"They were auf made from the alchemists who worked here," says Artemis. "The guy Kelpie says killed her maker is definitely not playing by Congressional rules."

"You would know, since it looks like you're a double agent," says Judy. She sounds less angry than exhausted, like she already can't stand to think about it.

"Yeah," says Artemis, with a sigh. "Does it help if I say I really didn't know? My host never steps forward, but I thought it was because she just didn't want to. I wasn't intentionally keeping her pushed down or refusing to let her rise. And after a while, it was just easier if I didn't try to force the issue. I had my own life. The years were passing, so she was further and further out of synch, and it's not like I've been keeping her a prisoner in her own mind or anything! This Reed fellow put a chain around her ankle and locked her to the bottom of our mind, and she couldn't come up until I was removed entirely."

"There's moonlight here, but it's different somehow," says Judy. "I can feel it better now that I've been inside the everything. Which reminds me." She turns, tapping her key against the wall. The gate vanishes, extinguished by her actions. "We found my window. That was my gate, I think because I tried my key first. Who's next?"

"I'll go," says David. "I think that when we try Artemis's gate, that's when we all go into the everything together. So we do hers last."

Judy nods and hands him the key. He takes a deep breath, Máni stepping up to take control of the moment, and as the air around him gleams with moonlight and frost, he taps the wall.

As before, no gate appears. Also as before, Artemis steps forward to repeat the gesture, and the gate blooms into being.

The pattern is different this time, less like calligraphy and more like rime blooming on frozen leaves. There are distinctions in the divinity behind the gods that unlock the gate. They're not normally this clear, because they're not normally opening in such quick succession, and not for the first time, Judy wishes she'd looked more closely at the gate Máni went through when he found Aske dead on the other side. Maybe then she would have known even before he came back that he was walking into someone else's space.

Máni steps through into the everything. Judy turns, and Chang'e offers her hand to Dodger.

"We need you to come with us again," she says.

Dodger reluctantly lets go of Roger, her hand lingering on his wrist, as if she's afraid to even break contact. Roger bumps her side with his elbow.

"It's okay," he says. "You came back, and everything re-entangled immediately. This isn't going to hurt us; it's just going to let us do what we came all the way down here to do."

"All right," she says, and takes Chang'e's hand, letting herself be pulled into the everything.

After that, all they can do is wait.

Mare Parvum

The everything is black lit with rainbows. Everywhere Dodger looks, she sees the flash and flare of dying possibilities. It's like she's standing at the heart of a living equation, one that might be the equation that controls the universe, the equation she was born to one day encompass and understand, but she doesn't want to understand it, not yet—she's not ready. She's afraid, on a deep, instinctual level, that once she grasps the underpinning mathematics of creation, she won't be able to be even as human as she is now . . . and she knows she's not as human as she used to be.

How could she be? She's half of a hive mind, and while she and Roger have taken complicated, sometimes painful measures to retain their individuality, she's slipping. Sometimes she loses track of which body is hers, at least for short periods, and they've been getting longer. Pretty soon, she thinks they'll spend their days ping-ponging back and forth, trading ownership of material shells without concern for who owned which one first.

She doesn't actually want that. Neither does he. They grew up thinking they were people with surprisingly solid imaginary friends, and they changed the universe so they could stay together, and staying together without merging into one means fighting to stay at least a little bit apart.

The equation that surrounds her, holding her up and beckoning her on at the same time, could either smash the last of the carriers between them and make them one person in two bodies rather than two people desperately trying to stay as separate as they can, or it could give her the tools no one was able to build for her and allow them to go back to the way things were before they manifested, without letting the Doctrine go.

This equation is the answer to everything, and to understand it is to be transformed in some way she can't know or define. She'll have to solve it eventually: it's what she was made to do. She wants to start working so badly that it's a sweet, metallic taste in her mouth, a burning tang like the aftermath of eating raw pineapple, and she never wants it at all. The combination of temptation and revulsion is hard to push aside. She tries to focus on the individual rainbow flashes instead, shutting out the silence in her head.

They're beautiful, and dizzying, and she never wants them to stop.

"Dodger? We good?" asks Chang'e. "This should be Máni's everything. Does it feel any different to you than the last one?"

Dodger blinks, shaking off her fugue, and looks toward the moon goddess. "I . . . Hang on." She looks at the rainbow flashes again, scanning them for something she doesn't have the words to explain to anyone outside herself. After a moment, she nods. "The underpinning geometry of the space is different. We're not standing inside the same piece of the equation. This isn't your space."

"Oooh-kay," says Chang'e. "So let's get moving."

Máni nods and starts to walk, and the others follow him as he treks through the everything. Dodger watches their surroundings intently, taking note of all the things her companions can't see. Chang'e described the everything as a rainbow path through nothingness, but Dodger knows that isn't so. They're surrounded by so much creation that the name of the space makes perfect sense, and it's not just a path; there are corridors branching off on either side, leading away from the route they're taking. She doesn't mention them, and neither do the Lunars; she's not entirely sure the Lunars know.

It seems odd that they would use this space so consistently for such a long time and not know everything about the way it works.

But when she blinks away the overlay of helpful figures that defines the space for her, forcing herself to see it as they do, it's more understandable: the rainbow flashes define the "walls," and it's easy to interpret them as linear things. There are no visible turns or doorways.

If she wasn't essentially the woodcutter's daughter who leaves her own trail of stones through the forest, she would be much more anxious about the idea of leaving the known safety of the path to the window.

Maybe they'll bring her back here when all this is done and settled, and together they can find out what's down those pathways into the rainbow dark. She'd really like to know.

For the moment, a window has appeared ahead of them, affixed to the wall when she looks at the everything the way she naturally wants to, at the equations and geometry of it all, and hanging unsupported in the air when she looks at it with only her eyes. This whole place is an optical illusion writ large, and it hurts her head to think about it too hard.

They approach the window, which has a hardwood frame and cotton curtains with a dinosaurs-and-rockets print. Máni's cheeks flush red, the color deepening his dark skin, and says, "I never thought about how juvenile my window is before. It's not like I can change the curtains, though."

"It's fine," says Chang'e, reassuringly. They approach the window, Máni first, Dodger close behind. She's the one who needs to chart their planned course, after all; she needs to see.

And on some level, she's hungry for another glimpse of the City she saw from Chang'e's window. It's as beautiful and strange and contradictory as the everything, with tall spires piercing the sky and streets paved in nacreous mother-of-pearl that gleams and shifts, as changing as the surface of a soap bubble. People move on those streets, alongside the occasional horse-drawn carriage; there are no cars. Indeed, she sees no signs of technological advancement beyond what's described in Baker's books, which stopped at the level common in the early 1900s.

She wants a closer look. She never wants a closer look. She's reasonably sure that looking too closely would mean forgetting how to look at anything else, ever, and even as she hangs back to let Máni unlatch his window and push it open, she loves and fears the City in equal measure.

The air that flows through the open window is entirely unpolluted by the modern era. Woodsmoke smudges its composition, but trees have always burned, all the way back to the beginning of time; the presence of a few bonfires doesn't imply an industrial revolution. She breathes in deeply, and tries to ignore the way the equations around them sharpen, coming into clearer focus as she comes closer to the City.

The Impossible City may be her destiny and inevitable destination. That doesn't make it her master. She moves to take Máni's place at the window, leaning out and scanning the nearby sky.

Stars gleam everywhere, little diamonds against the dark. She takes another deep breath of City air, and the diamonds become tetragons, some square, some rectangular, some with arched or domed tops, but all with four sides, perfect geometric shapes. Windows. Some are open, their owners already on their passage across the sky, and she wonders how the Lunars manage that, how they reconcile time zones and shifting sunsets to form a singular moon. She dismisses the question quickly. It's not her business, not her problem; she's here for the sake of the math, and she doesn't need to worry about the way the Lunars handle their own affairs.

She keeps looking, taking in the exact angles and designs of the windows, until she spots something familiar. She has to lean out much too far to see it, a white wooden frame about six feet to her left.

"There," she says, dropping back to the flats of her feet and stepping back before she can give in to the urge to steal another look at the City below. She indicates the direction in question. "Chang'e's window is over that way. Close enough that I'm pretty sure we could swing there if we anchored the rope right."

"So I can come see you when you're at work," jokes Máni, looking at Chang'e.

Chang'e smiles. "Assuming you feel like playing acrobat with a possible long, long drop, sure," she says. "Dodger, do you think you can estimate the location of Aske's window?"

"Not without the third data point, and it's Artemis's night anyway," says Dodger. "Let's go back to the others."

She's a little afraid to be in the everything with Roger. The two of them together, in this impossibly possible space, feels like it's something that ought to be forbidden. The feedback they set up between themselves may well cross the line into what they feared when they were children, when they hadn't wanted to meet because a single touch could have locked them into one another's heads forever.

But they need to be here. Both of them. She knows that, deep down, in the place where she keeps the equations that modify reality, the ones that somehow steal time from itself and bend causality like a strip of paper.

Máni shuts the window, and the three of them walk back to the gate, Dodger refusing to let herself look at the gaps in the walls that neither of her companions can see, Chang'e walking a little faster than the other two, like she's eager to get back to the underground lab where their friends—if they can be called friends—are waiting.

As they approach the gate, Máni makes a soft sound of protest, signaling a stop. Chang'e turns to look at him, curiosity taking ownership of her face.

"What is it?" she asks.

"Artemis," he says.

"What about her?"

"She lied to us when she got here, and I didn't meet her until after Aske was dead. Did you? Is there a chance that maybe this wasn't the first time Anna's managed to come back up to the surface? Because if Aske wasn't expecting another Lunar to attack her, she wouldn't have been prepared to fight back. Artemis tried so hard to make us not trust Diana . . ."

"I still *don't* trust Diana," says Chang'e. "Even if we can't trust Artemis completely, she's right when she says Diana doesn't do nearly as much of the administrative side of managing the local pantheon as she should. Judy's still a student, but Diana is happy to put all the maintenance and busywork on us, and she knows we'll do it—me because I don't want to see the pantheon fall into chaos, Judy because she understands my concerns. This shouldn't ever have been our job." She stops, silence taking a moment to grow heavy in the air between them before she finally says. "I don't trust Diana. I want to—this would be so much easier if we had someone powerful and trustworthy on our side—but I can't. Artemis has had plenty of opportunities to betray us. I think there's a good chance she is what Anna said she is. She's just someone who wound up in the path of the alchemists before she knew how to evade them."

"Sounds about right," says Dodger. "We'll see what we can do for her when this is all over."

"Artemis, or Anna?" asks Máni.

"Artemis," says Dodger. "I'm not sure there's anything that *can* be done for Anna at this point. Even if we could somehow pull off a miracle and get her a body she didn't have to share with someone she clearly hates, she'd be a hundred years out of the only time period she knows."

"Aren't you in charge of—" begins Máni.

Dodger fixes him with a glare before he can complete his sentence. "Don't even suggest it," she says, in a voice like ice.

"But you said you could control time," he protests.

She stops walking and sighs, pinching the bridge of her nose with her right hand and closing her eyes. "I can *reset* time," she says. "I can sidestep time, to a degree, just wrap myself up in the seconds dying all around me and disappear, or I can rewind us to any point within my own lifetime and let things restart from there. How much I remember when I do this is . . . well, it's not the most reliable thing ever. We did it a lot of times to get to this timeline. A *lot* of times. This is the best of all possible worlds, at least by the standards we have to work from, and I'm not going to risk all of that because you don't understand how the system works."

"We can't understand if you won't tell us," says Chang'e.

"All right, look at it this way." Dodger drops her hand. "You're always the same goddess, right? You have personal continuity, or continuity of personality at the absolute minimum. But you don't carry experiences and memories from manifestation to manifestation. If Judy dies, you'll find a new host, and you'll start clean, with only the things Chang'e knows, and none of the things Judy knew."

Chang'e nods, slowly.

"Seems inefficient to me. You should have a way of storing memories, so people can't just go around slaughtering Lunars the way they have been. Die here, manifest elsewhere with your saved game intact, immediately alert the rest of your pantheon. If I were in charge, that's how we'd do things."

"But then any god who'd incarnated more than once would overwhelm and swamp out their host," protests Máni. "We'd crush them as soon as we woke up."

"So maybe if I were in charge I wouldn't change anything," says Dodger. "Well, the way I manipulate time is sort of like what you're describing. I take us back to a preset time, and the version of me who did the taking ceases to exist. Then, if I do things right in the new timeline, she never gets the *chance* to exist, because I've bent things in a way that makes her impossible. Say I *could* go back to when Anna was an innocent little lamb who hadn't fallen into Reed's clutches or fully accepted Artemis yet. Say I *could* keep either or both of those things from happening. What happens then? Does Reed stay on the alchemical path that leads to my brother and I being created? Is there an Artemis here in Berkeley when we need a moon god who can actually fight? Do any of us exist? All of time is the butterfly effect writ large, and to be honest, I probably *can* do more than I think I can, but when there's a chance—any chance at all—that pushing my limits could wipe my brother out of reality, I'm sorry. There are risks I don't take."

"I didn't consider any of that," says Chang'e.

"Temporal causality is hard to think about without getting a headache, and most people never need to," says Dodger. She starts walking again, heading for the exit. "Let's go see if our backup has been captured by alchemists or eaten by aufs or something. I want to get this over with."

Mare Serenitatis

The ones waiting in the hall have not, in fact, been captured by alchemists or attacked by additional constructs, auf or otherwise. Roger is leaning against the wall, eyes on the ceiling, listening to the hum of the concrete around them and trying to figure out why it makes him think of the moon. There's something about this place that Erin isn't explaining to them just yet. Whatever it is, she's figured it out, he's sure of that; she looks like she's standing in a graveyard, arms wrapped around herself in a defensive posture.

He'd feel bad about making her wait here with the rest of them if not for the fact that Artemis and Kelpie are near the gate, talking in hushed voices. Kelpie doesn't move her hands much, and her facial expression doesn't give very much away, but her tail—maybe it's the lack of people with tails to have modeled herself after, or maybe it's just her natural body language. Either way, her tail is endlessly expressive. It lashes side to side as she and Artemis speak, and he finds himself staring at it, trying to decode the meanings of the individual motions. It's almost hypnotic.

Then, with a burst of sound and thought as loud and sudden as a shotgun blast, Dodger is back. She brings color with her, the hall and its occupants going from grayscale to full Technicolor like Dorothy stepping into Oz, and he wonders whether she even realized her depth perception was gone on the other side of that strange appearing, disappearing doorway. It's been so long since they were distinct from one another. He doesn't want to admit that he depends on the soft hum of her thoughts to go to sleep at night, but he does. The silence of her absence was nearly deafening.

As before, she flings herself across the space between them and into his arms, clutching tight and clinging for dear life. It's like she thinks she can burrow into his skin, like she's the hermit crab and he's the shell, and while he might normally try to remind her that he enjoys not having her nails digging into his skin, right now he only folds his arms around her and holds her in return. If the silence was as loud for her as it was for him, she probably needs the reassurance.

I hated that so much, she thinks, and it's the first coherent thought he's had from her since she emerged. Roger throws back his head and laughs, utterly delighted.

Dodger pulls back and frowns at him, clearly perplexed.

"You are so *weird,*" she says, letting go. She rubs her arms as she does, shuddering. "Let's never do that again. If I'm stepping outside the boundaries of normal reality, you need to come with me, or I won't go."

Roger nods. "I'd feel better if you didn't. And Dodge? We aren't going for another reset, there's only so much I'm willing to risk, but . . ."

"But we have to find a way to fix things for Kim and Tim," she says, finishing his thought. She sounds oddly relieved, and when he looks at her quizzically, she shrugs. "I was thinking that while I was inside the everything with the Lunars, and how is that a sentence that makes sense? It shouldn't be. Anyway, if having all that silence in my head was that upsetting when I knew you'd come back, what is it doing to *them*? To have all that silence there all the time? They were in each other's heads from birth onward, and now they're just . . . they're alone, Roger. We have to find a way to make this better."

"We will," he assures her. "Now that we understand what they're going through, we'll find a way to fix it."

While they've been talking, the Lunars have closed and reopened the gate once again, this time with Artemis making the first strike. She steps into the everything, and Kelpie follows her as Chang'e turns to face the others.

"It's time to go, if you're all ready," she says. "Erin, I can help you through."

"I've got Roger and Dodger," says Máni.

"You're sure you can handle them both?"

"I think if he holds her hand, she'll pull him through as soon as she's on the other side."

Chang'e can't argue with that, and so she simply holds out her hand, waiting for Erin to accept it. Erin looks at her with suspicion, but slips her cool fingers into Chang'e's own, even as Máni is taking hold of Dodger's hand, both of them pulling their passengers toward the reopened gate. Dodger grabs Roger's sleeve, pulling him with her. It's clear from how easily he comes that he would have followed anyway, but this way, they aren't breaking contact.

Erin looks back, sees him grimace as Dodger passes through the gate ahead of him, sees his face relax as he passes into the everything for the first time and their impossible connection is restored. They just need to be on the same side of the door.

(The gate, as opened by Artemis, is less Chang'e's glitter and calligraphed organic curves, less Máni's spiking mercury swirls of frost and rime; her gate is a silvery cascade of branches twisting together into knots that can't be broken, spirals without end. There are so many moon gods. Every one of them is different.)

Roger pulls his arm from his sister's grasp as he passes into the everything, straightening and turning a slow circle, eyes wide and mouth hanging slightly open in his awe. Chang'e watches him and smirks, just a little.

"Welcome to *our* version of reality," she says.

"The lights . . ." His voice lacks the strange harmonics it has in the outside world. It's still pleasant, still compelling in the way a charismatic person can be compelling, but it's not supported by an intangible need to do anything he says, all for the sake of keeping him happy. He seems to realize it even as he speaks, because he grins, a narrow tension slipping out of his posture and leaving him standing even straighter than before. "Can you read them?"

"Read them?" asks Artemis. "They're *lights*."

"I was able to spend some time studying with an older incarnation of myself before Judy's studies brought us here," says Chang'e. "She taught me the lights were possibilities the universe considered enacting and was unable to commit to. They come here to flare out and fade away, because they were never meant to be."

"If we'd had access to this place when we were still working on our perfect run . . ." Roger's voice trails off. He turns a slow circle, staring in open awe at the rainbows flashing around them. Then he stops, shaking it off, and turns his attention to Artemis. "All right. What do we do now?"

"I lead you to my window," she says. "Once we're there, Dodger tells us whether she can do the geometry we came here to ask her for, and then one of two things happens: either we swing over to Aske's window and find out what happened with her before I start my passage across the sky, or I start my passage. Either way, Chang'e and Máni will be able to walk you out."

"What about me?" asks Kelpie.

Artemis looks at her, expression softening into something lost and longing. "I'd like you to stay by my window until I get back, if you don't mind. We'll be coming out way underground, and there might be alchemists, or constructs. I want to walk you out myself."

"Wouldn't it be better if we *all* stayed inside the everything until you get back?" asks Dodger.

Artemis shifts her attention to the redhead. "I'll be crossing the sky for hours. It's almost time for moonrise and sunset to meet, and that's when my journey begins. You won't have food, or water, or bathrooms. You'll be bored stiff."

"And you want that for me?" asks Kelpie.

"You're a Lunar, or close enough that it doesn't really make any difference," says Artemis. "We don't experience any of those things in here."

"Neither do we, if I decide we don't," says Dodger, and it's such a calmly off-handed statement that it's terrifying in its implications.

Artemis considers a snappy comeback or a question, then dismisses both as bad ideas and gestures for the group to follow as she starts deeper into the everything. She walks the same way Chang'e and Máni did, following the same path. Dodger takes note of her steps, of the places where she deviates from the earlier journeys, the places where they stay the same. By the time the window appears ahead of them, she knows what's going on.

"The windows move," she says. "When you move in the physical world, they follow you in the everything. Chang'e and Máni manifested in two very different geographic areas. Their windows being close together could have been a coincidence. Yours being this close to both of theirs means it wasn't, and the windows move. We know there are windows on the other side of the sky. They shift with geography. Presumably they open when a new Lunar manifests, and close when a Lunar is lost."

Artemis's face falls. "So Aske's window might already be gone?"

"Depends on how fast things move around. How long have you all been in the area?"

"Since start of term," says Máni.

"Four years," says Chang'e.

"Three months," says Artemis.

"All right, and your window, while quite close, is still on the edge of the zone the other two are occupying."

"How do you know that? You haven't looked outside yet."

Dodger blinks at her, unable to figure out how she's meant to express the delicate, ongoing conversation between the flashes of light and the everything itself, which is not (contrary to appearances) the prismatic pathway glistening around them. It *is,* and it will be even when there are no more possibilities for it to contain, when it bridges the darkness as more of the same, alone and eternal. The everything and the potential for specific things are in endless dialog with each other, and that dialog is mathematical as much as linguistic: Roger can follow it as easily as she can, as easily as breathing. That conversation is what tells her Artemis's window is close to the other two. She doesn't need to look outside.

Still, she follows Artemis to the window, because she also doesn't need to argue. They're all tired and they're all stressed and they're all aware, to one degree or another, of the open gate behind them, beyond which is a nightmare maze of alchemical science and potential enemies. None of them were able to enter without the aid of a Lunar, but who's to say the alchemists will have the same constraints? Maybe they have a way of tricking the entrance into letting them through, something related to the moonlight held captive in the walls (and oh, Dodger is sure she'll be horrified when she finds out how they did that; horrified and maybe impressed, to a small, shameful degree. It's only natural that alchemists would do things in ways she instinctively understands—as their creation, she was designed to follow those same paths. That doesn't mean she likes it, or wants it to keep happening).

Maybe the alchemists lured the gate into their territory because they were hoping for this exact moment, when the window was open and its defenders were distracted.

She doesn't know, and speaking her concerns into the world won't make them any less real. Artemis opens the window. Dodger nudges her lightly to the side and leans out, into the bright City air.

Some of the other nearby windows—but not *too* near—are standing open, their owners already joining the slow journey from horizon to horizon. Dodger estimates their anchors as a hundred miles or more from their location, linked to Lunars who have no idea that any of this is happening, and would probably be rightly alarmed if they did. She really doesn't understand this system, or how it works for the Lunars who follow it, but she's not here to criticize; she's here to calculate.

Leaning out the window, she looks around until she spots the windows she knows belong to Chang'e and Máni. They're closer to each other than they are to Artemis's window, although they're still a good way apart. If she focuses, she can see the calculations in the air around them, the ones that tell her where they started and where they're going. They're seeking their permanent places in this section of the sky.

And she's just slowing things down by continuing to insist on seeing this scene the way a person would see it. *I'm sorry,* she thinks, enunciating the thought clearly enough for Roger to receive the words, and then she steps away from herself, deeper into the grasp of her domain.

(People who aren't like them—which is basically everyone except for Kim and Tim, and self-absorbed as they are, even Roger and Dodger realize how cosmically cruel it would be to try to have this discussion with their involuntary wards—assume constant telepathic communication must mean they get every thought the other has, fully formed and articulated. Instead, they receive every impulse and emotion, every feeling, and the words that are articulated internally with the same level of precision as they would be spoken. It's not a stream; it's a river. She feels Roger pull back to the limit of his ability to disengage, even as she descends into pure mathematics.)

The equations she's seen teased in the walls since their arrival snap into sudden clarity, and so do the equations in the sky, the calculated arcs of angle and ascent. She leans in to the numbers, finding comfort in what has always seemed to her to be the true proof of the divine, and she understands the way this sky works, the movement and placement of the windows, the reason everything fits together.

"It's beautiful," she says, or hopes she says—when she's this deep, she sometimes thinks she's saying something, but says something else entirely, some string of sums or formulae that, to her, express the same sentiment. She leans a little farther out, no longer concerned about falling, and scans the sky around her.

Based on the displacement and acceleration she sees written around her, Aske's window should be . . . She looks down. Not quite *straight* down, but close enough to be a short fall.

There, hanging in the air like all the others, is an open window, curtains rustling slightly in the breeze rising off the City far below, glass lightless. It doesn't gleam like the windows around it.

It is, in many ways, no longer a star.

Math and time are both Dodger's domain, and when she blinks, she sees the future of the window as clearly as any other equation: it will continue to dim, losing what little remains of its inherent shine, until it loses its grasp on the firmament and plummets. They're too close to the ground for atmospheric friction to cause combustive ablation, but still, it will flare and burn up.

She wonders if the inhabitants of the Impossible City understand that every time they point in delight at a falling star, they're marking the death of a Lunar. She rather hopes they don't. These are the people she will one day, inevitably, live among. She really doesn't want them to be cruel. If there's anything she can choose about her future, it's that she doesn't want the people she'll inevitably have to go and live among to be cruel.

So Aske's window is no longer a star the way the others are, but it's still here. Dodger pulls herself physically back, not only from her position out the window but from the mental state that allows her to see the world as pure numbers, no complications, no constraints.

"I found it," she says. "But we have a problem."

"When is there *not* a problem?" asks Erin. "What's the problem this time?"

"It's beneath us." She points, angling her finger so that even as she's pointing down, she's pointing with precision. "It's open, and I should be able to get there if I just lean out and let go."

"Why you?" asks Artemis. "Why not me, or Máni, or *someone* who belongs here?"

"Because of the other half of what I was about to say," says Dodger. "I can get *there*. I don't really see how anybody is going to get *back*. Even with a rope, we'd be asking someone to freeclimb about ten feet, when slipping would mean a potentially fatal fall. Unless you're signing up to splash, I don't really see anyone else doing it."

"You're leaving something out, Dodge," says Roger.

"I'm . . . Oh, right. I can find my way out of here if I need to. So unless you're sure, and I mean *sure,* that your little key trick will let you open a gate from inside the everything, if there's a chance our explorer gets stranded, it needs to be me."

Chang'e is drifting toward the window, moving slow and careful, conserving her steps to make it look as if she's not doing anything of the sort. Erin watches her go, and wonders, a bit, whether she should tell someone this is happening; whether anyone would care enough to stop it. She supposes Roger might. Chang'e's host is in his department, and he seems to like the girl. He probably wouldn't want her to splash across the City.

"Hey," she says, voice mild.

Chang'e doesn't stop or turn, only continues to drift toward the window, expression politely blank.

Dodger and Artemis are still arguing about who's going to go down to Aske's window, Roger and Kelpie looking on with near-matching expressions of indulgence on their faces. Máni is looking upward, into the rainbow dark. Out of all of them, he's the one who most seems to remember that Aske was a person before she died, and they're here because they need to know who killed her.

"Hey," she says again, more sharply, as Chang'e puts her hand on the windowsill.

Chang'e looks back at her, smiling politely.

"I'm the senior Lunar present," she says. "Any risks we're taking should be mine. Judy agrees."

She boosts herself up onto the ledge, looking back and down, and her smile broadens.

"I see the open window," she says, and pushes herself away, and falls.

Mare Spumans

Normally, when a Lunar slides out of a window in the sky above the City, they find themselves caught in the magnetic pull of the aggregate Moon. They drift gently upward, merging with the collective consciousness of every other Lunar who has come to share the sky, and they stay there until the moon sets in the location they started from. No one knows how the City sky can keep such perfect time, but it does. Age upon age, it does.

Tonight, however, Chang'e has entered the sky not to shine, but to fall, and fall she does, straight down, body held rigidly straight, stomach swooping to fill her mouth as the dizziness of descent kicks in. She has the presence of mind to reach out as she nears Aske's window, and she grabs hold of the open frame with both hands, jerking herself to a bone-shaking stop.

As Judy, she is always a physical being, a woman walking in the world. As Chang'e, a state she normally enters purely only in the everything, she is a divine creature, a combination of the heavens and the earth, immortal and untouchable. As she stops her fall, for the first time, she feels as if *she* were something temporary, capable of coming to an end. And in that moment, she understands a truth of the Impossible City: if she let go, if she actually fell all the way to the ground below, she would die. Not Judy, Chang'e. This manifestation of the goddess would wink away and be forgotten, lost to her believers, wiped from the collective consciousness of the world.

Is that what happened to all the forgotten gods, the ones who were but are no longer? Did they fall from their own windows into their own Impossible Cities, dropping down too fast to stop or save themselves?

Heart suddenly pounding and the copper-penny taste of adrenaline filling her mouth, Chang'e pulls herself up and over the window ledge, falling, limbs akimbo, into the everything on the other side.

The space is black as always, infinite, solidified void. But the rainbow flashes here are slow, sluggish, almost creeping along before they fizzle and die. This is what the everything looks like when it's cutting off a piece of itself, declaring a once-vital artery extraneous to needs. Chang'e straightens, pushes her hair out of her face, looks around . . .

. . . and screams.

There is a pool of silver-bright blood on the floor, not clotted or congealed in the slightest, as fresh and liquid as the moment when it was shed. There is no red, only silver, like mercury, and still she knows it for blood, because there's nothing else it could possibly be. She catches her breath, swallowing it to sit like a stone in her still-unsettled stomach, then moves closer, trying to understand the scene in front of her.

There's a lot of blood at first, a pool of silver that seems like it must be all the blood a body can contain. Drips and smears travel from it toward the window, and she turns to look. The mark of a grasping hand is on the ledge, desperately clutching at what must have seemed like a chance at salvation. Then it smears and drops away, grip lost, hope abandoned.

Aske was hit over there, and managed to crawl to here. She turns again, back toward the main pool, and begins following the drops in the other direction.

The primary wound wasn't dealt here. No. There are drag marks on the floor of the everything, which has never seemed so solid, or so unwelcoming; this is dead space. It doesn't want her here. It doesn't want *anyone* here. The everything that was once Aske's is mourning, no longer needed with her gone, not sure how it's meant to let her go.

The drag marks lead to a second pool, almost as large as the first, which must have been where the killing blow was dealt. Something hard and heavy was used to strike Aske, probably in the head, and she began to bleed out almost instantly. A footprint in bright silver stands out at the edge of the pool: Máni was here.

Drops of blood trail off into the distance, a gruesome reminder of the way she saw him approaching the gate, Aske in his arms. They mingle silver with mortal red, Aske's divinity bleeding out of her one drop at a time. Chang'e follows them, and at the end of the trail, she finds the terrible prize they've been seeking. Aske's body is still curled on the ground where Máni left her, eyes closed, limbs bent into the shape of a comma. It's almost obscene, how much it looks like she's just sleeping. Chang'e feels for her pulse, feeling a sudden flare of hope.

There's nothing. Aske is gone. Aske has been gone for quite some time. Chang'e turns her head to the side, revealing the smashed-in back of her skull, and grimaces. At least she knows now how the other Lunar died.

At least it wasn't an arrow.

She straightens, shaking her hands like she can shake away the feeling of tacky, undried blood and dead Lunar flesh. Then she turns and heads back toward the window, letting the blood trail guide her through the unfamiliar everything.

She can't control her relief when she sees the window floating serenely in the blackness. It's almost overwhelming, how glad she is to have the confirmation that she'll be able to get out of here. She almost runs the last twenty feet to the window, clutching the frame in both hands to reassure herself that it's real, she's not trapped, it's really *real*.

People are shouting above her, and she realizes how much she must have frightened them. She sticks her head out the window and looks up.

"I'm okay!" she yells. Saying it makes it true, or true enough that she breathes a little easier, stands up a little straighter, and repeats herself: "I'm okay."

"How are you planning to get back up here?" demands Máni. "What the hell made you go down there alone?"

Chang'e almost laughs. How can she say that it was out of the fear that if she took Artemis with her, she'd find Aske had been killed by an arrow through the heart, that she still doesn't trust the other Lunar, that she's tired of feeling like she's at the back of the line when it comes to handing out answers? How can she say any of that? She swallows her painful merriment, shakes her head, and says, "I have a plan. Step away from the window."

Máni vanishes, back into Artemis's everything, and Kelpie sticks her head out. "Artemis is crossing the sky," she calls. "She left right after you jumped. She said she was sorry, but she couldn't wait any longer."

"I need you to step back, too," says Chang'e. "I'll be right up."

Kelpie withdraws. Chang'e reaches into her pocket, closing her hand around the small, hard object nestled there. She pulls it out and opens her fingers, revealing a peach pit nestled in the hollow of her hand.

This is her main trick. She doesn't have a disappearing bow or control over the tides; she can't call a hunt or compel the truth. But she can grow an orchard out of nothing, if she wants one, if she has the seeds. She's never done it in the everything before, but how hard can it be?

Raising the peach pit to her lips, she kisses its rough, ridged surface gently, a tap of her lips against the shell, then bends to place it on the floor. It gleams silver, brought one step closer to divinity.

"If it pleases you, grow," she says, in a dialect of Cantonese so old that its proper name has been forgotten; it is a cousin to ancient Chinese, the oldest recorded form of the language, which also has no proper name, for when it thrived, it didn't need one, and when it died, its corpse was scavenged by its children and their cousins. "If it pleases you not, grow, for it pleases me."

The seed bursts as the peach tree it has always had the potential to become wakes and begins to grow with unnatural speed and vigor, becoming a sprout becoming a seedling becoming a healthy young tree which, at the softest brush of her fingers, bends and grows out the window, reaching ever upward as it becomes a monster of its kind. Its branches fork and spread, vaster than they have any proper business being, their boughs growing lush with flowers that bloom and drop away, a rain of petals for the City far below.

There are no pollinators here, but Chang'e's trees have never needed pollinators; she is their only symbiont, the only companion they require, and as the fruit begins to swell and ripen, impossible but solid, she smiles.

Above her, she hears shouts of surprise and delight. She sticks her head out the window, plucking the nearest ripe peach at the same time. The fruit is heavy in her hand, familiar and soft, and it makes her feel better as she calls up, "You can climb down. It'll hold you. And then we can all climb back up, but I want you to see the body."

"She's still *there*?" asks Máni, sounding utterly horrified.

"She is," says Chang'e. She steps back from the window. "It's clear."

One by one, the others descend, coming down the tree with peaches in their hands and leaves in their hair and, in Erin's case, an utterly ridiculous grin on her face.

"We should be able to solve everything by climbing trees," she says. "Roger, write that down for when you control the universe. Everything should be solvable by climbing a tree."

"I'll get right on that," he says, frowning at Chang'e. "What the hell possessed you to fling yourself out of a window?"

"Someone had to," she says, with a shrug. "Artemis needed to start her crossing. Máni had already seen the body—letting him see her again wasn't going to tell us anything new. If we had to leave whoever went down behind, better me than you, your sister, or Erin."

"Don't think about yourself like that," snaps Kelpie, who made her own descent with surprising ease, given her hooves. She brandishes a peach at Chang'e. "You're as essential as anyone."

"I'm one more facet of a very common god," says Chang'e. "Lose me, you'll have another within the week."

"And how does Judy feel about that?" asks Roger.

Chang'e doesn't answer.

"Seems like maybe Artemis and Anna aren't the only ones who aren't completely comfortable with the way you people have things set up," he says, and his voice is mild, but the inherent critique is not. "Nice trick with the peach tree, by the way. You do that often?"

"Not to full maturity, but peach trees are sort of my thing," she says. "I can grow an orchard in an afternoon. I only need the seeds."

"The body?" asks Erin, less patient and less comfortable with the situation than some of her companions.

Chang'e nods. "This way," she says, and turns to lead them deeper into Aske's everything. The rainbow flashes are continuing to slow, and the ground is taking on a mushy quality, like ice on the verge of breaking. It makes her nervous. She's fairly sure that's the right response to walking on something that feels like it's considering the virtues of ceasing to exist.

Dodger watches the walls as they walk, less rapt than fixated, intent. She still manages to avoid the blood, even without looking down. Chang'e isn't sure how that's possible when there's so much of it. She doesn't want to ask.

"Roger," says Dodger, voice gone soft. "Are you seeing what I'm seeing?"

"I am," he replies. "You have any ideas about how we're supposed to get out of here?"

"Can't we just go back up the tree?" asks Kelpie. "It's a good tree. It seemed really solid."

"That's assuming the tree is still there when we're done," says Dodger. "This place is breaking down."

"The everything can't break down," protests Máni. "It's always here, or we wouldn't be able to access the City, and without the City, I don't think anything else gets to exist."

"How much do you know about mushrooms?" asks Dodger.

Máni blinks before turning to Chang'e. "Is that a weird question?" he asks. "Because that seems like a weird question, but I no longer feel like I really have a benchmark for where 'normal' stops and 'weird' begins."

"Says the moon god to the moon goddess who just grew an adult peach tree in under a minute, while they walk through a channel of nothingness to look at a corpse," says Erin, almost singsong.

Máni flushes a deep red but keeps his eyes on Chang'e, waiting for her response.

She nods, not quite smiling. "Yeah, that's a weird question. What do mushrooms have to do with anything, Dodger?"

"I think that's basically what we are, all of us, except for maybe Smita, since she's still a human and not an anthropomorphic force of the universe. We pop up because the mycorrhizal network says the right conditions for our growth and survival have been met, and if those conditions persist, we survive. If they don't, or if there are more predators present than expected—meaning the alchemists— then we die."

"That's grim and a little terrifying as an outlook on life," says Chang'e. "What the hell's a 'mycorrhizal network'?"

"In forests, fungi tangle their mycelia with plant roots to form an organic internet. They communicate that way, full conversations via chemical signal. It's basically math as instinctive language, and it's gorgeous, and it lets the whole biome talk to itself. That combination of mycelium and root is the mycorrhizal network."

"And we're mushrooms?"

"Exactly," says Dodger, sounding pleased to have been understood. "We're mushrooms. Well, I think this—your everything—is the mycorrhizal network. We're walking through the channels the universe uses to communicate with itself."

"The universe being our version of the forest in this metaphor."

"Yup." Dodger shoots an oddly heated glance at Roger. "Stop gloating, asshole."

"I told you I'd get you to start using metaphors one day," he says. "My victory was inevitable."

"So is my fist."

He snickers and keeps snickering as Chang'e frowns, brows knotting together in dismay. "Okay, I mostly follow, I think, but why do you think my tree isn't going to be there when we go back?"

They're approaching the body, small, crumpled, and sad in its pool of red and silver. Roger speeds up, just a little, as does Erin; the two of them are the first to reach the fallen Aske, crouching down so that their bodies partially block hers from view. Kelpie looks relieved. She stops walking, and studies the peach in her hands, turning it over and over like it contains all the wonders of the universe. And maybe it does. Given the unsoil on which its parent fed its roots, this peach may contain the answer to all the questions ever asked.

"The mycorrhizal network tells the forest where mushrooms should grow, and when they sprout, they grow their own mycelia to add to the collective," says Dodger. "They put down roots, essentially, even though they started from a single spore. And then, if those mushrooms get plucked, some of their mycelia get absorbed back into the forest, but some of them just die. This slice of the everything was Aske's mycelium. And it's dying, because she's done. The everything as a whole will endure—that's why it matters that each of you has your own—but this piece of it is going to atrophy and be absorbed back into the soil. The universe, I mean, in this case. There's no more need for it."

"But . . . Aske . . ."

"Roger tells me she bled silver. That stuff we saw by the window, that was her blood. Is that correct?"

Chang'e nods silently.

"Then you have to know we were never going to be able to take her out of here and back into the material world," says Dodger. "She'd be the biggest prize we had ever dangled in front of the alchemists. A dead goddess, still leaking divinity? That's like rubbing catnip in your hair before you walk into a lion's den."

"Lions don't care about catnip," says Roger.

"Bite me," says Dodger mildly. She keeps her focus on Chang'e. "We have to leave Aske here, in her branch of the network, in her version of the everything. It's going to continue to degrade, and when it collapses, it'll take her body with it. If we can't return her to her family, I can't think of a better place for a Lunar to rest than here, in their everything."

"Oh," says Chang'e, very softly. "What does that have to do with my tree?"

"See how the flashes in the walls are slowing down? Like they're getting stuck?"

Chang'e nods.

"The possibilities that involve this place are narrowing to a single point, and when that finishes, away it goes."

"How do you *know*?"

"Because I can translate the equations the light traces out. This is the universe singing to itself, and the song it's singing here is a dirge. As soon as the light dies, this piece of everything is gone, and we need to not be here when that happens. We *really* need to not be halfway up a peach tree hanging over the void."

Chang'e blanches. "Okay. So how are we getting out of here?"

"Remember I said this was essentially the mycorrhizal network on a universal scale? The key word is *network*."

Chang'e shakes her head. "We only ever get a tunnel through the everything. A channel between the gate and our window. We didn't even know that we all had different iterations until Aske died and we couldn't figure out where her body had gone."

"You only ever *follow* a tunnel, because it's dark in here—which doesn't make any sense, by the way, I can see that it's dark, and yet I can see every person here perfectly well; it's like it manages to be light and dark at the same time—and you can't see the openings in the walls." Dodger shrugs. "I can. We can exit this everything and head into the next one over, and from there, we should hopefully be able to find our way back to Artemis's. Before she comes looking, or decides to climb down the peach tree herself."

"That reminds me; you probably shouldn't eat that peach."

Dodger lifts an eyebrow. "Oh? Why not?"

"These are the peaches of *immortality*," says Chang'e. "Just one won't make you immortal, but it'll probably stop your aging for a while. In a god, a single peach lasts for about a decade. In an anthropomorphic personification? I have no idea."

"It's cute that you don't think I stopped our aging a while ago," says Dodger. "There's nothing wrong with getting older, but Smita makes incredible curry, and I don't want to deal with that thing where every white person I know who's physically over forty gets horrific heartburn any time they eat something with a decent level of spice. Time and I are good buddies. I negotiated a ceasefire as soon as we finished looping through our lives, and it's holding pretty solid for right now."

Chang'e blinks. "That's . . . You're . . . How can you be so *casual* about that?"

"You just informed me that eating one of your special magic peaches from the tree that didn't exist an hour ago would make me stop aging for a whole-ass decade. I don't think you have the high ground when it comes to 'things we should be less casual about.'" Dodger raises her voice, calling, "Hey, Erin, you two about done over there? Because I want to get us heading for the next room over before this one starts eating people."

"She died of a blow to the back of the head, hard enough to fracture her skull," says Erin, straightening. There's not a drop of blood on her, which should be impossible, given the way she was touching the body. "One good thing about that as cause of death: she wouldn't have had much time to suffer."

"That's not as comforting as I think you want it to be," says Máni.

"Was it the alchemists?" asks Chang'e.

"Not unless they have a way of getting through that gate without another Lunar to help them," says Roger. "There are three sets of footprints in here, from where the person walking couldn't avoid the blood. One of them is yours, and one of them is Máni's. The third is someone I can't recognize. Small feet, though. Definitely not the man we saw before."

"Is there anything else we can learn by staying here?" asks Dodger. "Because if not, I don't think we should be. The window of safety is closing fast."

The rainbow flashes in the walls have slowed so much, they're only coming every few seconds, in contrast to the constant flow in

Artemis's everything. The others turn to look at them, registering the unhappiness in Dodger's tone. Roger glances at her.

"You're sure?"

"Am I ever wrong about this sort of thing?" asks Dodger, with evident disgust.

He shakes his head. "Not normally."

"Good. Now, is there anything else to learn from the body?"

"No. Just that she died fast and brutal, and she managed to drag herself back to the window before she did. Someone was waiting for her near the gate."

"So it was someone who understood the system enough to know when her guard would be down. Great. Come *on*."

Dodger starts to walk, steps brisk and sharp. The first few are stable. On the third, her foot seems to sink, as if she's stepped into a small divot in the previously smooth floor. She winces, and keeps going.

"You're about to walk into the—" begins Chang'e, just as Dodger makes a hard right turn, and disappears.

"—wall," finishes Chang'e, awkwardly.

A split second later, Dodger wraps her hand around what suddenly looks like the edge of an entryway and sticks her head back into view, asking, "Well? Are the rest of you assholes coming with me?"

"We're coming," says Roger, and gestures for the others to follow as he goes after his sister. Only Chang'e seems to notice how he closes his eyes as soon as he starts to walk, while Dodger fixes her attention on the ground, watching their feet. Oddly, he's the only one of them not to stumble on his way to the turn. They all avoid the divot that caught Dodger, but at one point, Kelpie steps in a hole that goes halfway to her knee, while Chang'e catches her foot in what feels like a pothole, stumbling and falling behind the group.

The ground is mushier with every step, until it feels less like walking on ice about to break than it does like walking on cornstarch mixed with water, like it's becoming something that's only solid under direct pressure, and returns to a liquid state as quickly as it possibly can. It feels like it's eroding around the edges of her foot, slipping away into nothingness. She walks as fast as she dares, unwilling to risk running when the ground is this unstable. Falling, she feels, would be a terrible mistake. Quite possibly the last one she'd ever have the opportunity to make.

Roger reaches the turn before any of the rest of them, and turns, eyes still closed, to offer them his help in clearing the floor. As Chang'e approaches, he leans out, shouting, "Jump!"

It's a direct command. She can no more refuse to obey than she can suddenly figure out how to fly. She digs her feet as deep into the dissolving ground as she can, leaping for him, and feels the moment when it drops out from beneath her. For a moment, she feels like she's flying after all. She always thought the everything was built on blackness. Now, hanging above true darkness, she understands how wrong she was.

In that split second, she's genuinely afraid she's about to die. Immortality doesn't do much good for someone who breaks every bone in their body, and part of being twinned with mortals is dying. Chang'e knows that. She never meant to lead Judy into the abyss.

And then Roger is catching her, swinging her around to safety before settling her feet on solid ground. They're standing in a new corridor, identical to the last, at least to her eyes, although this one still has rapid flashes dancing in its walls. Not as many as she expects there to be; compared to her own iteration of the everything, this is still a lightless, lifeless place. Roger lets her go and steps back, finally opening his own eyes.

"There you are," he says, sounding quietly satisfied with himself.

"How—" she squeaks, voice breaking on that single syllable, denying it the chance to become the question she intended. She pauses, swallowing hard, and tries again: "How did you know?"

"Sometimes what I see isn't as important as what my sister sees," he says.

"And vice versa," Dodger agrees. She leans to the side, looking around the pair of them, and winces. "I really hope no one dropped their keys back there."

Chang'e looks over her shoulder. Aske's body is gone, as are almost all signs of her demise. A few splashes of silver-red blood remain, back in the direction of the window, until the ground drops out from beneath them and they, too, fall into the void.

"No," she says, faintly.

"I think the place was already collapsing, but putting all of us inside it put pressure on it that it wasn't equipped to withstand," says Dodger. "Okay, everyone. This is where you follow me, and you don't argue anymore. Got it?"

"Yes, ma'am," says Kelpie.

"Come on," says Roger, offering Chang'e his hand.

More shaken than she knew was possible, she takes it and holds on firmly, letting him guide her through the dark.

*   *   *

They stay clustered close as they walk, following Dodger's lead. She walks a mostly straight line, but when she steps to the side or takes a larger step than usual, she pauses and looks back, watching them. It's hard to mind that very much. The consequences of her *not* watching out for them are too dire.

"What if the tree's still there?" asks Kelpie, sounding worried all out of proportion with the question. The reason follows immediately after: "What if Artemis gets back and sees it and climbs down, but doesn't realize the ground's mostly missing?"

"I thought you didn't want to belong to her," says Máni.

"I don't want to belong to anybody," says Kelpie, fiercely. "I'm a person, and that means I'm not property, no matter what the ones who made me were trying to do. But if I'm going to wind up with an Artemis no matter what, I'd rather be with the one I already know, and not have to spend all my time wondering whether some stranger is going to stroll in and try to . . . to claim me or something. So, what if the tree's still there?"

"This space is part of the universe, but it's outside the universe at the same time," says Dodger. "We're walking on the bottom side of the Möbius strip. Anywhere else, I wouldn't have to run just because the floor was disappearing from underneath me. I'd tell it to cut that shit out, give it the mathematical proof that it already had, and keep on going. Here, I can't do that. I'm limited by the nature of the reality around us."

"And isn't it amazing?" asks Roger.

Chang'e winces a bit at the delight in his voice. He sounds far too happy to be told that he's been placed under some incomprehensible new limitation.

Erin nudges her with an elbow. "Ignore them when they get giddy about things no one reasonable would be happy about," she advises. "They're so used to the world being made of folded paper that they get excited when something refuses to rip just because they're pulling on it."

Dodger makes another turn.

This hallway has more flashes in the walls, more lights in all directions; it's almost as vibrant as the active everythings Chang'e and Máni are accustomed to. There's a distinct upward tilt to the floor. Dodger nods, looking satisfied.

"It's doing that to make us comfortable," she says. "There's no actual 'up' or 'down' here—Artemis's window being higher up was just the way the sky arranged itself, not anything to do with where your branches are. But the everything knows we expect certain things from linear space, and it's trying to be linear for us. I don't know what would happen if you brought an actual normal person in here. Whether the everything would collapse or fold in on itself, or just become a compressed plane and smash everyone inside." Her tone turns speculative at the end.

"No using other people's bolt-holes as your science experiments," says Roger.

She sighs. "You never let me have any fun."

"We're walking through the infinite darkness on the other side of reality. I let you have all the fun in the world," says Roger.

Dodger huffs, and they keep on walking.

The journey is mostly uneventful. Every turn takes them to a new level of rainbow flashes, the activity ramping up bit by bit, until they come around a bend and see a window hanging in the air. This one is painted a cheery shade of sunshine yellow, with curtains covered in rainbows and unicorns. Chang'e blinks.

"Our windows take the form of the room our hosts occupied when we first became a part of them," she says. "I hope whoever's room this is still likes rainbows and unicorns."

"Who doesn't?" asks Máni.

"People who got bludgeoned with them as children," says Chang'e. "It's more common than you'd think."

"Damn," says Máni. "Any idea whose window this is?"

"Not Diana's, if she's the senior Lunar in this area. I recognize that fabric. It's based on a show that came out about twenty years ago," says Erin. Roger and Dodger turn to look at her. She shrugs. "They kept me in the lab, but I was still a kid, and sometimes Leigh would reward us for good behavior. Take the cadaver apart in under five minutes, get an hour of screen time, that sort of thing. The main difference between my childhood and a horror movie was that I couldn't turn my childhood off."

"We keep moving," says Dodger. "The window's closed, but we don't know whether it's actually in the same time zone as the one we started with. If it belongs to someone in Hawaii, they could enter the everything at any moment. Even if it doesn't, it's probably rude for us to be here without an invitation. Come on."

She wheels and steps through another hole none of the rest of them can see, and they follow her into another upward-slanting corridor.

They walk along it until Dodger makes another abrupt turn and they find themselves looking at Artemis's window. The tree is gone, leaving a scattering of leaves and a few fallen peaches on the ground. There's no way of knowing whether Artemis came back and climbed down, or hasn't come back yet. But the window is still open, so they know it's one of those two.

Dodger moves to the window and leans out, bracing her hands

on the sill and looking down. When she leans back into the main space, she's smiling, clearly smug about something.

"There's no window below us," she says. "We must have gotten out just in the nick of time."

"Why do you look happy about that?" demands Kelpie. "Artemis—"

"Wasn't down there."

Kelpie stops. "What?"

"Time is moving faster in here than it is in the normal world. I'd say about three to one, or something in that neighborhood. It has to be, for this whole system of moons and Cities to work even as well as it is right now. Still." Dodger steps back from the window and picks up one of the peaches. It's barely starting to show a bruise. "This fell off the tree when the tree fell away, and it happened almost at the same time as us losing the floor. Do not ask me how I know this. When the woman who is the living incarnation of time itself tells you something happened at a specific time, you listen to her. You don't ask her to show her math."

She tosses the peach gently to Roger, who snatches it out of the air and turns it over in his hand before he nods. "Works for me. Chang'e, Máni, any questions?"

"No," says Chang'e.

Kelpie gulps a breath, visibly calming herself. "All right. Thank you for getting us out of there."

"You can thank me after we finish waiting for your boss to get back," says Dodger. She sits down on the rainbow-streaked ground, leaning back against what appears to be nothing, and stretches her arms up over her head. "Anyone need me for anything, or can I take a little nap?"

"How can you sleep here?" asks Chang'e. "We're in the void!" She's been traveling the everything for decades, but she's never lost sight of the fact that it's a tunnel through infinite nothingness, and today's reminder was something she could really have done without.

"You can sleep anywhere if you really try," says Dodger. "I did a sleepover in the Sutro Baths shortly after we manifested. That place burned down before we were born, but I asked it nicely to exist again for the night, and it did."

"There was a time when she said we were going to go live there," says Roger, fond and weary and absolutely accepting in the way that only truly comes to someone whose life has been reshaped to make statements like "I asked it nicely to exist again" make perfect, reasonable sense. "I talked her out of it, thankfully. A little house in Berkeley with a negotiable number of rooms is a much better place for us than a collapsed bathhouse that has to be constantly reminded not to disappear into the ether. I like floors that actually exist whether or not you ask them to."

Dodger wrinkles her nose at him, then closes her eyes, relaxing into whatever unseen surface she's leaning against. Roger looks around, then sits down cross-legged, resting his elbows on his knees. Erin flops to the ground not far away, leaning on her hands and looking like she was happier when the floor was dropping out from underneath them. At least then, something was actively going on.

"The way I see it, we have a braid of problems," he says, without any preamble. "Your friend's dead, and that sucks, and we need to figure out who or what killed her; we have an asshole alchemist running around making monstrosities and attacking people who haven't done anything to warrant it; and we have a group of alchemists who seem to have mostly been wiped out by the aforementioned asshole, who were making accessory packs of existing Lunars in a really complicated attempt at a honeypot. Does that sound about right for a summary?"

"What's a honeypot?" asks Kelpie.

"Usually a woman wearing her underwear as eveningwear being sent to seduce a professional spy," says Roger dryly.

Kelpie blinks.

"Ignore him," advises Erin. "The rest of us do, and it works pretty well for the most part. That sounds accurate to me, Roger. Missing some nuance, but what summary isn't?"

"Any nuance that matters?"

"They're doing this all ahead of an eclipse, and it's all but guaranteed that it's an attempt at claiming the Impossible City."

"They're not going to give up on the City," says Roger. "If we stop them this time, they're just going to step back and take another run. Is this the rest of our lives? Lurching from alchemical attempt at the City to alchemical attempt at the City, until either we slip and they get in or we admit that there's one way to stop this and move into the City ourselves."

"That sounds about right," says Erin. "But until we have to file change-of-address forms, we have pizza, and we have cable television, and we have time to figure out a better way to do this. For right now, we focus on the murdered girl, the local alchemists, and the Lunars."

"It's what works," says Roger.

Chang'e sits down next to him, letting Judy slip a little closer to the surface than she normally does when they're inside the everything. Judy reaches over to take his hand, tangling their fingers together, and holds on tight.

"I'm sorry you got dragged into all this," she says.

"I'm not." He shrugs. "This is the most fun I've had in weeks, and even if it wasn't, without Dodger playing *Minesweeper* back there, you would all have plummeted into the abyss, assuming you could find Aske's everything in the first place. I'd rather be a little inconvenienced than never know you because you'd died in the everything."

"That's . . . oddly sweet."

He grins. "Oddly sweet is my superpower."

The others sit in turn, and comfortable silence falls as they wait in the dark, surrounded by the rainbow light of unfulfilled potential, and hope that they haven't already missed their chance to set things right.

Palus Persici

Everyone has drifted off by the time Artemis comes through the window. They're not all necessarily asleep, but they're dozing, disassociating, nicely removed from the situation. She slides off the ledge, getting her feet firmly planted as she takes in the scene; the bodies either sitting or sprawling on the unseen ground, the litter of leaves and bruised peaches that remain, even in the absence of the tree. After a long pause to see if anyone will notice her arrival, she plants her hands on her hips, and demands, in a carrying voice: "What the actual fuck is going on here? I thought this was a murder investigation, not a slumber party!"

Chang'e jerks awake. She dozed off with her head on Roger's shoulder, dreaming a complicated, confusing mixture of Judy's dreams and her own, and it is surprising and pleasant to realize how many of those dreams were the same. She turns to the window, eyes wide and still bleary from sleep, then scrambles to her feet as she realizes who's there.

"Artemis!" she exclaims.

Kelpie rubs her eyes as she wakes, and rises with startling grace, offering her hand to Máni as she does. Both of them face the goddess of the hunt and the moon, who looks refreshed and invigorated by her evening's activities, full of light and vigor.

"I'm so glad you're all right," says Kelpie.

Artemis's expression softens, like she wasn't expecting that and doesn't quite know what to do with it, but is happy to accept it all the same. "Why wouldn't I be?" she asks. "I've been doing this for a long time." Her attention flicks to Chang'e. "I see you didn't die."

"No, I made it through Aske's window," she says. "I grew a peach tree from there to here, so everyone else could come down and join me."

"Oh? And how did that work out?"

"I'd need to wake Dodger to explain, and the Doctrine may not be quite human, but it's not Lunar; they still need to sleep. I'd rather not upset her. Basically, we each generate our own individual branches of the everything, but they're all connected. Dodger understands them sort of instinctively, and when Aske's started collapsing, she got us out before we could fall into the void."

She's leaving out so much. She doesn't feel like this is the right time to explain.

"Was Aske still there?"

Chang'e sighs. "She was. Blunt-force trauma to the head. She died quickly, but she made it back to her window before she did. I think she was trying to reach the City. That, or whoever attacked her dragged her there, and was trying to open the window, but it wouldn't open without Aske."

"She was definitely attacked inside the everything?"

"It looked like it. And since her window is gone, we can't go back for another look. But the way the blood was splattered made it pretty clear. Can I see the bottom of your shoe?"

Three sets of footprints. Aske's, Máni's, and a third set which left smaller tracks. Looking bewildered, Artemis lifts her foot and shows Chang'e the sole of her shoe.

The shoe's too big. It's too big, and it looks like it fits, and she can't imagine anyone would put on shoes that were too *small* in order to commit a murder. Chang'e untenses, shoulders slumping.

"Thank you," she says.

"No problem," says Artemis, sounding bewildered. She puts her foot back down. "Did you learn anything else?"

"Dodger understands the everything better than anyone else I've ever met, I think because it's linear and mathematical in a way that doesn't make sense to most of us; she says it wouldn't be possible for someone who's not a Lunar or accompanied by one to get into the everything. Because of the way we work the buddy system, someone would know if Aske had pulled somebody into the everything with her; she went in alone."

"Which means we're looking for a homicidal Lunar?"

"Yes, and it wasn't you."

Artemis blinks, slowly. "I would like you to please explain, in very carefully selected words, why you feel like you need to specify that I didn't kill one of our own."

"Anna," says Máni. Artemis turns to him. "She's not you, but you share a body. Chang'e told me Judy was able to enter the everything when she was first trying to figure out what was happening. If Judy can get into the everything, Anna could do it too, if she managed to surface long enough to seize control. We know she was working with the alchemists when they suppressed her and let you take over solo. If they wanted Aske dead for some reason, they could have pulled Anna to the surface, set her loose, and let you come back as soon as the deed was done. You'd have no idea what had happened, and could honestly say you weren't there."

"But it wasn't the alchemists who killed Aske, and I don't think they're the ones who ordered her dead," says Kelpie fiercely. The rest of the Lunars turn to her, frowning. "Oh, don't look at me like that. I'm not defending them. I know they're bad people, even Margaret, no matter how nice she was to me. But they're *alchemists*. If they were the ones who'd had Aske killed, we would never have found her body."

"They would have broken it down for raw materials and put her to work, because that's what alchemists do," says Erin, opening her eyes and pushing herself to her feet. "They don't leave good components laying around for other people to make use of."

"So what could they have *wanted*?" demands Chang'e.

"They wanted the everything," says Dodger.

The Lunars—and Erin—turn to look at her. She's still on the ground, eyes still closed; if not for the fact that she's talking, it would be easy to assume she was sound asleep. "What do you mean?" asks Artemis.

"Her branch of the everything collapsed as fast as it did because there was too much weight on it. It was falling apart before we got there, but it was stable, mostly because she was still in there—I'm not sure it could tell the difference between living and dead without something to compare it to. It could have endured that way for weeks, or even months, just empty and floating mired in the sky above the City. When we made it realize Aske was dead, that *it* was dead, it gave up and dropped away." She sighs, finally opening her eyes. "Don't you see?"

"See what?" asks Chang'e.

"Get a Lunar to kill another Lunar on your behalf. Leave her where she falls. Create an empty everything that still has a window but doesn't have an owner. Make yourself a synthetic Lunar who doesn't have a window of their own," she nods toward Kelpie, "and send them into the abyss. Zib was able to take the graveyard path into the City and open the doors from the inside, and it was made very clear that anyone who opens the doors can let people in. So you send your synthetic in, and they let you in. Then you have access to a stable window, with no one to stop you."

"And how is that Lunar supposed to even get into the everything, if they don't have a key?" demands Artemis. "If they *did* have a key, how would they open the door to someone else's everything?"

"Blood," says Dodger. She shrugs. "That's how alchemists do everything. Get enough of Aske's blood, and even if they can't fool the universe into accepting someone natural as a Lunar, they can fool it into accepting a synthetic Lunar as Aske. There's a lot of blood in an adult human body. Approximately one and a half gallons, for most people. Well, I only saw a little under a gallon while we were in there. Was Aske a blood donor?"

"She never mentioned it to me if she was," says Máni.

"So she would presumably have had the normal human amount of blood," says Dodger.

"Because knowing how much blood that is, *and* being able to estimate how much blood someone has lost with a glance, that's a normal human thing," grumbles Máni, sotto voce.

Chang'e elbows him. He grimaces, unrepentant.

"Let me see if I'm following you here," she says. "You're saying the alchemists had Aske killed because they had Kelpie and thought she would be able to access the City via Aske's window, as long as Aske's iteration of the everything remained accessible. And that by using blood collected by the Lunar who did the actual killing, they'd be able to convince one of our keys to open Aske's gate into the everything, meaning they'd have an unprotected point of access, without any Lunar actually taking the step of betraying the City itself." Chang'e isn't sure it's *possible* for a Lunar to betray the City. She has the feeling, vague and unformed, that the City would stop them if they tried.

Dodger stands as she nods. "Yup. It's convoluted, but alchemists *like* convoluted. They think a simple plan is destined to fail, because the universe abhors a straight line. Give them a labyrinth with a finish line at the end, and hoo, boy, they are your new best friends."

"There's just one problem."

"What's that?"

"How were they planning to access the everything without a key? There are only three in the city, and before Aske died, I would have told you there were only two. I'm certainly not handing mine to a stranger."

"I'm not either," says Artemis.

"Who has the third key?"

"Right now, I do," says Máni. "I was supposed to hand it to Artemis—clearly unnecessary—and then she'll give it to whoever comes next in the rotation."

"Diana," says Chang'e, slowly and with dawning horror.

Máni frowns at her. "But Diana doesn't cross the sky very often."

"She said she wanted to go the night before the eclipse, to remind herself why it was so important," she says. "Diana put herself down for the next crossing."

"Meaning I, in my guise as Losna—a minor moon goddess with

no allies and no real protection—would be meeting her alone with a key in my hand and no witnesses." Artemis gives a small, hard shake of her head. "Nope. That's a trap. I know how to recognize a trap when I see it, and that's a trap right there. I was supposed to walk into it without hesitation."

"Diana gets the key from 'Losna,' douses it in Aske's blood, and gives it to the alchemists." Chang'e frowns at Kelpie. "But you're not quite right."

"I'm orange and I have hooves," says Kelpie. "How am I even remotely right?"

"No, I mean you're not a synthetic Lunar in the sense they'd need. You're imprinted with Artemis's Hind. They'd want to use something completely empty."

"Margaret had a project in a locked room," says Kelpie slowly. "She was building the ideal human body, she said, and if we couldn't figure out how to fix the damage my accident had done, she'd see about transferring me into it. At the time, that sounded like the nicest thing anyone had ever offered to do for me. Now I'm wondering what parts of me would have been left out."

"Take an empty vessel, infuse it with just enough bottled moonlight and symbolic folklore to attract the universe's attention, and pump it full of stolen Lunar blood," says Dodger grimly. "Or hell, if the body didn't make it out of the lab for some reason, do it with an auf. All you'd need to do is empty it out a bit more than they normally do before they wake the nasty little fuckers up."

"So Kelpie's a Plan B, not a component of Plan A?" asks Artemis. Dodger nods. Artemis does as well, looking fiercely grateful.

"Good," she says. "I don't want her back in the line of fire unless she insists—and if she insists, I'm still going to argue. Someone deserves to get through all of this unharmed. Even if it's not necessarily going to be one of us."

"Artemis . . ." says Kelpie.

"You may not be mine. I know you don't want to feel like you *belong* to anyone. But you were made for me, and everything I am tells me to protect you, even from your makers."

"You really think this Diana lady's crooked?" asks Erin.

Artemis nods. "I've had my suspicions for a long time. I wasn't kidding when I said that Artemises don't come around Berkeley, because your Diana is territorial. And we talk. Just like every other flavor of Lunar, we talk."

"Do we confront her?" asks Chang'e. "Or do we wait for tonight, and then see who shows up at the gate?"

"If they open a channel into Aske's everything, they're going to die," says Dodger. "It's not there anymore, and now that the universe knows it's gone, it won't take kindly to someone trying to play that kind of trick on it."

"Right, so we don't let them go through."

"Or maybe we do, and this becomes a self-solving problem."

Chang'e stares at Dodger for a moment. "That's horrible."

"That's practical. I'd rather be a little horrible and alive than untarnished and dead. But hey. You do you, I guess."

"All right," says Artemis. "Let's not fight. Here's what I say we do: we get out of here."

"At last someone's talking sense," says Dodger.

"We all go home, and we go about our normal business, we don't let on that anything's out of the ordinary—we don't spy on Diana, or avoid her if we would normally see her around campus, or anything ridiculous like that. And then, come moonrise, I go to the clocktower, assuming the gate is back where it belongs, and I wait to see who shows up. If it's Diana alone, we're good. If it's Diana and the alchemists—which sounds like a rival band from *Scooby-Doo*—then she and I settle this like alpha goddesses."

"Meaning?"

"I pull her hair, kick her in the tits, and run like fuck," says Artemis. "I'm in pretty good shape; she's an art professor. I can outrun her."

"And I'll be there, which gives you a power boost," says Kelpie.

Artemis looks at her, mouth opening like she's about to object, and stops as she sees the look on Kelpie's face, which is sternly determined, a deep line between her eyebrows as she scowls.

"You'll be there," she agrees. "I'll be happier with backup."

"We'll be there too," says Chang'e. "Aske was our friend, not yours. She deserves to have people show up to avenge her."

"Do you want me to just take out an ad in the newspaper?" asks Artemis.

"That would be an excellent idea," says Erin. "We can include the address where the alchemists can come to collect your corpse, and save ourselves a lot of trouble. Are all moon gods as bound and determined to get killed as you lot?"

Máni shrugs. "We know we're actually immortal. Why not be a little inclined to taking risks while we're here on Earth?"

"Because the human halves of you aren't immortal," says Erin. "What do they have to say about this?"

"Judy's fine with it," says Chang'e. "She feels like we failed Aske."

"David was planning to ask Eliza out after the end of the semester, when he was sure she had her feet under her and didn't need a friend more than she needed a partner," says Máni. "He's furious with himself for not doing it sooner, and if this was Diana, he wants a chance to explain to her that Aske was never meant to be collateral damage."

"Anna doesn't get a vote," says Artemis.

"Plan is to just go home, then? And those of us who live together get to deal with the traumatized widow and her son—and their dog—that we've suddenly acquired? Great," says Dodger. "Erin, go wake my brother up, if you would be so kind. Kelpie, are you staying at our place tonight?"

"If you don't mind," says Kelpie.

"If you're not careful, Smita's going to decide that you live there, and then what I do and don't mind is going to be entirely irrelevant," says Dodger. "Artemis, this is your everything. Can you get us out of here?"

"I can," says Artemis.

Erin wakes Roger, who rises groggily and with many small sounds of protest, then falls into line with the rest of them. Even half-awake, he's learned to watch his words, not saying anything that could be viewed as either a request or a demand. It must be a hard way to live. Chang'e watches him, and understands both why her human half finds him so fascinating and why he cleaves so closely to his sister, who doesn't seem to be as affected by his voice as the rest of them.

They fall into a line, Artemis at the front, Chang'e and Máni close behind, Kelpie after them. Roger and Dodger come after her, and Erin brings up the rear, a final defense that will hopefully go unneeded. They make their way back to the gate, Dodger watching the rainbow flashes in the walls with rapt fascination. As they're nearing the wavering square of light that will lead them back to the alchemists' lab, she clears her throat, then calls, "I want to try something. Can we hold up for a moment?"

Artemis stops, and the others stop in turn. Dodger, meanwhile, breaks away from the line and walks a few steps deeper into the blackness, then reaches out and begins to play her fingers over the air like she's tracing patterns on a screen. The rainbow flashes follow her fingertips, increasing in brilliance and frequency, until they coalesce into a sheet of vivid brightness, scintillating through every color and no colors at the same time. It hurts to look at. She presses her palm against the center and it shatters back into a cascade of rainbow streaks, racing off to join their fellows in the walls.

Dodger turns, a satisfied expression on her face, back to Artemis. "I think that worked," she says. "Let's try the gate."

Artemis gives her the sort of patient look normally reserved for very small children and for pets that have done a clever trick. "All right," she says. "We'll try it."

She resumes her passage toward the gate, looking through its distorting transparent membrane, and blinks, recoiling slightly. "That's not the lab," she says.

"Nope," agrees Dodger.

The gate is looking out onto the blackberry snarl behind the carnival house, briars and even boughs bending inward under the weight of their fruit visible through the distortion.

"How—?"

"I moved it," says Dodger, with an easy shrug. "Now that I know where both ends are, it wasn't hard."

Roger looks at her fondly. "Please stop terrifying our new friends for fifteen minutes, if you would."

"Fuck you," says Dodger, in an amiable tone. She gestures to the gate. "After you, moon people. I promise I won't stay in here and reprogram the universe while you're not looking."

Oddly, this doesn't seem to be as reassuring as she wants it to be. Artemis frowns as she looks back to the gate, not moving until Kelpie pushes past her and steps out. Then she follows, and the others follow her, leaving Roger and Dodger alone in the everything.

She looks at the gate and doesn't move, agony in her eyes.

"Dodge," he says.

"I don't want to go back," she says. "I know we've always said we wanted some time to be normal before we went ahead with doing what we were made for, but I don't want to go back. Everything here, on this side, feels . . . unlimited. In a way I can't really describe yet, but want to spend more time figuring out."

"We don't know if they have farmer's markets in the Impossible City. Or potatoes, even. Baker was an American author, so I'd assume potatoes, but she was writing in a very European tradition. Maybe we get there and we don't have access to anything they didn't have in pre-Colonial London. Are you ready to go without internet? Without your journals? Because I don't think I am, and this is one of those things we do together or we don't do it at all."

"I know." Dodger shrugs. "I'm still allowed to want to stay."

"You are. You just can't do it yet." He offers her his hand. "At least now we know we'll have company."

"Yeah, maybe you can ask your new girlfriend to drop care packages every time she's the one up in the sky."

"She's not my girlfriend," he demurs.

Dodger laughs and prods him with her elbow. "She's going to be. I know the signs, and I know you've been lonely. She can't keep up with you, but no one can, not even me, and she's about as close as it's going to get. Preternaturally empowered linguist who also happens to be a part-time god? That's your type. Even if you didn't know it two days ago, that's your type. You nerd."

"I nerd, you also nerd," he says, reaching out to take her hand and pull her with him out of the everything. She doesn't protest, although she glances back at the lines of rainbow light with longing in her eyes, watching them until she's on the other side of the gate and they vanish, lost in the blackness and the blur.

Roger lets go of her hand. She turns with a sigh to the gathered Lunars and Erin, who are watching her with varying degrees of wariness.

The whole night has slipped away while they were in the everything, leaving them standing in the last vestiges of darkness before the sunrise. Dodger wasn't kidding about time moving differently in there; what felt like three or four hours has proven to be at least eight, maybe more, and the lights in the house are still on. Smita and the teens must have stayed awake, waiting for them to come home, unable to sleep when they didn't.

"How did you do that?" asks Artemis, and then: "Can you do it again?"

"I negotiated with the possibilities until they agreed it was possible they might have placed the gate on the back fence," she says. "Not the easiest conversation I've ever had, but not the hardest, either. It was easier because someone else had already done it. The gate was supposed to be on campus last night."

All of them turn then, looking at the fence where the gate is anchored, standing open and barely visible in the watery pre-dawn light. It will vanish soon enough, whether or not it's formally closed. Artemis pushes past the rest of the group, remarkably careful not to knock any of them into the thorns, and taps her key against the frame.

The gate spirals inward on itself and is gone, leaving only the fence behind. She looks over her shoulder at Dodger. "What do you mean, someone had already done it?"

"I mean, someone convinced the gate to show up in the lab, underground, rather than where it wanted to be. It'll be back on campus tonight."

"Who could have done that?"

"Is Hecate in town?" asks Artemis.

"Not unless she snuck in the same way you did," says Chang'e. The glitter in the air around all three of the properly divine Lunars is more apparent in the small, dark hours of morning, haloing their heads in sparkling light.

"Hecate isn't a sneaker," says Artemis. "You'd know."

"Who else does doors?" asks Máni.

"Diana is also the goddess of crossroads and passage to the underworld," says Erin, in an aggravated tone. "With the way you go on about people using their other aspects, could the Diana you've all been worried about have done it somehow?"

"If we call the bottom of a ladder into a secret alchemical laboratory 'the underworld,' I suppose we could, sure," says Artemis. "She would have needed to know where the gate was intended to be."

Chang'e shrugs. "I do the divinations at the start of the moon cycle every month, and then I make a shared calendar. Diana has access."

"A shared calendar," says Artemis.

Chang'e nods.

"The modern world has brought us nothing worth preserving," says Artemis.

Kelpie snorts as she laughs.

"I need coffee," announces Roger, starting for the house. The others follow, since none of them has a better idea. Dodger, who seems to want coffee even more than her brother, trots ahead of him. She's the first one up the stairs, the first into the kitchen, where Smita has fallen asleep at the dining room table, where she stops and turns to motion the others to be quiet as they follow her inside.

"Smita," says Erin. "We're home."

"Oh, thank fuck," says Smita, sitting up without opening her eyes. She stands, motion jerky and stiff from hours spent dozing in a hard wooden chair. "I'm going to bed," she announces, and stumps out of the room, finding her way by muscle memory alone.

Roger smiles as he shakes his head. "They worry about us."

"Of course they do," says Dodger. "If we die and the Doctrine doesn't immediately pass to Kim and Tim, they're homeless. This house mostly exists because I've convinced it that it doesn't have a choice in the matter. If we go poof and the Doctrine isn't right at hand to maintain my equations, the house as it currently is goes poof with us."

"Leaving . . . ?" asks Kelpie.

"A one-bedroom with mold stains on the ceiling that hadn't been given basic maintenance in roughly fifty years," says Dodger. "Really, it's best if we don't die."

"Back to Diana, *please*," says Chang'e. "Do we honestly think she could have moved the gate?"

"We do," says Artemis. "Before we had the tools to chart where the gates would appear, and in the absence of anyone as damned useful as my Hind apparently is, the gates were set by Diana. She'd tell them where to open, and they'd anchor there, so that whoever was going to make the passage could open them at their leisure. She would need an old rite to move a gate, the sort of thing most people don't know about or use anymore, but she could do it."

"The sort of thing an alchemist might have in their files?" asks Erin. The others look at her. "We know the alchemists are behind this, because the evidence says so, and their history confirms it. The alchemists are behind basically everything when you dig deep enough. Say they needed to get a Diana on their side, and figured out what would get around her defenses. They come in with proof that she would have been a lot more powerful once, and they've got her. I guess." She pauses, then, frowning deeply. "What the hell does this Diana of yours even *want*, anyway?"

"That's what we're about to go find out," says Chang'e, looking toward Máni and Artemis. "Kelpie, you might want to stay here for now. If she's working with the alchemists, we don't want to let her know you've found us."

"I don't like you going off without me, but you're right," says Kelpie. "I'll stay here and make sure Isabella and Luis are okay when they get up. Be careful."

"Careful is for people less awesome than we are," says Artemis. "We'll be fine."

As she and the other Lunars leave Kelpie and the other alchemical constructs behind, Kelpie wonders if Artemis even knows how boldly she was lying just there.

They may not, in fact, be fine.

BOOK V

Full

The graves stood tenantless, and the sheeted dead
Did squeak and gibber in the Roman streets;
As stars with trains of fire, and dews of blood,
Disasters in the sun; and the moist star
Upon whose influence Neptune's empire stands
Was sick almost to doomsday with eclipse.
                    —William Shakespeare, *Hamlet*

I'll dance the Moon again as long as she's the piper
I was her acolyte, but have become her partner
When I've done dancing with her,
Then I'll tend her flame
Just like her, some things change
But others stay the same.
    —Talis Kimberley, "Raspberry Leaf and Lemon Balm Tea"

A woman emerged from the opening at the top of the stairs
and started languidly down, one hand resting on the rail to
steady her. Her skin was very pale, with a faint grayish cast,

like the Page of Ceaseless Storms, or Niamh; Niamh was more blue than gray, but they could still have been related, however distantly. Her hair was long and white and unsnarled, despite the fact that it hung loose down her back, where it should have been heir to countless tangles. She wore a gown of flower petals and mist, and that was one more thing that should have been impossible but somehow wasn't, because where this woman walked, nothing was impossible.

Avery looked at her and was lost, his eyes going wide and his hand slipping out of Zib's to dangle by his side, even as his mouth fell slightly open. He looked at the Queen of Swords like she was a bowl of ice cream on a summer afternoon or a perfect grade on a math test he'd forgotten to study for, like she was the most impossibly flawless thing to ever have existed in an imperfect world.

"Welcome," she said, in a voice as sweet as the rest of her, and just as perfect. "Welcome, children, to the Palace of Storms in the Land of Air. I have been waiting for you for a very long time indeed."

"Hello, Mother," said Jack. "I have one of your little pets here."

The Crow Girl whimpered again, burying her face in the side of his neck this time, as the Queen of Swords finished descending the stairs and walked, slowly and grandly, toward them.

"I see that," she said. "One of the Crows, isn't it? Crow Girls are so easy to make that I scarcely keep track of them all, and they're flighty enough things that it's best to let them fly away and seek other aviaries when the desire strikes them. Nothing good ever came of trying to contain a Crow who didn't want to be kept. Did I make this one so small?"

"She's lost quite a few birds," said Jack. He gave his mother a challenging look. "The kind thing to do would be to open a cage of blank birds and let her keep the core of herself as it stands. But you won't do that, will you?"

"It's the nature of Crows to be changeable, unless they can be careful," she said, waving a hand, like she was brushing something away. "She'll rebuild her murder the way they all do, with birds who need a flock to belong to, one by one, until she reaches the size that keeps her comfortable."

"Kindness has never been your strong suit, has it?" asked Jack.

"I don't know, my beautiful boy. Did you think it was kind when I pulled your heart out of your chest and built a rookery in its place, a spot for the jackdaws to roost and rest and keep you company? You're never alone, thanks to me. You're not my finest monster, but you're my most precious, and you'll never fly away from me."

"Only because you left me with a name."

"A flock with a name will never roam too far from home," she said, crisply, and turned her attention on the other three. "A drowned girl, hmmm. Someone else's monster, and not mine, unless I read you wrong. . . ."

—From *Into the Windwracked Wilds*, by A. Deborah Baker

Mare Frigoris

They walk through the city as the sun rises, streets shading into shadowed view around them, early-morning inhabitants beginning to stir and leave their homes for the duties of their day. None of the three speaks as they walk, the glitter around them decreasing steadily as they step down and allow their mortal halves to take over.

(Not Artemis. While her glitter decreases as it should, Anna is no more present than she ever is, than she's been since they were gawky teens together. As she walks, Artemis wonders whether she should have asked more questions about that, raised more alarms— "Artemis never steps fully down when she's on the hunt" had been a convenient excuse in its day, but she's never truly believed it, has she? There's always been the little question of what, exactly, Artemis considers a hunt, as she's been unable to step down even when doing things as simple as looking for a certain kind of cereal at the grocery store. Anything can be a hunt, if you define the term broadly enough.

It makes her feel sort of slimy inside, like she's been unknowingly complicit in the oppression of a person who should have been her partner—even if Anna's few minutes of ascension made it quite clear that she was never looking for a partner, would never have been able to find a peaceful accord with Artemis. Still, that's a conflict they should have been allowed to have for themselves, in their own time, not had dictated for them by alchemists.)

Judy watches the rising mist of morning as it clears from the streets, and wonders how she could have been so foolish, how she could have missed the way Diana removed herself from the local community, how she could have overlooked the signs. She doesn't know what they were, even now, but she's certain they existed, that there was some indicator Diana might be planning to turn against her own kind. It shouldn't have taken a corpse and a stranger to make those connections. Aske should still be alive, and the fact that she isn't is her own fault. Or Chang'e's. The temptation to push the blame off onto her other half is strong; Chang'e interacted with Diana more than Judy ever did with Professor Williams. Maybe if she'd been an art major, that ratio would have been reversed. Maybe she would have noticed something, before it was too late.

Maybe.

David walks in refreshing simplicity compared to the others. He is angry, for his friend's sake, and for his own; he and Eliza might never have been anything more than friends, but they were good friends in the time they had, and he feels they would have stayed good friends, even if she'd turned him down. They had a whole future together, whether romantic or platonic, and these alchemists stole it from them. If Diana helped them, as he genuinely believes she did, she can be a target for his anger. She may be a more powerful and popular goddess than he is a god, but he has Chang'e and Artemis on his side, and he's willing to believe they can take her down together. His anger is a clean, straightforward thing, and it burns all the stronger for that simplicity.

By the time they reach the final approach to campus, the Telegraph Avenue street vendors are out and setting up their carts, positioning their wares to shine and sparkle in the morning sun. They begin to call out to the trio, to wave them over to gawk and appreciate, but they stop before the final invitations can be uttered. Street vendors are, by and large, a canny lot, with finely tuned instincts for danger. They have to be, to survive their chosen callings. Each and every one of them looks at the group as they walk with solemn unity toward campus, and they let them pass.

By the time the first students are arriving on campus to begin their days, the trio has reached the art building. They approach in a line, heading for the rear door, as if they fear their quarry might make an impressively coincidental escape if they come via the front. Artemis falls back, letting Judy take the lead.

Judy strides up the steps and through the door as if she does this every day, as if this were her department and place in the ebb and flow of college life. David and Artemis are close behind. Down the hall she storms, until she reaches the half-ajar door of Professor Williams's office.

She does pause then, to knock. The rules and rituals of school are so deeply engrained in her that anything else would be unthinkable, even if she feels foolish the moment she does so. They'll be going in whether they're invited or not.

But then, they don't want to confront her with a student in the room. Knocking lets them verify that she's alone. Judy knocks, and then they wait, all silent, to hear the call to battle.

"Come in," calls Professor Williams.

Judy pushes the door fully open and steps through, watching the older woman carefully. She's a good actress, is Professor Williams, but not quite good enough to conceal the slight thinning of her lips, the narrowing of her eyes, as she sees Judy.

Judy smiles with all the saccharine sweetness she's learned from an adulthood spent in Academia, dodging the sexist assumptions of old white men who think they're doing her a favor by seeing her as a delivery system for tits and ass rather than a racial stereotype. "Hello, Professor Williams," she says, every inch the respectful graduate student. "I just wanted to let you know that last night's passage went perfectly as scheduled, and Losna is safely home in her dorm room. I was a little surprised not to find you waiting for the hand-off."

It's a calculated guess: the gate originally opened underground, in what can only be described as enemy territory. If Diana went to wait for them there, without being intercepted or fleeing from the dead auf in the hall, she was openly admitting to being on the side of the alchemists. But given that Judy has no panicked texts about arriving at the clocktower to find the gate missing and the key missing with it, she's reasonably sure Diana simply didn't show.

"Did it, now?" asks Professor Williams. The tension around her eyes is only getting worse. Whatever she agreed to do for the alchemists, she clearly didn't expect to be required to deal with the consequences.

Gotcha, thinks Judy, and there's no triumph in it, only regretful recognition that she's never known this woman, not really, not the way she should have. "Have you met Losna, by the way? It feels like I've been falling down in my duty to introduce you to our newcomers. She's very eager to be helpful, and she has lots of good ideas about how we can move the pantheon into the modern era."

"I . . . No, I haven't met Losna yet. I keep meaning to, but . . ." Professor Williams waves her hand vaguely. "You know how the time slips away from us."

"I certainly do," says Judy. "Why, it seems like just yesterday I was the new kid on campus, and you were already the senior Lunar, taking care of all us juniors. That's something I always respected about you. The way you genuinely cared about our well-being."

Professor Williams is looking more uncomfortable by the second. "I know my duty as senior Lunar in the area," she says. "You'll have to do it yourself, one day, I'm sure."

"After I graduate and move on, I hope. I would never want to replace *you*." Judy turns to the door. "Losna! Professor Williams is ready to meet you now!"

"Awesome!" In bounds Artemis, eyes once more the untroubled, deeply layered blue of the sea near Tuscany, an expression of almost-frantic eagerness on her face. "Professor Williams, it's a genuine honor to meet you, I've heard so much about you, and you're not buying a word of this, are you?"

Professor Williams is no longer seated behind her desk. Professor Williams is on her feet, back to the wall, staring at Artemis like she's just seen her worst nightmare entering her office. Her eyes narrow, and in a strangled voice, she manages to spit, "*You.*"

"Me," agrees Artemis, tone mild. "You. This is a fun game. Do we loop Judy in now, or do we just keep going back and forth forever?"

"This is my territory, my pantheon," says Professor Williams, and the air seems to almost bend with the force of her stepping up, Diana becoming manifest in their midst. She doesn't get any taller, but she towers all the same, a mountain, a monument to godhood, untouchable, unstoppable, immortal.

Artemis lifts an eyebrow, unimpressed, while Judy has to fight the urge to quail away. "Step up," says Artemis, tone mild. "I need the support. David?"

But it's not David who busts into the office. It's Máni, charging in and stepping up at the same time. The divinity in the small space is becoming choking. Judy steps up almost in self-defense, Chang'e gently nudging her aside to take her place.

"You moved the gate," Chang'e thunders, interposing herself between Artemis and Diana. Her fury is as great as theirs, and her cause more just. This is *her* campus, seniority be damned. "You had every cause to believe a junior goddess would be making the passage, and you *moved* the *gate*. Why would you do such a thing?"

"I'd heard a rumor. That a corrupted incarnation of Artemis was attempting to infiltrate our pantheon in the guise of Losna," says Diana, glaring daggers past Chang'e to Artemis. "I thought to catch her out. No one else would have been hurt. But if she could find the gate at all, that would prove she was other than she claimed to be. No incarnation of Losna would be able to enter the lion's den and survive."

"You would have left the City unattended, had you been correct and she been unable to access entry," says Chang'e, fiercely. "You broke every creed we stand by."

"One missing Moon does nothing to harm the City," says Diana. "It might have once, when each of us was unique in the night. Now, there are a hundred Chang'es scattered around the world like stars in the sky, a thousand Dianas, and one of us missing changes nothing. We just need to show up so that one missing doesn't turn into a dozen missing, or any other number that might dim the light that shines upon the City. We're less essential on our own than you would make us out to be."

"Tell yourself that if it makes you feel less like a traitor," says Artemis. She reaches into the air like she's grabbing at a flying insect, and for a moment, she's holding the shadowy outline of a hunting bow. Then her fingers pass through it and ball into a fist, and the bow is gone. She looks, bewildered, at the place where it briefly was.

Diana laughs.

"You can't draw your weapons during the day, little huntress, or did no one teach you the rules of your position before they sent you to challenge me? You're powerless here, while I, on the other hand, am in my own domain."

"You're as tied to the moon as the rest of us," snaps Chang'e.

"True. But I'm a tenured professor in my own office, and you're a bunch of students threatening me for no reason." Diana's smile is thin and cold and does not reach her eyes. "I would run, if I were you."

Chang'e shakes her head. "I respected you," she says. "I thought you must be the best of us, to have held your position for so long."

"The best, or the most trapped," says Diana. "There's no promotion from 'goddess of the moon', Chang'e, no way to move up in the department. You get chosen, and that's your tenure, and then you're stuck doing the same thing over and over again until you die. I was going to be a great artist, once. I was going to change the world with my brilliance. And what am I now? A middle-aged art teacher trying to make people understand that I'm more than just an easy A in a discipline that matters so much more than they want to believe it does. The Moon isn't our friend. It's our abuser. It lures us in when we're young and innocent, and it uses us up, and it never knows our names. The City doesn't need us. The City just needs something to shine. We're an affectation at best, an infection at worst. It's long past time something changed the system. You can't blame me for seeking a better way, can you?"

"I can blame you for Aske," says Máni, voice cold and thick with fury. Chang'e hears David in his voice, god and man united in their anger. "She had nothing to do with anything you think you've been burdened with. She was young and kind and eager to see what kind of life she was going to have, and you took that away from her!"

"I did nothing of the sort," says Diana.

Artemis looks at her coldly. "We were in her everything. We saw what you did. We know you're working with the alchemists, and we know you killed her."

Her voice is steady, her words clear. She may be exaggerating how absolute their evidence is, but she's doing it well.

Diana doesn't recoil. She does, however, sink deeper in her chair. "Do you have any idea what you're risking?" she asks. "How dangerous this is?"

"Not unless you tell us," says Chang'e.

"I was supposed to be a famous artist," says Diana. "I was supposed to reimagine the world. When I was called to serve the City, I thought, well, this might slow me down for a little while, but it'll be something new for me to bring to my art—something innovative. I went willingly and with joy, and when it became clear that I wouldn't dream anymore, wouldn't find the inspiration I needed to be truly great—and you can't sell paintings of the City, people just assume you're trying to be a children's-book illustrator, they don't take you *seriously*. Well, then, I thought I might as well make the best of it. I had technique if I didn't have inspiration, and so I started teaching, and I suppose I liked it well enough, at first. I met a man who taught history, and we were happy, he and I, for a very long time. I told him, eventually, what I was, why my clock never changed while his rolled around the wheel of hours, and once he believed me, I started bringing him peaches, so he could stay with me."

Chang'e recoils. "That's . . . You know that isn't . . ."

"You're young, you have a lifetime of mistakes ahead of you, you have no idea how malleable the rules become when following them would mean sitting back and watching the people you care about suffer. You say we serve the City. Well, when has the City ever served *us* in return? We cross its sky nightly, but it gives us nothing. We wouldn't even have immortality if not for your damn peach trees, and when there's no Chang'e to be found, we sicken and age like anyone else. It's an unfair system. You can't blame me for wanting out of it."

"And that justifies bludgeoning a student to death where her parents will never be able to know what happened to her?" demands Máni. "Lying to us, working with *alchemists*?"

"Oh, you think you know everything, don't you?" asks Diana, her own tone mild. "Well, then I suppose there's not much left for me to say. You could call campus security, but there's no way you can prove I did anything, since it didn't happen in this reality. Or you could call the police—oh, same issue. What are you going to do?"

"We're going to stop your friends," says Artemis.

"Good luck with that," says Diana, and reaches for a notebook on her desk, apparently dismissing them. Chang'e frowns, then turns to the door, which closed behind Máni when he came into the office. She gestures for him and Artemis to follow her, moving to exit.

When she opens the door, the man from the lab is right outside, an unnervingly calm smile on his face. She stumbles back, knocking into Artemis, who steadies her before she can fall.

"You really should have listened when I told you to run," says Diana.

Lacus Bonitatis

K elpie isn't tired.

She ought to be—she didn't sleep while they were waiting for Artemis to take her trip across the City sky, and even if she had, they'd been running around for a while before that. Adrenaline is exhausting under normal circumstances. She should be tired—but she's not. She feels fine.

That's a problem, because everyone else is asleep, even Erin. The amount of time she and the siblings spent dozing in the everything doesn't seem to have been enough to prepare them for the day, and all three went to their rooms to collapse after the Lunars left. Except for an ancient orange cat that strolled into the kitchen, creaked at her several times in apparent expectation of breakfast, and then left in disgust when Kelpie failed to feed it, she's the only thing awake in the whole house.

She's not sure she's ever been this bored in her life.

Boredom is a relatively new discovery. She never had much time for it in the lab, where she was continually needed for one task or another. Margaret had likely been trying to run her too hard for her to realize how many holes there were in the story of her situation. And after leaving the lab, of course, everything had been new and terrifying, overwhelming in ways she didn't have the experience to understand and easily deal with. So this is the first opportunity she's *had* for boredom, really, and while it hasn't been that long, she's already pretty sure she doesn't like it.

Leaning as far back in her chair as she can, until she feels the front legs lift off the floor and the back of her head is resting against the wall, she stares at the ceiling and wonders how long she's supposed to endure this before she's allowed to start waking people up. That's probably one of those social rules you learn through osmosis when you're allowed to actually be a part of the world and not just an adjunct to everything that's happening around you.

"Kelpie?" Luis's voice is thick with sleep. She whips around, the front legs of her chair thudding back to the floor, and finds him standing in the kitchen doorway, rubbing his eyes with one balled-up fist and blinking at her. In case it wasn't clear enough that he just got up, his hair is sticking out in all directions, lending him a comical air. "What are you doing here?"

"I, um. I'm staying here too," she says. "Did your mom not tell you?"

She's not sure what Isabella will have told him, or what she *can* have told him. Does he even know his father is dead? Do *they* know who has the body? If the alchemists have him, friendly, non-magical Juan, they can bring him back as an auf, they can turn him into the weapon he never asked or deserved to be—

But that's a problem for later, for people more accomplished and experienced than she is. For right now, she only has to deal with Luis, who has stopped rubbing his eyes and is looking at her plaintively, as Bobby comes up behind him and starts nudging the back of the boy's knees with his cold, wet nose.

"I was going to take Bobby out. Is there breakfast when I get back?"

"Not the kind your mom will make when she gets up, but I bet we can manage toast without setting the kitchen on fire."

Luis nods and heads for the back door, and Kelpie rises to begin looking for things they can eat without using anything more complicated than the toaster. Bread, milk, and cereal are all reasonably easy to locate, and she can only hope she's not stealing someone's specifically earmarked food as she toasts the first few slices and begins searching for jam and butter.

Luis comes back in a few minutes later, and for a little while, things are easy. Food is simple. He seems enchanted by the novelty of cold breakfast and sugar cereal, and doesn't ask her any more questions, which she views as a small mercy at the beginning of what's likely to be a long and terrible day. She's rinsing their bowls in the sink when she hears Artemis scream.

The sound of ceramic shattering against the floor is almost drowned out by the agonizing wailing in her ears. She claps her hands over them and whirls around, seeking the source of the sound. She finds nothing. She and Luis are alone in the kitchen. He's staring at her, frightened and confused by her sudden panic.

"Kelpie? What's wrong?"

Artemis is still screaming, but the sound is distant, for all that it's deafeningly loud. It's almost enough to knock her down. She forces herself to straighten, to take her useless hands from her ears—they weren't doing anything to block the sound, anyway; it's not the sort of sound that stops with a physical barrier—and looks to Luis.

"When Roger and Dodger get up, tell them I had to go," she says. "Tell them I'm sorry, but it was important. Can you do that?"

"I don't . . ."

"Can you *do* that?"

Luis stares at her for a few more seconds, then nods, slowly and deliberately.

"I can do that."

"Thank you," she says, and turns, and runs, racing toward the sound as hard as she can. She hits the front door without slowing more than absolutely necessary, and then she's outside, running toward campus, running across the city she doesn't really know, through crowds of people who can't see her clearly because of what she is. And for the first time, she isn't thinking about the ones who *can* see her. She's just running, moving as fast as she can with screams ringing in her ears and threatening to overwhelm her.

The cereal and toast she ate with Luis are a stone in her stomach, heavy and unyielding. She'd stop to vomit, but that would slow her down, and she doesn't feel like they have the time to waste on something as trivial as her nausea. Artemis is still screaming, and so she's still running, following the sound, which isn't a sound at all, but a feeling, like razors being dragged along her nerves.

She hits the edge of campus hard and keeps on running, letting the screams guide her, arrowing in on their source as accurately as an actual arrow, like she's been loosed from Artemis's bow, designed to fly straight and unerringly to her target.

Her path takes her to a large brick building with students gathered outside. None of them give her a second glance. She expects, momentarily, to charge inside, but instead, the screams lead her around the building to the creek beyond, a channel cut through campus, flanked by high muddy banks. Hooves don't give her a lot of traction on the slope, but they dig in enough that she doesn't need to slow as she plunges down, into the water, through a faint gleam in the air and into someplace entirely other.

Diana of the moon; Diana of the underworld. There's a reason Diana is among the most powerful Lunars, and as Kelpie stumbles to a stop on the wide stone floor of a seemingly endless cavern, she understands the reason better than she ever has. The alchemist who killed Margaret is there, as are Chang'e, Máni, and Artemis. The latter isn't screaming. She's bound and gagged, tied to some sort of stone spire growing straight out of the floor. Máni and Chang'e are back to back, their eyes fixed on the auf surrounding them. These auf are less human-looking than the two former members of Margaret's research team, but Kelpie recognizes them all the same; they're the members of Isabella's coven, seized and gutted by the man with the cadaver's smile.

Diana is there, fully stepped up into her divine aspect, the air around her sparkling like purest moonlight. She turns to Kelpie as she hears the other woman's hooves clatter on the cavern floor, and she beams with satisfaction and pleasure.

"Ah, the little runaway hind," she says. "I wondered if you'd be joining us today."

"Kelpie, get out of here," yells Chang'e.

"Don't be silly: she can't leave," says Diana. "She's our guest of honor. The Lunar with no alignment. She'll open the door to Aske's everything, and we'll be able to end this. The light will be restored to the tower, and all will be well. Forever."

"The light will guide us home," says the alchemist, and somehow that's the worst thing of all, hearing the words Kelpie once thought of as a sacrament transmuted into the threat they always truly were.

Artemis glares daggers at him. Kelpie stumbles to a stop, looking wildly around the room they're all occupying.

"What are you *doing*?" she demands.

"Oh, it's very simple," says Diana. "Tonight's the last time the City will be accessible before the eclipse. So we're going to send you to open Aske's everything, and let your creators in. They'll open the gates for their fellows, and cut the tie between the City and the Lunars. We'll be free. We'll retain our divinity, but we won't be servants anymore. We can finally be the gods we were always meant to be."

Kelpie hesitates. Diana's right; she can't run, not with Artemis right there, trapped and tied and needing her. She glances over her shoulder. It wouldn't matter if Artemis *wasn't* there, because more auf are behind her, blocking the way out. If there even *is* a way out: there's no tunnel or doorway there, only more cavern.

She looks back to Diana. "You can't really intend to give the City to the alchemists," she pleads. "They'll do terrible things."

"Everyone does," says Diana. "Mr. Rapp?"

The man with the skeleton smile steps forward, withdrawing a jar from his pocket. It's filled with silver-red fluid, surrounding a silver key. He thrusts it at her, and Kelpie takes it automatically, having been long trained to obedience and good behavior.

"The gate is this way," says Diana, gesturing for Kelpie to follow her. "Do as you're told and we might leave Artemis ascendant when we're done. Or we could banish her entirely—she's had quite long enough—and give the body back to her mortal aspect. Doesn't Anna deserve a chance to live?"

"I don't . . ." Kelpie stumbles after her, glancing helplessly at the cornered Lunars.

Máni grabs Chang'e by the shoulders and shoves her forward, hard, right through the circle of auf. They look momentarily confused, but their orders must have been both narrow and clear, because they don't follow her, only begin to close in on Máni and Artemis, as Chang'e runs to Kelpie's side, grabbing her hand and glaring defiantly at Diana.

"Synthetic or not, she's a junior Lunar, and that makes her my responsibility," she snaps.

"Go with her, then, for all I care," says Diana. She gestures to the cavern wall. "Touch the jar to the stone, and we'll finish this," she adds.

Chang'e slips her hand into her pocket while Diana's attention is on Kelpie, sneaking something out. She looks at Kelpie and nods, and Kelpie, trying not to shake, does as she's been told.

The gate blossoms into existence, a series of complicated swoops and spirals like flower petals etched in shining light sketching itself outward, not from the key in Kelpie's hand but from Chang'e's fist where it rests against the stone. Kelpie realizes what she's done as the other woman takes her arm and the two of them step into the everything.

Diana realizes the truth an instant later, following them. And Chang'e, who left a peach pit behind the last time she was in her own everything, stamps her foot against the ink-dark ground, and the tree bursts into life.

Diana is the senior Lunar. She's held her position for decades. Her power eclipses Chang'e's as much as a floodlight will eclipse a candle, and Kelpie has no power to speak of. But for all that Diana is a tower of strength, she's also a human woman, and Professor Williams is as mortal as any other human. She's made of flesh and bone, and neither of those things is made to endure a peach tree growing directly up and through her body. It pierces her lower back and keeps growing, following the command it has been given.

Diana is in the act of reaching for Kelpie, making a strangled sound as branches begin to break through the skin of her abdomen and torso. The leaves glisten dark with blood. The fruit this tree bears will taste of slaughter. Chang'e stops to look back at her, flinching at the sight but not turning away.

"You shouldn't have betrayed the City, Diana," she says.

Diana makes that horrible, inhuman sound again, thrashes, and goes still. Chang'e sighs.

"Think the Doctrine will help me get her out of here?" she asks. "I don't want a corpse in my everything forever." Kelpie is staring at her. "She would have done the same to us, you know. Now come on."

They step back out of the everything. The auf are closing in on Máni and Artemis, while Diana's alchemist ally watches, still smiling. Chang'e steps rapidly down again, back toward humanity, and Judy places her fingers in her mouth, whistling shrilly. The alchemist's head snaps toward her, attention wavering.

"Máni!" she shouts. "Release her!"

He nods, turning to rip the ropes away from Artemis. They're thick cable, but they freeze where he touches them, shattering to shreds under his hands like they were made of nothing substantial, and he spins to charge at the nearest auf, shoulders down like he's trying to cross the football field.

Artemis straightens, shaking her arms out. This time, when she reaches for her bow, she finds it easily, and takes aim at another auf, releasing half a dozen arrows in quick succession.

The alchemist with the skeleton smile stops smiling for the first time, looking almost concerned. He turns to Kelpie. "We *made* you," he says. "You have to see the wisdom of allowing us to take the City. We're undoing the damage Baker did. We're . . ."

"Monsters," she finishes, before he can. "Maybe I am too. I don't think it matters all that much. Artemis is going to kill you now, and I'm going to spend the rest of my life forgetting that I ever saw your face. You made me, but I'm the one who decides what that means. I don't work for you."

"Anna," he begins, desperately.

"Is dead," says Artemis, as she releases another arrow. He stops mid-sentence, unable to speak with the arrow through his throat, and stares at her as she advances. "You people killed her, and now we'll never know who she could have been."

He reaches for her. She puts two more arrows after the first, until his labored breaths begin to slow. Even the apples of Iðunn won't save him from this.

"I hate it here," says Kelpie.

"Me, too," says Chang'e. "Let's go."

And they walk away, three moon gods and a constructed companion, closing the door on an artificial underworld occupied by half a dozen dead auf and one dying alchemist, and not a one of them looks back.

Not once.

Mare Finale

The carnival house feels empty with Luis and Isabella gone. Roger gave them the keys to their new house this morning, apologizing profusely that it had taken him so long to find something suitable. Erin had rolled her eyes and muttered about him being completely out of touch with the way the world worked for literally everyone else if he thought finding a house in Berkeley in six days was a long time, but she'd been smiling as she said it, so Kelpie supposes she wasn't actually annoyed.

Isabella invited Kelpie to come with them, but Isabella's still grieving, still choked by her loss and waking screaming in the night. Luis is even worse. Once he realized his father was dead, he started crying, and didn't stop for two days. He's just numb now. They've both been damaged by their brush with the alchemical world, and they may never recover. Kelpie thought it was better if she stayed here with the other constructs, and the blackberry tangle in the yard that never scratches her or runs out of fruit. Still, she's going to miss them, even Bobby and his endless begging for table scraps.

She's in the front room, looking for something to read, when the doorbell rings. Dodger's out at another of her seemingly endless farmer's markets. There's one every day of the week, or at least it seems that way. She never seems to buy much of anything, but spends hours browsing and returns looking fulfilled in a way Kelpie can't understand but isn't going to question.

Roger and Judy are in his office, and Kelpie's not going to bother them just because someone wants to sell them cookies or something. The lab is gone, destroyed by the alchemists themselves, and she's seen no evidence of lingering activity. That doesn't mean there isn't any, just that she doesn't know about it, but it certainly feels like they're getting a chance to catch their breath.

She has a lot of learning to do, about who she is and what she is and who she wants to be. But she's safe here while she does it, and there's time. Finally, there's time.

Kelpie pauses to pat the ancient orange cat—he's sitting on the stairs, much happier now that the dog is gone—on her way to answer the door, and she's unsurprised to find Artemis waiting on the porch. There's been no sign of Anna since the underworld, and even Roger thinks that going to another layer of reality, apart from the everything, may have been enough to knock her loose somehow, letting her go to the afterlife she'd been consigned to by one James Reed decades before.

Artemis has been keeping busy since they defeated Diana. With access to Diana's records on the local Lunars, and her notes about Diana's dealings with the alchemists, she's finally figured out the disappearances of newer Lunars that have been plaguing the community for the past several years. The alchemists have been taking them for building materials, apparently, and won't be doing that anymore now that the pantheons are on guard. Kelpie isn't sure she quite understands what's been happening, but that's all right; as long as no one else has to die.

Artemis has also been keeping her distance, giving Kelpie space. Now, the goddess looks at the Hind awkwardly, rubbing the back of her neck with one hand, making no move to come in off the porch.

"Um. Hi, Kelpie," she says, awkwardly.

"Hi," says Kelpie.

"I was wondering . . . now that we're not running for our lives, you want to get coffee? I feel like we should figure out a few things."

Kelpie pauses, then slowly smiles. She didn't want to be compelled to spend her life with this woman, but a compulsion and a choice aren't the same thing, now are they? There's no reason she can't try it out, see how she likes it.

"Let me get my coat," she says.

There's hours to go until moonrise, and the City stands.

Through everything else, the City stands.

About the Author

Beckett Gladney

SEANAN MCGUIRE is the author of the Hugo, Nebula, Alex, and Locus Award–winning Wayward Children series; the October Daye series; the InCryptid series; and other works. She also writes darker fiction as Mira Grant. McGuire lives in Seattle with her cats, a vast collection of creepy dolls, horror movies, and sufficient books to qualify her as a fire hazard. She won the 2010 John W. Campbell Award for Best New Writer, and in 2013 became the first person to appear five times on the same Hugo ballot. In 2022 she managed the same feat again!